KATHIE

KATHIE

Dora Taylor

Edited by Sheila Belshaw

PENGUIN BOOKS

PENGUIN BOOKS

Published by the Penguin Group
Penguin Books (South Africa) (Pty) Ltd, 24 Sturdee Avenue, Rosebank, Johannesburg 2196, South Africa
Penguin Group (USA) Inc, 375 Hudson Street, New York, New York 10014, USA
Penguin Group (Canada), 90 Eglinton Avenue East, Suite 700, Toronto, Ontario, Canada M4P 2Y3 (a division of Pearson Penguin Canada Inc)
Penguin Books Ltd, 80 Strand, London WC2R 0RL, England
Penguin Ireland, 25 St Stephen's Green, Dublin 2, Ireland (a division of Penguin Books Ltd)
Penguin Group (Australia), 250 Camberwell Road, Camberwell, Victoria 3124, Australia (a division of Pearson Australia Group Pty Ltd)
Penguin Books India Pvt Ltd, 11 Community Centre, Panchsheel Park, New Delhi – 110 017, India
Penguin Group (NZ), 67 Apollo Drive, Mairangi Bay, Auckland 1310, New Zealand (a division of Pearson New Zealand Ltd)

Penguin Books (South Africa) (Pty) Ltd, Registered Offices:
24 Sturdee Avenue, Rosebank, Johannesburg 2196, South Africa

www.penguinbooks.co.za

First published by Penguin Books (South Africa) (Pty) Ltd, 2008
Copyright © The estate of Dora Taylor, 1951

ISBN 978 0 143 02569 6

Typeset by PieRat Design in 10.5/13.5 pt Palatino
Cover design: mr design
Printed and bound by Pinetown Printers, KwaZulu-Natal

For all those South Africans whose broken lives inspired the writing of this novel, at a time when there appeared to be no hope for them on the horizon.

Throughout her life, Dora Taylor worked passionately to gain human rights for the people of South Africa – a dream she never gave up.

Quoting from her diary, Dora dedicated all her writing:

'To and for the people'

CONTENTS

Book 1 – A HOUSE DIVIDED

Book 2 – THE INTERWEAVING OF LIVES

Book 3 – HARVEST

Book 1

A HOUSE DIVIDED

CHAPTER 1

The Little Mother

Kathie's mother named her new baby daughter Stella because she was so fair-skinned and pretty. And because Stella meant 'star'. All the neighbours marvelled at her fair skin, as she wasn't like any of the rest of the Liedeman family. Kathie had a gold-brown complexion; she and her father were the darkest. Andrew, though he was lighter than Kathie, was dark too, more like his mother. So people wondered where Stella had inherited her fair skin from. It must be through her grandmother, Mrs Fraser, who behaved as if she thought she was a lady.

Kathie had always been the Little Mother to her sister Stella. There were eight years between them and from the day Stella was born the girl had dedicated herself to her chosen task with all the solemnity of her passionate little nature. Mrs Liedeman was always busy and was glad to be relieved of some of the burden of looking after the baby.

Kathie never forgot the day Stella was born. The terror and the joy had stamped themselves on the child's mind as something she had never felt before, opening up a quality of experience that was strange and fearful. She remembered her mother's face as she lay on the bed, a face grown unfamiliar through pain and exhaustion. Unfamiliar sounds came from her throat. The child did not know that a human being could utter such sounds. There would be silence and then a low moaning mounting to a cry of pain. The breath was drawn more rapidly, the cries deepened, communicating their fear to the tensely listening child. The sound rose and quickened to a shriek of uncontrolled agony, then subsided to a merciful silence, taut with the expectancy of the next onslaught of pain.

It was a difficult birth and her mother nearly lost her life. Afterwards Kathie understood all this, but young as she was she knew that her mother was going through the travail of childbirth. In the crowded district where she lived, babies were very common and her inquisitive gaze had seen many things which a child of her age was not supposed to understand. Her mother had lost two children: a boy who did not survive the first year, having caught a sickness of the stomach in the early summer and died after a few days; and then a baby girl who was stillborn. The doctor had said she shouldn't have any more, but Kathie knew that a woman couldn't help these things, because she had heard her mother saying it to a friend.

And Kathie knew that at the end of this agony there would be a little baby sister or a brother. It was a baby sister she wanted.

She dimly remembered her baby brother before he died. She slept in the same room as her mother and father, her brother Andrew who was two years younger than herself, and the poor little baby. In his short span of life he had always been sickly and used to wake her up with his wailing. Kathie had no doubt that a baby sister would be far more agreeable.

She had stood in a corner of the room unobserved, full of expectancy yet filled with a pity and fear she was never to forget. When the midwife burst into the little house at the last minute she scolded those who were present and bundled the child out of the room. Kathie had to stand outside the door where breathlessly she waited for something to happen, her pity and fear stronger than her joyful expectation. For, with her keen imagination, to stand shut out and see nothing was worse than if she had been present. The vague sounds, the cries and the silence magnified her concern.

At last she heard a new sound – the high, shrill sound of a

newborn child. Her heart leapt. Her baby sister! Or her brother.

When she managed to slip back into the room it was to the old cot, refurbished to receive the newcomer, that her eyes first darted. Sure enough there was her baby sister. For the moment she had the little one all to herself because the other people were all hovering over her mother. She gazed at the baby's face. It was very red and the hands were tiny and crumpled. Moved by a deep feeling of protectiveness she pushed her finger into the crumpled fist, which immediately folded over it. Fearful of disturbing the baby Kathie stayed motionless, tasting the magic of this new sensation. She felt she could stand there forever. Forever protecting her baby sister.

The spell was broken by the voice of her grandmother. She lived a long way off and had just arrived, looking very excited.

'What on earth are you doing here, Kathie?'

'I've got a baby sister!'

'Now don't you go meddling with her.'

'I'm not!' protested Kathie.

But even her grandmother couldn't hurt her at this moment. Her wish had come true. Spellbound, she gazed at the sleeping face and then went obediently out. Nobody could take from her this helpless little being, who had clung to her finger like the tendril of a flower as if she would never let it go.

Thus Kathie became the Little Mother.

Kathie liked the name Stella. It was just right for her pretty baby sister.

Drawing in the cheeks of her long narrow face in the prim way she had, Mrs Liedeman had said, 'I'm not like those people who call their children after some relative or other even if they have an ugly name. There are enough troubles in the world but you can always have a pretty name.' She herself had been called Irene by her mother, who said it meant 'queen'.

'What's all this nonsense about names?' snorted Kathie's father. But he let the women have their own way.

After the christening, Kathie's grandmother had taken the baby in her arms and then she had said a funny thing to her mother: 'Now let her father do what he likes. This is our child!'

Kathie saw her mother and her grandmother look at each other over the baby. Secretly she said to herself, 'She is my baby sister,'

not knowing then how the birth of Stella would change the lives of
everyone in her father's household.

CHAPTER 2

Johannes Liedeman

East of towering Table Mountain, on the fringes of the Cape Flats, Johannes Liedeman lived with his family in a predominantly coloured quarter of Lansdowne, one of Cape Town's sprawling suburbs.

He was a short, square-set man with a leaf-brown skin, an uncompromising look in his dark brown eyes, and a deep full-throated voice. As a lorry driver for a wholesale firm, he was better off than most of the coloured people in this crowded neighbourhood – superficially squalid and noisy, yet vitalised by a heroic will to survive.

For them it was a precarious existence. Unskilled jobs and fitful terms of employment, together with low wages, ensured the inevitable pattern of poverty for this section of the population. Although Johannes Liedeman didn't get a white man's wage, he earned enough to keep his comparatively small family with their heads above water, except for one problem – his bouts of drinking.

Discontent and a sense of frustration gnawed at him, though he couldn't have explained why there was a hunger in him that made him turn to the drink. Once it had even made him lose his job. Now and again he'd curse his bosses for the mean dogs they were. They thought they could kick him around just because he was a coloured man. He was as good as any man, he insisted, whatever his colour.

The question of colour always sent his temperature up. Proud of what he was, he was enraged by his mother-in-law's false gentility on the grounds of being near-white, and the snobbishness of both his wife and her mother towards those who were darker in colour than themselves. His father's elder sister had married a white man, by the name of Baaskemp, and their son in turn had married white and was now a well-to-do white farmer in the Free State. But Johannes would never allow their name to be mentioned in his house.

Yes, Johannes Liedeman was a proud man, with a strong sense of justice and a hatred of pretension or hypocrisy in any shape or form. Drink brought no ease. In fact it sharpened his tongue so that he would jibe at his wife and her mother for their praying and psalm singing in and out of season.

His rages were something terrible to see. When his dark moods were on him he spread such an atmosphere of silent fear through the house that Kathie would long for him to be gone. She sensed a hatred between her father and mother, though she had no means of understanding it. There were so many things this large-eyed, serious child tried to understand and could not. Her mother would sit crying – a sight that so enraged her husband that he sometimes struck her. The sound of blows beat on Kathie's ears till they felt like bursting. How much of her knowledge throughout life came to her through her too keen senses and spoke to the heart that welled too easily with feeling.

'*God man*, stop your blerry whining!' Johannes would shout. 'It's driving me mad!' And seizing his hat her father would fling himself out of the house, the door banging after him.

For a long time after that her mother would sit, just sit, till Kathie would approach her timidly, holding out her hand with a piece of fudge she'd bought with the penny her father had tossed to her, joking and laughing loudly when he came in from drinking at the Royal. The child feared him because his kindness alternating with his rages bewildered her, providing her with no solid ground for her affection.

And yet Johannes Liedeman loved his eldest child, who not only had a physical likeness to him but also had so much of his own nature in her. He would draw her towards him and stroke her curly black hair with a rough tenderness. 'You're my *meisie*, Kathie – my little girl,' he said one evening when he came home from work. 'And you must be proud of what you are. Never forget that.'

'No, Pa.'

'Promise me.'

Kathie promised, though it was not clear to her what she was promising.

'Don't listen to what they say,' he continued. 'They have a lot of damn silly ideas in their heads about us coloureds. Yes, and about themselves most of all. And I'm telling you, Kathie, it's very wrong, the way they think. They're going to cause a lot of trouble.'

Kathie puzzled over this. Her father had spoken with strong feeling, his eyes smouldering at something that angered him. What was it made him so angry? 'They' referred to her grandmother and her mother, she was sure.

Kathie didn't like her grandmother. A child's senses are acute, recognising even without words whether a grown-up is sympathetic or not. Kathie instinctively felt the lack of real human kindness in Mrs Fraser. Perhaps the long, yellow, pale face with the narrow lips had something to do with this impression. She associated her grandmother with a trim, even prim, black dress fastened close to the neck with a big silver brooch, the sharp corners of which seemed designed for pricking the skin. Her grandmother was very proud of the brooch, saying it was real silver and had been presented to her by a European lady on her deathbed.

Kathie didn't require to be told that there was no love lost between her father and her grandmother; even if he hadn't spoken as he did she would have known it. She had observed that her grandmother visited mostly when her father was at work. Once when he had come home earlier than usual, he had declared almost before the door had shut on her: 'Didn't I tell you I won't have that blerry woman snooping around my house? Always poking her nose into other people's business! When she isn't praying.'

But the two women did not change their habits. The visits continued, in spite of this incident. At the hour when Kathie's father was due to return, Mrs Fraser would look up at the clock, roll up her knitting in a white silk handkerchief, gather the rest of her things together and say she'd better be going. Then she would peck her daughter on the cheek and call for Andrew, if her grandson was anywhere near, in order to bestow on him a similar salutation, though he was usually nowhere to be found. But to Kathie it was always: 'Now, child, be a good girl to your mother.' She would then make her way out of the house, past the neighbours without greeting them, and so up the street, shoulders stiff, eyes front.

The home of Johannes Liedeman was a house divided against itself. But as he saw it, the evil genius disrupting his home was his wife's mother, who exercised an ascendancy over the mind of her daughter even after her marriage to him. He suspected that they kept up their relationship in spite of his veto, for he hadn't gone so far as to forbid them outright to visit each other. But the very fact that his wife's mother was invisible, yet powerful in her influence, lent her a sinister aspect in his eyes.

The battle between him and Mrs Fraser involved much more than that which arose simply from two strongly antagonistic natures. With the birth of his youngest child Stella this conflict reached more serious proportions.

CHAPTER 3

The Englishman's daughter

Mrs Fraser was a tall, lightly coloured woman who never forgot that she was the daughter of an Englishman. Hence the meticulous care she always bestowed upon her person to emphasise at once her degree of whiteness and her claim to superiority. But, though she herself tried to forget it, a strong physical legacy had also been left to her by her 'Malay' mother, who was a beautiful product of the admixture of various peoples who had inhabited the old Cape Colony: the Malays, who had been brought over from the East Indies as slaves, their Dutch masters, and the indigenous Hottentots. Not all Mrs Fraser's careful make-up could submerge this legacy.

On the eve of her marriage to a South African of Dutch descent, her engagement had been broken off owing to strong objections by her prospective in-laws, in spite of the money her father had left her. On the rebound she had accepted a young coloured man's proposal, Tony Fraser, who was earning good money in the printing trade. Soon she was pregnant, but in spite of the fervency of her prayers the child did not turn out to be as fair as her mother had expected, bearing a striking resemblance to her Malay grandmother. However, Mrs Fraser had her daughter christened Irene, because she had heard that it meant 'queen', and hoped for better luck next time.

But there was no next time. Providence had very unkindly planted a TB germ in her husband's lungs. It appeared that it had been lurking in his lung tissues even before she married him, so either Tony or the germ had been guilty of duplicity. When her husband died she had bravely faced life alone with her little Irene. She vowed to herself that next time she would marry with extreme care, combining prayerfulness with her own natural shrewdness, with which she was well endowed.

Perhaps the dictates of the latter proved overcautious or perhaps her faith in prayer had to be put to the test, but whatever the cause, she never married again. She found a position as a housekeeper to a childless couple who allowed her to keep her daughter Irene on the premises, since she was so well behaved. She held this position for many years, becoming – as she expressed it – one of the family, and when her employers died they left her a small sum of money. Her virtue was rewarded.

Now she was able to live without working, cautiously but comfortably, and only did some better class dressmaking for a city firm. She took a small house in a respectable terrace situated at the edge of a white locality, next to the railway line that ran from Cape Town to Simon's Town. Coloured people with light complexions favoured this area. With its magnificent eastern view of the bulging slopes of Table Mountain and Devil's Peak, its only drawback was that it was so near the railway line that the noise of the trains was very trying to the nerves. But one couldn't have everything.

The narrow house with its narrow stoep was separated from the street by well-painted if somewhat ramshackle palings. The corrugated iron roof was also kept well-painted, though it was very hot in summer. The lace curtains covering the windows showed a pretty pattern to the outside and effectively concealed the inside.

Mrs Fraser never allowed anyone to see her looking untidy. Though otherwise parsimonious, she always spent more than was necessary on her cosmetics. Not that she was made up in any way unbecoming to her age. Everything was done discreetly. She liked to think of herself as one of nature's ladies.

In her widowhood, two means of solace were open to her:

religion and domination over her daughter. With the early death of her husband her naturally domineering character had to have an outlet. Her two interests worked well in combination, for in the process of teaching Irene the Christian virtues, she took care to lay the most emphasis on docility. This was easy, since the girl showed a pliable nature and was not particularly possessed of intelligence. Throughout the impressionable, formative years of childhood, when the young mind is at the mercy of whatever adult hands it falls into, she was free to mould her daughter's character and set its basic pattern for all time.

This domination continued for more than twenty years. Mother and daughter spent a good deal of time together at the same occupation, both being excellent with the needle. Irene Fraser was attractive enough in her youth with her delicate narrow face and long, deep black hair. She dressed well, too, if rather primly; she had been well trained by her mother, but lacked her style. Her chief defect was a timidity of manner and she did not make friends easily.

The fact is, Irene was never the woman her mother was. Though similar in some characteristics she lacked her mother's strength of character. Mrs Fraser's sense of superiority expressed itself in aloofness from others; she never allowed people to become friendly with her, as if she feared they might deprive her of something. She lacked sympathy for others. Yet over and above all this she attached a great deal of importance to what people thought of her. So did her daughter. But Irene's attitude to others was not rooted in the same self-confidence.

In their dependence on religion, too, there was a difference. Irene's nature was particularly sympathetic to the dictates of religion. Her mother on the other hand, if she was not a hypocrite, at least subscribed to the motto: Heaven helps those who help themselves.

Even when Irene was in her early twenties her mother continued to feed her egotism on her daughter's dependence.

Then the unexpected happened. Irene became infatuated with Johannes Liedeman, a young man whom she met at a dance, and not all her mother's arts of bullying or persuasion could shake her out of it. One might have expected Mrs Fraser to be pleased at the prospect of marrying her not very attractive daughter off to someone, but from her point of view he had one fatal drawback. His complexion was darker than her daughter's, so that, according to her standards, he was beneath Irene in the social scale. He seemed to be earning a steady wage, which was indeed a rare good fortune among the coloured youth, and he might have a good character, though Mrs Fraser doubted it. But this one defect put him clean out of the running as a suitor for her daughter. The one factor with which he might have challenged her, on her own ground, was that he was related to a family – the Baaskemps – who passed for white. But he did not even trouble to mention it at this stage.

Mrs Fraser did not prevaricate. She was rude to Johannes Liedeman; she had to be rude to be kind or her daughter might make a fool of herself – and her mother.

What would people say about such a marriage? She was confident she could persuade Irene to see sense, but whether out of devilment or real affection for Irene, Johannes Liedeman persisted in his attentions. Mrs Fraser proceeded to paint him even darker than his complexion and succeeded only in bringing out a hitherto unsuspected trait in her daughter's character: stubbornness. It was most exasperating.

In defiance of Providence and all Mrs Fraser's dire warnings of disaster, Irene Fraser and Johannes Liedeman were married.

Strong in her self-righteousness, Mrs Fraser endured the blows of fate and in due course received her reward. Under any circumstances two such natures as those of Irene and Johannes were bound to clash and destroy each other in the process. Irene was handicapped in the first place by a constriction of her whole character and outlook, largely due to her mother's training. Her very mannerisms became a source of intense irritation to her husband, while to her his robust and forthright nature seemed merely coarse. Even the fact that he usually spoke a down-to-earth Afrikaans, whereas her mother had always insisted on English as their home language, became an added source of friction. With no key for the understanding of each other, their mutual antagonisms brought out the worst in each character, so that they became incapable of seeing each other except in a distorted light.

When her husband temporarily lost his job, Irene felt the full impact of poverty all the more galling. Compelled to live in a crowded district among Africans and coloureds of all sorts, she saw her mother's home in retrospect as a haven of blessed gentility. Her brief spark of independence went out in a flood of tears.

Mrs Fraser seized the opportunity to drive home the moral lessons of experience, the sin of disobedience and the folly of marrying a social inferior. When Johannes created what she described as vulgar and disgusting scenes, Irene was all for running home to her mother. This, however, did not exactly suit Mrs Fraser's purpose. Irene had made her choice and would have to live with it; if her mother out of the largeness of her forgiving heart was ready to supply a feather mattress of sympathy and advice, she must at the same time ensure a goodly stock of the thorns of marital discord by way of chastisement.

When Irene became pregnant, both women prayed that a fair child be vouchsafed to the daughter of Mrs Fraser. It was necessary to practise secrecy in this matter, since Johannes, having a strong suspicion as to what was afoot, roared and railed at them, saying that to pray for the fulfilment of such a desire was nothing less than blasphemy – a remark that convinced them that it was he who was guilty of that terrible sin.

The birth of Kathie, so unmistakably her father's child, was a sore disappointment. It was obvious that Irene's term of chastisement was not yet over. But as there is usually some good in every evil – according to Mrs Fraser – Irene's dependence on her mother became as great as it had ever been. With the steady fall in her daughter's domestic fortunes, there was a gratifying rise in Mrs Fraser's parental stock.

Two years later Andrew was born. He was almost worthy to be her grandson, except that the texture of his hair and his features revealed too strongly his father's heritage. Until the birth of Stella he was his grandmother's favourite. Not that he was particularly appreciative of the fact. If being a favourite involved frequent reprimands for being an untidy boy, he would have preferred to fall out of favour. He was a happy-go-lucky child more responsive to his father than his mother liked to admit and unfortunately more than his father took the trouble to realise. Johannes never went out of his way to make friends with his son.

Mrs Fraser's influence continued to be felt in many ways: in Irene's conduct of her home, in her stand-offishness with her neighbours, in her punctiliousness in religious observance, which she imposed also on her children at an early age, though she bewailed the difficulty of her task in view of the godless example of her husband. In these matters Johannes Liedeman was indifferent. For him, religion gave no answer to his problems. But that was no reason why it should not provide solace to the women, as long as they did not interfere with the peace of his home. Peace! That was what a man wanted most of all at the end of a gruelling day behind the wheel.

There was one respect, however, where his mother-in-law's influence created a profound disquiet in his mind. For the two women the question of colour had become an obsession. It dominated their thought, dictated their manners, became their religion.

Six years after the birth of Andrew, Stella had been born. To her mother and grandmother she was the miraculous fulfilment of their desire – a child with blue-grey eyes who looked almost as fair as a European. One day – who knows? – this delicate being would scale the towering racial cliff and cross to the other side. It was too early to judge from the innocent face of babyhood what her appearance as a young woman would be, but the words of her grandmother spoken at her birth voiced their conviction.

'Now let her father do what he likes! This is our child.'

The words expressed a fanatic conviction and to Johannes Liedeman they flung a challenge.

Colour. How potent was that word in its influence on the destiny of every member of the Liedeman family, and a thousand others like them? A racial creed, which segregates people along the colour line, had placed Mrs Fraser, her daughter and all their kind below that line, beyond the social pale. It is a white man's creed, and in its name he imposes on the non-white – by written and unwritten laws – conditions of poverty which speak powerfully to the eye and stink in the nostrils of the privileged. Is it any wonder then, that colour and inferiority become identified in his mind? It is the creed on which he is nurtured, so that he does not stop to examine the great gap in his logic that allows of such an error.

But what shall we say when a non-white also embraces this racial creed? He himself suffers from all its injustices, its discriminations, its insults. Every day he tastes the bitter bread of its humiliation. He sees it cast a blight on feeling, split a man's moral nature in two and distort his thinking; in its presence love between two human beings may sicken and die, or fear to be born. All this it can do and more. For how is it possible that the non-white, the victim of that racial

16

creed, can also have his thinking distorted by it? Yet so it is. Indeed it is a two-edged sword, destroying both those who wield it and those who cower under the blade.

CHAPTER 4

The dark and the fair

Baby Stella seemed to be born for happiness. With her pretty face and her pretty ways she endeared herself to everyone. For Kathie, her presence created new sensations. The pent-up affection of the girl's nature, bewildered by her father's erratic behaviour and often chilled by her mother's, found an outlet in her devotion to her baby sister. Sometimes when her mother had to go out, Kathie stayed away from school to look after the child and proved so efficient that her mother came to rely on her. She softened in her manner towards her eldest child, treating her as if she were older than her years, as indeed she was. How proud Kathie was of that trust! Basking in the double glow of giving and receiving affection, she felt that her little world was a happier place than it had ever been.

Andrew, too, petted this little angel in his rough and ready way – when he was given the chance. For Kathie would boss him and shoo him off, telling him boys didn't know how to handle babies. He would go off in a huff, muttering that he would get his own back on Kathie one day.

One Wednesday evening when Mrs Liedeman had gone to a church meeting with her mother and Andrew was already in bed, Kathie sat reading a book of fairy tales while her father lolled in his chair reading the evening paper. Baby Stella lay in her cot in the corner. She was not yet asleep as good babies ought to be but was busy trying out the strength of all her limbs simultaneously, tossing off her blanket and making warm little sounds that brought a smile to Kathie's lips even though she did not look up from the page she was reading. Now and again Johannes lowered his paper, stretched out his legs still further as he leant back in his chair, and glanced over at the baby and then at Kathie's bent head. It was a scene of rare contentment and peace in which he felt he could relax completely in every pore of his body.

Suddenly he rose, stepped quietly over to the cot and stood gazing at his youngest child. What delicate thing was this that had been born of his seed? The secret pride of fatherhood welled up in him and his features softened with a gentleness too long absent from his face. For Johannes Liedeman was a man in whom the well of affection, as deep as it was in his daughter Kathie, had been poisoned by the bitterness of estrangement from his wife and the dim consciousness of a life frustrated in its strongest desires.

Slowly he reached out and with one careful finger softly touched the child's cheek; the bright eyes caught the movement and the little limbs quickened their play. The father smiled, moving his lips with unaccustomed endearing sounds, to the child's gurgling delight.

Kathie looked up from the table, and without saying a word came and stood beside her father. Together they gazed down at the baby, then simultaneously turned to each other and exchanged a glance – a moment of such understanding and mutual pleasure that Kathie forgot all her former fear.

'Oh, Pa!' she cried.

Leaping up she flung her arms round his neck and hugged him.

The cry spoke not only of affection but pleading – pleading against the harshness she feared, the bitterness she sensed in him but could not explain. But above all it expressed their common devotion to the child. Their love was without taint of any kind; it was affection in its purest essence. Hand in hand they stood beside the cot. The baby kicked and cooed. Father and daughter smiled.

Johannes Liedeman had more than an inkling of what the birth of Stella meant to his wife, though he could not wholly guess how fanatically she was building her dreams around her youngest child. On one point, however, he was determined: his wife's mother would never have the care of Stella.

It was more difficult to keep her out of the house now, for she doted on the little one and always brought her a present. He could see that already in her mind was the idea that she could assist the family by offering to look after her youngest grandchild. He knew the arguments beforehand: a better upbringing for Stella than in the squalid conditions of her father's house; a much better locality, so respectable and genteel. Very kind of her indeed! Be damned to her! He would let no child of his fall into her clutches. She would be putting ideas into Stella's head, making her think there was something inferior in being coloured. She would have the child looking down on her father one of these days. *O God man*, and her mother, too, and all of them! He had seen it happening in other families; children ashamed of their parents, disowning their own brothers and sisters. He had seen it happen too often. But not in his home. Not if he knew it.

Johannes spat viciously at the thought. Suddenly he realised he had been letting himself be carried away by his fears. There sat the innocent babe in the pram her grandmother had bought, as happy a sight as ever blessed a father coming home weary at the end of a day's work.

In her possession of Stella, Irene Liedeman felt recompensed for all she had suffered in the past. She had been an unhappy, humiliated woman, despised by her husband. Yes, he who so much deserved her contempt could make her feel that he despised her. But now she had Stella. It gave her a fierce sense of pride, a feeling of independence she had never experienced before. She even resented her mother's possessive attitude towards the child, becoming impatient with her continual interference. Irene Liedeman had plans for her youngest born and nobody would stop her from carrying them out. God would help her. Every night she prayed to him. If God had sent her this fair child, it was for a purpose and she would be doing less than her duty if she failed to carry it out. She would give Stella every chance – starve herself if necessary to give her a good education that would lift her out of their world. There was nothing she wouldn't do for her, even to sending her out of this house, if it were for her good. Though it would break her heart.

Throughout those early years of Stella's childhood her mother nursed her ambitious dreams with a passionate but secret tenacity.

But the storms and conflicts lay far off in the future. Now it was almost as if they did not exist nor would ever bear their poisoned fruit.

With the presence of the sunny-natured Stella in the house there came a halcyon period within the Liedeman family circle. In those first years, with little to impinge upon her from the outside world, protected with loving care from the frosts and winds of her social environment, she gave and received happiness, growing like a flower. The affection bestowed on her flowered in turn through the happiness it gave.

It was to Kathie most of all that Stella clung. It was a rare sight to see two such children together, the dark and the fair, with an indefinable but unmistakable family likeness between them. The solemnity with which the Little Mother guarded her charge called forth smiles of friendly sympathy amongst the neighbours, who would comment to Mrs Liedeman on the prettiness of her youngest born and the sweetness of her eldest. Whereat Mrs Liedeman smiled too, lost some of her prim reserve and warmed to her neighbours. Maybe, she thought, she had kept to herself too much. They were very kind, she remarked to her husband.

'What did I tell you?' he said. 'Take people as you find them. Treat them decent and they'll treat you the same. If you show them any side, it only puts their backs up. I'm glad you're learning some sense at last!'

Johannes didn't express himself very tactfully, but his wife took what he said in good spirit. It was quite a while since he'd had any of his drinking bouts and that meant more money coming into the house. Things were looking up. If only they could get a house somewhere in a better district, like the area her mother lived in. There was Andrew growing into a big boy and every day more out of hand, always wanting to be out in the streets. She dreaded him falling into bad habits with the *skollie* type that lounged about the alleyways, living in vice and sin and ending up in the reformatory or in jail. And there was Stella – this district was no place for her. If only her mother and her husband weren't at daggers drawn they might even put up at her place, small as it was. But Johannes was so pig-headed, he'd never hear of it. She wasn't so sure she'd like it herself. Her mother was so bossy over what she should and shouldn't do where Stella was concerned. The best plan would be to look for a house of their own. If Johannes kept steady the way he had been doing for some time past, there was no reason why they shouldn't afford it.

The next few years slipped past unperceived, in comparative happiness. There were the usual stresses and strains between people compelled to live with one another, but the sum total formed a pattern neither light nor dark, but rather in greys and subdued colours. It is such a period as seems monotonous while it is being lived through. One may even have a passing mood of discontent and long for something to happen to break the monotony. Yet when it is past and the pattern is violently broken, when one looks back on it, it takes on a totally different colour. If this, the unhappy present, is life, one would willingly push it away and escape back into the security of the past. One cries out for the peace that is certain never to come again.

Stella was now seven years old. It was time to send her to school. Her physical being had already taken shape and form, and for the rest, if affection could create what was good, she promised well and fair. She had a smooth olive complexion against which her well set grey eyes, with their long black lashes, under shapely dark eyebrows, were strikingly beautiful. She had the rather broad face of her father, but the nose had delicate narrow nostrils. The fair down that had covered her head at birth had grown into a mass of soft dark curls. Nature had done her work admirably, as if she had found pleasure in blending the features of widely differing ethnic types into a well-defined beauty that was a joy to contemplate. The lips were full, though a touch of petulance at the corners marred their expression. She had been a spoilt and petted child. What promise of a full ripening beauty lay in this bud of childhood.

It was Kathie who first brought up the question of sending Stella to school because she was looking forward to taking her little sister to her own school. As she had been Little Mother to her since babyhood, it was she who must take the child by the hand and lead her into this new world, guarding her from the strangeness of the first days.

Kathie was nearly fifteen, not very tall for her age but sturdily built, with a figure already maturing. Her dark brown eyes were arched with the same strong brows as her sister. Her skin was smooth and brown as the sunlit depths of a pool, her lips full and firm, tinted like her cheeks with the bloom of youth. If Stella's eyes made you look again because of their colour, Kathie held you by her straight, intelligent glance, perhaps a little disconcerting in its directness. While she was her mother's right hand – for she was one of those who assume responsibilities as naturally as others shelve them – she was also very fond of reading. She had expressed a wish to continue her studies into high school, but her mother grumbled at the unnecessary expense, since what would the girl do with the extra education when as like as not she would be going into a factory?

'Oh, Ma, don't nag so!' remonstrated Kathie on one of those occasions when Mrs Liedeman said it was time Kathie was leaving school. 'I have a good chance of winning a bursary that lasts for two years.'

'A bursary won't feed and clothe you, my girl. It won't do much more than cover the expense of those books you're always wanting. Besides – '

At this point her husband broke in. 'You leave Kathie alone. Bursary or no bursary, I'll give her what she's set her heart on, and that's education. I'd have thought you'd be proud of the idea, as you are always thinking you're better than most people around here.'

'Where's the money coming from, I'd like to know?' Irene said. 'There's Andrew growing so fast there's no keeping him in his clothes and look at the number of shoes he kicks through in a year.'

'They're made of paper,' interrupted Johannes.

'Maybe that's my fault,' Irene snapped.

'*O magtig!* We're not talking about shoes! Kathie's going to get the best education I can give her, as long as I'm alive to do it!'

His wife stared at him. Since when had he been interested in education? But then Kathie always had been his favourite. 'There's Andrew's education, too,' she said sullenly.

'I never said he wouldn't get as much education as her – if he has the brains to take it in.'

'His brains are all right,' she said in defence of her only son.

Johannes laughed. '*Ja, wragtig,*' he said. 'He is *my* son!'

Glancing up from her book Kathie spoke up. 'Ma, I'll do all I can to manage on the bursary money. I know there's Stella's education too.'

Johannes Liedeman looked sharply at his wife. His lips tightened. 'I wouldn't be surprised if that's why you're always harping on Kathie leaving school. You've got something up your sleeve!'

Irene didn't want to speak in front of Kathie. She looked at her husband as though she could kill him. 'Stella must be educated,' she said.

Innocently Kathie continued. 'Ma, let me take Stella to school. I must see her started in my school before I go into high school.'

'We'll see,' Irene said, not looking at either of them.

'Please, Ma. Let me take her. It's time she was going to school.'

'You shut up now. As if I didn't know what was best for Stella!' Irene said, her patience beginning to run out.

'Why shouldn't Kathie take her along?' challenged her husband. He glared at his wife, but she remained silent, her lips pressed together with frustration.

'Spit it out, woman! I know what's in your head.'

Irene narrowed her dark eyes. 'How can you go on like that in front of Kathie?' she asked through clenched teeth.

'What is going on? Just you tell Kathie what you mean to do. At least, what you think you'll do.'

Kathie looked from one to the other. Here was a battle flaring up between them, just as it used to do. What was it all about?

Johannes laughed bitterly. 'Your mother thinks you and me aren't good enough for her precious baby. She wants to get her in with the blerry white sheep, and you and me and the rest of us can stay among the goats.'

Kathie stared at her father, but said nothing.

Irene strained every nerve to keep control over herself. She had long planned getting Stella into a European school by concealing her race. In this she was taking the first step in the fulfilment of her ambition for her youngest child. Now, she told herself, she mustn't lose in the very first round of her battle with her husband. She had often thought what she would say; in her imagination she had seen herself wheedling Johannes into accepting her plan, for didn't he dote on Stella as much as anybody did? But she had been taken unawares and she was disconcerted by Kathie's presence. Not that she couldn't ordinarily manage her teenaged daughter. The girl had plenty of spirit, but where her affections were concerned she was surprisingly docile. She would lie down and let Stella walk all over her if necessary.

Irene sighed deeply. She didn't need to consult a mere girl about her plans, she told herself. For one thing Kathie probably wouldn't understand what it was all about. But now her husband was trying to set Kathie against her.

She took a deep breath and glared at her husband. 'Do you mean to tell me you wouldn't be glad to see Stella having a chance to get out of the rut the rest of us are in?'

'Not your way! Not by teaching her to look down her nose at her own people!'

'You're talking nonsense!' said Irene.

Ignoring his wife Johannes looked open-mouthed at his daughter. 'Kathie, your mother thinks she can take Stella away from us. But we won't let her, will we?'

'It's not true, Ma, is it?'

'Of course it isn't. Your father's making a big fuss about nothing. I only want to send Stella to a decent school.'

'Decent!' Johannes exploded. 'A coloured school is good enough for Kathie and Andrew, but not for Stella! Is that what you mean? Let me tell you, woman, you're seeing the whole business upside down. I want all my children to get education, the same education as any other man's child. I want no coloured school for Stella, any more than you do. But we shouldn't have to send Kathie and Andrew to a coloured school either! What has a white child got that mine haven't – all three of them – except opportunity? It's a crazy world. But you're not going to put anything right by splitting up the children, sending Stella to a white school and Kathie and Andrew to a coloured school. Hell man. No! You'd be stuffing Stella's head with a false pride – ja man, and a false shame – '

'You've been drinking,' his wife said coldly.

'*O magtig*! You'd drive any man to drink.'

Kathie had stood all this time petrified at the hatred blazing up between her parents, sickened at their quarrelling about Stella, struggling to take in its meaning.

'All this fuss,' her mother continued, 'because I want to send Stella to a better school.'

'Ma, will they let her in?' Kathie asked softly.

Johannes jumped to his feet. He stood in front of his wife, his broad shoulders quivering with rage. 'Ja. That settles it! They won't let her in to the white school. And we aren't beggars to be turned away from any man's door.'

'I'll get my mother to take her to the school,' said Irene.

'Your mother!' There was an indescribable contempt in his voice. 'I knew she had a hand in this.'

Mrs Liedeman burst into tears.

'I'm only thinking of what's best for Stella,' she sobbed. 'God knows it's the only happiness I live for, to work for my child's happiness.'

'You are going a funny way about it, teaching her to be ashamed of her own people. You're aiming to destroy my child, that's what you're up to, though you're too crazy to see it. But I'm warning you. I'll whip the skin off your back before I'll let you do anything in this *verdomde* business.'

Kathie looked at her father and hugged her arms. He had the same smouldering look in his eye that used to frighten her.

'Stop your snivelling, woman. I'm getting out of here!'

Before Kathie could speak, he was gone, without a glance in her direction.

Left alone with her mother, Kathie was moved to pity. Poor Ma, she thought. Poor Ma. Involuntarily she recalled the experience that had most strongly affected her in childhood – the birth of Stella and the tortured face of her mother in the pangs of labour. It was something she could never forget. It was what always made her shrink from seeing pain in others.

CHAPTER 5

The battle is on

Nothing more was said for some days, but Kathie guessed that something was brewing between her mother and her grandmother. Nearly every afternoon her mother put on her neat Sunday suit and went off, leaving Kathie to prepare the supper. She had no friends in the neighbourhood whom she was likely to visit, so she must be going to Grandma's house. She came back in time for supper and changed her dress before Johannes arrived. Kathie said nothing, but she had her thoughts.

A gloom had hung over her since the day when the subject of Stella's schooling had been brought up and she had seen the hatred distorting the faces of her father and mother. The gloom was not in Kathie's mind only. It pervaded the house like a chilling fog and only the innocent cheerfulness of Stella, the cause of it all, was untouched by it. In the very silence there was an unnatural restraint, behind which forces seemed to be gathering themselves, ready to burst out again.

As Kathie had feared, her father returned home drunk on the

night of the quarrel and she found it hard to overcome the disgust she felt at his behaviour. As if nursing a secret shame, he avoided her in the days that followed. Possessed with one of his old sombre moods, he would flare up at a word from anyone. Her heart cried out to him, but she felt helpless, too young to take the initiative in speaking to him, too ignorant of life to realise the necessity to break the barrier between them and make contact at all costs. In a state of divided allegiance, she was the more bewildered by her mother's uncommonly gentle manner towards her. Where her father was violent and erratic, her mother had the air of long-suffering endurance. Johannes perceived this and it made him uneasy; it was so much simpler to explode and have done with it. His outburst had done nothing to shake his wife's resolve, for though weak in many ways, she clung with stubborn tenacity to her ambition for Stella. And now the sight of her husband's drunkenness only strengthened her feeling of self-righteousness.

One night when Kathie and her mother were sitting in the kitchen, Andrew and Stella already asleep in the only other room in the house, Johannes came in late and obviously the worse for drink. Silently his wife placed a plate of food in front of him. With a violent movement of his arm he sent the plate flying off the table.

Surveying the mess on the floor, Irene said calmly: 'Fetch a cloth and wipe up the mess, Kathie.'

The girl obeyed. As she bent down the smell of drink and hot sweat from her father's body sickened her; she tightened her lips and her eyes hardened with the effort to control her nausea.

Her father glanced up and caught the look. He glared at her, then lifted his hand and gave her a ringing blow on the side of the head.

'Leave it alone! Get out of my sight!' he shouted.

Numb with the physical pain and still more with the blow of her father's words, Kathie withdrew without a sound.

Johannes turned on his wife.

'So that's what you've been up to, you sneaking bitch!'

'I don't know what you mean.'

'What have you done to Kathie?'

'Ask yourself what you have done,' she retorted.

'There are rats in this house!' He spat on the upturned food. 'And there's an old rat outside who's doing a damn sight more harm than the rats that are in here. I'll wring her neck one of these days. The old bitch has lived too long!'

'If you so much as lift a finger to my mother I'll have the police on you!'

'The police?' He laughed. He was so struck with the moral depravity of his wife for harbouring such a thought that he was silent, gazing at her as if she was some obnoxious insect. Her glance wavered. 'I believe you would,' he said at last.

'Well, it's time your mother and me settled accounts. I can't call this house my own. I can't call my children my own. There's nothing she'd like better than to see a bust-up between us. But this is my home and I'm going to keep it mine. *God man*, you aren't much joy for a man to come home to. But I'm not going to give her the satisfaction of getting the better of me.'

'I don't know what you're talking about. My mother doesn't come here. That was what you wanted, wasn't it? To shut the door in her face.'

'Rats have long teeth.' Without looking at her he reached for his hat.

'Where are you going?'

'It's none of your business.' He slammed the door as he went out into the street.

With a frisson of alarm Mrs Liedeman stared at the door, then reassured herself that her husband had probably just gone off to see some crony of his; in his drunken state he had only been trying to frighten her about her mother. He took pleasure in it.

'Kathie,' she called. There was no answer from the next room. She called again. Slowly the door opened and Kathie crept towards her mother. Her dress was crumpled; her eyes were dry.

'Not in bed yet?'

Irene took a quick look to see the extent of the bruise on her daughter's face.

'I'm not sleepy.'

'Come, I'll bathe it for you.'

'It's nothing,' said Kathie, shrinking from her mother's touch.

'Are you trying to stand up for your pa?'

The girl did not answer.

'Kathie ... ' Mrs Liedeman hesitated. She wondered if it would be wise to take Kathie into her confidence. She was a big girl and old for her years. She would soon be working and able to bring in some money.

'Kathie, I know how you feel.'

Her daughter looked straight at her, yet through her.

'Nothing can excuse your father for what he did to you. I can't find it in my heart to forgive him. Maybe your grandma is right.' She paused. 'It's my duty to separate from him. For the sake of my children. For your sake, Kathie.'

'You mean leave Pa – '

'It's my duty.'

'Oh, no, Ma! He's fond of us really.'

'You can say that after what he did tonight?'

Kathie had no words to explain to her mother what she felt.

'I must give you a home. A real home, Kathie. Away from all this violence.'

'Where?'

'With your grandma.'

'With Grandma? Oh, Ma!'

Mrs Liedeman ignored the dismay revealed in Kathie's remark.

'It won't be easy making ends meet. But Grandma has promised to help us. And you'll soon be able to get a job, Kathie.'

'But Pa promised I could go to high school!'

'You'd see your mother working herself to the bone while you play around with books?'

'Oh, Ma, you don't understand.'

'I was a fool to take you into my confidence at all.' Mrs Liedeman drew in her cheeks. 'You'd better go to bed.'

'Ma, we can't just leave Pa all alone. What would he do without Stella – he's so fond of her?'

'Stella!' Her mother laughed wildly.

'Couldn't I stay with Pa and look after him?'

'Then you won't see your little sister again.'

Kathie felt the cruelty of her mother's words.

Mrs Liedeman stood up and with staccato movements started tidying the table. 'Don't be silly, Kathie. It's no one like *you* your pa wants to look after him. Now go to bed.'

When Kathie had gone, her mother fell back into her chair. Silently, with her head in her hands and her shoulders heaving and an ache that tore her heart asunder, she wept.

CHAPTER 6

The house by the level crossing

As he walked the streets on his way to his mother-in-law's house, Johannes sobered up completely. His heart had been inflamed at the sight of Kathie's disgust, and he had struck out blindly, but as to 'settling accounts' with Mrs Fraser – when it came to talking, he was no match for the womenfolk. He had acted on the spur of the moment when he said he'd have it out with her.

But he didn't turn back. Better walk a bit and clear the fog out of his brains anyway.

What did trouble him was the fact that he had struck Kathie. *Allemagtig*, why had he done it? Poor Kathie. She hadn't said a word. She had never been one to whine, like her mother. *God*, but their married life had been a sorry mess and now it was getting worse. A queer thing how spiteful a woman could become. Once his wife got an idea into her head, there was no knowing what lengths she'd go to. She had the devil's own cunning, for all that she was as stupid as you could make them.

This idea of sending Stella to a European school. He had tried to put it to Irene as he saw it, but she hadn't listened to a word of it, he was sure of that. He would have to be very firm in the matter. Meantime that damned mother of hers was busy stoking the fires. It made you feel like cracking up, man, all this dirty business going on behind your back. Yes. Yes, perhaps he'd better have it out with her after all.

It was a long walk. His mother-in-law's house was alongside the railway line, diagonally opposite a level crossing. Johannes hated level crossings; hated the booms and the red flashing lights. Thank goodness he didn't have to cross the line on this occasion. So often, especially when he was driving, he would be kept waiting at these level crossings, cursing the fellow who stood safely out of earshot in his signal box, certain that he kept the booms down on purpose to provoke him.

Ah, there was the house, just below the line. He couldn't remember when last he had been in it; the pretentiousness of the place smacked too much of the woman herself for him to have any liking for it.

There was no light on in the front room. Most likely she'd be at the back. Perhaps she had gone to bed, in which case she'd have to get up again, for he had no intention of going home till he'd had it out with her. He gave a good tat-tat on the door and was in the act of repeating it when the door was opened a little way, revealing Mrs Fraser in a dark green dressing gown.

She was surprised, if not apprehensive at the sight of her visitor, especially at this time of night. She opened the door a little wider.

'Has anything happened?' she asked.

'I want to talk to you,' he answered abruptly.

The neighbours had not yet gone to bed and Mrs Fraser had no desire for a scandal. The man had probably been drinking, she thought, quickly letting him in and closing the door after him. Without waiting for her he walked along a narrow passage to a door leading into the front room.

There he was arrested by a curious phenomenon. The light had not been switched on, but the room was not in darkness; it was illumined by a strange red glow that pulsed, strong and weak, strong and weak, with a disturbing regularity. It was as if he was aware of his own heartbeat magnified in some supernatural way. Glancing towards the window with its flimsy lace curtain he realised that the boom lights from the railway crossing were on now, giving warning of an approaching train. What a maddening effect they had! Their powerful rays must penetrate the room all night long unless you took care to shut them out. It was like his mother-in-law to have such a thing in her vicinity, he reflected quite unreasonably, without pausing to consider that residential segregation severely limited her choice of abode no less than it did his own.

She came forward and switched on the light. The brown patterned linoleum covering the floor reflected the light with an unpleasant glare, but did little to dim the strong red beams from outside. Only when she had drawn the inner curtains was the insistent rhythm of this powerful irritant shut out.

'You don't ask me to sit down,' he said, pulling forward a straight-backed chair and seating himself.

'You make it unnecessary,' she said, coldly.

'It's a cosy room you've made for yourself,' he remarked, though the room had the chill air of not being lived in but carefully preserved. The oval oak table, looking as if a homely cup of tea had never violated its varnished surface, was barricaded by four high chairs, though Johannes had rudely broken the symmetry by planting himself on one of them. An uncomfortable looking easy chair and small settee to match had crocheted antimacassars where clearly no human head had ever rested.

On the easy chair Mrs Fraser now sat stiffly waiting for her son-in-law to state his business.

'Do you mind if I smoke?' said Johannes taking a squashed cigarette from his back pocket and lighting it.

Wisely she refrained from either granting or refusing permission to a fait accompli while he puffed a few soft rings of smoke in her direction – incongruous forerunners of the hard words to follow. She waited, her small dark eyes watching his every movement as the rumble of a passing train filled up the silence.

Johannes was himself surprised at his own coolness. He wished that his wife could see him at this moment. Pity he hadn't faced up to the woman long ago instead of allowing himself to get all worked up inside. Of late he'd been feeling the strain of driving the van long hours every day, but it was the worry that aggravated it. Now he felt master of the situation.

'You're a clever woman,' he began.

With this statement Mrs Fraser fully agreed. No comment was

necessary.

'Since the day I married your daughter you've been meddling with my affairs. I sent you packing years ago but that didn't stop you from worming your way in. You couldn't stop the wedding – I grant you it would have been better for me if you had and since then you've aimed at one thing. To smash my married life.'

Mrs Fraser regarded her son-in-law with a look laden with disdain. 'I think you've done that pretty well yourself. Time has proved I was right when I told Irene she was preparing a bed of sorrow for herself in marrying the likes of you.'

'Marrying the likes of me, as you call it, was a damn sight too good for her. But it would have worked. It would have worked if you'd left her alone.'

'She came running back to me because you put the fear of death into her those first weeks of her marriage.'

'You have a dirty mind!' he said with venom in his voice. 'That's the way you wanted her to feel.'

'If you can only hurl abuse at a respectable woman, the sooner you take yourself out of my house the better.'

'Respectable woman? You're a hypocrite! If to be a Christian is to be mean, spiteful, narrow-minded, then thank God I'm not a Christian! If loving your daughter means to grab and grasp her all your life long, twisting her mind the way you want it, then the Lord save us from all such loving! I'd rather have a snake squeeze me to death. In all your dirty scheming it wasn't her happiness you were thinking of.'

Carried away by his own eloquence, Johannes might have continued indefinitely if he hadn't been stopped short by the look of shocked amazement on his mother-in-law's face. Was it possible she had hoodwinked even herself into believing in the purity of her motives? He went on more quietly.

'What you've done to Irene I can't mend. But one thing you're not going to do and that is interfere with the bringing up of my little Stella. Hands off, I say!'

'Irene has as much right as you in deciding what is best for Stella,' said Mrs Fraser with a smirk on her face.

'Not with you behind her. For you'd corrupt the child's mind. Teach her to look down on her parents. *Ja*, and teach her to look down on herself!'

'You are crazy.'

'What's good for a white man's child is good for mine too, whether it's Stella or Andrew or Kathie. Take note of that, you *verdomde* hypocrite. But I'm not sending Stella to a European school on your terms. Not sneaking in expecting a clout on the head if she should ever be found out.'

'It's because I want to save Stella from your kind of life that I advised Irene to act as she is doing,' said Mrs Fraser calmly.

Johannes sprang to his feet, almost sending the chair flying across the room. 'You! Save her? I don't understand your language, woman.'

With her lips almost in a straight line, Mrs Fraser continued. 'Only a strong sense of duty, which I instilled into her, has made Irene put up with the degraded life, yes, the degraded life she has led with you. But now a stronger duty calls her – her duty to her children. I may as well tell you I have advised Irene to seek for a separation. And she has agreed.'

Signalling that there was no more to be said, Mrs Fraser lifted her chin and forced the air out of her lungs. As she rose from her armchair the man's fist shot out and landed her a blow that sent her staggering against the table, so that she fell, striking her head as she crashed to the floor. For a moment she lay stunned. Cursing, Johannes bent down to help her. He had never meant this to happen. As soon as he touched her she came to herself, struggled to her feet and gave him a look of such hate that he stood back aghast.

'You'll pay for this,' she said through her teeth.

To Johannes she looked grotesque and yet something in her venomous tone chilled him to the heart.

'Ughhh! I didn't mean to dirty my hands touching you. Good night.'

And with that he let himself out of the house, walking away as quickly as he could.

Approaching the level crossing before turning left and heading east towards Landsdowne, the boom lights almost blinded him. Switching steadily from side to side, they aggravated his already overwrought mood. The train wasn't even coming yet, was nowhere in sight and he shook his fist at the invisible signalman for holding up the cars waiting impatiently to cross. Just then he heard the siren of the oncoming train and couldn't help himself stopping to watch it, mesmerised by its overwhelming force.

The purely physical effect of its passing, the rush and rhythm of this looming object with blankly lighted windows and unseen faces, the thunder of the powerful turning wheels so close to his body, the very tremor of the ground where he stood, and the ceaseless to and fro movement of the red lights at the booms, all produced in him a vague apprehension, a sensation of being overwhelmed, engulfed by forces over which he had no control.

Ordinarily he was not given to morbid thoughts. He was by nature simple and straightforward, strong in his feelings, stirred easily to anger, irked by frustration. He did not willingly come face to face with the problems of existence in the sense of consciously grappling with them or even formulating them. The impact of life from day to day was as much as a man could cope with. But the events of the last week had given him no respite. *God*, why must a man be so tormented! What could a mere fist do against tortuous ways of thought?

The train passed; the booms lifted; the red lights dimmed and were still. Johannes walked on absent-mindedly and was vigorously cursed by the driver of a red MG screeching to the left after speeding over the crossing. Hooting loudly, it swerved to avoid him. He didn't know what it was all about, but he gave good measure back as the driver flung his abusive epithets in the wake of the retreating car. With this slight relief to his feelings he walked on, his head bent as he soon became immersed in his thoughts again.

Johannes realised that he was up against the fanatic determination of the two women. His wife could be obstinate; her tactics would exasperate him and wear him down. Her martyred expression would invite his blows, made in sheer self-defence, with the odds in her favour. But he told himself that he mustn't let her get away with it this time. There was too much at stake; the future of Stella, and Kathie and Andrew too. But especially Stella. He must talk to his wife again, try to keep calm and work it all out and show her exactly what she was doing. He had said she was aiming to destroy his child. And by God, it was true!

All the way home his thoughts went on milling through his head. By the time he came to the street where he lived he found it dark and deserted. A mongrel dog barked and came up to him, then wagged its tail obsequiously at the familiar touch and the sound of his voice. Turning in at his gate he suddenly became aware of how tired he was.

There were no lights on in his house.

CHAPTER 7

Father and daughter

Next morning, no spoken words passed between husband and wife. The usual morning scramble to get to work did not encourage speech at any time, but this morning Johannes was so charged with what he wanted to say that he didn't know how to begin, and decided it was better to wait till he came home in the evening. Besides, he had a lousy head.

Kathie, with her bruised face, avoided her father. Shame for him and for herself made her hide out of the way.

Mrs Liedeman eyed her husband furtively. There was something in his manner that made her anxious. She wondered if he had gone to her mother's house the previous night after all. If so, what had passed between them? Had her mother told him? Not likely, or he would have made a row when he came in. He could never keep a thing like that bottled up. Not like her. He had to come out with it, or burst.

Just as he was going out he stood over the bed where Stella was still fast asleep. A gentle expression came over his face and very tenderly with his strong coarse fingers, he slowly lifted a curl away from her eyes. Then without even a 'so long' he hurried off into the busy street. Thinking of his gesture after he had gone, his wife felt a momentary pang of pity. For all his rough ways he was fond of the child. He would miss her. But she mustn't go back on her decision now. For the sake of Stella she had to leave him and the sooner the better. She would discuss it with her mother, where she had decided to go as soon as possible in order to satisfy her curiosity as to what had happened the night before.

Johannes had a trying day. Everything went wrong that could go wrong – or so it seemed to him. First he had words with the clerk who gave him his orders for the day – a pale-faced European fish who lorded it over him. Blast his eyes! The fellow said he'd lodge a complaint with the boss. For what? Because Johannes had dared to speak up for himself? Let him complain and be damned to both of them! Then he had trouble with the van. Nothing much, and luckily he knew about the mechanics of a car, so he didn't have to take it to a garage. It had been his pride when he was younger to fiddle around with gadgets and get the hang of them all on his own, and now his knowledge came in handy. All the same it had meant him getting down under the van and sweating his guts out before he had it going again. A traffic cop had told him to get a move on. *Magtig*, there was no end to the ways in which people interfered with you and you just wanting to do your job and leave others in peace. Swallowing a sharp retort that would have only landed him in more trouble, he put the van in gear and shot off at a good speed. Maybe they'd have him up for that next, but he must make up for the time he had lost.

At the back of his mind was the gnawing worry of his home affairs. He would have to argue it out with his wife that very night, clear the air and come to some understanding. 'Hey!', someone roared at him, and he stopped the van so suddenly that the youth who travelled with him nearly shot through the windscreen. He hadn't noticed that the traffic lights were against him.

'Whew! That was a near shave!' the youth exclaimed, wiping his mouth with the back of his hand as he glanced sideways at Johannes.

'Steady,' Johannes told himself. Keep your eyes glued on the road and don't let your thoughts wander so much! He moved off amid black looks and threats of being reported.

'You coloured bastards should be kicked off the road,' said one driver whom he saw taking his number. That was always the way. They blamed it on you for being coloured.

Johannes glanced over at his companion. 'A good thing the brakes are in order. You all right, son?'

'Okay,' the youngster replied and they laughed together with relief now that the danger was over.

When he entered the kitchen about six o'clock that evening he was surprised to find Kathie alone. She greeted him with constraint and hurried to set a plate of food on the table.

'Where's your ma?' he asked.

'She's gone out.'

'She isn't usually so late. Where's the kids?'

'Andrew's still out playing. He's had his supper.'

'And Stella?'

'Ma took Stella with her.'

'Oh. When was that?'

'In the afternoon.'

'Gone to her mother's, I suppose.'

Kathie didn't answer. He glanced at her sharply.

'What's up? Did she say when she'd be back?'

Kathie came up to him. He saw that her eyes were brimming with tears she had been trying to hold back.

'Oh, Pa,' she said. 'Ma came home in the afternoon in a terrible state. She said you nearly killed Grandma!'

'Nonsense. That's one of her lies. The old woman angered me so, I gave her a clout. She deserved worse.'

'Ma came in and began packing some things in a case. She was crying all the time. She told me to get Stella ready because she was taking her to Grandma's. She isn't coming back tonight. She says you'll do something terrible to her ... and to Stella too.'

Johannes looked at Kathie gravely. 'Do you believe that?'

Kathie was silent. Her dark eyes returned his look.

With a shock he remembered that he hadn't given the child much cause to trust him. He thought of what he'd done to her last night. He moved closer and gingerly stroked her head. She winced. He swallowed hard wondering if it was because of the bruise. Could she really be afraid of him when all he thought about was how best to protect her and Stella from that woman? How little his daughter knew him! And how little he had tried to win her confidence. But she had stayed here and prepared his food. Had that been for her mother's sake?

'Don't worry, Kathie. I'll do them no harm,' he said gently. 'Your mother wants to take you and Stella and Andrew away from me.'

'I know,' she said in a stifled voice.

'Did your mother tell you?'

'Yes.'

'And what did you say?'

'I don't want to leave you, Pa.'

He gripped her hand, holding on to it as though it were a lifeline and he was drowning.

'Listen to me, Kathie. You're too young to understand what it all means. But what your ma and grandma want to do is not a good thing. This business of them wanting to send Stella to a European school and make her so that she won't be your sister no more – that's just the beginning of it. Heaven knows what would be the end of it if they had their way! But I must stop them, Kathie. Do you understand?'

'Yes, Pa.' She said it to comfort him.

'Will you help me, Kathie?'

She nodded, holding her lips tight so they wouldn't tremble. 'Yes,' she said. Then after a moment she asked: 'Will you go and bring them back tonight?'

Johannes hesitated. If he went now his wife would be sure to refuse. With her mother to support her she would make a scene. He couldn't face another scene. He'd had enough of them.

He slumped down into his chair, too tired to eat, too tired even to go to bed and rest. 'I'm tired out, Kathie. I think I'll let them be for tonight.'

Kathie looked at her father anxiously. With all her heart she wanted to remove this trouble that was weighing on his mind. But what could she do? Her affection told her he was a tormented man. She did not judge him. It frightened her to see her father and mother hurting each other the way they did. Why must it be this way between them? Feeling forlorn, she knelt down next to him and laid her head against his shoulder. Without lifting his head he put his arm around her.

When Andrew burst into the kitchen some time later, hot and panting from a street fight, and full of how he'd got the better of his opponent, Kathie helped him to clean himself up a bit and packed him off to bed, not without remonstrances on his part.

'Pa's tired,' she said. 'Can't you go to bed quietly for once?'

The boy looked at his father and something of the man's utter weariness penetrated even his unimaginative mind. He felt uneasy and subdued but not for long.

His mischievous young spirit prompted him to pull his sister's hair when she wasn't looking, whereupon she smacked him and tucked him into bed. His last friendly gesture was to put out his tongue at her and then pop his head under the blankets before she could retaliate.

Returning to the kitchen she found her father sitting at the table as she had left him.

'Do go to bed, Pa,' she pleaded. 'You look so tired just sitting there.'

'*Ja*, okay,' he answered, his voice flat and despondent.

For a long time Kathie lay and listened to his breathing. At last he was asleep. Then she, too, slept.

In the morning Kathie woke her father in time for him to go to work. Still tired and half asleep, he flung on his clothes. As consciousness and memory came back to him, his spirit sank. There was Kathie bustling about for him like the little mother she was, but where were his wife and Stella? He missed them. *Ja*, even the woman who had given him so little happiness, he missed her.

He wondered what would happen in the course of the day. How would she feel after staying away for the night? Would she want to get back to her own home after all? It wouldn't be so easy getting used to being with that domineering mother of hers every day, not after having a home of her own. There was nothing like your own home. Well, he must be off. He'd be late if he didn't hurry. He'd go and see his wife in the evening when he came back from work.

Kathie watched him go, sadness filling her whole being. He looked back and waved and she waved in return.

Going back slowly into the kitchen she continued to think of him.

She felt closer to him than she had ever done in her life before. Maybe – she stood still at the thought – maybe she could do something to bring her mother and father together again. If only Grandma didn't hate her father so much. She was afraid of Grandma ... But no, first she must get Andrew off to school.

Kathie had more than one bad mark at school that day. She was accused of being indifferent to her work, absent-minded and careless. When asked why she hadn't done her homework she answered: 'I forgot.' The teacher rejected her excuse and said she was lying. In the playground the girls asked her what she was moping about. She said she wasn't moping and would they mind their own business. They gave her a push, laughed and ran off to play. Indeed, what was the matter with her? The teacher asked her a question and she didn't hear it. Then she was punished for being impudent, but really she hadn't heard it. She was thinking how she would go and see her mother tonight and tell her how sad her father had been last night. She was missing Stella. She couldn't imagine herself being deprived of the thousand and one things the two of them did together. She was sure Stella would cry if she couldn't be with her big sister Kathie.

She gave a sigh of relief when school broke up and without waiting for any of her friends she ran on, eager to reach home. What would she find there? Her father wouldn't be back till it was almost dark. Would her mother and Stella be there after all? Her mother would have to come back, as she would never leave Andrew. There were all her things in the house, too. When two people separated like that, what happened to all the household things they had collected together, the dishes and the table and the chairs and all the little things they'd bought for fun when they had something to spare? It must hurt, leaving them behind. If she knew her mother, it was she who would take most of the things away with her. Poor Pa!

Her hopes rose as she neared the house and she sped like the wind down the last street, her dark hair flying, the books in her case dancing up and down. Out of breath, she tried the door. It was locked, just as she had left it.

She entered slowly, pushed her school hat off the back of her head, and letting her case slip unheeded from her fingers, sat by the table on the chair her father had occupied the night before. On the table were the crumbs, and a few dishes she had left unwashed after Andrew had finished his hurried breakfast; the place looked untidy and forlorn. No, she didn't want to do a thing. Andrew could look after himself when he came in. She wished it wasn't so long before her father came home. Poor Pa! He too, like her, would hurry home expecting, hoping, and when he opened the door quick and eager and saw only Kathie ...

She didn't even feel hungry. She would sit a while and when it was near the time when her father usually came home she'd make something nice for him.

So the afternoon wore away. Andrew arrived, dumped his books, grabbed some bread and was gone again as always. It was growing dark and still her father hadn't come. Kathie began to be anxious. Sometimes he was kept late when there was an extra delivery to one of the outlying suburbs. Maybe he'd gone to the Royal for a drink. Her heart contracted at the thought, remembering what had happened two nights ago. He'd forget last night with its kindness between them and grow sullen and sore ... Maybe he would go straight to Grandma's house.

Long after the mountain was no longer silhouetted against the sky, she sat down reluctantly at the table and ate a little of the rice she'd prepared for her father. He would scold her if she waited for him and would ask what nonsense was this. Sometimes her mother shouted when he came in late and that would anger him. Why should he come in on time for a meal? he'd say. Women were always fussing.

Afterwards she washed the dishes, wishing her father would hurry up and come now because the food was getting spoiled. Just then there was a knock at the door. Kathie started. It wasn't a friendly knock. This knocking was sharp and hard. It came again. On opening the door she saw a policeman standing outside and drew back a step. Instantly she thought: what had her father done now? To all coloured people the police are a symbol of attack or threat of attack against their well-being, their liberty, their person. Dimly she saw people hovering behind him, curious to know what had happened. Gruffly shooing them off, the policeman asked if this was where Mrs Liedeman lived.

'Yes,' said Kathie, even more perplexed now.

'Is she in?'

'No.'

'Are you her daughter?' Kathie's lip trembled. 'Yes.'

The policeman took a step towards her. 'Do you know where your mother is?'

If he wanted to speak to her mother then her father *had* done something terrible. Should she tell the policeman where her mother was? No, she wouldn't.

'Hurry up,' said the policeman. 'I can't stand here all night.'

As though turned to stone Kathie made no move.

'There's been an accident,' said the policeman.

'An accident! My pa?'

Kathie never remembered clearly what she did after that. Yes, something had happened to her father and her mother had to be fetched and taken to the hospital as quickly as possible. She didn't remember when her mother came or how. She never saw her father again. The accident was at one of those railway crossings that didn't have the booms. Death had been instantaneous. She never knew exactly how it had happened: whether it had been his fault, or he hadn't seen the train coming or something had gone wrong with the van when it was on the line. She could never bring herself to speak about it to anybody. Not even to her mother.

CHAPTER 8

'You're different'

For a long time after her father's death Kathie's manner was subdued and sullen. People remarked that she had changed; she used to be such a sweet-natured child before her father died. Her mother scolded her for being sulky. But she wasn't sulking. She had suffered a profound shock and the very strength of her affections prevented her from throwing off its effects quickly, as the young usually do; where her affections were concerned she was tenacious, even stubborn. All her life she lived through her emotions; through them she experienced her greatest happiness and suffered her deepest sorrow; they were her understanding, her wisdom – and perhaps her folly. They were the touchstone by means of which she knew the worth of man or woman; through her affections she would love or hate, pity or forgive.

While she never spoke about her father until long afterwards, during those first months after his death her thoughts constantly turned to him. She pictured the last time she had seen him, hurrying off to work; how he had waved and she had waved in return. She recalled how she had felt that day, as if oppressed with the shadow of foreboding – for so it seemed to her on looking back. She remembered with a pang how she had prepared for him the food he liked – and he was already dead. What had his thoughts been before he died? Had he been wondering how he would solve his problems, when it happened? Thinking hard, as she had been thinking in school when she didn't hear the teacher asking her a question?

Over and over she recalled the night before he died. What he had said then was sacred, because they had been his last words to her. *You are too young to understand,* he had said. *But what your ma and grandma want to do is not a good thing. That's just the beginning of it.*

The beginning of what? She couldn't figure this out clearly. She had told him she understood, but that was just to make him feel easy about it. He'd said something about Stella not being her sister any more, but how could that ever be? Stella loved her more than she did anybody, Kathie told herself with fierce possessiveness. Even more than she loved Ma ...

And then she recalled how her father had said: *I must stop them, Kathie.* But he hadn't been able to stop them. He was dead.

The fact that he had confided in her, young as she was, gave her a feeling of responsibility that she nursed within herself. His death had cut him off from whatever it was that he'd wanted to do. How terrifying death was, making an end so suddenly. All that had troubled him about her sister, all he had meant to do, he would never do. What the nature of it was she did not yet know. What she did know was that for his sake she must guard over Stella and give her all the love of which she was capable. But then she had always done that.

Her mother and her grandmother tried to get Kathie to talk about her father, but she had shut her lips and kept her counsel. Only when her grandmother suggested that Johannes had probably been drinking before the accident was she moved to a violent contradiction of such a suggestion. At the same time they were careful not to hide from her certain conversations they had as to the ways of Divine Providence and the way things turned out for the best even if at the time they seemed hard to bear. It was natural that a child should miss the father she had been fond of; she would probably forget his faults and magnify his virtues. But she must not forget how he had made her mother suffer when he was alive. And, said her grandmother, the very day he was killed Kathie bore on her face the marks of the blow he had given her. This hurt Kathie, for where her heart had almost instantly forgiven, it seemed as if her flesh had been too willing to remember.

The death of her father had brought a revolution in Kathie's life that was more than simply the loss of a parent and the removal of the mainstay of the family. The material circumstances were much the same; the family had exchanged an obvious for a more genteel poverty. The death of Johannes had resolved his wife's problem in one way – she had no choice but to go and live in her mother's house; always excellent with her needle, she would assist her mother with the dressmaking and earn her keep that way. The family was more crowded than it had ever been, but, as Mrs Fraser said, it was better than living in a dreadful slum.

For Kathie the transference to a home dominated by her grand-mother, and more than that, to a locality so different from the one she'd been accustomed to, involved a change in spiritual atmosphere in which the young girl pined as from a sickness, without knowing why. It hadn't been easy living in her father's house, for he had been a violent man. But he was also a warm-hearted man. There had been storms, but there was laughter too; there was poverty, but in him no meanness. It had been a home in which the spirit could still breathe freely.

In the genteel terrace where the family now lived things were always done with an eye to appearances; the lace curtain, which covers and conceals, was its symbol. The keeping up of outward appearances demanded cheese-paring economies and meannesses. It was on the whole a mean and petty world. There was a keeping of oneself to oneself, yet everyone knew everyone else's business. Such and such a neighbour would be considered undesirable because his or her occupation was not of the genteelest; this one's sister had a reputation for – well, you can draw your own conclusions when you see no obvious means of livelihood. And as for that one's brother, he was far beyond the limits of acceptance. There was a punctilious carrying out of religious observances, but the customary expressions of humility and trust seemed to have no bearing on human relationships. Here flourished jealousy and envy, malice and spite. The woman next door but one didn't go to the right kind of church; you were English Presbyterian while she was only Dutch Reformed.

To procure a more handsome piece of furniture was to score a point against your neighbour, even if the monthly instalments landed you deep in debt. If your neighbour's child, because of his lighter skin colour, contrived to be admitted into a white school, while yours, though only slightly darker, was denied entrance, it was your righteous duty to inform the headmaster of the fraud being perpetrated against the white community, and you would have the satisfaction of seeing the child withdrawn. The resulting feud between the families was in imminent danger of violating all the laws of gentility, for vulgar brawls were practically unknown in this locality.

In this world of pretension the gentler virtues pine and die; suffering itself is deprived of nobility and endurance is inglorious. Indeed the privation of the spirit is its most deadly aspect, even more than the physical privation. The struggle for existence is all the more relentless for being disguised. It is in this stratum of society, wherever social or racial disability – or both combined – impose on the individual a desperate effort to climb up to a higher stratum, that one fears most for the survival of human kindness. For all these pitiless and pitiful efforts are based on a false conception of values; an aiming at the show of things rather than the substance. Humanity can better survive where conditions have reached rock-bottom and existence is unashamedly that of tooth-and-claw. There, where everything seems designed to crush the last vestige of human dignity, an act of kindness may suddenly blossom in the midst of brutality, thus demonstrating humanity's defiance of all attempts to destroy it.

So the transference from a home of her own – whatever its tribulations – back to her mother's house did not make things easy for Mrs Liedeman. Mrs Fraser saw herself as a generous benefactor and expected interest on her outlay of capital – and compound interest at that. There was much talk of gratitude, or more often reproaches for ingratitude, a form of tyranny practised by the ungenerous on the victims of their self-indulgence, who can never till the end of time discharge their debt to such benefactors.

The relationship between Mrs Fraser and her daughter, especially at this stage, was of an ambivalent nature. It had complexities and contradictions often to be observed between two people who are closely bound together and too dependent upon each other. If love is the bond between them, it does not exclude elements of hate, jealousy or resentment. It frequently finds expression in irritation or cruelty; it is capable of deceiving; and the only thing alien to it is indifference. Johannes Liedeman had been right when he said that his wife would not take easily to being under her mother's roof again. The pattern of relationship that had existed during her youth could never be exactly repeated. She had been a wife and a mother and, happy or unhappy, this gave her rights and privileges, needs and claims of which the unmarried girl had known nothing. For a mother to attempt to impose her former tyranny was to create an undercurrent of resentment on both sides, since the mother was aware that her realm of authority had shrunk while the daughter jealously guarded such freedom as the married state had bestowed on her. The older woman, with some of her own comforts curtailed by the presence of three obstreperous youngsters, inevitably criticised her daughter's management – or, as she would say, mismanagement – of her children and when she interfered too much her daughter would resent it. Their close proximity in the small house, each tied for long hours to the same occupation, aggravated the tensions between them and resulted in continual petty bickering. Johannes Liedeman had indeed too effectively removed himself, from Mrs Fraser's point of view, for he had deprived her of much of the justification for her benevolent tyranny.

This, then, was the spiritual atmosphere in which Kathie grew up during the years following her father's death. It was a crucible in which the qualities of her nature were tested and struggled to survive. In this battle her intelligence stood her in good stead; her sensitiveness at once exposed her to hurt and sharpened her awareness of people, while her affection was more an enemy than an ally. Her memory of her father was something she kept alive in the midst of her present mode of life and as she matured she realised that the things he stood for were different from those that dictated the actions of her mother and her grandmother. Not that he had been a man to formulate his ideas; as a worker he had no time nor inclination for that. But his very simplicity and straightforwardness of character were positive qualities which were all the more valuable to the girl because she felt an alien in her present environment.

Her chief source of happiness was in her devotion to her sister Stella, and the wholehearted affection that the child gave her in return.

But it was not long before this fount, too, began to be poisoned.

The reason for this was already inherent in the pattern of relationship within the Liedeman family, a pattern that revealed itself more clearly with the death of Johannes and the removal of his influence on the fate of his children. Now Kathie was the inheritor of her father's standpoint; in her lay the potentiality of upholding it. But she was as yet too young and immature, herself weak and unprotected; and incapable at this time of formulating what was taking place. How could she, then, protect her sister from those ideas which her grandmother and her mother proceeded to implant in her mind? Ideas which in the last analysis accepted the racial myth of the inferiority of colour. Incapable of any subtleties of argument, crude in his speech, his wisdom acquired from the harsh experience of life, Johannes knew the myth to be false and with simple dignity claimed equality for his children with those of any man. In his awareness of the perverted ambition for Stella on the part of the two women, he had cried: 'They are aiming to destroy my child!' and he had appealed to Kathie to help him prevent it. Yet in the nature of things, what a burden to place on her young shoulders, and how impossible for her to carry out her role of Little Mother, to which she had dedicated herself with such fervency. With the new disposition of forces within the family, Kathie, being darker than any of the others, was in a particularly isolated position.

Indeed, the two sisters became the pivot of an ever-growing conflict. It is a conflict that has its roots deep in any society where one race dominates another, a society cleft in two on every plane by the dread concept of colour.

Mrs Fraser and her daughter, with their acceptance of the racial myth, saw above and beyond them a paradise of privilege – the white world. But it was not something they thought of claiming as their natural right, or something to be fought for together with their brothers. For them it was a world to be entered into through a narrow door, one by one, surreptitiously, fearfully, anonymously. They themselves, having the physical traits which too clearly excluded them, could not hope to enter this world; all the more eagerly, therefore, did they pin their hopes on Stella achieving what they could not do. They would make sacrifices in order to prepare her to enter this world of white privilege, with its very substantial benefits. As for themselves, they hung between two worlds and in turn looked down on those who were darker than themselves. For them, the galling thing was that Kathie, one of their own, both by her appearance and her attitudes, as she grew older, clearly proclaimed her allegiance to the mass of their people, and at the same time emphasised their own precarious footing. In her own family she did not quite belong. This she was made to feel again and again with an anguish she was never to forget.

On the other hand, in pursuing their ambition for Stella they did not ask themselves on what tortuous path they set her innocent feet, nor what store of spiritual suffering they were laying up for her and for themselves, the frustration and the gnawing sense of insecurity, the bitterness and the sheer futility of a mother's self-sacrifice. In all that followed there would be the warping of a once sweet nature and not all Kathie's devotion would be able to protect it from harm.

A truly bitter harvest.

The question of Kathie's schooling was the first to come up for discussion. Mrs Fraser was all for sending her out to work as soon as possible. At least she could make her contribution to the family income. This meant the end of Kathie's ambition to continue her education, which her father had supported.

One day it was announced at school that those who intended to continue the following year into high school must hand in their names. Kathie's heart leapt. It was now or never. All the way home from school she asked herself what her mother would say and remembering what she had already said on the subject, before her father died, she had very little hope. Oh, if her mother would only understand how she had set her heart on continuing her studies! Perhaps if she could talk to her mother alone when Grandma wasn't there, she could persuade her.

To Kathie's disappointment, the two women were together in the kitchen when she came in. They glanced up, but without a word she went and helped herself to some bread and peanut butter. She felt too excited to speak and dared not risk an immediate no to her request.

'Sulking again?' remarked the older woman.

'Oh, no, Grandma!' replied Kathie.

'Andrew and you certainly have big appetites.'

'It's only natural with them growing so fast,' said Mrs Liedeman.

'I wasn't complaining. Only it's a good thing you and me are such small eaters.'

Meantime Stella, hearing Kathie's voice, ran in from the other room where she had been allowed to amuse herself on her grandmother's old piano. Except for the companionship of her big sister she was a lonely child who had always been jealously guarded from contact with 'undesirable' children. Even in her new home there was no neighbour's child near enough to her own age and at the same time considered good enough for her to play with, so she spent a great deal of her time indoors.

Entering the kitchen, Stella danced up to her sister, demanding her customary toss in the air, which the sturdy teenager proceeded to give her. She was a dainty child and her light body responded easily to the lift of her sister's arms, carrying through the movement on her own momentum and joining in Kathie's laughter.

'You'll do that once too often,' commented their grandmother. 'Stella isn't a baby any more.'

'I'm a big girl,' the little one declared.

'Such a big girl!' Kathie agreed. 'And she can read, and play the piano already, can't she?'

'I can read Kathie's book,' announced Stella to her grandmother, boldly but not quite truthfully.

'That's very nice.'

'Listen, Kathie!' said Stella, running back into the other room whence in a moment the discords could be heard from the piano.

Kathie came close to her mother.

'Ma ...'

'What is it?'

'I have to tell them at the school this week whether I'm going to high school or not.'

'What's that? I can't hear you.'

With less confidence Kathie repeated her statement. Her mother went on sewing, more slowly now than before.

'Say yes, Ma.'

Mrs Liedeman looked over to her mother, who had pricked up her ears at the word 'school' but had not heard what was being said because of the noise from the piano.

'Be quiet, Stella!' she called sharply. The discords did not cease and she called again, whereupon Stella made the petulant sounds of the spoilt child who doesn't see why her wishes should be crossed. Her grandmother had to get up and go to her before she accepted the fact that on this occasion she couldn't have her own way.

Kathie took the opportunity to whisper to her mother: 'Please, Ma! I do want to go to high school.'

Mrs Fraser returned, pulling an unwilling Stella by the hand and bidding her sit quietly on a chair without opening her mouth for five minutes.

'Now what's this about your school?' she demanded.

Kathie explained.

'That's easily settled,' said her grandmother in her clipped English. 'You're leaving at the end of the term. Your mother and I have already discussed it.'

'Oh, Ma!' Kathie's tone was full of reproach as she saw her dreams evaporate into thin air.

'We didn't really decide,' said Mrs Liedeman.

Mrs Fraser glanced at her daughter with surprise. Irene really was weak. It had all been nicely cut and dried and now she was in danger of giving in to Kathie. The girl would be bossing her mother in a year or two if she wasn't careful.

'Now then, Irene, there's no point in going over the old ground again. You agreed with me it's time Kathie was going out and earning something. We need the money, with three hungry mouths to feed, besides ourselves.'

'We manage along,' said Irene.

'And who have you to thank for that?'

'I do my share, sitting and slaving at this machine.'

'Oh! So you and me must slave so that a big strapping girl like Kathie can go and play at high school, must we?'

'I'll work hard. I'll get a bursary!' cried Kathie.

'Be quiet,' snapped her grandmother. 'Look here, Irene. You agreed Stella must go to school next term. We can't put it off any longer.' At these words Stella bounced off her chair and seized Kathie's hand.

'Kathie! Kathie! You'll take me with! I'm going to school! I'm going to school!'

Kathie restrained her sister with a strong grip of her hand. Oh, how she wished her father were here. She looked from her grandmother to her mother, remembering the harsh words that had passed between her mother and father before his death. Feeling every muscle in her body tense, she looked straight at her mother.

'Ma, where are you sending Stella?'

'One thing at a time,' interrupted Mrs Fraser.

'Kathie, you're hurting me!' cried Stella, pulling her hand away from her sister's tightening grasp.

'Go back to your seat and be quiet,' said her grandmother, and with an impudent toss of her pretty little head, the child obeyed.

Mrs Fraser continued: 'Don't forget, it'll cost a lot of money, with Stella at school.'

'Not at the beginning,' said Irene.

'There's her clothes.'

'I'll make them myself.'

Mrs Fraser turned slowly to face her daughter. 'What are you getting at?' she asked, narrowing her eyes.

'I've been thinking Kathie might have another year at school.'

'Oh, Ma!' Kathie threw herself down on her knees and grasped her mother's hand. 'I'll work hard! I'll help you, just see if I don't!'

'Will you be quiet!' said Mrs Fraser.

'Kathie's clever at her lessons. And if I'm willing to pay for her schooling, that's my business,' said Mrs Liedeman.

'You forget it's my house.'

'I'm never likely to forget it.' Her tone was half tearful, half defiant.

'And *what* do you mean by *that?*'

'Ma's upset! Can't you leave her alone?' said Kathie.

'You impudent girl! Don't speak to me like that.' Then she turned to her daughter. 'I don't expect gratitude, Irene. But I do expect a little common sense. Here you are letting Kathie tell you what you should and shouldn't do – why else should you have changed your mind all of a sudden? When that husband of yours – '

'Don't you dare say anything about Johannes!'

Mrs Fraser stared at her in amazement. 'Well!'

For Irene her mother's short exclamation contained volumes. She continued more quietly. 'This has nothing to do with Johannes. Kathie's a good girl and I see no harm in letting her stay on another year at school. Stella's schooling won't be so expensive to begin with and I can always take Kathie away if we can't manage.'

'Not if she gets her own way, as she is now!'

'Oh, Ma, don't go on so!'

With grim martyrdom on her face, Mrs Fraser snatched up her sewing and marched without a word to the front room.

Kathie looked speechlessly at her mother. For months she had been nursing sore, hard feelings against all the world; now she felt herself brimming over with love. Tentatively she slid her arm round her mother's shoulders.

'I must get on with my sewing,' said Mrs Liedeman, pushing her daughter away.

It is difficult to say what it was that prompted the mother to accede to the girl's desire, contrary to the former stand she had taken. There is no doubt that Kathie herself had influenced the decision. But it was not so simple as that. If her most fanatic ambitions were centred in Stella, Kathie was her daughter too, and it gratified her vanity to know that she did well at school. Her surreptitious resentments against her mother had also something to do with it. Unconfessed to herself, Mrs Liedeman felt the position of her eldest child in this near-white household. In this precarious little world where to be as nearly white as possible was the hallmark of respectability, she herself did not pass the test.

Whatever the cause, in this instance the victory went to Kathie. Her horizon had unexpectedly taken on a rosy colour that would have been untarnished if it hadn't been for this other question of a school for Stella. Her father had made it quite clear that he did not want his child to enter a white school under false pretences. She had no doubt that he had attached very great seriousness to this step. 'It is the beginning,' he had said.

Feeling now more confident in approaching her mother, she ventured to bring up the subject one day when Irene sat as usual at her machine. Kathie observed that she was making a new dress for Stella. For a few seconds she watched, fascinated by the swift whirling of the machine wheel.

'Ma ...'

'Yes?'

'Is Stella going to school soon?'

'Yes,' said Irene, not looking up from her work.

'Where?'

'I'm not sure yet.'

Kathie's cheeks began to burn. 'It isn't a white school, is it?'

'And why shouldn't it be?' The question came sharply.

Kathie flinched. 'But Pa said – '

'Your pa didn't know what he was talking about.'

'Why can't she just come to my school?'

'You're different.'

Different?

Kathie stood as still as a statue, her eyes fixed on her mother, trying to grasp the enormity of that word's significance, taking the full force of its cruelty.

'You know what I mean,' her mother said lamely, realising that she had spoken without pausing to consider the effect of her remark.

Kathie turned and went quietly out of the room.

Different?

The word beat on her mind. Was her mother ashamed of her? But how? No. It could not be. She recalled her father's words, spoken once long ago. 'You must always *be proud* of what you are.' And she had promised. Yes, she was proud. If she was different, she was glad she was different.

Experience had once more touched her to the core. This new thing – she took it to her breast as a mother takes her child, with pride and with something of pain and fear.

Undressing noiselessly so as not to wake her sister, who was already asleep in the little box room they shared together, Kathie got into bed beside her. For a long time she gazed at her sleeping face. Then putting out the light she slipped back into bed.

When she fell asleep her arm rested lightly, protectively, over her sister's body.

CHAPTER 9

Stella

Stella was sent to the white school. Her grandmother took her the first day and no awkward questions were asked. It all happened so easily, so simply, that Kathie might have asked herself why she had been so apprehensive about it. For Stella, school was a new and thrilling experience. She loved her teacher, who praised her and was surprised that she could read so well. Stella explained that Kathie had taught her and when the teacher asked who Kathie was she told her she was her big sister, who was at high school. The teacher said she didn't remember Kathie being in her class, so Stella told her she had been at another school.

When Stella in all innocence recounted this incident in front of her grandmother she was scolded for speaking in school about her sister.

'But why shouldn't I?' she said. And then Grandma was really cross. Stella must just do what she was told, that was all. So Stella promised not to mention Kathie's name again and meantime tucked away in her mind something that puzzled her. Her first impulse was to ask Kathie when she came home because her big sister always explained things to her. But then she forgot and the question was never asked.

Often in the afternoons Stella held audience in the kitchen at home, chattering to them all about what she did in school, while they listened with admiration and pleasure. She was a talkative, confiding child who came out with everything, having an implicit trust in other people's interest in what she did. This was chiefly due to the affectionate indulgence with which Kathie had surrounded her since babyhood. She was the more thrilled with school and the new contacts she made there because up to then she had lacked companions of her own age. Some natures are self-sufficient, drawing upon their own inner resources for sustenance; some need companionship as a plant needs water; they live through the eyes of others, popularity and praise are the breath of life to them and if they should lose them, they wither and pine away. Stella's nature was essentially of this latter kind. She basked very much in the approval of others. During her early years her own family had provided the sheltered nook in which the tender plant had grown; her mother's ambition and her sister's affection had combined to protect her from the ordinary influences of her environment. It was difficult to be ungentle towards her; her charm expressed itself chiefly in a grace of movement and a smile that courted approval. Even her brother Andrew, who had been subjected to the rough-and-ready school of the street more than the home, petted her as softly as a lioness gambolling with its young.

So far in her little life she had not often been crossed in her wishes; selfishness had been encouraged as if it were a pretty whim, adding to her charm. There is no doubt that the little lady was spoilt. On the rare occasions when discipline was unavoidable the darling of the family showed a nasty temper and it required all Kathie's patience to restore her to smiles again.

Up to the time of going to school, Stella's strongest affection had been for her sister Kathie, but with her newfound friendships at school her need for her big sister became less. This was perfectly natural and Kathie was glad to see the child happy with friends of her own age. One day Stella wanted to bring one of her little friends home with her from school. She was her very special friend and her name was Elizabeth. Her mother put her off, saying she was too busy; besides, they lived a long way from the school and the house where her friend lived, so there would be all the trouble of seeing her home again. She was sure that Elizabeth's mother would never let her go so far. These arguments upset Stella, though she did not become stubborn over the matter. It seemed quite natural that she should go to her friend's house instead, since it was so close to the school, and as long as her mother knew where she was she needn't worry. Stella loved going there and Elizabeth's mother liked having her, since the two children got on so well together.

Stella came home after these visits full of descriptions of the beautiful house that Elizabeth lived in, much more beautiful than *her* house. In fact her house was ugly. She looked round, surveying it with new eyes. The rooms were small, the walls were hideous, and why didn't she have a bedroom all to herself like Elizabeth, with a lovely little white bed and a dressing table painted white too? Elizabeth's room had pictures on the walls, a cupboard full of toys and such lovely books, not torn old books like the ones Kathie gave her. She didn't like Kathie's books any more. Old, dirty things. She asked Elizabeth to lend her one of her books and brought it home. To her shocked surprise her mother smacked her bottom and told her to take it back to Elizabeth the very next day. Meantime she must put a cover on it to keep it clean. Stella didn't want to be bothered, so Kathie covered it for her. Then suddenly she didn't want the book any more; she even disliked it and threw it against the wall and when she saw that it was damaged at the corners she was glad. Next day she gave Elizabeth back her book, but didn't apologise for the broken edges. A feeling of envy came over her at all the things her friend had and she hated her. With a growing feeling of resentment she asked herself why *her* mother didn't have a big house and give her nice new books and toys.

When prize-giving day came round at the end of the year Stella brought home the announcement that all mothers were invited to attend. She had won a prize for reading and her heart swelled with pride at the thought of walking up to receive her prize before a crowd of people. She was going to wear the new white silk dress her mother was making, and Kathie was going to put a big white bow in her dark curls. Great was her surprise, however, when her mother said she wasn't coming. She was too busy to leave her work. Stella swallowed her disappointment; she could see herself in all her finery curtseying before the lady who was going to present the prizes. They had been practising it that morning in school. And she forgot to feel let down any more.

Such incidents when they occurred conveyed nothing to the child, but the time was not far distant when the fact of colour was to be borne upon her. Then all the small, apparently unperceived incidents, gradually accumulating, would fall into place with damning significance.

Meantime Kathie was rapidly growing up. She had gone to high school which was something she had set her heart on; she had won the bursary and she had stayed the full course.

She was not beautiful, but a thoughtful observer might have said she had something more. A quality of mind, personality, spirit – or what you will – that makes the difference between the beauty that merely satisfies the eye and that which makes the eye linger, warms the heart and excites a kind of divine dissatisfaction in the beholder. She had a certain gravity of expression that did not harmonise with the bright bloom of youth in her cheeks – that bloom which beckons the glances of the lover and innocently provokes his advances, and whose companions should be gaiety and admiration. Her gravity enhanced her attractiveness, but made her less approachable. Here was a flower blossoming in the desert, its worth unperceived, yet the process of ripening went on, both physical and spiritual, and paradoxically, the very barrenness of her environment did something to sharpen the spiritual hunger of a nature that would demand a great deal before it would be satisfied.

There was the problem of what she would do after she left school. Proud of Kathie's success, her mother suggested her becoming a teacher. There wasn't much else that a coloured girl, who had received more than the usual education, could become. There was something that Kathie really wanted to do, but it was so wild and fantastic that she did not even mention it to her mother, or anyone. That was, to become a doctor. It was a dream that had its origin, perhaps, on that memorable day when Stella was born and she had been the unobserved witness of her mother's travail. She feared the sight of pain in others, yet she desired with the deepest fibre of her being to heal it.

Of course her family would never hear of her taking up such

an expensive course as that of a doctor. As a non-European, she would have to go overseas for most of her training because the white hospitals would give her no facilities. Not even in death could the white body be touched by the non-white hand. The nearest Kathie could come to fulfilling her desire was to become a nurse. For some reason her mother didn't want her to take up this profession. She said it was more genteel to become a teacher, only she stipulated that it must be the shortest possible teaching course. To this Kathie submitted, while secretly refusing to relinquish the possibility of one day fulfilling her ambition to at least become a nurse.

Stella got on well in class and continued to earn the praise of her teachers. She was conscientious with her lessons and hardly needed her mother to encourage her to be neat and tidy, for that was the way she liked to be. Her bosom friend at this time was Hester, the daughter of well-to-do parents, judging from their big, double-storeyed house in Newlands to which Stella quite frequently went after school.

A servant working there caught Stella's attention because she had a slight look of her sister, Kathie. One day when she came home Kathie was aware that the child was observing her very earnestly.

'What is it, pet?' she asked.

'Oh, nothing.' There was a peculiar embarrassment in her manner that did not escape Kathie.

'Weren't they nice to you at school today?'

'Nice?'

Kathie spoke teasingly. 'Were you naughty?'

'Not particularly,' said Stella, shrugging her shoulders.

Returning to her book, Kathie was aware that her sister's glance continued to hold a question, and she had a suspicion of what it signified. For a long time she had asked herself if she shouldn't speak to Stella. But how? Of what? If only she could talk things over with her mother. Even as the wish came to her mind she knew that it was impossible. Mrs Liedeman was not a woman who would take anyone into her confidence, least of all her children. What could she say to her mother? Here was something you didn't talk about, though it penetrated to the very core of your existence.

Her mother had once told Kathie she was 'different'. It was a word that had seared itself into her mind. Her whole being rejected it. Her father would have explained it all to her if only he had lived.

She and Stella, born of the same father and mother ...

Kathie knew that because of her family, the white people themselves would not want Stella to be at a school for Europeans only. Her fear was that something would happen at the school to hurt Stella; if she were to be shut out, left out in the cold, how frightened she would be, she who loved so much to be with others. But supposing Kathie were to speak to her, what could she say? A feeling of helplessness and anger stirred in her against this intangible thing that hung over them, permeating their lives.

Now she wondered from Stella's manner if something had really happened to upset her. Surely her sister trusted her enough to speak about it? Kathie decided eventually that she was being fanciful and overanxious and for the time being dismissed the matter from her mind.

The following weekend Stella was spending the day with her friend Hester. Hester's mother was having some ladies to tea and bridge, as her custom was, and the children were being allowed to help with the tea, if they were very good. On this particular occasion Hester's mother was holding forth in an excited manner to her guests about coloured people in general and the dreadful character of coloured maids in particular, whereupon the others joined in, letting loose a flood of reminiscences concerning their remarkably similar experiences with their coloured maids.

The two children were all ears.

It appeared that the previous evening the maid, who had already caught Stella's attention, had absconded with all her belongings, and some of her mistress's as well.

'It's your own fault,' said one of the ladies to Hester's mother.

'I always thought you were spoiling her, letting her off every time she asked, as well as her Wednesdays.'

'And every Sunday, too.'

'What did I tell you? They simply don't appreciate kindness.'

'They don't understand the meaning of gratitude,' chimed in her partner from the other side of the table.

'These coloured people are a hopeless lot,' said the fourth of the bridge party. 'I never met anyone so lazy as the last maid I had. She kept her room like a pigsty and when I gave her a telling-off about it she had the impudence to say I didn't give her the time to clean her own room.'

'What can you expect? It's what they're used to. If you put them into decent houses tomorrow, within a month they'd turn them into a slum. A dirty, dishonest, drunken lot, that's what they are.'

All of the bridge ladies seemed to have had unfortunate experiences with their maids, though one had contrived to keep her present maid for a whole year.

'Touch wood,' she added, fearful of breaking her good fortune by boasting of it. The others exclaimed with envy.

'She's a native girl. Trained in a mission institution,' she explained. 'So she knows her place. Of course now that she's in town there are all sorts of bad influences and I'm just afraid she's going the way of all the rest. She eats an awful lot, but at least she's honest.'

'You never know,' interrupted Hester's mother, smarting from her own recent experience.

'Oh, I watch her, don't you worry. One thing that bothers me is that there's a native man hanging around the place. I told him to clear out, because of course I don't want anything indecent going on in my house.'

'I'd be scared to death if I was you.'

'Oh, my husband has a revolver. Besides, there's our big Alsatian. It was screamingly funny the other afternoon. It was my maid's day off and this native – at least I think it was him – was standing outside the gate waiting for her, when Rexy suddenly got wind of him. Did that dog let fly at him or didn't he! And did that native run! We nearly died laughing.'

Hester's mother and her friends all laughed at this picture. Hester nudged Stella and giggled. But Stella had hardly heard the last part of the conversation. She was thinking about the maid and the nasty things they'd said about her. She remembered how she had looked, quite different from what they were saying about her now. Suddenly she felt sad. She didn't want any more cake, thank you. Perhaps she should go home now because her mother was expecting her. Hester was offended and said she needn't have come if she didn't want to stay and her mother told her not to be rude to her friend. She asked where Stella lived and when Stella named the street, Hester's mother turned to her friends and asked if any of them knew where that was. But they looked doubtfully at each other and said they didn't know. Stella hastened to tell them that she could easily find her way home herself, so Hester's mother very kindly pressed her to have the piece of cake and let her go.

'You're home very early,' Stella's mother remarked when she came in.

'I don't think I like Hester any more, Ma.'

'Now why should you say a thing like that? You're silly.'

Stella did not explain. She could not. But she tucked the incident away in her mind. The next day she had forgotten and played with Hester as usual.

Stella had made friends with another Elizabeth, only she was called Liesbet because her people were Afrikaans. She was a fair-haired girl whose father had something to do with a government office, though Liesbet herself wasn't sure what it was. At any rate he wasn't nearly as well off as Hester's pa, who had a big car and a big house. Liesbet had once invited Stella to her house and Stella knew by just looking at it that this was different; it was better than her own home but it wasn't nearly so grand as Hester's. She didn't really know Liesbet very well, but they discovered that their birthdays were on the same day and there was some talk of maybe having a joint party, at least Liesbet thought it would be great fun. Her mother seemed to be a very sweet lady with the same golden hair as her daughter and when Liesbet asked her about the party she said she might think about it, if Stella's mummy didn't mind. With this in the air, the two girls – as girls will – became as thick as thieves for the next few days.

Not that Hester was forgotten; she was still Stella's 'best' friend till one day, as she and Liesbet were walking arm in arm, Liesbet passed a strange remark about her.

'Did you know Hester's a Jew?'

'A Jew? What does that mean? Is there something wrong with her?'

'Her father may be well off, but my father said he was a dirty Jew and I mustn't be seen playing with her.'

'Why not?' said Stella. 'I play with her and there's nothing wrong with her that I can see.'

Liesbet snatched her arm away from Stella's, tossed her head and said: 'I only thought you ought to know. Other girls might talk about you playing with Hester. But if you want to, it's all the same to me!'

As she walked off Stella wanted to run after her and plead with her not to be cross. Tears sprang to her eyes. What had she done to offend Liesbet? What did it mean, 'dirty Jew'? Hester had dark hair and a complexion darker than her own. Could that have something to do with it? Whatever it was, after that she didn't feel happy about being seen with Hester.

Hester noticed the change in Stella's manner towards her. 'Why don't you play with me any more?' she asked. As they stood together someone ran past them very fast and called: 'Dirty Jew!' and was gone, almost like a shadow. Hester turned swiftly, her face burning, her glance wounded, apprehensive. Stella was silent and embarrassed. Hester looked as if she would burst into tears and without a word ran inside. Stella did not follow her.

Liesbet and Stella quickly became bosom friends. Having a birthday on the same day created a special bond between them, like being twin sisters. The joint party was the chief topic of conversation and it was agreed that it would be held at Liesbet's house this time and Stella's house next year. A happy solution, for when she had mentioned the subject at home her grandmother had said, without wasting any words: 'Out of the question!'

The party was a great success, particularly for Stella, whose mother had made her a new dress, lovelier than anything she had ever had before. Liesbet's mother said what a sweet little girl she was and asked who had made her dress.

'My mother. She's a dressmaker,' Stella explained proudly.

'A dressmaker?'

Judging by the astonished look on Liesbet's mother's face it seemed that for some reason she had said the wrong thing.

Next day as the girls passed through the school grounds together, Liesbet suggested going home with Stella for a change. A perfectly natural request, yet Stella was conscious of her friend looking surprised at her hesitation. Her mother had never encouraged her to bring anyone home, saying she was too busy. But of course Stella knew that wasn't the reason; it was really because the house was too small and not as impressive as other people's. But Liesbet must think it queer that she never invited her, especially after that lovely party. It was too much that her mother was always telling her not to do things, and with a sudden spark of defiance she said: 'All right, let's go.'

When they reached the railway crossing the booms were down and the red light flashed from side to side.

'It's not far now. Just over the line,' said Stella.

'So near the trains? Doesn't it get on your nerves?' asked Liesbet, using a favourite phrase of her mother's.

Stella shrugged. 'We get used to it.'

The train approached and the girls involuntarily drew back, laughing. The current of wind lifted their hair and billowed out their dresses, then the booms lifted and the girls ran across, hand in hand.

As they entered the street where Stella lived she cast a sidelong glance at her companion. Walking with Liesbet gave her new eyes; eyes which made everything shrink and look shabby. She wished now that she hadn't brought her. If only she had listened to her mother or told her beforehand she was bringing a friend. She found herself hoping that Kathie wouldn't come home till after Liesbet had gone.

At their gate she fumbled with the catch. 'I wonder if anybody's at home. My grandmother lives with us.'

'Oh?' said Liesbet, following her through the front door.

Instead of making straight for the kitchen as she usually did, Stella led her friend into the front room, just as a figure disappeared quickly at the other end of the passage.

'Do sit down,' she said, startled to hear her own voice using that stilted phrase. What must Liesbet be thinking of her? 'I'll see if there's any tea.'

'Oh yes, I'd love it,' exclaimed Liesbet ecstatically, her voice exactly like her mother's.

Stella left her visitor and went to the kitchen. As soon as she saw the faces of her mother and her grandmother, her heart contracted; her grandmother looked daggers at her while her mother's face was a picture of distress.

'Didn't I tell you never to bring any of your school friends home?' said her grandmother sharply.

'No, you didn't!' Stella said.

'You'll be punished for this, you disobedient brat. Irene, I told you not to spoil the child, but you wouldn't listen to me.'

'You're blaming me, I suppose!' Irene said miserably.

'Shh! you fool! The girl will hear you!'

Stella looked from one to the other. She had done something wrong, far more serious than she could have imagined. A sensation of fear and insecurity took possession of her.

'I came for the tea,' she said in a small voice, all her joy and confidence gone.

'I'll bring it through,' said her grandmother. 'You go back now.'

Slowly Stella went along the passage. Her little world had darkened; it held dangers hitherto unsuspected and undreamed of.

'Tea's coming in a minute,' she said, forcing a smile.

'Oh, you shouldn't have bothered, really you shouldn't.'

'Wouldn't you like to see some of my books?'

'I'd love to.'

'I'll bring them to you.'

Stella didn't want Liesbet to see the tiny little room she had to share with Kathie.

When her grandmother entered with the tea she greeted Liesbet most effusively, and the girl was unnaturally polite. Nothing could thaw the atmosphere into anything resembling naturalness; Liesbet just wished she could go, while Stella was torn between two conflicting impulses, to force her friend to stay or to tell her to clear out.

'I really must be going,' said Liesbet, using yet another of her mother's phrases.

'Do you know how to get home? I'll see you to the bus.'

The two girls left the house without seeing anyone. They walked towards the looming mass of Table Mountain, the irregular line of the blue-grey colossus topped with a cascading tablecloth of late afternoon cloud. Coming to the crossing they had to wait yet again; the lights jerked to and fro and the passenger gate clapped shut.

'I do think the man keeps the gates shut on purpose!' exclaimed Stella impatiently, unconsciously repeating something her father had complained about so often when he was alive.

As she spoke she caught sight of Kathie waiting at the gate opposite; she was the only one standing there.

Kathie waved. For some reason she could not have put into words, Stella did not wave back.

'Who's that coloured girl waving to?' Liesbet asked, looking round and seeing nobody behind them.

Stella shook her head. There was an unwilling compulsion in all her movements as she fought for some divine release from what suddenly seemed an impossible situation. What would she do when her sister came up to her and Liesbet?

The train thundered past, and still the gate did not open. Another train came from the opposite direction. The booms lifted. The journey towards Kathie began. It was the longest journey in Stella's life.

She was afraid of every step that took her towards the other side, afraid of what her sister would do, praying that she would make no sign, panic-stricken lest she would stop and reveal to the white girl who she was. And beneath it all she was terrified at the thought of what Kathie would say to her afterwards.

Why, why, why hadn't she waved back to Kathie in the first place? It would have been quite easy and Liesbet probably wouldn't have noticed. She glanced at her companion now, but Liesbet was quite oblivious of the coloured girl approaching her.

They were coming nearer. Stella threw a swift look at Kathie's face, which had become a blur. Now they were abreast. Stella looked straight ahead, resisting an almost overwhelming impulse to turn her head. Now they were past.

Nothing had happened. Kathie had made no sign.

The sensation of relief was succeeded almost immediately by a rush of questions so that she hardly knew where she was going. Had Liesbet noticed anything peculiar in her manner? When they passed each other had Kathie been ready to speak and smile? Or had she, too, looked straight in front of her? Would she understand and forgive her? Or would she be nasty about it? Never had the girl's mind been in such turmoil.

At the Main Road bus stop alongside the tall, elegant houses, surrounded by high hedges and brick walls, with huge gardens stretching towards the thickly wooded slopes of the mountain, she said goodbye quite gaily to Liesbet. Already she was learning to play her part, and promised to see her next day, though she knew perfectly well that she would not. With a feeling she had no means of analysing she watched the bus disappear into the busy main road traffic, then turning unwillingly towards home, she walked on, the shadow of thought on her face. Had Liesbet suspected anything? Would she say anything to the other girls? If she didn't suspect anything, at least she despised Stella for the kind of house she lived in. She was sure of that. But who was Liesbet anyway? She didn't live in such a grand house herself. She was a nasty, spiteful girl. She had called Hester a 'dirty Jew', probably because she was jealous of her. Yes, she hated Liesbet! Oh, why did this have to happen to her? She wanted to cry out with the anguish of it. A feeling of resentment against Kathie surged up in her heart. She hated Kathie too! She hated her mother! She hated them all! She would have to go back into that house where her grandmother would probably start nagging her, but she would show her she wasn't going to stand for it. Tears of helpless rage filled her eyes, blurring the pavement in front of her.

The crisis was the more painful for Stella because she had so far led such a sheltered existence, with a view – ironically enough – for this very destiny. She had existed thoughtlessly, light-heartedly, unselfconsciously; her vanity had been fed by indulgence, but that too had been on an unselfconscious plane. Now something had happened that compelled her, if not to look at herself, at least to become conscious of herself. It was indeed to be her tragedy that she would never come frankly face to face with herself; striving henceforth to appear other than she was, she would be deprived of solid ground under her feet; her very self would sometimes seem unreal.

Self-consciousness, then, came at her like a blow. She had observed many things, but they had remained unrelated like fragments of a puzzle waiting to be put together, their meaning implicit, not explicit in her consciousness. Not that she understood the situation even now. What she did know was that she must conceal her family connections because with colour was associated some mysterious veto or ban that shut one out. She was different from other girls at her school – but only because other people thought she was different. She really belonged; she looked the same as the other girls, though some, like Hester, for instance, were darker in complexion; she was dressed the same as all the rest, except that she was more neat and trim than many of the others. It was all very confusing.

Yes. The world was a hostile place. She must be on guard against it. The unknown stretched before her feet and she had to walk warily because there were pitfalls, uncertainties, vague terrors ...

Stella entered the house hoping to avoid everybody, especially Kathie. It was the thought of Kathie that perturbed her most. Since babyhood the bond between them had been of the strongest, even if, with the natural thoughtlessness of childhood, she had taken her big sister for granted. The bond of sheer animal comfort is a powerful one. Now, in spite of herself, she had disowned Kathie. Would Kathie hold it against her? But she couldn't help herself, really she couldn't.

Stella was relieved that Kathie was nowhere to be seen. Andrew would only come in for supper: he was hardly ever there, anyway.

'Come here.' It was her grandmother's voice. Reluctantly Stella obeyed, half turning her body towards where the two women sat.

'What is it?'

'What is it? Listen to her. What is it? It's time you learned how to speak to your elders, my girl.'

'Did you meet Kathie when Liesbet and you went out?' her mother asked abruptly. 'She came in just after you'd gone.'

Stella looked down at her feet. Kathie can't have said anything, she reflected, thinking quickly. 'No,' she said nonchalantly.

'Of course you know you did a very wicked thing, bringing the girl home without asking permission,' said her grandmother, suppressing her sigh of relief.

'I didn't know.'

'You ought to have known.'

Stella glared at her grandmother. 'How should I have known?'

'You aren't a fool. At least, until today I thought you had plenty of sense. But your mother has done her best to spoil whatever sense you've got.'

'You've no right to say that.' Mrs Liedeman's voice was shrill and full of venom.

'I have plenty right. Isn't it me that had to take the girl to her school because you can't show your face?'

Startled by this remark, Stella looked at her mother. She saw the hatred for her grandmother burn in Irene Liedeman's eyes. Stella was seeing her mother for the first time.

'What do you think will happen if tongues start wagging?' continued the grandmother.

'I think you're making a fuss over nothing,' said Mrs Liedeman. She was in revolt at her mother's insensitiveness and could not trust herself to say what she really thought. 'And if you'd stop interfering, I'd manage Stella in my own way,' she concluded boldly.

The older woman was outraged. 'Well, of all the ungrateful bitches!' she exclaimed. This word had not been heard since Johannes Liedeman's death. The base ingratitude of her daughter and her granddaughter had made her forget herself, thus adding to their guilt.

Into this fracas burst Andrew, now a lanky youth to whom his grandmother had given her height and her complexion – and too much at that, in his opinion, for he had no desire to owe her anything.

'Where's my supper?' he asked.

'You can whistle for it,' replied his grandmother, and his mother sent him packing till she and Stella had made it ready.

'Okay. You needn't all look so glum about it,' he flung back as he retreated through the door.

His mother sighed. She had never been able to manage Andrew, nor impose on him either her standards of gentility or her religiosity, a failure for which she blamed her dead husband. Actually he was a normal, well balanced youth with his feet more firmly planted on the ground than any of them. He had done with school, flatly refusing to sit any longer in a stuffy, overcrowded classroom, and was particularly emphatic on his rejection of the same old platitudes, dates and lies dished up in the name of history year after year. The problem then had been what to do with him. His grandmother had wanted him to slip into some white collar job. But how? These things didn't come the way of coloured youths and the same restrictions applied if he wanted to become apprenticed to one of the coveted skilled trades which were open to the white youths of the same age; he could only enter them perhaps by the back door, at a lower wage level.

In the limited field open to him he had tried one job after another. As a telegraph messenger in one of the suburbs where more coloured people lived than in his grandmother's street, he had fancied himself in his uniform and prided himself on being the world's ace cyclist when it came to nipping in between traffic. He even thought of entering a big cycling race, but how was he to get hold of the latest sports model? Certainly not from that close-fisted lady, his grandmother, he told himself. Like all healthy youth he had his daydreams of how he would find himself a place in the sun. For all his devil-may-care temperament, however, he had shied clear of the *skollie* gangs, those antisocial products of a vicious system of frustration of non-European youth. As a small boy he had been terror-stricken at their violence. They had sneered at his pale skin and that had puzzled him. Late one day when his mother was still out he had run home to Kathie all bloodied and torn and gasping as if his lungs would burst. He wouldn't tell her what had happened, but clung to her until his terror had subsided. All he could say was: 'Don't tell Ma! Don't tell Ma!' Kathie understood, and together they had washed away as much as they could of the traces of violence. She never asked what had happened, but she had mended his clothes for him in secret. Ma always made such a fuss.

After being telegraph boy he had got a temporary job as messenger to a business firm, which had meant a slight step up in wages, though he lost the uniform. What riled him most was the fact that he was at the beck and call of young women whom he considered to be no better than he was but who eyed him with an insolent mixture of 'hands-off!' and 'what-about-it?' He had reached the stage when he was very particular about the creases in his one suit and spent as long over the set of his tie as a girl in the manipulation of her curls. It was a stage that filled his mother at once with pleasure and trepidation of that unfortunate fate of every mother's son – marriage. 'You be careful the young hussies around here won't be hooking you,' said his grandmother.

'The females around here?' Andrew's look was enough.

There was no doubt that the girls were casting provocative glances in his direction. His cheerful and reckless manner, which covered a solid ambition to get on in his own way, made him a source of attraction to more than one – though he was in no hurry to be caught.

If he had a passion for anything it was in messing around with gadgets, learning for himself how the little wheels and the big wheels go round. Machinery thrilled him. He fancied himself as a motor mechanic so he next contrived to get taken on as little more than handyman at a garage. He was determined, however, to pick up every scrap of knowledge he could and perhaps one day, if miracles could happen, he would set up on his own. During his spare time he fiddled around doing repairs that came his way. 'You never look clean,' said his grandmother, his dirty overalls being a perpetual defiance of her standards of cleanliness even after they had emerged from the washtub.

He wasn't one to think things out, any more than his father had been. The pride his father had had was his too, but without the bitterness or the despair. He was himself and that was all there was to it. He took things as they came. He was fond of Kathie in his careless, brotherly way but didn't go out with her anywhere. Stella he petted for the pretty thing she was – and was usually pushed away because his paws were dirty. At this he would laugh. He wasn't bothered.

On the day that had brought crisis to Stella, Andrew perceived nothing out of the usual. Popping his head in at the kitchen door, he demanded the freedom of the kitchen sink since he wanted to wash the day's dirt out of him before he went out after supper.

'Where's Kathie?' he asked.

'This is her night at the tech,' answered his mother.

'Can't she stop and give herself a rest?'

'Did you want anything done?' his mother asked, translating his brotherly concern for Kathie.

'Stella, be an angel and iron my shirt,' was his reply.

'Out of the question! We're just going to have supper,' exclaimed his grandmother.

'I can't do it as well as Kathie,' said Stella, 'but hand it over.'

'You can't learn too young, little sister.'

'Now don't you be cheeky or I won't do it at all,' she replied, while Andrew proceeded to bury his face in soapsuds.

Supper was a constrained meal. Grandma said grace and the four of them ate in silence; only Andrew seemed to be completely unconcerned. At mealtimes in Mrs Fraser's house there was none of that light-hearted exchange on the doings of the day, the backchat and the hearty teasing by which an affectionate family demonstrates its essential unity. Neither was there that effervescent interchange of ideas, the verbal sauce that so pleasantly aids digestion.

'Don't gobble!' said Grandma to Andrew.

'I'm in a tearing hurry,' he replied.

'Have some respect for your stomach,' said his mother.

'My tummy's made of iron.'

'You won't say that in ten years' time,' warned Grandma.

'It's my tummy, so you needn't worry.'

Silence followed this philosophic retort.

'Don't pick. Eat up your food,' said Grandma, this time to Stella.

'I'm not hungry.'

'There's no need for you to be in the sulks.'

Stella did not reply, but got up and ran to her room.

'What's it all about?' Andrew asked between gulps of tea. 'Well, so long,' he said, not staying long enough for an answer.

He blew out like a small hurricane, leaving his grandmother shaking her head and wondering what the young generation was coming to, and why her daughter was cursed with such disobedient children.

'For heaven's sake, stop nagging at me and the children! I'm sick to death of it!' said Irene.

She had been upset by the afternoon's incident, fearing lest the inquisitive and snobbish child Liesbet, while not perhaps fully understanding, would carry tales to her mother, setting the monster – rumour – into action and thus destroying her plans for Stella. Her head ached, her eyes ached, her back ached and a positive nausea came over her at having to return to her place at the machine immediately after the meal. Her mother, she reflected bitterly, had the easier part; she knew how to take care of herself – bullying them because it was her house. Maybe it would have been better if Johannes had lived ...

What Irene Liedeman did not pause to consider was her child's feelings in all that had happened that afternoon.

About an hour later Kathie came in from her class. She had embarked on her teacher's course and being determined to pay for it as much as possible herself, had chosen to learn typing.

So far, not many non-European girls had qualified as teachers for the simple reason that openings were few, but Kathie had persisted in her choice to further her education in spite of opposition from both her grandmother and her mother.

Entering the kitchen she cast a quick glance round, wondering where Stella was, but keeping her own counsel as she had done earlier in the day.

'I've kept some food hot for you,' said her mother.

'Thanks, Ma.' Then noticing another plate, she asked: 'Who's this for?'

'Stella left it,' said her grandmother. 'The child seems to have taken it into her head to starve herself. But don't you interfere. It'll do her no harm to go hungry for once.'

Kathie frowned at her mother, who did not lift her head from her sewing. Best say nothing, she thought, in case she said too much.

'She's gone to her bed,' added Mrs Fraser. 'Just leave her.'

Consumed with curiosity, Kathie wanted to go straight into the room that she and Stella shared, but forced herself to sit down to her work. It wasn't long though, before her thoughts wandered back to the incident at the railway crossing.

She had been fully aware of her sister's behaviour. Stella's failure to return her greeting might have been accidental, but the very stiffness of her demeanour beside the white girl disillusioned her; then as they approached each other from opposite sides of the crossing she had looked unwaveringly at her sister, hanging to the last second on the chance that she would stop and greet her. Neither of the two girls had cast a glance in her direction; Stella from compulsion and Liesbet because she had been trained, not necessarily to avert her glance, but simply not to see a non-European person. If Stella had turned and met her sister's eyes at that moment and received the full force of the feeling they contained, the situation might have been very different. For in that moment the sisters lost each other – and for Stella childhood came to an end.

Kathie had not looked back. As she walked blindly on, a tumult of feeling had taken possession of her, of which it would have been hard to define the exact quality. Her first impulse was one of violent anger and contempt. Her head throbbed as she recalled her sister's averted face – the face she had loved and watched since that first day in her mother's room. But how to express the thousand moments of tenderness, playfulness, happiness outraged in that one second of time? Since Stella's babyhood their lives had been intermingled in the indefinable intimacies of daily contact, made possible by Kathie's affection. Could this be destroyed in a flash? Did she hate the child? No. That was impossible. But had Stella realised what she was doing?

Thus one question had jostled another in quick succession as Kathie groped her way out of the pain the incident had caused her. She found herself asking what she would say to her sister when they met. Would she ignore what had happened? No. She couldn't. Surely this was what her father had meant when he had spoken to her that night ... Would she tell Stella about her father?

It was of her father she was thinking now as she bent over her books at the table.

'Kathie!' The girl started out of her reverie.

'You aren't doing a stroke of work.'

'I'm tired, Grandma,' she answered.

'Better get to bed, then, and rise a bit earlier in the morning.'

Kathie gathered her books together, only too glad to obey.

'Good night, Ma.'

'Good night.'

'Will I leave Stella's food?'

'She's probably sleeping by this time.'

'Good night, Grandma.'

'Good night, child.'

The bedroom was in darkness and Stella apparently asleep. Without switching on the light, Kathie undressed and lay down beside her sister, who was at the far edge of the three-quarter bed. This in itself wasn't a good sign. Kathie listened and could catch no sound of breathing. She knew that Stella was not asleep. Softly she settled herself, gently pulling the blankets, then after a few minutes she put out her hand and touched the body beside her; it was rigid and still. A body relaxed in the merciful balm of sleep would have responded in its very unconsciousness to the familiar touch. Kathie withdrew her hand as softly as she had placed it there. What loneliness there is when two people who have known the intimacy of companionship are compelled to lie side by side in physical nearness, but separated by a great gulf of feeling.

But at last for very weariness Stella slept, though her body retained some of the tenseness of the mind's distress. Her limbs twitched slightly and now and again a faint sound escaped her lips.

Unable to sleep herself, Kathie rose and tiptoed to the window, drew back the curtain and pressed her forehead against the cold glass. It was a back window, where the invading lights of the railway crossing did not penetrate, and opening it she let the cool night air caress her tired body. A myriad stars pierced the black dome of the sky, the moonlit mountain a dense featureless backdrop that in its ever-changing mood was the essence of the Cape Peninsula. Glancing back into the room lest the noise had awakened Stella, she became aware of the familiar objects silhouetted in the faint light that now penetrated from outside – familiar yet ordinarily unobserved: the bed that she and Stella had shared for years, though there were repeated promises that now they were such big girls they must really have a bed each; the little home-made bookcases, one for Kathie and one for Stella, that Andrew had furbished up out of old paraffin boxes, and which contained a few precious books; the dressing table be-frilled with gaily coloured chintz, with their few toilet things lying side by side.

Looking at them, Kathie felt a pang, a sense of something lost, never to be recaptured.

With a sigh she turned to the window again. Dark shapes of houses loomed in front of her, with jagged fingers stretched taut. The branches of a solitary oak tree, black in silhouette, swayed to and fro, to and fro, as if compelled by an inward motion that would not give them rest. The heavy movement fascinated her, becoming part of the movement of her own troubled spirit. Beyond the huddle of houses her glance travelled upwards to a sky pulsing with stars dimmed by the light of a young moon imperceptibly mounting the heavens. As she watched, a small cloud visited the moon and received the benison of its light, giving to it in return the mystery of its tenuous, ever-changing shape that dissolved and passed like a dream. The night soothed her. No profound thoughts came to her as she stood there gazing into the darkness. It was simply that the beauty of the night laid a caressing hand on her senses and gave her comfort.

At school next day nothing untoward happened. Liesbet did not ask Stella to her house, but Stella's own manner was unfriendly to her bosom pal of yesterday. Looking to read in her child's face the events of the day, Mrs Liedeman was reassured, though nothing was said. There was no doubt that she and her mother had been exaggerating the whole affair.

As for Stella herself, finding that the world had not the smiling face she imagined it had, she began to feel a vague distrust in place of her former unthinking trust. People did unexpected things, she thought. The confusion in her mind, combined with her uneasiness and her sense of guilt where Kathie was concerned, compelled her to adopt a hostile attitude towards her. At the same time she was already pushing the whole incident to the back of her mind.

It was the following evening before the two sisters came face to face. Kathie came into their bedroom to find Stella reading a story book. At her entrance she looked up quickly and then back again to her page without greeting, so Kathie referred casually to the story as if nothing were amiss and Stella answered in the same tone. With the atmosphere thus at ease between them, Kathie spoke.

'Stella, what happened yesterday?'

Stella looked blankly at her. 'Yesterday?'

'Come, Stella, you know what I'm referring to.'

'Oh, that!' She assumed an indifferent tone. 'I thought you'd understand.'

'Understand what?'

Stella hesitated.

'Well, I was with a friend. Did you expect me to stop in the middle of the railway line and introduce you?'

'I'm not trying to quarrel with you,' replied Kathie.

'I see nothing to quarrel about.'

Kathie controlled an impulse to be angry.

'I'm not blaming you,' she said, 'but there's something I want to say.'

'I have a lot of homework to do.'

'How about the story you were reading?' said Kathie, smiling and indicating the book in Stella's hand. Then, more seriously: 'It'll only take a minute, darling.'

How should she talk to her sister now, she who had been Little Mother all these years so that Stella ran to her more than to her own mother? How could she explain what their father had said? Would it not seem disloyal to their mother?

'It's not just what happened yesterday. I'm thinking of you, and how difficult things are going to be for you.'

'I can look after myself,' said Stella.

'Do you think it's a good thing never to be able to invite your friends here? Never to let them see your family? To be afraid to invite them?'

'I won't listen to you! Leave me alone, I tell you! Leave me alone.'

'I'm so afraid that some day the people at that school will hurt you, out of some fool notion that they're better than you. Do you know what Pa once said? He was a good man, Stella – '

'I don't care what he said! And if you're trying to tell me I must leave my school, I'll never leave it! Never!'

'Stella – '

'I'll never leave it! Never! I'll prove I'm just as good as they are!'

'You don't need to prove it. Why should you prove anything to these people?'

But Stella wasn't listening to her. She had gone up to the mirror and was staring at herself in a strange way.

'I look the same as they do. My eyes are the same colour. I smile like them ...'

Stella peered at herself. It was as if she was talking to her own shadow. She touched her face and smiled back to herself.

'Don't, Stella!' cried Kathie, seizing her arm.

Kathie felt she had failed in what she wanted to say to her young sister. It was a task beyond her years.

In that simple, apparently childish statement: 'I'll never leave it! Never!' Stella had made her choice. She would never be one who could question ideas. Having gained a foothold in the European world, she clung to her determination to possess in full its racial privileges. She saw a goal and made for it, regardless of the cost.

Against Kathie she hardened her heart. Henceforward she saw, not the companion of her childhood, but a figure far removed from reality – a figure she was under compulsion to create in her mind in sheer self-defence. For Kathie by her very existence seemed to her not only a threat to the success of her plans, but in her convictions she was an enemy, hostile to Stella's ambition and wholly opposed to the path she had taken. To her feeling for Kathie, more than to any other, she had to do violence.

It was unfortunate, yet inevitable, that Stella's deepening consciousness of colour came at that difficult transitional period between childhood and womanhood. It is a time when emotion cannot sufficiently guard itself with thought and reason; imagination has wings, feeling itself capable of overcoming every obstacle, yet with this sense of power goes also a terrifying sense of weakness. Then the turbulent young heart loves or hates, dreams or despairs, and without compromise. Everything is subjective, seen in relation only to the supremely sensitive ego – sensitive for itself, but blindly insensitive for others.

In Stella, half-child, half-woman, the process of transformation took place over a number of years. Nevertheless the incident at the level crossing marked the turning point. The necessity to live in two worlds, the necessity to conceal what she was, affected her personality as certainly as the storm bends the tree even when it does not split the wood asunder. How subtly did the changes come, unperceived by those who lived in the same house together! The estrangement between the two sisters did not manifest itself in any dramatic or spectacular way; a process of growth or destruction seeks imperceptible ways of fulfilling itself, which make it seem at the same time inescapable. This it is that sometimes gives the sense of doom to life, though it is no more than the dynamic interplay of character and experience, operating in turn to bring about new events. Kathie became more reserved towards her sister, more wary in offering her affection, and it was all too easy for Stella to interpret this reserve as hostility. Yet Kathie felt no bitterness towards her. Actually, she experienced a curious sense of guilt, as if she had somehow failed Stella. And Stella went her way, untroubled by the estrangement. The days of innocent childhood were indeed over.

Her school years passed uneventfully. If some of her companions had their suspicions they did not in this instance express them with the crude vulgarities of speech with which children sometimes ape the barbarities of their parents. She made herself popular. She had a craving for friendships, but they were short-lived, and this was usually through her own fault. She feared intimacy and was extremely sensitive to offence, real or imaginary. A rebuff was intolerable to her.

Alas for the innocence of childhood past and gone.

Book 2

THE INTERWEAVING OF LIVES

CHAPTER 10

The dance

The dance was in full swing. Supper was over and the tables that had been adorned with good things had a dishevelled and deserted look. Up on the platform the coloured band, the best in town, with throats well lubricated and the blood nicely kindled, had got into their stride. Bows were going faster and more furiously, drums throbbed and the saxophone shrilled with strident gaiety; feet and shoulders abandoned themselves to their own rhythm, faces were stretched to a grin or set in an expression of solemn ecstasy. The encircling dancers swung like puppets at the end of a magic thread. With everything else forgotten, musicians and dancers swayed under the spell of one hypnotic impulse – the sheer joy of physical rhythm.

Most of the young women were in evening dress and only a sprinkling of younglings, too poor to afford the sweeping silks and taffetas of their sophisticated sisters, sported gaudy Sunday frocks, through which their undeveloped forms, like saplings, showed their unalluring contours. Conscious of their adolescent gaucherie, they danced with each other or with youths no less gauche than themselves. The young women, some of them shop girls or factory girls by day, queened it in their flowing dresses as gay as a garden in the sunlight as their sinuous forms wove in and out of the dance. Their faces with their arched brows, the crimsoned cheekbones and the full painted lips were as varied in tint as the wines from the vineyards of Constantia valley.

One of the last to emerge from the dining hall where she had been having a hurried cup of tea after helping with the supper, was Kathie, escorted by a very attentive young man. How happy she looked, how sparkling her eyes, how light her step! Above the emerald green of her dress the rise and fall of her breast revealed the pulsing life within. She had the stamp of maturity upon her, concentrated in the full, firm lips and the clear glance of the eyes.

Without a word her companion piloted her into the circling crowd, his hand on her elbow. Without a word she accepted the clasp of his hand, nestling slightly into the curve of his body as they slipped into the dance. More than one pair of eyes amongst the older folk who found vicarious pleasure in watching the young ones whirling and swirling in the maze before them, lit up with an appreciative smile at the rapt expression on Kathie's face. It was so womanly, so grave, and yet so happy. She was not looking at her companion, though his eyes were upon her. Then she met his gaze, a smile lit up her eyes, and he smiled back.

Alan Nel was a good dancer. That was not all there was to him by any means; like other non-Europeans whose parents could only afford to give them a limited education, he had continued on his own after acquiring the minimum to become a teacher. But it was as a dancer that he had awakened in Kathie a love of rhythmic movement she had hardly suspected she had, for she had rarely given herself to the unthinking pleasure of the moment. This common love of the dance constituted a peculiar bond between them. He felt the pride of one who had stirred something to life, while she tasted the simple joy of it. They had been teachers together in the same school during the two years she had taught in a small country school not far from town and now that she had given up teaching to become a nurse he had managed to get a transfer to the city.

Kathie might have laughed if anyone had taxed her with being in love with Alan. He was a little too vain to be altogether manly, and dressed with a care almost ostentatiously discreet. But there was something about him that appealed to her, perhaps because she was more mature than he was. At the moment, however, there was no thought in her heart but the joy of their being together at the dance. She yielded herself to the slow strains of the music as if she and he alone moved to its spell.

'Kathie,' he said, 'did you know you were beautiful?'

'Hush,' she said, smiling with mock reproof.

'You are a beautiful woman.'

She shook her head slightly, but her body yielded to his enfolding arm with a softer abandon.

'What have you done to yourself tonight?' he said.

'I am with you,' she replied simply.

'And you very nearly didn't come to the dance at all.'

'Don't pick me out for that now,' she teased. 'I am here.'

'What are you doing tomorrow?'

'Tomorrow? Let me see.' She danced a few steps before answering. 'I'm not sure.'

'Then I'll come for you about eight.'

'Oh, Alan, I forgot. What's tomorrow?'

'Thursday, silly.'

'Thursday, of course. And I have to be on duty.'

'You're making that up,' he said, frowning.

'Honest, I'm not.'

'You said it as if it didn't mean much to you anyway.'

'Oh, Alan, that's unkind.'

'Sorry, Kathie.'

They danced a few steps in silence.

'Just look at the man who's playing the violin,' said Kathie, her heart warming to the player's enthusiasm. 'How he loves it! Look at his face. Look at his hands.'

But her partner looked only into her eager face. The music stopped. There was a roar of 'Encore!' then it started up again and once more the dancers slipped into an enchanted world. From Kathie's expression one would have said she had forgotten her surroundings.

At this moment a latecomer arrived. She was dressed all in white, in a full flowing taffeta dress and a white wrap framing a pretty face almost dead-white itself, except for the crimson lips. Her handsome escort wore his dinner jacket and sleek black hair with an air. The glamorous pair stood at the entrance as if expecting homage for their late arrival. They certainly received numerous stares, some appreciative, some envious.

Catching sight of them, Alan gave a half amused exclamation. 'There's a stunner!' he said.

Kathie turned to see what had excited her partner's comment.

It was her sister, Stella.

'She looks as if she has dropped in by mistake,' said Alan in the same half amused tone that made it quite clear to Kathie that he guessed she was one of those who sailed near the colour line.

'That is my sister,' said Kathie.

Alan suppressed a further exclamation. 'You never told me,' he said.

'Shall we sit down?' said Kathie.

Stella had disappeared but returned almost immediately, without her wrap, her creamy shoulders above her strapless gown challenging the glittering lights to reveal their smooth beauty. Slowly she sauntered the length of the hall beside her escort, inclining her head from time to time and smiling her set smile.

Kathie followed Alan's glance and together they watched her approaching.

'So that's your sister,' he commented. He was obviously struck with admiration. Her sophistication appealed to his vanity.

'That's my little sister.'

He laughed. 'Not so little.'

'Would you like me to introduce you?' Her voice had a guarded tone that was completely lost on Alan.

'Sure.' Then half jokingly he added: 'If you think she wants to know me.'

'Why shouldn't she?'

'Don't tell me you're here, Kathie, dear,' exclaimed Stella when Kathie stood in front of her. Her voice was light and hard; her eyes gave the impression of seldom being still.

Kathie introduced Alan Nel. Stella appraised him at a glance, found him not unattractive, though a shade too dark, and acknowledged the greeting in the manner of the grand lady.

Stella then introduced her companion, Mr Hakim, who coldly acknowledged the presence of the others.

'This is my big sister Kathie. Who always looks after me,' added

Stella, amid that brittle laughter considered suitable for the occasion. 'In fact, it's quite a family gathering,' she went on nonchalantly. 'I can see my brother Andrew in the corner, surrounded by a bunch of lovesick dolls.'

As it happened, the girls were casting glances at her – as she was well aware – and trying to flatter Andrew through his sister. With a hint of malice in her tone one of them on the outskirts of the group remarked that the dark one standing beside Stella was his sister too.

'You never see them together,' the girl went on. 'Stella Liedeman thinks she's too good for everybody around here.'

'I don't think much of her partner,' remarked the other.

'He's got money,' was the reply.

'I say, I rather like the Romeo next to him.'

'You mean the one that's making sheep's eyes at Stella Liedeman?'

'You've said it.'

Alan himself would not have been flattered at the impression he was giving to the group of interested spectators. But there was no doubt that he showed signs of having been bowled over by the sudden appearance of Kathie's glamorous sister. And he was not long in seizing his chance.

With an air that outdid that of Mr Hakim, he asked Stella for the next dance. With a flicker of her eyelids Stella hesitated barely a second and then swept into the dance on Alan's arm.

Kathie, left standing beside Mr Hakim, felt the blood mounting into her cheeks. Courtesy bade him ask her in turn, but the invitation was not forthcoming. The boorishness of the well-dressed gentleman did not upset her, however, and she was just on the point of making her escape when a young African seized her and whisked her away.

'At last!' he said, smiling into her eyes.

Paul Mangena gave the impression of wiry strength. Though he was rather thin, his broad shoulders gave a fine balance to his height. The face, too, bore the marks of a strenuous existence either physical or mental, or both, and its power was in the wide forehead, concentrated especially between the brows. The slightly aquiline nose was broad at the nostrils; the lips curved in strong, full lines, but were mobile and not hard. His dark brown features and his neck were shining, for it was hot work matching his vigour to that of the musicians. But he was enjoying himself, especially now that he had

Kathie in his arms.

'What is the meaning of this?' laughed Kathie, recovering her breath.

'I saw the trapped look in your eye. It was enough,' replied Paul.

She laughed again. 'I am really grateful.'

'There you stood,' he said with mock solemnity, '"wasting your sweetness on the desert air." It was too much.'

'Desert air is about right,' she agreed, casting a glance in the direction of the bored Mr Hakim. He had not deigned to ask anyone to dance since Stella left him to go with Alan, but stood against a pillar, nonchalantly smoking a cigarette.

'Now tell me what mischief you've been up to?' said Kathie. 'I haven't seen you for a long time.'

'I'm glad it seems a long time,' he taunted, at which Kathie unclasped her hand from his and gave him a playful little slap.

'First of all, *you* tell *me* what you've been up to?'

'Working hard,' she answered lightly.

'As usual.'

'Not really. The wards are always full,' she said, settling to a graver tone. 'Some of the mothers have even to sleep on the floor because the hospital has never enough beds. But what gets me down most –'

She stopped herself from continuing.

'Yes?'

'You're cheating. I asked you what mischief you'd been up to.'

'Working hard,' replied Paul with a look of exaggerated innocence. 'As usual,' he added.

'You expect me to believe that?'

'You, Kathie, can believe anything you wish. You are privileged.'

'Thank you.'

'Let's get out of this mob,' he said.

'It's your fault we're in it,' she teased.

She put her hand on his arm and smiled into his face. Paul drew her outside to the balcony, away from the noise and heat of the drab dance hall. The sky was dark but from where they stood they could look across the spider's web of city lights, dancing like jewels on sunlit waters on one of those mellow, windless days of late summer. Kathie gave a sigh that was half of pleasure and half a reaction to a feeling of tension she had not realised until this moment.

'Tired?' Paul asked.

'No. Not at all,' she answered rather hurriedly.

'You know, I don't think you always stick to the truth. I don't trust you.'

'Don't you?' Her voice had a world of tenderness in it, as much as to say: *There's nobody you can trust more, and you know it.*

In the half-light she was aware of his gaze upon her. It was a look that completely answered her tone, belying the light badinage that had passed between them inside the hall. But it disturbed her a little.

'I've been thinking about your young friend Nontando,' she said.

He acknowledged her desire to change the subject.

Nontando was a young African girl of about sixteen of whom Paul had spoken to Kathie the last time he had met her. She could see that he was very fond of the girl and indeed wondered a little curiously what his real attitude to her was. It wasn't quite that of the big brother; he was too consciously protective towards her for that.

'I've been thinking a lot about her,' continued Kathie.

'Have you? I wish she knew that. She needs a friend like you, Kathie.'

'She has you.'

'She needs you more.'

'I wonder. From what you told me she gives me the same impression of waywardness as Stella does.'

'Stella?' Paul showed surprise. 'There's nothing sophisticated about Nontando.'

Kathie smiled at his defensive attitude.

'They both need a guiding hand,' she said.

'Stella doesn't strike me as being particularly in need of that.'

Kathie was aware of the criticism, even hostility, in his tone and again felt the need to change the subject.

'How are your studies getting on?' she asked.

'Not so good. I need more time. The evenings aren't enough.'

Paul had contrived to become articled to a firm of Cape Town lawyers, while at the same time he was preparing for his examinations on his own.

'It must be pretty heavy – fitting them in with your work at the office.'

'That's the snag. The load of sheer donkey work they give me hardly leaves any time to study the law itself.'

'How does the rest of the staff behave itself these days?'

Paul shrugged. 'As well as may be expected. But I don't know which is worse, the condescension of the Englishman who wants you to know it's jolly decent of him to swallow his colour prejudice, or the downright rudeness of the Boer who makes no bones about wanting to kick you out. Sometimes it makes me want to give up the whole business – '

'No, Paul! You mustn't do that. No matter how they treat you, you must get your law degree. There's so much at stake.'

'Because an African doing law is a nine-days wonder?'

'Oh, Paul. We know there should be thousands more. You're leading the way.'

'I sometimes wonder if I'm not deceiving myself.'

'How so?'

'I'm beginning to think law's a dirty business anyway.'

'All the more reason why you must be able to help our people to get out of its clutches.'

'Maybe I'm a fool thinking I can make any difference.'

'What's come over you, Paul? What are you beating yourself up for?'

'I've been missing that sharp tongue of yours,' he replied.

She looked up at him, her eyebrows slightly raised. 'And whose fault is that? If you will hide yourself away for so long.'

'I had an idea you were busy – '

'I'm always busy, but not so that I can't see a friend.'

'I meant busy in another sense.'

He did not speak Alan's name, but she knew what he meant.

'Oh.' Her voice dropped to a constrained key.

'Isn't it so?'

'I don't think so, Paul.'

She turned towards him a clear, simple gaze, yet even as she spoke she remembered the pang that went through her at the look on Alan's face when he went off with Stella on his arm. It had been the look of a man oblivious of everything but the spell of the moment. Could he forget in a flash what he had whispered in her ear only a few minutes before?

'Shall we go in?' Paul asked.

'As you wish.'

Her voice had caught his constraint.

Paul did not need to be told where her thoughts had strayed. He had the sharp eyes of one who loves and knows that he is not loved in return.

Kathie did not see Alan again that night and it was Paul who took her home. He accompanied her to the gate of the house beside the railway crossing, but he did not go in.

Kathie had known Paul for more than a year. It had been at a social evening that they had first met and been attracted to each other, chiefly because they found they had ideas in common. At least that was how Kathie saw it. She was two or three years older than Paul and, without defining her feelings, she had adopted an attitude that slightly suggested the elder sister. She had the endearing capacity of listening willingly and sympathetically – the eyes soft yet keen with interest – to what one had to say about oneself. After his first evening with her Paul had gone back to his small, airless room in District Six feeling that he was someone of importance, more confident than he had ever been in the work he had undertaken, more determined than ever to overcome the impediments that stood in his way as a black man breaking his way into a profession reserved almost exclusively for whites. That was the rare gift Kathie had. And he worshipped her for it, though he covered his feelings with a bantering tone and matched his wit with hers when it came to argument. Indeed he had a keener mind than she possessed, so that her assumption of maturity was hardly justified.

This she was to learn in the course of time.

CHAPTER 11

Rivalries

Kathie lay in bed, her eyes wide open, the tormented tendrils of her thoughts curling round the complex lives of each member of the Liedeman family. The events of the months and the years preceding the fiasco at tonight's dance swam haphazardly before her eyes like the pieces of a broken kaleidoscope, now and then slotting into focus, until just before dawn when she finally fell asleep.

After being away for two years teaching in a school near Stellenbosch, she had returned to her mother's house while she undertook her training as a nurse. She'd had a curious feeling of compulsion about returning; the ties of affection binding her especially to her mother and to Stella were too firmly knotted for her to break them easily. Yet at the same time she never completely felt that she belonged. Her grandmother had died the previous year, but had left a legacy of gentility and colour prejudice rooted in her daughter's mental outlook. The old woman lived on in her daughter Irene, and in Stella too, though superficially none would recognise the slightest relationship between the stern, self-righteous grandmother and her sophisticated granddaughter.

Her grandson Andrew had been a disappointment to Mrs Fraser. Though nearest to her in appearance, his light-hearted nature, with a solid basis of sense, had little time for her social pretensions. Yet he had a strong ambition to get on in the world and had imbibed the family pride more than he knew. While Kathie was away he had set up a small garage business in partnership with an older coloured man. His mother might grumble at his perpetually dirty overalls, but there was no denying that his feet were planted on the ladder of business success. He was prepared to work hard and with a fair amount of luck he would achieve that independence which few non-European people could claim.

Andrew was unaware of Kathie's loneliness. Between work and pleasure he was completely preoccupied with his own concerns. His affections were shallow, otherwise Kathie would have been better able to seek his support in a house where she never quite fitted in. She asked herself more than once why she continued to stay on in her mother's house. Her two years as a teacher had sharpened her awareness of things; through her disappointment at the frustrations in the calling she had chosen she had grown more critical, more observant, more dissatisfied and to a certain extent harder. If she had had any illusions as to what she could do for others through her teaching, she was quickly disillusioned.

She had reached the stage where a sensation of positive sickness came over her when she had to enter the school door. How she hated the dingy classrooms! Empty, they looked forlorn and bare; the dirty, grey walls were smudged with fingermarks, pencil scrawls, streaks of mud where the rain water had flowed through the rusted roof during the winter. Pictures out of newspapers that had been pinned up as much to hide the cracks and the dirt as to interest the children, had faded and curled up at the edges and only added to the general air of decay. The school equipment was of the scantiest and all Kathie's appeals to the headmaster for more were met with a shrug of indifference born of hardened despair; for years the school had been waiting and asking for more. The powers that be were stone deaf – so why waste your breath? Everybody gets used to it in time.

If the classrooms breathed decay when they were empty, what could she say of them when the mob of children had flocked in after prayers held in the shed they called 'the hall'? In winter, bare feet on the concrete floors were mottled with cold; faces were pinched; wet clothes had a fetid smell. The children stamped their feet and pressed their hands under their armpits in an attempt to fight the chill in their hungry bodies, for some of them had walked a long way to school on an empty stomach. In summer the heat under the creaking corrugated iron roof melted one's brains. Under such conditions, teaching was a mockery; attention wandered and what was called naughtiness spread like a contagion throughout the classroom.

Day after day Kathie's anger mounted. Why must it be like this? she asked herself. Whom could she blame? The headmaster? The school management? Or that sacred overruling body, the education department, impersonal, indifferent, remote? Or was there some other authority she knew nothing of, some power brooding like a monster over the fate of these naughty innocents, making them hungry, cold, indifferent, rebellious, apathetic? Could she blame their parents for sending them to school like this? No. The parents in many cases were desperately poor, but struggled to give their children an education. Education! Poor souls, how they were deceived! They skimped and scraped and went hungry so that their children might have this travesty of education.

Unable to bear any longer what she considered to be a false position, Kathie made up her mind to give up teaching. This, she knew, would mean a battle at home. Hadn't her mother made sacrifices so that Kathie might fulfil her ambition to become a teacher? And was she now going to give up a secure position all for a whim? What ingratitude! Kathie knew the arguments, but she stuck to her determination to make a change. She couldn't go on as she was. Restless and frustrated in her work, she looked for a new channel of activity.

That old desire to become a nurse came back to her. Why shouldn't she undertake the course? It wasn't too late to change. She had saved a little while teaching and would just manage to cover the expense if she did some private coaching at the same time. Thus she had come back to town, taken the course as a nurse, specialising in maternity cases and now was doing her first year at St Mary's hospital.

On her return she found that Stella had shot up suddenly into a sophisticated young woman and more than ever removed from her. Stella had demanded to leave school, though her mother had wanted her to take another year. She was sick of school, she said, and wanted to get out into the world and prove her ability to get on. What did she want to be? She wasn't sure. She laughed and said she wanted to get married. 'Don't be in a hurry,' her mother said. 'You spoil your chances if you are in too great a hurry. You must learn to pick and choose.'

'I'll do that, don't you worry!' said Stella with the arrogant confidence of youth. That she would marry white, she had no doubt whatever. Meantime the chief thing she had to do was to groom herself for the part.

She had found employment in a European dress shop that catered for the well-to-do. She was highly pleased at her success, her sense of style having made it possible for her to get the job. Her rather un-English appearance, without being unduly provocative, suited the pretentiousness of the establishment.

This meant that she continued to live in two worlds. She did not make friends with her white co-workers, and the last thing she could do was to reach that stage of intimacy when she would have to invite any of them to her home. They for their part found her to be 'stuck-up', and were secretly envious of her unmistakable good looks.

Sometimes Kathie contemplated her sister's pale face with its dark brows and heavily rouged lips, and tried to probe the thoughts that went on behind it. But Stella had learnt very well to mask her thoughts and feelings. For her there was an ever-present need to protect herself against others, especially Kathie. Occasionally in the evening she went out with her mother, but never with her sister. Thus for them to meet at the dance was one of those rare accidents that Stella for her part went out of her way to avoid. Unable to mix socially with the Europeans, she gravitated towards the genteel coloured, who more or less had the same aspirations as herself. While feeling superior to many of them, out of necessity she made the most of their company.

Such tensions developed between the three women in the house that Kathie sometimes wanted to run for her things, bang the door behind her and never return. To see the girl who had once been her joy and care put on a pose of superior sophistication infuriated her, and her resentment and anger only widened the breach between them. But when it came to violent words, something like despair overcame Kathie, for the dreadful thought entered her mind that Stella hated her. It could not be! It could not be! she told herself. Yet the fear remained. At the same time, for all her loyalty to her mother, there were undercurrents of criticism in her attitude, making her harsh in spite of herself. Her father had said that her mother's ambition for Stella was an evil thing, and so to Kathie it seemed to be. How often her feeling rose up against her mother and her sister, only to give way to remorse that she could harbour such bitter thoughts. On every side she had a growing sense of frustration. Her experience as a teacher, her experience as a nurse, the suffering she saw in the course of her daily work, the pitiful, shabby tragedies she encountered in the lives of the women whose babies she delivered – all beat on her consciousness. And when she looked for an explanation for it all, she could find only chaos.

In an attempt to still her inward uneasiness, Kathie threw herself into her work. She was an efficient and popular nurse. People liked and respected her more than she knew, and while the amount of confidences poured into her all too willing ears added to the burden of her knowledge of men, they were a measure also of her popularity. It was not uncommon for her to be teased about being too particular where men were concerned. She was a handsome young woman and not married yet, so obviously, averred the wise old women, it was entirely her fault. Perhaps there was some truth in the observation. There was no doubt that Kathie was hard to please.

Perhaps instinctively she protected herself against the single-mindedness of passion, for with her strong nature, when she did love, she would do it wholeheartedly and without measure. At the same time it was not easy for one with Kathie's intelligence and upbringing to find a suitable mate amongst the young men she met. The very insecurity of life and the severely restricted channels for earning a livelihood tended to breed a type of youth that was unstable and cynical, unable to give a woman like Kathie the feeling she would demand, and unfit for the responsibilities of married life.

She counted herself fortunate, therefore, in meeting Alan Nel. Without admitting to herself that she was in love with him, she treasured his friendship, which had lasted more than two years. They had been separated when she first returned to town, but having obtained a transfer to a new teaching post, he renewed his contact with her and in the course of their last few meetings the increased ardour of his feelings had filled her with a secret joy. Impatient of the fact that she led such a busy life, he grudged the time spent away from him. Since town life was new to him, she hoped that time would not hang too heavily on his hands and was glad for his sake when he told her of various entertainments he had enjoyed, though she herself had not been able to be present.

Kathie would have been surprised and even shocked to learn that she excited envy in Stella. Stella saw her being successful in her profession. She was aware that people liked her without any effort on Kathie's part; her mother, having reconciled herself to the change in her occupation, didn't hide her pride in her elder daughter's success. Stella herself had a consuming desire for popularity; she did not dare to admit the possibility that anyone should turn away from her. Immediately she asked herself: Why don't they like me? Her sense of confidence depended on the approbation of others. At the same time her air of superiority certainly did not make friends for her. In women she had not the slightest interest and never made a confidante of one of them. But the attention she received from men was manna to her soul; it fed her vanity and sense of power. She always dressed with extreme care, with just a sufficient touch of the unusual to draw attention to herself without any violation of good taste. She was not as fair as she had been in childhood yet a combination of fair and dark in her, the grey eyes veiled in thick, dark lashes, the olive pale skin against her well-groomed curls caught many a glance as she tripped to her work on her high-heeled shoes.

What Stella did not realise was that the very provocativeness of her beauty attracted a certain type of man among the Europeans. She who desperately sought security allured those who were themselves bankrupt of it; the pursuer was pursued, but by those who had nothing to give.

When she first obtained a job in the dress shop her daydreams took easy flight into the arms of handsome business managers, who, having accompanied their wives into the superior establishment where she worked, and having once seen her, did not rest until they made an assignation. Not that she had any intention of selling her charms too cheaply; the enamoured business manager would be but a stepping stone to more solid benefits. But superior as it was, this dress establishment did not attract business managers prepared to martyr themselves as escorts to unattractive wives on shopping sprees, so that they never discovered the reward that awaited them in the person of Stella. She had to content herself with something less.

She was particularly attractive to young men who were determined to keep the cup of pleasure forever bubbling at the brim, men to whom women were a series of conquests – never woman in the singular – and to whom the idea of settling down, since it would be synonymous with defeat, was a consummation devoutly to be shunned. For them boredom was an implacable foe to be kept at bay with ceaseless effort, yet forever threatening to be the victor. A few of the more intelligent among them were cynical. They hoped for nothing, they believed in nothing, they lived for the present and damned the future. Some of them also dabbled in the arts. They were those familiar inmates of Bohemia, the parasitical hangers-on of the arts, who would pluck its fruits, but abhor the toil without which no seed may grow nor fruit ripen. Theirs was the philosophy of young men who had no incentive, indeed no roots in life. Whatever jobs they had, had been theirs for the asking, by virtue of their white skin. Their work contained no challenge, but only another boredom to be escaped as quickly as possible. Unawares, they behaved like men who, believing in nothing, not even themselves, were hollow inside. The smell of decay was in their nostrils, for their society had ceased to nourish them. Their behaviour was as predictable as the behaviour of a fungus under a microscope.

Among their womenfolk they occasionally patronised colour, provided it flattered them by being what they considered exotic. Slaves of their own ineffectuality, they liked to imagine that they were free of the inhibitions of their class; it gave them a feeling of superiority.

Weighing up her various options, Stella's hopes began to settle on a young man, Ralph Leighton, who was a supervisor in a shoe factory. He frequently spoke to Stella about his imminent advancement when the manager returned from his overseas sojourn. She gathered that he was assisting the assistant manager and she is not to be blamed if she nourished the conviction that one day Ralph would be the manager. She was encouraged in these ambitious daydreams – which, as she thought, concerned her own fate – by the very attractive appearance of Ralph, with his athletic body and curly fair hair, and more particularly the careless elegance of his sports suits.

Ralph painted a bit in his spare time and they used to meet in the house of a bohemian friend, the favourite meeting place of a 'gang' of young men and women. He purchased a little red Fiat and they began going out together at the weekends, always choosing a different place from among the many beauty spots the Cape has to offer. In summer they basked and played in a secluded spot they found by walking miles down Strandfontein beach, and looked a lovely pair, thought Stella, with their tanned skins, he in his bathing trunks and she in the most up-to-date bathing costume.

Her mother scolded her for exposing herself so much to the sun and thus darkening her most precious asset, her ivory skin. But Stella laughed a joyful laugh and said that Ralph was just as sunburnt as she was. He was the manliest man she had ever met. She adored him. The cup of life was almost as full as she had dreamed it would one day be.

Walking one sunny day hand in hand with Ralph through the Company Gardens, they stopped at the open-air 'Europeans Only' tea garden for some refreshment. Her view was bounded, not by Table Mountain and Devil's Peak that loomed like rampant monsters in the brilliant sunshine, or by the blaze of colour in the flower beds that encircled them, but by the strip of lawn dotted with tea tables, all in one pattern, where young women in no way distinguishable from herself sat with their escorts, while coloured girls in trim uniforms ran to and fro with trays of tea and cream scones. This was the freedom she had dreamed of. This was the life she was entitled to. A feeling of exultation thrilled through her, all the stronger for the knowledge that several people were glancing in her direction. It gave her beauty a hard, bright quality that made Ralph's eyes rest on her with undisguised desire.

During the New Year holidays he suggested camping together. Everybody did it. He knew a lovely secluded spot near The Strand. The rest of the gang were going to Silvermine; there would just be him and Stella. What about it? Speaking as casually as she could, she informed her mother that she would be away over the New Year.

Lifting her narrow, yellow-brown face from her sewing, Irene looked at her daughter with a tightening of the lips. She had a pinched look, not of hunger, but of a constant habit of anxiety.

'I don't like it,' she said. 'I don't know the young man.'

'That's not my fault,' retorted Stella. 'Would you like me to bring him here?' Her mother let the taunt pass.

'What do you know about him?' she asked.

'Plenty. He talks a lot about himself and what he's going to do.'

'But where does he come from?'

'I told you. His people are in Jo'burg.'

'What do they do?'

'I can't go asking about his people all the time, can I? He doesn't ask about mine.'

'Can you trust him?'

'I can look after myself. I'm not a baby,' snapped Stella.

'If you let anything happen ...'

'Oh, shut up!'

'I've brought you up a respectable girl. I've done everything. Everything!'

'And who says I'm not respectable?' Stella's tone was defiant. 'I suppose Kathie's been saying something –'

'Oh, no. Kathie never says a word.' Irene's tone was conciliatory.

'Oh, you make me sick!' Stella flung herself out of the room and went to sort out her clothes for the holiday.

Stella did not ask herself exactly what she expected of her week with Ralph, but her hopes were high. He hadn't gone so far as to speak about an engagement between them, but there was no doubt about his infatuation for her. While she waited for the day to arrive she knew what it was to walk on air and was sweetness itself in her relations with other people.

She parted gaily with her mother and set off to meet Ralph at a bus stop on Main Road, her haversack slung over her shoulder. The weather was ideal for camping, which was lucky, for the southeaster often blew a gale at this time of year. It had died down and a still warmth took its place, giving them the pleasure of knowing that it would be sweltering in the city, but here by the sea it was perfect. On the way from town Stella had noticed a camping site, one of the few set aside for non-Europeans, and the people were packed like sardines in a tin, though judging from the amount of noise they were making, with banjos and drums, they seemed quite content. She and Ralph chose a secluded corner all to themselves among the protea bushes, and less than a five minute run through the sand dunes took them down to the sea.

That first night the moon was in half circle and they had a

midnight swim. Stella was the first to leave the velvet softness of the water. Running up the sands laughing and panting, she flung herself down and looked back. How wonderful Ralph's body looked in the silvered darkness of the waves. The movement of the waters excited her. She shivered a little. He was coming across the sands towards her; she got up and ran on, but he caught her foot and they wrestled together, their wet bodies smooth and glistening in the moonlight. Suddenly she gave in, clinging to his body as he carried her to their hidden shelter.

The rest of the week was spent in a dream, a dream which she told herself was real life. No need now for her to put on a brave front to the world. No more need to find refuge in daydreams of luxurious living. The Cinderella story that she liked best in the films had come true ... well, not quite true. Her mother had warned her, but what did her mother know of life and ecstasy? Poor, ignorant, anxious Mother! There was nothing wrong with what she was doing. How could there be, when she felt so happy? All her life they had deceived her – her puritan mother and her mean, religious grandmother. Why were people afraid of happiness, jealous of happiness? But now she knew. She smiled to herself half sadly, grave with this new knowledge of her womanhood. She thought of Kathie. Poor Kathie. She took life so seriously.

She would never know love like this.

Their holiday had come to an end and in spite of herself Stella felt the chill of reality at the thought of returning to town. A doubt slipped into her mind. Of course, as she had told her mother, she was able to look after herself. Wasn't it best this way? Now she had a hold over Ralph. He couldn't let her down after this. How soon would they be able to get married? She wished that the manager would come back from overseas because then Ralph would be sure to get his promotion. Back in town, Stella told herself that she had played her cards very well.

They didn't see so much of each other as they had before their holiday. Ralph said he was busy and Stella understood that he was going all out to prove himself indispensable at his job. It wouldn't be long now before the manager returned. Her heart was more at peace than it had ever been, except in her innocent childhood. She had a feeling of inner confidence that had been sadly lacking all her life. There wasn't the same need to defend herself against people, to be always on guard. At the dress shop her companions laughingly teased her about going in for the next beauty competition and hoped she would remember them when she took that trip to Hollywood. Towards Kathie her manner softened and Kathie responded in double measure, catching a glimpse of the Stella she had once known.

Stella was aware of her mother watching her, her questions unexpressed and unanswered. The girl was almost playful in her manner towards her, as if teasing her. She could guess what she liked. Stella didn't care. But one day soon she would tell them all the joyful news that she was getting married. She nursed the thought in her heart with secret exultation. Let them wait. All in good time she would tell them. Then they couldn't blame her for anything. They would have to admit how clever she had been.

In this way some months passed by. The manager at the factory had returned, but he didn't seem to have become aware of Ralph yet. Of course he must be very busy, having been away so long and perhaps the assistant manager was a mean fellow who was taking all the kudos for himself. The peculiar thing was that Ralph talked less and less about what he did at the factory and when Stella tried to broach the subject he became irritable and said he was fed up with the whole concern. Poor Ralph, he must be feeling sore at not getting recognition for all his hard work. She decided that she must do nothing to irritate him. She tried to tell him she didn't really mind if he didn't get promotion immediately, but to her surprise that made him more rattled than ever. She told herself she would be willing to start their married life no matter how small his salary was – according to her standards, whatever a white man earned must be munificent. She would veer the conversation round to the subject that was pressing on her heart, only to discover that Ralph had become elusive, even secretive.

Then one day Stella woke up to the fact that she had been nursing her hopes entirely on what she herself had been able to give them. She had run on ahead like a foolish child while Ralph was walking slowly far behind her, and soon, if she was not careful, he would disappear from her sight altogether. She must retrace her steps, carefully, warily. She must do nothing rash. She mustn't frighten him. Oh, God! Were all her ambitions and dreams to fall in the dust just when she had thought to put out her hand and grasp them? She became even more careful with her appearance, if that were possible; she wore the colours which she knew his artistic nature liked; she blended her face powder with anguished skill to enhance her beauty. But nothing could cover the fear that now invaded her heart.

One day Ralph rang her up at the dress shop to say he wouldn't be able to see her that evening after all. She tried to keep her tone light and indifferent, but her heart beat in her throat, so fast that she almost lost her voice, with the result that he had to ask her with some irritation to repeat what she had said. She repeated it obediently, though it sounded silly saying it a second time and almost immediately afterwards he rang off, saying he was in a hurry but would ring the next day.

All next day she waited, starting at every call that came through. Oh, if only the phone didn't ring so often! These stupid women seemed to think she had nothing else to do but attend to their silly orders. They had cars and phones and husbands, they had everything, while she ... Then during a lull when the phone was silent, there was such a noise in her ears, she thought she would go crazy. The clock drew near to five, the hour at which the factory closed, and she realised that she would lose her chance of contacting him that day, if she waited any longer. True, he might ring her after he left the factory, or he might not ring at all. She did not know where he lived.

Without stopping to think, she approached the manageress. Please, would she let her off early? Her mother was ill and she felt very anxious about her. She would stay late next day to make up for it. The manageress stared at her. Stella certainly did look distraught. Very well, she would let her off this once, but she mustn't make a habit of it. Hardly waiting to express her thanks for the grudging favour, Stella darted off to get her coat and hat. Within fifteen minutes she was outside the factory. She had never been there before and for a second her courage failed her.

Ralph never let his personal affairs be known at the factory. She remembered him saying that he had made no friends there, considering himself superior to the rest of them. His private life was his private life and no man's – or woman's – business. Perhaps she oughtn't to have come. Supposing he had rung up the dress shop after she had left. She ought to have waited. But it was too late now to go back. It was exactly five so he couldn't have gone yet. Factory buildings all around her were disgorging their workers and groups of coloured girls were streaming past her in a laughing chattering crowd. They jostled her as they passed, some looking at her with a keen stare. And one of them recognised her. She had never thought of that. She must walk on as if part of the crowd. She saw the same girl make a remark to her companion, whereupon both turned to stare. Oh, she ought never to have come!

At that moment Ralph came running down the steps of the building. He was in a great hurry. She must catch him before he disappeared. Completely forgetting the crowd of coloured girls around her, she separated herself from them and went towards him. At sight of her he halted in surprise. She tried to read his face, but he quickly masked his expression and spoke with an assumption of lightness.

'Why, Stella! What are you doing here? Is anything the matter?'

What indeed was the matter? How could she answer him?

'I – wasn't at the shop and I thought I might have missed your phone call,' she murmured.

Without answering, he indicated where his little Fiat stood.

'Get in.'

Neither of them spoke while Ralph threaded his way through the traffic. Then he took the road up to De Waal Drive, through town and up towards Kloof Nek. Her confidence in her action completely evaporated; she did not know what to say to him. He was stubbornly silent.

'Were you going anywhere?' she ventured at last.

'It doesn't matter.'

'I'm sorry if I –'

'I said it doesn't matter.'

Stella felt an overwhelming impulse to burst into tears and sob out all her sorrow on his shoulder. But his gaze was fixed ahead, just as if she wasn't beside him. Oh, if she could only confess what was in her heart he would understand and forgive her. She looked at his averted profile, remembering how the touch of his face had thrilled her that first night beside the sea. Now he stared straight in front of him, his hand nonchalantly on the steering wheel as the red Fiat climbed towards the nek, the great craggy buttresses of Table Mountain looming ever closer.

'What's it all about?' he said.

'Oh, Ralph, I ... you must think me very silly ... '

He made no response to this.

'Have you been worried about your work?' she hazarded.

'Not at all. I've been busy.'

'I thought it was that,' she said, though it was far from the truth.

'How do you mean?'

'Ralph ... ' She hesitated. 'I've been feeling lately you don't confide in me the way you used to.'

'That's nonsense.'

She tried another line.

'Did you ring this afternoon?'

'What's this cross-examination for? What are you getting at?'

'Then you didn't ring?' Her voice hardened.

'Must I ring as a duty?' he asked coldly.

'A duty!'

Her heart sank at the cruel question.

'You know I don't want you to ring if you don't want to.' The words seemed to be dragged out of her.

'Exactly.'

She had never heard this tone from him before. What had she done? She had never meant this to happen. Oh, why had she obeyed that foolish impulse to intercept him at the factory? He must think she had no pride. Now she would spoil everything. What should she say? Laugh it off? Take the blame on herself? Assume a haughty manner?

'Where are you taking me to?' she asked, suddenly aware that they were descending on the Atlantic side of the mountain with the sea spread out before them.

'Where do you want to go?'

'Nowhere.' Her voice was almost inaudible.

'Then I'd better take you back.'

He stopped at the next lay-by, letting the tyres screech as he turned the car. 'You haven't told me what you wanted to see me about,' he continued.

'I ... I just wanted to see you.'

'At the factory?'

There was accusation in his tone.

By this time they were on their way back to town and he seemed to come to a decision.

'I'm going away,' he said.

'Going away?' There was no expression in her voice.

'I'm going overseas.'

'For the firm?' Stella's mind struggled between hope and fear. Was this the longed for promotion?

'No. I've decided I want a break. I've waited too long. I'm getting into a rut here.'

'How long?' she breathed.

'Oh, maybe a year. I might even stay for good if I like it over there.'

'I see.'

'Well, aren't you going to wish me luck?'

'Oh, yes! It's wonderful! Overseas. Yes!' Wildly she obeyed the suggestion of his bantering tone.

'I'll be frightfully busy the next few days,' he rattled on. 'You wouldn't believe the thousand and one things I have to see to at the last minute. I'm leaving next Friday.'

Then he'd been hiding it from her? An overwhelming sensation of anger swept over her. What a fool she had been and she had actually been feeling ashamed that she had approached him at the factory.

'What about me?' she exclaimed.

'You?'

'Yes. Me. Don't pretend you don't understand. You can't do it. You can't do that to me.'

'My dear child, what are you talking about?'

'I'm not a child.'

'Then don't behave like one. Look here, Stella. I didn't mean to say anything. But you've asked for it. People like you and me ought to be able to separate quietly, decently. I always took you to be a girl of sense. We've had good times together – '

'Good times! You think you can just throw me over when it suits you – quietly – decently – and I won't make any trouble!'

'Now, now, don't tell me you didn't have any fun out of it.'

'How dare you!'

'Come off it, Stella, it won't do you any good. I like you. You've been a good sport. Now don't go and spoil it all.'

'Do you think I'd have let you touch me if I'd known?'

'Touch you! Good God, woman! Who do you think you are?'

'What do you mean by that?' Stella seized his arm.

He flung her off violently.

'Look out, you fool. Do you want us to have an accident?'

'What do you mean?' she repeated.

His hand held the steering wheel lightly; his eye on the winding road was more alert.

'Don't tell me you were kidding yourself I didn't know what you are?'

'You – ' She suppressed a terrible impulse to drag the wheel out of his hand. Let them crash … Any pain but this.

'You're mad if you think I would marry you.'

'You – you rotten double-crossing rat!'

He shrugged.

'Let me out of this car.'

'Now you're talking. Just say the word.'

They were back in town. He drew up at the side of the road.

'Mind the robot,' he said. 'The police don't like jaywalkers.'

Ralph Leighton changed his women as he changed his jobs, with a restless fear of boredom. He was unfit to marry any woman. He was afraid of marriage. In this instance it had been a simple matter for him to discard Stella because, while he might flaunt the freedom of the so-called bohemian by associating with a lightly coloured woman, when it came to fundamentals he was at one with his class. It was unthinkable that he should marry a coloured woman. His jaded senses had found stimulation in the girl's richer type of beauty, but that did not alter his attitude towards her.

As for Stella, nothing could soften for her the bitter realisation that because of her colour she had been treated no better than a prostitute. It became an obsession in her thoughts. And in her helpless fury she hated her mother, she hated Kathie, she hated everything that bound her to the coloured world. How could she revenge herself? It was not only the insult that rankled, but the dashing to the ground of all her cherished hopes of security and escape – the quicksands on which her life had been built.

She had fancied herself in love with this white man – her first love. Love! She laughed bitterly to herself. There was no such thing as love. It was a case of every man for himself – a filthy, dirty game. She would know better next time. Never again would she let a man have the whip-hand of her. Next time *she* would be top dog. She had learned her lesson.

For her it was white against colour, herself at the mercy of the white man, and it stirred in her an unexpected hatred. Next time? Her thoughts were as bitter as ashes.

For days no one could get a word out of her. Her mother did not dare to ask her any questions. More than once she surprised her daughter looking at her and was frightened at what she saw. Was it possible that the child hated her, who had devoted her whole life to her well-being? Hadn't she made sacrifices for her, worked her fingers to the bone for her – the only one of her children who was really dear to her? Andrew went his own way, and Kathie – she tried to be fair to Kathie, who never gave her any anxiety at all. Never. But she knew, and Kathie knew, that her heart was given to the welfare of her youngest born.

Kathie, for her part tried to break the impenetrable shell, but every gesture of friendliness was repulsed. In company Stella had never seemed so vivacious, so poised. Her laughter was frequent, but when she heard it Kathie wanted to put her hand over her ears and shut it out. Kathie guessed that there had been a crisis in the affair with Ralph Leighton, which her mother had told her about. She had feared its outcome from the start, but knew that any word from her would only strengthen Stella in the course she was taking.

Angered by the pity she thought she detected in Kathie's eyes, Stella hardened herself still more against her sister. Caught on an endless wheel of bitter thoughts, she saw Kathie as the one who, more than anyone else, bound her to the doom of the coloured world. She, with her youth, her beauty, her intelligence, had stood on the edge of that other world; she had thought to enter it on the arm of Ralph Leighton. And now?

It was not long before Stella's acquaintances were commenting on her latest boyfriend. Abdul Hakim, the son of an Indian merchant who had made his money in Durban, seemed to have no particular occupation except attending college now and again and escorting well-groomed women.

This mode of existence might be said to be more of necessity than choice; for, while the racial barriers operating against all non-Europeans severely narrowed the field of his activities and contacts, his wealth accentuated his futility and made the racial barriers the more galling in view of the fact that wealth normally opens every door. He had more in common with Ralph Leighton than might at first seem possible.

The friendship between him and Stella ripened quickly. Paradoxically, it had a fairly solid basis in a mutual cynicism. Both knew what they were about and each had taken the measure of the other; both knew the rules of the game and would give as good as they received, neither more nor less. When Stella's mother once again remonstrated with her, warning her about 'these rich Indians', she told her to mind her own business. She wasn't frightened by old wives' tales about Indians. People were just envious of them because they made money. They were as clever as the whites at that game, so the whites did all they could to blacken them and silly people like her mother fell for it.

Abdul was a pleasant young man and a pleasant friend. Her mother then tried what to her was an irrefutable argument. Stella mustn't allow herself to become too deeply involved with an Indian; she was thereby throwing away her chances. It was positively dangerous. Was this what her mother had made all her sacrifices for – to see her daughter falling for an Indian?

Stella turned on her in fury.

'You and your sacrifices!' she screamed. 'Day in and day out you fling them in my face. I didn't ask you for your stupid sacrifices!'

'If you marry an Indian,' her mother shouted, 'I'll never forgive you.'

'Marry!' Stella laughed. 'Don't you worry. I know what I'm doing.'

And she went her way before her mother could say another word.

Hakim had the company of a woman who flattered the eye, and she might well say the same of him. There was a mutual satisfaction to their vanity. Sure of success, greedy for pleasure, and he supplied it. As far as luxuries went, he was able, within the racial pale, to provide her with far more than an overseer in a factory had done. She remembered Ralph Leighton with contempt. Sitting beside Hakim in his gleaming Cadillac that skimmed the surface of the road like a bird, she turned her face from the European roadhouses where she and Ralph used to stop and have iced drinks or cream teas or toasted chicken sandwiches. She and Hakim always carried with them a de luxe hamper filled with dainties and had their tea in a secluded spot miles into the country. Stella felt that her horizon was expanding. She was mistress of the situation. People must envy her.

Stella could not have said at what precise moment it entered her head to win Alan Nel away from her sister Kathie. Probably she would have denied any such intent, beyond the exercise of her charm and beauty. Nobody could blame her for that. Still less could she be blamed if Kathie was so little able to hold her man that he fell for her sister's more powerful charms the moment she beckoned. When they had met at that otherwise boring dance, it was Alan who had in fact issued the first challenge – to Hakim! Stella had liked his spirit. And he was attractive enough for her to carry on the game as long as it amused her. Only she had to be a little careful where Abdul was concerned, since he resented anyone encroaching on his preserves.

What she had not expected, or desired, was that her conquest over Alan would be so complete as it was. After the dance they had met frequently and there was no hiding the fact that he had cooled off where Kathie was concerned. Had he really been in love with her? Stella hoped that her sister would have the sense not to be cut up about it. She wasn't sure just how far the affair between Kathie and Alan had gone, except that they had been friends for about two years and he had followed her up to town. Of course he was obviously a bit green.

He couldn't have met girls like Stella in the country and Kathie wasn't exactly the type to bowl a young man over. Living all his life in a country *dorp*, except for the period of his training, he must have a pretty narrow outlook and it would do him good to rub shoulders with Stella and her kind. He ought to be flattered. But he must know his place, Stella said to herself.

Now he was actually presuming to be jealous of Hakim. The idea! Why must men be so stupid and possessive instead of just enjoying the good things of life as they came? Stella wriggled her shoulders with exasperation. He gave her presents that he could ill afford and that fell pitifully short of satisfying her extravagant tastes, accustomed as she was to Hakim's gifts.

Stella told herself that she had no particular desire to hurt Kathie and in fact she began to be sorry that she had ever embarked on her flirtation. It was getting out of control. Kathie was very quiet and this made her sister uneasy. Kathie had strong feelings and was uncompromising in her sense of right and wrong. Stella called it being narrow-minded, nevertheless she had a wholesome fear of what she affected to despise.

In trying to extricate herself from the toils of her own making, Stella adopted a new tactic. She would talk to Alan about himself, about his plans for the future and she would bring Kathie into the conversation, referring to her with a patronising kindness, the assumption being that though Stella was younger, she knew much more about the world than her sister. To anyone not obsessed, as he was, with an overmastering passion, all this would have appeared laughable, but he was merely embarrassed by this feline kindness towards Kathie. For the time being he was completely at the mercy of a sexual madness, ruthless in its need, and refused to listen to reason. The little world to which the Liedemans belonged watched the petty drama between the sisters with that mixture of sympathy and secret pleasure that the suffering of others so often excites.

Especially where the conflict is a sexual one, it stirs in the on-lookers unsuspected and complex sensations. They gossip head to head, snapping up the sordid details (many of them invented) with relish; their pity has a gloating quality; their condemnation of the wrongdoer is uttered with coarse laughter and their censure is self-righteous yet filled with a sneaking envy. They are thankful not to be in the mess. If this is life, they are glad it has passed them by, but they bear it a grudge all the same.

Mrs Irene Liedeman had always kept herself aloof from her neighbours, so she would have been surprised to learn how much they knew about her and her family. Mrs van Zyl, the plumber's wife who lived next door, called on her neighbour Miss Slabber on the other side, and together they held a private court on the whole business.

'It's time that stuck-up *meisie* was taken down a peg or two,' announced Miss Slabber. 'She'll play with fire once too often.'

'If you ask me, that whole family has it coming to them, from that snob of a mother downwards, always fancying themselves better than any of us,' said Mrs van Zyl. 'Did you ever meet old Mrs Fraser – the grandmother?'

'No. She died before my time.'

'You should have seen her walking down the street, with her back like a poker – and as mean as they make them.'

'It always turns out bad when you set one member of a family above the rest,' continued Miss Slabber, who seemed to have it most in for Stella.

'No wonder the two sisters are ready to tear each other's eyes out,' said Mrs van Zyl, smirking.

'Did you see the nurse coming up the street with a native last week?' Miss Slabber went on.

'Nurse Kathie? With a native! What's the world coming to?'

'Maybe it's all she can get, now that her young man's hooked up with her sister.'

'Their brother Andrew doesn't seem to like it,' said Mrs van Zyl. 'He threw the young man out on his ear last night, when he came to the house drunk.'

'Drunk! What did Stella say to that?'

'What should she say? It's her doing. But that's not all. I saw the Rolls Royce at the door yesterday.'

'Cadillac. Not Rolls Royce,' corrected Miss Slabber.

'Whatever it is, it isn't decent ... '

There was one onlooker who occupied a position outside all this intrigue, yet who suffered the pangs of one who stood at the very centre of events. This was Paul Mangena. His love for Kathie might have welcomed the fact that her sister Stella had been the instrument for revealing the true character of Alan Nel, whom he had always considered totally unworthy of her. He might even have rejoiced at the young man's fall from grace, as being to his own benefit. Stella's behaviour kindled such a flame of anger in him that he could not rest until he had spoken to her. He did not stop to argue what good he could effect by doing so. It had become a burning necessity.

It was no easy matter for him to bring about a meeting between himself and Stella. She was a fully occupied young woman who did not believe in sitting at home in contemplation of the four domestic walls. In fact she had a dread of it. But even if her time was not fully booked up, the last person with whom she would have imagined herself spending an hour was the African, Paul Mangena. She had once been introduced to him by Kathie and had coldly acknowledged his existence.

She despised Kathie for the association. She had no business to let a native hang around her. If she had any consideration for the family she would send him packing. Their brother Andrew ought to see to that. What could Kathie have in common with him, even if he was studying law? He was probably insufferably conceited. It was one of those peculiarities of Kathie's, picking up odd people and taking pity on them. Stella supposed it had something to do with her being a nurse and always helping lame ducks. It was true there was nothing of the lame duck about Paul Mangena. He had looked at her in a positively insolent manner when she had met him, so all the more reason why she should keep him in his place.

Paul for his part contemplated Stella from afar with an amused kind of wonder. He told himself that he would like to see inside that vain little head and try to understand its peculiar workings. Queer, he thought, that Kathie should have such a sister. Kathie, so warm and glowing of heart, so quiet, so strong and, yes, so simple and straightforward.

Paul knew that Stella was very dear to her sister and in talking to him about her, unburdening herself of certain heavy thoughts, Kathie revealed to Paul more of Stella's nature than she realised. Paul had been content to let their friendship grow thus imperceptibly; it was all he asked or hoped for as yet. That she could speak simply of what concerned her convinced him that he meant a good deal to her. At first he had thought that all the benefit of their relationship was on his side; she was such a listener, listening as patiently as the shadow of a stone cast on the water, while he unfolded his experiences, his plans and dreams to her. In those countless imperceptible moments spent in talk between them, sometimes serious, sometimes gay, slipping away as the sand slipping through one's fingers, two lives and two worlds were being interwoven, with all that touched them in these separate worlds when they were apart.

Only about Alan Nel she was silent and he respected that silence. But he had seen enough to know what was happening between the man and her sister. His own hopes of winning Kathie made it hard for Paul to admit that she had given her heart completely to Alan, though it didn't require much imagination to realise the blow it must have been to her to be betrayed by both her sister and her friend. What must her thoughts be? He feared her quietness. Being so completely lacking in self-defensive egoism – indeed too much lacking – she would not weep and mourn that the world had come to an end because a man had played a dirty trick on her. If Paul knew her – and how devotedly he made it his business to know her! – she had too many resources within herself ever to be destroyed by what man or woman should do to her. Yet that did not take away the pain. For this Paul could not forgive the arrogant girl and the infatuated young man.

What surprised him was that Kathie seemed to be more concerned for Stella's sake than anything else in the whole affair. This was hard to understand. Condemnation – yes – most people would think it natural if she slapped the girl's face for her treachery, but from the way she talked, she actually found it possible, if not to forgive her sister, at least to find excuses for her behaviour.

Paul and Kathie were one day snatching time off from their various duties to walk in the Company Gardens, their favourite meeting place. It was a cold June day and at this time of year the once gay beds of flowers wore a subdued mantle of brown, while caged birds in the aviaries flaunted the flowers of their tropical plumage as they flitted chattering to and fro. Kathie watched them for a moment, her face pensive, and then Paul drew her away to a quieter spot. They walked slowly – it was too chilly to sit – and Paul had never so much wished that he had somewhere to take her. His room in District Six he considered out of the question and he was aware that Kathie could not invite him to her mother's house without aggravating the relationship between herself and her mother. Mrs Liedeman had no time for natives.

'Paul,' Kathie said at last, 'I find it so hard to understand Stella.'

'Why should you try?'

'But I must. Who will, if I don't?'

'You will never be able to understand her. You are as different from her as night from day,' he answered.

'That's not going to help her, Paul, speaking like that.'

'Does she need your help?'

'Yes, yes she does!'

'I don't know another girl who seems better able to look after herself. She's as hard as nails.'

'You're prejudiced against her.'

'Perhaps I am. And I have reason to be. When I think of what she has done –'

He stopped, unable to trust what he would say next.

'Oh, Paul, she doesn't know what she's doing.'

'She's old enough to know.'

'But she's deceiving herself all the time. She makes out that she's hard and worldly wise –'

'That's precisely what she is. Isn't it you who are deceiving yourself? Aren't you taking a rather sentimental attitude about your little sister?'

'You aren't helping me much, Paul.'

'I'm sorry, Kathie. But she makes me so mad!'

Then, as if following a train of thought, she resumed: 'Stella is very unhappy –'

'So she ought to be.'

'Paul, are you going to let me say what I want to say, or aren't you?'

'I am dumb,' he replied contritely.

'I've been thinking a great deal about Stella. She doesn't know where she's going. She doesn't know what she's doing. I think, Paul, maybe she feels desperate inside … I mean, she feels up against everyone all the time.'

'Isn't that her own fault? She thinks about herself all the time. She can't forget herself.'

'She can't forget herself because she's never sure of herself. That's what I think, Paul.'

'Stella not sure of herself! Then tell me who is!'

'I find it difficult to explain it to you, Paul, though I've tried to before. Oh, I know what she has done. Sometimes I feel very bitter about it. But that doesn't help me. Nor her either … I used to carry her in my arms, Paul. That's something I can't forget, even if I wanted to.'

They walked on in silence.

When she spoke again he knew that her thoughts had gone back into the past, a past of which she had once before spoken to him. As if assuming he could fill in what she had not spoken aloud, she continued:

'And it's I who should have protected her. But I haven't.'

'How could you, Kathie? You were too young, then. You couldn't have gone against your mother.'

'No. I couldn't.'

'It's no use blaming yourself. You're forgetting one thing. Stella herself chose the way she wanted to go.'

'I wonder.'

'Of course she did! Didn't you?'

'Yes. But I'm different.'

Even as she spoke, her mother's phrase came back to her. *You're different.* But that wasn't what she meant.

'In what way are you different?' Paul asked. Kathie considered a moment.

'Well, it wasn't easy for her to think for herself.'

'Is she such a weakling? I don't think so, Kathie.'

She had no answer to that.

'Paul, I told you about Ralph Leighton, remember?'

'I remember.'

'I'm not sure exactly what happened. But I think she loved him.'

'Because he was white?'

'It's not like you to speak so harshly.'

'When I see you tormenting yourself over her, I must, Kathie.'

Her lips trembled.

'Paul, I shouldn't have spoken. I didn't mean to bother you with all my troubles.'

He knew it was useless to argue with her any further, once she had made up her mind.

'It's time I was going,' she said.

As they parted she looked into his eyes almost reproachfully and it was all he could do to refrain from speaking her name in the way that one does not do in the open street.

Absent-mindedly wending his way through the milling crowds in Government Avenue Paul found himself asking what motive could have prompted Stella to behave the way she had done. On the face of it, it was hardly in her own interest to entangle herself with Alan Nel. He had nothing to give her, if Paul judged her rightly.

He suddenly resolved to speak to her himself.

He had to wait some days before the opportunity offered itself, though in the end it was his sheer determination that brought it about. He met her apparently casually in the street as she was returning from the dress shop and on the inspiration of the moment he addressed her, saying that Kathie had asked him to speak to her.

(He hoped Kathie would forgive him the lie.)

The very unexpectedness of the meeting and the unusualness of his request caught Stella off-guard and gave her no time to refuse. Kathie had not spoken to her for days and she had some curiosity as to what her sister might want to say to her – and through such an ambassador. Besides this, there was a look in Paul's eye that did not brook a refusal.

Paul and Stella walked along in silence, not without several eyes taking note of the tall African accompanied by the well-dressed, pale complexioned girl. Paul took her to an Indian cafe, one of very few places catering for the better class non-Europeans.

'It should be pretty quiet here at this time of day,' he said. He piloted her past some Indian and coloured youths who were sitting at glass-topped tables in the front portion of the cafe, their mouths joined to their bottles of Coca-Cola by long yellow straws, while others had cheap cigarettes dangling from their lips. The youths barely threw them a glance, but went on with their conversation interspersed with spasmodic bursts of laughter and exaggerated jerking of shoulders.

When the two had sat down in a secluded part of the cafe a coloured girl with a rather unfriendly manner took their order. Stella slowly removed her black gloves, looking as nonchalant as she knew how. Paul, however, was in no hurry to begin. Noting her pose, he smiled inwardly, appreciating the eternally feminine in her.

The tea arrived.

'Well?' Stella said.

'Will you pour?' asked Paul. 'Two sugars,' he added.

Suppressing her irritation, she obeyed him. Why on earth had she consented to come with him in the first place? For the life of her, she couldn't imagine how it had happened. He was a cool customer.

'Have you had a busy day?' he asked politely.

She ignored this.

'You have something to say to me?' she said.

'I've heard a lot about you from Kathie.'

'That's very kind of her.'

He let the sarcasm pass.

'I feel as if I've known you a long time.'

She lifted her eyebrows.

'Kathie's always talking about you. I mean, about when you were a kid and the things you did together.'

'Is that what Kathie told you to tell me?'

'She didn't tell me to tell you anything.'

'Oh, so you brought me here on false pretences?'

She half rose from her seat.

'Not at all,' he answered. 'Sit down.'

Reluctantly she resumed her seat. She wasn't accustomed to this kind of behaviour.

'I brought you here,' he said, 'because I have a perfectly honest desire to help Kathie. Who is my friend,' he said deliberately, looking straight at her.

'And I thought – I hoped – you could help me.'

'Me?'

'Yes, you.'

'What do you mean?'

There was a hint of apprehension in her voice, but if she thought he was going to refer to Alan Nel, she was mistaken.

'Kathie is worried about you,' he said.

She did not hide her amazement.

'I don't understand you.'

'I suppose not. Your sister thinks you are unhappy.'

Paul could see that Stella was completely nonplussed. These subtleties were beyond her.

'Look here,' she exclaimed. 'If this is a joke – '

'*Are* you happy?'

'This is ridiculous! Happy indeed!' Her hard eyes glittered defiance. 'I don't believe for a moment Kathie said such a thing about me. Why should she think that I'm – I'm – unhappy?'

'Perhaps you think *she* is.'

Her eyes clearly asked: How much do you know?

Paul went on. 'Can you imagine what a feeling it is to make someone else happy? To give all you've got and not ask for payment?'

This was more confusing than ever.

'Happy! Happy!' she burst out. 'What's all this talk about happiness? It makes me sick. As for Kathie worrying her heart out about me, tell her she can keep her worrying to herself. I've had enough of it. Since you've put yourself to so much trouble you might as well know what I think.'

'I'm deeply interested.'

Stella looked up sharply. There was no trace of mockery in Paul's tone, and he continued with the same gravity. 'Stella,' – neither of them noticed his use of her name – 'there's one thing you must know. There's nobody in the world, neither man nor woman, who will ever give you the same completely selfless love as Kathie does, and always will. If you don't know that, you know nothing, for all your cleverness.'

Stella was silent. Would she drop her defences?

She began to pull on her gloves with care.

'Is there anything more you had to tell me?' she asked, then added: 'You're a sentimental bloke, aren't you?' And with that she rose.

Paul paid for the two teas and they parted at the door of the cafe. Neither of them had mentioned Alan Nel. He didn't seem to be important any more.

Stella did not admit to herself that Paul's meeting with her had affected her in any way. She resented his tone and considered that she had put him in his place. All the same, there had been something about him ... How dare Kathie speak to him about her! She was always interfering with her sister's life ...

Suddenly, however, she decided she would send Alan Nel packing once and for all. The very thought of him nauseated her. He had taken to drinking. It was disgusting. Kathie could have her beloved Alan back, and good luck to her. Perhaps she could reform him. Stella did not stop to consider that you don't send a jug back to its owner after you've cracked it, and expect it not to leak.

She reflected that she had been rather neglectful of Abdul of late, which perhaps wasn't too wise of her. There had been a shade of coolness in his manner the last time they had met. Or was it her fancy? Of course there was no harm in letting him see that she could be independent of him. Once make yourself too cheap ... She shrugged her shapely shoulders and sighed. Ah, well, having starved him a bit she'd step up the temperature and all would be well. She would ring Abdul this very evening. There was still time.

Hurrying to a public telephone she wondered which dress she would put on that evening. After a long wait in the smelly telephone booth a voice that sounded like a servant's answered that Mr Hakim had gone out for the evening. Could she take a message?

'No message,' Stella replied and flung down the phone.

She spent the evening at home in a dark frame of mind. Kathie was out and her mother looked pleased at the prospect of having her favourite to herself.

'Shall we go to the bio?' she suggested timidly.

'No,' said Stella.

'I'm going to bed,' she said a few minutes later. 'If that Alan Nel turns up, tell him I don't want to see his face. It gives me indigestion.'

Her mother said nothing.

As she brushed her hair with her customary assiduity Stella promised herself to make matters right between herself and Hakim tomorrow. Meantime she must get some beauty sleep. An early night once in a while wasn't a bad thing.

Next day brought home to Stella the fact that one's actions have a nasty habit of acquiring a momentum of their own. They may even career downhill before you know where you are and knock things over in the most heedless fashion. Briefly, in the matter of Abdul Hakim she had miscalculated badly. Whether out of fickleness, or because his pride was piqued or because he was genuinely hurt – whatever the reason (and it didn't really matter) – when Stella crooked her finger to beckon him back, there was no bird to answer the call.

After the first shock of discovery, however, she picked herself up, held her head a little higher and went on her way. There were other fish in the sea besides Hakim, and besides, as her mother had said, she had been endangering her chances by attaching herself to an Indian, however wealthy. But she found herself remembering Alan Nel with hatred. And it was Kathie who had introduced him to her. *Kathie*.

Paul had reason to fear Kathie's quietness. For the time being she did not again speak about the thoughts that were troubling her concerning her sister. Of Alan Nel she dared not speak. What she suffered on that score she never revealed to anyone. But Paul was right when he said she would not bemoan her loss, losing herself in self-pity. The chief outward sign was her apparently tireless physical energy; her refuge – physical exhaustion.

She hoped she would never meet Alan Nel again. However, one day she saw him in the distance not far from her home. He was stumbling and staggering. She turned and hurried away, overcome with the shame of it; with a shock she realised that this thing she had thought she had conquered was not done with after all. She had actually been thinking only of herself and had completely forgotten what all this would involve for Alan Nel himself. She had not reckoned with the extent of Stella's unscrupulousness – in fact, she told herself, she had been a romantic fool. This new realisation made her harden her heart against her sister. What should she do? Speak to Alan? No, a thousand times no! He could not possibly want to see her, least of all now.

One thing the sight of him had brought home to her with a cruel finality: the last spark of her love for him had been extinguished. Perhaps, if she had never met him again, she would have gone on secretly nursing the image of him with a vague regret of what might have been. Now not even that was left to her.

But could she be completely indifferent to his fate? This was Stella's doing. Surely it was no concern of hers.

One Saturday afternoon Kathie asked Stella if she could spare half an hour as she had something she wanted to say to her.

What now, thought Stella. Why couldn't they leave her alone? However, it was difficult to say no to her sister without seeming downright rude.

'What is it?' she asked.

'Let's go into the room.'

'The room' was that front room where the curtains were always drawn, where the flashing red lights of the level crossing still penetrated, where her father had once confronted her grandmother and commanded her to leave his child alone. It had changed little in all these years, for it had the chill, characterless air of a room that is not lived in but is only kept for show.

As her two daughters left the kitchen, Irene looked at them enquiringly, her eyes roving from the fair face to the dark and back again. But neither of them spoke to her. They passed on into the room, and Kathie shut the door.

Stella took a nail file from her bag and began manicuring her nails. Kathie waited, suppressing a sharp word, and watched those rose-varnished fingernails.

'Stella,' she said softly.

Her sister looked up, raising her brows with a characteristic gesture.

Kathie decided on an indirect approach.

'I haven't been seeing Abdul around,' she remarked.

'He had to go back to Durban.'

'I just wondered.'

'His fat father refused to dole out the cash if he didn't come back and report.' This was a malicious invention on the spur of the moment.

'I'm glad,' said Kathie.

Stella didn't ask her to explain the source of her gladness. The nail file flashed back and forth with its irritating grating sound.

'Stella, I'm rather worried.'

'So Paul told me.'

'Paul!'

'Do you mean to say you didn't hear all about it?'

'Hear about what?'

'I must say I thought it was a cheek.'

'What did he say?'

'Oh, I've forgotten.'

'Was it about – ?'

'If I've forgotten, I've forgotten, so what's the use of asking? But one thing is obvious – he's soft on you.'

Kathie's eyes flashed.

'Shall we leave Paul out of it?' she said quietly.

'With pleasure. And if you're wasting your time worrying about my affairs, you needn't. I'm quite well able to manage them myself.'

'You misunderstood me just now,' replied Kathie. 'I wanted to speak to you about Alan Nel. Have you seen him lately?'

'No.'

'That's the trouble, Stella.'

'What do you mean?'

'He can't take it.'

'Must I be held responsible for every fool who wants to hold my hand?'

'You can't push it away like that, Stella. If you could see him now I don't think you would have gone so blindly into the affair. For that's all it was to you.'

124

'Well?'

'You – we – have no right to hurt any man like that … ' Kathie paused, finding it difficult to express herself.

'What exactly are you getting at?'

'Couldn't you see Alan?'

'And then?'

'I – don't know. Somehow I think he would listen to you if you spoke to him, tried to get him to pull himself together. He wouldn't listen to me.' She spoke without rancour.

She went on hesitatingly: 'It's not … nice to see a man losing his grip. It's a terrible responsibility, Stella.'

'If you want somebody to talk to him, why not put this Paul Mangena on to the job?'

'Stop this stupid posing!' said Kathie, her anger suddenly flaring up. 'Who are you to play about with anyone's affections and then toss them aside because you have no further use for them? Who do you think you are? All the time pitting yourself against others. What are you afraid of?'

'How do you mean? Afraid?'

'Why do you put out only claws when others hold out a hand to you?'

'I don't know what you're talking about. I won't listen to you any more. You're always in the right, aren't you? I'm going out of this house. I've had enough!' And crying hysterically, Stella snatched her things and went out.

Kathie heard the front door banging. She walked slowly into the kitchen, her heart heavy with the sense of her failure.

'What have you been saying to Stella?' her mother demanded. 'You know how touchy she is.'

'I'm sorry, Ma.'

Irene was going to say more, but her daughter's manner silenced her.

She watched Kathie prepare to go out.

'Goodbye, Ma. Don't keep supper for me. I'm on late duty.'

Her mother sighed and went on with her sewing.

Kathie had that desperately lonely sensation we feel after quarrelling with someone we love. If she was looking for a counter-irritant in the contemplation of the lives around her it was all too easy to find it at St Mary's. Physical pain, mental anguish, dull endurance met her daily in this so-called place of refuge for those non-European women and unmarried mothers unfortunate enough to have transgressed the moral laws of society. What she found hardest to bear on this particular day was the look of dumb suffering, of silent bewilderment on the face of a young girl in the maternity ward. Whichever way she moved the dark eyes followed her. She went up to the bed and touched the hot forehead with a cool hand; the young mother was suckling her baby and Kathie said a soft word about the child, drawing a faint response from the girl. She is as helpless as the little bundle of humanity huddled in her arms, thought Kathie. No. Even more helpless, for he has his mother's breast to suck from, his mother's body to nestle into, while she is bereft of every moral and spiritual support.

It came to her that the girl was no older than her sister, Stella. It might be she who was lying there. Alone, helpless, shunned by her people, deserted by the man whose child she had borne. Perhaps without even the human pang that a faithless lover inspires but only the dumb callousness of one who has never known the touch of love – only the brutal need of the male, the coarse laughter, the drunken embrace – one whose earliest memories grew in a crowded, fetid room, without privacy, suffocating ...

No, it was not Stella who lay there. She had never suffered these degradations, and never would.

Kathie shook herself free from her morbid thoughts. An urgent voice spoke at her side. It was a young nurse.

'Sister Kathie!'

'Yes, nurse?'

'Nurse May says will you please come quickly. There's a native woman in ward three who's in convulsions.'

'I'll come at once.'

By the time she arrived the woman was in a coma. A quick examination convinced her that her condition was very dangerous indeed.

'Didn't the patient receive the injections this morning?' she asked.

'No, Sister,' Nurse May replied. 'Dr Stowe said she didn't need them.'

'Didn't need them! Where is Doctor now?'

'He's due to arrive any minute, Sister.'

'Go and see if he has come. Tell him to come straight here.'

The other nurse went off with the message.

Kathie bent over the comatose African woman. With cool, experienced fingers she felt her pulse and passed her hands over the taut abdomen.

'The baby is dead,' she told Nurse May. 'And she is too weak to bear it. You should have called me sooner.'

'We thought it was all right, Sister.'

'You had no right to think so.'

'Doctor said –'

'Yes?'

'He said these – these – creatures go into the bush and have them and think nothing of it.'

'And you believed him?'

'Well, I've heard of that myself.'

'Look at her. Look at her face!' demanded Kathie. 'Perhaps you haven't had time to look at it before.'

Nurse May looked fearfully at the African woman as if indeed she had not looked at the face before.

'It is a woman's face,' said Kathie with a strange look in her eyes. 'Remember nothing else when you tend her.' As she spoke she passed her hand over the clammy forehead and the closed eyelids fluttered.

A short, thickset man, with a small growth on the bridge of his nose, bustled in, his white coat flapping. The young nurse was at his heels.

'You wanted to see me, Sister?'

'Yes, Dr Stowe.' Kathie indicated the African woman.

Without speaking, he made a cursory examination. All his movements were abrupt, like his manner of speaking. Kathie watched him intently while his fingers seemed to stub themselves against the woman's flesh.

'There's not much we can do,' he said.

Kathie glared at him. 'Nurse May tells me she did not receive an injection this morning.' Her voice contained as much reproof as she dared.

All of them standing beside the dying woman knew that she should have received treatment.

'The stock is low. You know the struggle I have to get supplies. I can't waste it.'

'Waste?'

The nurses looked at her fearfully.

'There is no time for sentiment in a place like this. You ought to know better,' said the doctor frowning at her impertinence, the growth on the bridge of his nose shifting inward. Then nodding to Nurse May: 'You will see to her, Nurse.' And with that he departed, the young nurse hastening at his heels.

After he had gone there was a moment's silence.

'I will watch,' said Kathie.

'Very well, Sister.'

Nurse May went off to another patient and Kathie remained behind the screen.

A tumult of revolt beat in her breast, all the more painful because of the cold decorum that her position and her uniform demanded. The ferocious disregard for human life had never come home to her so sharply. She stood with her eyes fixed on the woman's face, its colour more grey than brown. All was quiet in the ward and the only violence seemed to be in Kathie's breast. For the patient, the tumult and the violence was over. How easy it was to do nothing when the victim herself yielded with the inexorable acquiescence of mortality. It was useless to blame the nurse for what had happened. Could she even blame the doctor? It was the common attitude to non-Europeans. And how familiar were the arguments: These creatures are more animal than human; they don't feel pain like Europeans. You needn't waste pity on them either. You'll only get a curse for your pains instead of a word of gratitude for all you are doing for them. And if they die, so much the better! Far too many of them already. They breed like rabbits. Bury them like cattle! Push them under the earth and forget them. Don't dig deep. A shallow grave and a sprinkling of earth is all they need. The worms will quickly do the rest.

For the remainder of her period on duty Kathie went about her work with a hard, stubborn expression on her face. Then at last she was free, free to go to her own room, free to be herself. Slowly she took off her uniform. She sat on the edge of the bed, her arms inert, her head drooping. She was conscious of an aching throat as if she had been talking incessantly and wildly for some hours, though actually she had restricted herself to abrupt monosyllables when she had been forced to communicate with her fellow workers.

Suddenly she burst into uncontrolled weeping. The stress and strain of the day had been too much for her; the quarrel with Stella, the sight of her hard, mocking face; her experiences in St Mary's; the doctor's abrupt tones: 'There must be no waste.' Waste, waste, waste of human life. 'Let the woman die . . .' Waste of human life and happiness . . .

Kathie spoke aloud to the empty room.

'Paul! Paul!' she cried. 'I cannot bear it any more.'

It was as if she summoned him with all her heart and soul into her presence.

CHAPTER 12

Paul

At work the next day a message was brought to Kathie that she was wanted on the phone. It was Paul. He was speaking with that deep voice of his, but today it was unusually gentle.

'How are things?' he asked.

'Oh!' She tried to speak lightly. 'Not so good.'

'Very busy?'

'Yes, very busy.'

'I just wanted to hear your voice,' he said.

She didn't know how to answer. On the spur of the moment she said: 'I've been rather lonely, Paul.'

'Are you sure you can't get off for even half an hour?'

'I'd love to. But if you were to step into this place right now, you'd know how impossible it is.'

'I can imagine it all right. Only, I don't want to see you cracking up. You are too precious, you know.'

Kathie tried to keep the trembling out of her voice.

'There's no fear of that,' she assured him. 'I must ring off now,

Paul. You'll understand.'

'Sure. But don't forget, my shoulders are pretty broad, if there's anything on your mind.'

She laughed. 'I won't forget.'

'Goodnight, then, Kathie.'

'Goodnight.'

'Until tomorrow.'

'Until tomorrow,' she echoed.

The words had been commonplace enough, but the undertones, the implications of deep feeling, the gentleness in the usually strong voice ... They left no doubt in her mind as to where she stood with Paul.

And she?

If this was love it filled her with both joy and fear, a great sense of trust and a longing such as she had not known before.

When Stella had made a mocking reference to Paul how quickly she had sprung to guard him from her sister's taunting tongue. It had revealed herself to herself. She realised that for a long time she had taken him for granted, yet the very fact of unburdening herself to him of her anxiety concerning Stella had drawn her closer to him. The sorrows that bound her to her sister had been the bitter-sweet soil for the enrichment of their love. She wondered now what had held her back so long. She ought to have known that Paul was her true mate.

Of course she knew the attitude of Stella and her mother towards natives. It was the attitude of her people, who considered themselves superior because they had European blood in their veins. It was not done for a 'superior' coloured girl to associate with Africans, and still less to marry one. She herself had not entirely escaped this influence, for it was all around her. Perhaps that was why she had adopted the elder sister manner towards Paul – as a kind of protective measure. However there were other factors making it easy for Kathie to obey the dictates of her heart. There was not only her natural impulse to think only in terms of men and women wherever she might be; there was also a strong need to override the barriers of race and prejudice. For at the core of her experience was the conflict that had arisen in her family over Stella, the unnatural estrangement between the sisters and her own isolation in the family.

She herself did not reason it all out – that was never Kathie's way. But she knew quite simply that henceforth the whole tide of her being was set towards Paul, come what may.

Paul understood that Alan Nel no longer stood between them, and Kathie knew that he knew. It was not necessary to put it into words.

The next day being Sunday, Paul and Kathie spent most of it together. Taking a bus as far as Kirstenbosch – the botanical gardens where masses of spring *vygies*, yellow and purple and red, spread their fleshy succulent leaves with abandon at the foot of the sombre mountain slopes – they walked for a mile or two beyond it to a small glade in the Constantia valley. Before turning in to the little path leading off the highway they stood and gazed across the famous valley of the vines, the blue sky fading to a mist that was the sea lapping the shores of Africa. The sun-drenched valley was asleep, the vineyards brown and bare, with no hint of the rich summer harvest to come.

The path led the lovers deep into a glade of oak tree and bluegum. It had been raining the night before, but the rain had yielded to the sun and now the raindrops gleamed on every bush and glistened on the darkling leaves of the gum trees while the young oaks were as luminous as a young girl dressed for a festival. Where the foliage was deep and had resisted the rain they found a sheltered spot where they could sit and look up into the chequered canopy shot through with the September sun; the leaves made a hush-hush-hush of sound, twinkling and vibrating with light. A bird called to its mate; there was a quick rush of small wings and then another in pursuit. Paul and Kathie looked at each other and smiled, revelling in the light-heartedness of nature and the sheer joy of being in each other's company; they loved as if they thought that none had ever loved before them.

They talked and talked and talked; what infinite variety of mood and thought they found in each other, what gaiety and what profundity!

Paul talked of the past, of his early days in the country, of the mother he had never seen, of Nonceba, the big sister who had been mother and father and all to him.

'I think I'd be rather afraid of her if I met her,' said Kathie.

'Afraid!' Paul laughed. 'She only pretends to be a bear. Wait till you meet her. You'll see.'

'I hope she'll like me.'

'I'll disown her if she doesn't,' said Paul, thereby announcing his certainty that two such women as Kathie and Nonceba, who by some miracle both adored him, would understand each other.

'What a feeling it is to make someone else happy,' he said.

'Do I make you happy?' she teased. But he did not respond to her laughter.

'And no greater pain than to hurt the beloved,' he went on. And they sealed the thought as lovers do.

Later Kathie began to ask about those early days when he first came to town. Like all lovers, she wanted to know the past, which did not belong to her. But he was reticent. She realised that he had buried deep within him the experience and feelings of those days when an obscure but none the less heroic battle had been fought in the city jungle, with none to observe the anguish and the restraint involved for this young African coming into contact with it for the first time. Gradually he began to speak, spasmodically, unwillingly, and as she sat beside him listening and waiting for the words to come, she watched how he crumbled a twig of oak leaves between his fingers when memory came too near the quick of what he had gone through.

During the days that followed he spoke more and more freely. In the rare harmony of this relationship where the personality of each blossomed and expanded at the touch of the other, they discovered with a naïve wonder an endless well of common thought and feeling. And often while at work the fleeting image of Paul would leap to Kathie's mind, strong and sometimes harsh, but to her always gentle. His words and turns of expression would come back to her unbidden, for he had a searching quality of mind, a restless probing quality that readily communicated itself to her. He made those experiences of the past so vivid that he communicated, too, his angle of vision. And sometimes it startled her. It was like her own, yet much clearer than her own.

She had a strong impression of the deep humanity of the man, his sense of human worth. How had he contrived, she wondered, to come through the city jungle – a favourite phrase of his – neither warped by the cruelty he encountered there, neither cowed nor vicious nor cunning – unless it be the cunning of an Odysseus encompassed by pitfalls and extricating himself with the infinite cunning of the quick mind? *He has the makings of a fighter*, she said once to herself, though she did not pursue the thought further nor ask herself how he could be a fighter.

Unconsciously she began to be interpenetrated with the life that had been his so that it was intermingled with her own and seemed to be part of her own. Some of it she knew from his own words. But there was much that she did not and could not know. There was the white man, Hans Farben. What Paul said about him excited her and made her want to know more. And there was the girl, Nontando. Early in their friendship he had spoken about her in a way that indicated that she meant a good deal to him. In spite of herself, Kathie suffered a twinge of something very like jealousy. Not that there was anything in his manner that suggested that he was hiding something from her. But she was not satisfied. If she could meet Nontando, perhaps she could solve the mystery ...

Kathie would eventually know almost everything that happened to Paul before he met her, though there were some things she would never know. Just as there were some things Paul could never know about Nontando ...

Paul Sipo Mangena, later known simply as Paul – that being his first name but not the name used by his family – was born on the outskirts of Lukalini, a village in the Ciskei. Unlike the majority of Africans, he had lived in comparative security in his early years. His father had been a teacher in a local school, and had also possessed some land and cattle. The boy had been brought up mainly by two sisters much older than himself, to whom the memory of a fine mother, dying at his birth, had been the light that guided them in their relation to him. This thread of feeling to womankind had been woven into the pattern of his young days and was to influence him throughout life in his relations with women.

His father died when Paul was still a boy and ancient tribal custom saw to it that his children were swindled out of their bit of land. The younger of the two sisters had left home and she, too, had died, so that he had been left in the care of the elder sister, Nonceba, who was also a teacher. She was a strong-minded woman whom he both feared and loved, and though earning but a pittance in a one-teacher school, she continued to send him to Lovedale College in order to

134

prepare him also to become a teacher, according to his father's wish.

As he grew older Sipo realised what a struggle it was for his sister to continue to pay the fees for his schooling and, seeing other boys of his age going off to the town, he informed his sister one day that he, too, was going to the big city. Her rage, when he told her, was a fine thing to see – and hear – if he hadn't been the victim of it. What was wrong with wanting to go to the city, he wanted to know. And from the way she talked about it one would have thought it was a place full of ravening wolves that tore out your entrails and left you to perish where you lay. So for another year not a word about the city passed between them. But at the end of that time she fell sick. He pleaded with her and promised and assured her that all the cunning and wisdom of the Mangenas was lodged in that round head of his – which was his mother's head as Nonceba was fond of telling him – and proud woman that she was, she had to give in and let him go. She was not relinquishing her ambition to make Sipo a teacher; this was only a temporary capitulation to cruel fate; and Sipo too, intended to work and study at the same time. For was he not as strong as a young ox that has been to rich pasture? If there were obstacles his shoulders would be broad enough to take them. Nature had made him that way.

So, at the age of eighteen Paul went to Cape Town, ready to conquer its mysteries. That was a long time ago. He had been a boy then, but now he was a man. His elders might still speak of him as a boy – but the city makes a man, or mars him.

Those first months were not easily described in the language of men. Afterwards, when he looked back to this period of his life, he could never clearly remember how he had lived and how he had survived. Like a man hanging over a precipice, he simply hung on with a grim tenacity. Having a certain solidity of character and the mental shock absorbers of a naturally resilient nature, he had contrived to keep his head above the swamp. He had not written to his sister. He dared not. He quickly discovered that his very existence in town was a crime; the laws made it so; and to exist at all a black man had to violate the laws. If he starved, it was no man's business, but he was fair game to any policeman who took it into his head to demand the pass showing that he had permission to work in the city. And if he lost his job they might jail him and bundle him back in the Bombela train – a truck for human cattle – to where he came from.

Poverty he knew in the district to which he belonged. It was the common lot of Africans. But not this debasement of savage existence such as only the city can produce. He himself tasted for the first time the rigours of poverty; his dreams of saving money vanished; he soon found that you cannot scrape and save anything off a bare stone. His sleeping quarters, little more than a closet shared with an already overcrowded African family in District Six, bit a fair slice out of his weekly pittance; food was exorbitant in price, especially as he had to buy it in small quantities, and by the time he had paid his poll tax, he was down to rock bottom.

But poverty was not all. He was a pariah to the whites; he was alien to the coloured and the Malays of the city, who, while not on the whole hostile to the blacks, were not friendly either; and to most of his own people he was something of a queer fish. For they had become inured to the savagery of town existence. On a Saturday night, seeking some rest, his senses were stretched on the rack by the sounds of violent living seething round him; the drunken altercations, the shrill voice of an angry woman, the wail of children, the wild gaiety of a jazz song on a cheap record, the thud of a falling body. And more than all the rest, the debasement of woman in this environment shook his faith in human worth in which he had been nurtured. His sexual battles he told no man, then or afterwards. Though virile and passionate he was at the same time fastidious and had unconsciously acquired a tendency to idealise women – thanks to Nonceba's influence. To see them now more fierce than the men who degraded them had been a shock to Paul, making him lock up his own passions for very fear of them.

He had tried one job after another – such jobs as were open to blacks: handyman in a bazaar, messenger, houseboy. But he never kept a job for long. There was something wrong with him, from the point of view of the bosses. They couldn't exactly say what it was; they admitted that he was scrupulously honest, clean, and willing enough, qualities they were always bemoaning the lack of in their servants; but something about his manner made them uneasy. Insolent, one employer called him, though Paul hadn't opened his mouth. 'A bad kaffir', said another, and damned him out of hand. An educated 'kaffir' was a 'bad kaffir'. So get rid of him quick, without any explanations, before there's any trouble.

Unconsciously, Paul was a traitor to the master-and-servant

relationship expected between white and black. He had not learned to be servile, docile, subservient. In a word, he did not know his place. In the white man's world every step he took exposed him to insult, if not brutality, sometimes overt, sometimes surreptitious, very often unconscious on the part of the white man himself. He himself did not seem to know how to behave towards a black man, his manner vacillating between familiarity and a complete aloofness, so that you did not know where you were. In his necessary encounters with officialdom (since a special department was set aside for dealing with Africans), in a post office, in a train station or even in the street, wherever the petty official reigned supreme, he was the butt of petty tyranny; his skin colour was the red flag to any young bull from the backveld. In this peculiar world, to be ignored was to count oneself lucky. But unfortunately for Paul, whether it was his height or the carriage of his head, his very appearance seemed to break the regulations. (Kathie smiled at his phrase when he used it. It was so like him to find the individual expression – which was part of the very difficulty he was describing, for he never fitted in to the expected pattern of behaviour considered proper for a black man.)

He was learning fast, but apparently not fast enough, and perhaps never would completely learn, to assume a mask in the presence of the white man. He might set out in the morning with the best intentions in the world to be the most silent and efficient cog in the industrial machine of this remarkable system. But before he knew where he was he had shattered the standard racial pattern and had to take the consequences. It might be some woman behind a counter who behaved towards him in what seemed to him a particularly rude or stupid manner. If he retorted without thinking, simply as a man, the outraged expression on the official face would suddenly reveal his mistake. If he was lucky he would assume the proper mask in time to save the situation, but if he failed to clamp down on his natural impulses, he would be shown his place in no unmistakable terms.

Every day bristled with problems of contact that sprang up when he least expected them. For two months he had contrived to keep his position as handyman in a bazaar; it was characteristic of such jobs that his duties were undefined, provided they were menial. Sometimes he would have to fetch and carry from the store to the shop or from one department to another, or he might have to sweep the floors or remove empty boxes.

One day he was standing in front of one of the counters where he had deposited a pile of pans when the white girl behind the counter called out:

'Hey, John, you might sweep up this mess behind the counter.'

Paul went on with his work, ignoring the voice.

'Hey, you! John! Are you deaf?'

Paul looked coldly into the face that was plentifully powdered, its thickly coated lips outlined with a down of dark hair.

'Are you speaking to me?' he asked.

'Now, John, don't you get cheeky.'

'My name is not John.'

For answer, the girl and her companion cackled with laughter.

'That's too bad!' she said.

She leaned over the counter with a look, half of provocative insolence – recognising him as a male – and half of cold dislike, that declared the conscious superiority of the poor white over the black.

'Sweep up this mess, John, and look slippy about it.'

'I don't take orders from you,' said Paul.

'Well! Of all the cheek!'

The two girls, no longer cackling, exchanged a look of outraged dignity.

'We'll soon see about that,' the girl replied. Whereupon she marched off to report 'John's' insolence.

Paul lost his job.

You had to have the skill of a tightrope walker in this mad world, thought Paul.

Perhaps unfortunately for him he was able sometimes to stand aside and look at the people he came in contact with, both black and white, and it didn't make things any easier for him. Sometimes he wondered if it wasn't he himself who was mad. If the white man's world was a jungle where he had to walk warily, or perish, District Six, where he lived, seething with outcast humanity, was no less of a jungle. For it derived from the larger jungle. It was its offspring, cast in its own image. If the beasts of prey battened on the weaker, they in turn devoured those who were still more defenceless. In the hairs of the monster a vicious battle for survival went on, and woe betide the one who lost his footing.

Once his spirit came near to breaking point.

He was out of work. He was hungry. The woman from whom he rented his room was herself desperate for money to pay the rent and made it clear to him that she couldn't wait much longer. It was hard on him, but she had to think of herself and her children, didn't she? Paul bowed his head and agreed with her.

There were relatives he might have looked for in town, though he hadn't met them yet. Nonceba had told him there was the family of his mother's brother who had come to Cape Town many years ago. But a stubborn pride forbade him to show his face in his present condition. He ought to have written to his sister. How wroth she would be with him for his stubborn silence! How gladly would she give her last penny to help him! But she had warned him of the city and he had laughed at her warnings. Now he could not admit himself to be beaten. So he was silent.

Then he saw an advertisement for a 'houseboy' and decided to answer it. He had always told himself he would never do woman's work in a white man's kitchen. He had despised those he had come across when he had occasion to deliver groceries at back doors. Dressed in their white uniforms, they had adopted a ridiculous air of superiority towards a mere delivery boy, though he was one of themselves. With their white coats they seemed to have donned the appropriate mentality; accepting their position as 'boys' – though they might be men of mature years – they looked down their noses at lesser 'boys'. ('It's a mad world,' said Paul, 'when even language becomes distorted with slavish thinking.')

But now he was desperate. He would answer the advertisement. It was a Sunday evening when he had borrowed the newspaper and he was so afraid that he would miss his chance if he waited until Monday morning that he decided to try his luck there and then. The address was in a suburb where he had never been before. Dusk was falling; it was raining and after walking a long way he had to admit that he was lost. The few people who had ventured out in the rain eyed him suspiciously. Once he spotted a policeman at a corner ahead of him. Quick as a shadow he dodged into a side street. He hadn't a scrap of paper on him authorising him to look for work. If it meant only a night in jail, he could take it, though he was a Mangena. But if they shunted him out of the city, it meant the end of his ambitions.

There was no sound of pursuing feet behind him, so he slackened his pace and considered seriously what he should do next. His stomach was empty; from the feet up he was chill and his one respectable jacket was becoming soaked through with the steady rain. Should he give up and return to his room? He shuddered. He might as well push on, seeing he had come so far. A white man passed him, but it was out of the question to stop him and ask the way ... Ah, there was a coloured man. The man gave him the directions. Paul thanked him and within five minutes he was on the doorstep of the house.

A dim light came from one of the front rooms, so somebody was in. The door of mottled glass before which he stood, was dark; then someone switched on the light and he could just make out a figure moving inside. The door opened; a woman appeared. With the light behind her he could not see her face, but at sight of him she stepped back quickly. Her movement made Paul realise that, with the light full upon him, his face wet with rain, his coat bedraggled, he must cut a sorry figure. But it was more than that.

'What do you want?' she said sharply. There was an edge of terror in her voice.

With a shock Paul realised that she was afraid of him. Instead of answering her, he stood arrested with a sudden awareness of the hopelessness of his position. It was one of those moments when the objective world falls away and one has the sensation of standing over an abyss. What he saw was real, horribly real, but beyond the grasp of human understanding. Here he was, Sipo Mangena, young, warm-hearted, with eager, ambitious thoughts coursing through his veins. All he wanted at the moment was work and food. But here was a woman who saw in front of her only a black face, a thing of terror. Paul felt that terror in every fibre of his being and it filled him with shame. Of whom? Of what?

'What do you want?' she repeated.

Paul stammered that he had seen an advertisement and he had thought ...

At the tone of his voice the terror of the woman gave way to fury.

'Get out of here,' she cried, 'or I'll call the police. How dare you come to my house at this time of night! If you're really looking for work you should have come in the morning.'

With that she banged the door in his face.

With all this, something of a revolution was taking place within him. The natural balance of his personality was being shaken. His confidence was being undermined; his sense of himself as a man, an individual, had suffered a kind of rupture. He no longer felt secure within himself, his pride no longer carried its head high, afraid of no man.

Was there really something wrong with him? Was all the world mad or was he alone going out of his senses? Again and again the exercise of his natural impulses brought him into conflict with those around him. At first he had been amazed and angry, then he grew wary. He closed up like a man clenching his fist on something precious that he will not lose at any cost. When he went out in the morning to face what the day might bring, he told himself that he left his being, his very name behind; whatever rude hands would touch, it would not be him, his essential self. This no man could violate.

He was learning fast, but still not fast enough. He became a messenger in a big department store, where he and another 'boy', an African of about fifty, had the handling of ladies' dresses and coats. His senior had been a long time on the job in more senses than one, for Paul began to discover that he had made a fine art of stealing the dresses and getting rid of them among his women friends. He was generous enough to tip Paul the wink, but as soon as Paul indicated that he was not interested, he became nasty and Paul decided that his safety lay in quitting his job. His employer, having found Paul to his liking, shook his head at the unreliability of these 'boys' who were here today and gone tomorrow, even when you treat them well and give them a good wage. It was better to treat them rough after all, like most of the other firms did, for all the good you got out of treating them decent. Didn't Paul like his job? (Paul was dumb.) What then? With a shrug of exasperation the boss let him go.

When, a week or two later, a retired army captain and his wife, from India, took him on as cook-garden boy, he made up his mind that he would behave as correctly as he could think how to do. He accepted the uniform they put on him; he could no longer afford to despise the menial tasks. The first few days he tried to do everything that was expected of him. Nagged at for his slowness, railed at for his stupidity, reproached for his extravagance with the leftovers in the kitchen and refusing to eat 'kaffir-food', suspected, also, of pilfering, he swallowed his manhood and bent his head to the petty humiliations of his position. His master and mistress prided themselves on treating their servants better than most of their neighbours did, and gave Paul to understand that they would be glad if he would show some appreciation and gratitude on this score.

Every afternoon the old captain took the pedigree dachshund for a walk. His wife said it was good for her husband as it gave him an appetite for dinner. One day, however, the Captain being indisposed, his lady summoned Paul to the lounge.

'Yes, Madam?'

'Master has such a bad cold; I want you to take Judy for a walk. Come here, my pet,' she said to the dachshund. 'Promise me you'll be good, Judy, dear. Don't let other nasty dogs come sniffing at her. You must take great care of her. Is anything the matter?' she asked, for Paul had not made the customary responses.

'I – It's not part of my duty, Madam.'

'You are here to do whatever we ask you to do. You can't complain we give you too much to do.'

'It's the bitch, madam.'

'Do not speak rudely, please.'

'I –'

'You mean you refuse?'

Paul was about to voice his sense of outrage when he remembered the woman at the door on the occasion he had gone in answer to an advertisement for a houseboy. It was hopeless, he decided, to try to communicate with such people.

'Very well, Madam.'

'I'm glad to see you behaving so sensibly. You're a good boy, if only you weren't so slow.'

Paul set out with the dachshund at the end of a lead. After he had got over the humiliation of it, he looked round him only to discover that the passers-by were completely oblivious of his existence, though they were obviously appreciative of the dachshund's points. One or two children made friendly approaches to the dog without being aware of him at the other end of the lead. Somewhat reassured, Paul became lost in thought, a habit that had been growing on him since he had come to the city, and only when he felt the dog pulling at the lead did he realise how late it was. Good heavens! Where was he? It was getting dark and he'd have to hurry back.

An irate mistress greeted him at the entrance. She had feared the worst for her dear Judy. Alternately gushing over the dog and shouting at Paul, she pursued him into the kitchen. Suddenly his endurance snapped; unable to stand the din in his ears he flung down the dish in his hand so that it broke into a thousand pieces. The torrent of words dried up and the woman's face fell open at this atrocious act of insubordination. Demanding his money, he received amid silence the exact amount, and departed.

One day an African of his acquaintance came to him and asked if he would take over a job from him.

'What kind of job?' Paul said, suspiciously.

The man explained. He acted as messenger and general assistant in a small bookseller's shop, receiving for this a better wage than an African usually received.

'What's the snag?' Paul asked.

The man explained that he wanted to go to his home in the Transkei. His father had died, his mother was afraid of what was happening to the small plot of land they had and she was asking her son to come home and settle their affairs. She had heard that they would lose their bit of land.

'Is it true you will lose it?'

'I don't know,' said the man.

'I would like to know about it,' said Paul, concerned for the man.

'If I come back I will let you know.'

'What about this job?' Paul was no longer suspicious.

'I'm sorry to lose it. The work's easy enough. The boss even lets you look at the books.'

'That would suit me!'

'The boss isn't a bad sort. Only he's a bit – peculiar.'

'How is he peculiar?'

'He tries to be nice to you.'

'Nice?' Paul had to laugh at the man's expression. But he knew what he meant. If the African had to conform to the general pattern of behaviour expected of him, so had the white man. Otherwise it excited suspicion; it operated both ways.

Paul interviewed the bookseller, a wiry little man with a beady eye, by the name of Hans Farben, who, as Paul learned later, was a Swiss not long arrived in the country. The first thing that struck Paul when he came into his presence was that he looked him straight in the eye. This he was not accustomed to from the bosses and officials he had hitherto encountered.

Paul gave as good as he received. He felt interested at once, though still on guard.

'So you want the job?' The man spoke abruptly; this was familiar.

'Yes, sir.'

'Are you willing to work?'

'I think so, sir.'

'You think so?' Hans Farben laughed, shaking his shoulders, which were rounded like those of a man habitually bent over a book. 'Then we'll get on. I hear you're fond of books.'

Paul wondered what his friend had been saying.

'Yes, sir, I am.'

'Educated?'

'At Lovedale.'

'Never heard of it.'

'It's a college for non-Europeans only, sir.'

'Non-Europeans only, eh?' Again the man laughed. Paul wondered why.

'And your teachers, were they black too?'

'No, only one or two.'

'I see.'

Paul wondered what he saw.

'And you're aiming to be a teacher too?'

Paul reflected that his friend had been talking too much.

'I was, sir, but –'

'I see. No money. Like me!' And again he laughed.

Hans Farben was certainly behaving 'differently', said Paul to himself, but he had no key as to what it meant. He'd watch and see and perhaps he'd find a clue in time. Of course he might change any minute, so he'd better be on guard. Paul didn't admit that a grave lack of money was one of his chief difficulties. 'Well,' continued the bookseller, 'I'll treat you straight if you treat me straight. That's fair enough, eh? But don't let me see you with your nose too much in the books, eh? Everything in its proper place. You're here to work for me. See?'

So his friend had been wrong about the man letting you read his books. Paul felt disappointed, as if he'd been cheated out of something. He looked round him wistfully.

'Never seen so many books all at once before, have you?' remarked the bookseller, whose eye was as quick as it was small.

'Great things, books are, eh? "The precious lifeblood of a master spirit." Did you ever hear that?' Then he went on in a kind of sing-song, obviously tasting the words: '"Who kills a man kills a reasonable animal, but who destroys a good book, kills Reason itself ... " Do you know who wrote that? A poet in Cromwell's time. Ever hear of Cromwell?'

'Yes, sir.'

'Oh, so they do teach you something at Lovedale?' And he laughed again. 'It's good to cultivate the reading habit,' he continued. 'It broadens the mind.'

'Yes, sir,' said Paul, catching the spirit of the man and forgetting his caution, his suspicion. 'I think so too.'

'You do, eh?' Farben flashed him a look that brought Paul back to a realisation of what he had come for – a job, from a white man.

'Well, we'll talk some more. Get moving now. You can see the place is in a mess.'

Paul saw that the place was indeed in a mess, and whether that was the fault of his friend who had got him the job, or of the boss, he could not be sure. He resolved to work with a will, for the man's conversation had stimulated him, even excited him. He remembered his friend's jocular remark that this foreigner tried to be 'nice', and, while he warned himself that he must still be on guard against him, this wasn't quite the way he would have himself described the man's manner. It was unusual, not to say eccentric, yet he didn't seem to be particularly bothered about what effect he was having on Paul. His manner was too abrupt to be merely 'nice'. Perhaps it had something to do with him having come from Europe. Yes, he was a European. Paul found his imagination wandering to this far unknown place, but baulked at the very vagueness of it. Would he ever be able to visit it one day?

As his hands touched the books in their piles, Paul experienced an almost painful sensation of pleasure mixed with longing. He glanced up quickly lest he had betrayed himself to the white man. But the little bookseller had forgotten his existence and was himself immersed in a volume propped up in front of him. Paul had some inkling of why Hans Farben could say he had no money. He was obviously no salesman.

In the days and months that followed Paul had ample opportunity to watch Farben, to observe his untidy habits, his un-businesslike methods, his moods, his love of the books he was supposed to sell and above all to listen to his conversation. This last would come unexpectedly, sometimes after days of silence during which the man brooded with a louring face as if, thought Paul, watching him, all the bitterness of all the world's folly had curdled the blood in his thin body.

The man is angry at something, Paul said to himself, but had no key as to why a white man should be bitter about anything. Life was easy for the white man in this country. It is the black man whose blood should be bitter ...

He had never heard a man speak as this man from Europe did. The words excited him, sometimes depressed him, filled him with a deep uneasiness – as well as a desire to hear more. Yet he had difficulty in overcoming his suspicion of the fact that a white man should talk to him. 'What is he doing it for,' he would ask himself. 'Why is he talking like this to me? What does he think he'll get out of it? What *can* he get out of it? I have nothing to give him.'

But gradually he became so absorbed in these discussions that he forgot to be suspicious, till eventually his mistrust seemed absurd. This European talked to him as man to man. He had a consuming desire to pursue the point of discussion touched upon in their necessarily brief meetings. Often he did not understand them and at night they would come back to him, challenging him to find their meaning.

He never admitted to the white man that he did not always understand him, but cunningly, cautiously, he would bring the conversation back to the point where the meaning had become obscure and occasionally he would be rewarded by him falling right into the trap; leading him on, pretending more stupidity than he was really capable of, even at the risk of irritating him (for he was very irascible) Paul would get him to hammer away at a point till it was clear to him. Sometimes the bookseller would turn the tables on Paul, probing him, breaking down his defences, even taunting him a little, till he, too, became angry. Ah, but this was how men should be! Wrestling with ideas, hammering away at them, beating each other with them, so long as they arrived at the truth. What was the truth? Paul was but a boy; the man was twice his age, and each one had a mind that was a match for the other. If only Paul knew and could study much more than he did. Then they might arrive at some truth together. But Paul knew so little. He was so ignorant.

In time, Farben lent him books to read.

'Have a look at that,' he would say, carelessly tossing the book on the table where Paul was busy sorting out bundles for postage.

'Not now,' he would add. 'No stealing from business hours. Lose some sleep on it, if you like.'

Paul didn't tell him that it was almost impossible to read because of the noise in the house where he lived in District Six. It was during his lunch hour and in the evening that he would slip into the public library at the foot of the Company Gardens, where non-Europeans as well as white people were allowed to use the reading room. Of course reading in bits and pieces was not conducive to earnest study and if Farben thought that Paul was unduly long in returning a book, he would taunt Paul for his laziness. This would put him on his mettle, forcing him to try to master the book faster than his mental stomach could digest it. But at last they would have discussions on it, in the course of which the little man would grudgingly admit that Paul was no fool.

'You have the makings of a brain, Paul,' Farben commented.

And Paul smiled. He was beginning to understand this man. There was no condescension in the remark.

Farben continually harped on the need to broaden the mind and fight against mental and spiritual stagnation.

One morning he fixed Paul with his small, sharp eye and became more eloquent than he had yet heard him to be. 'Beware of the narrow mind, Paul,' he said. 'Having no vision, it becomes capable of all evil. Be it ever so upright, it becomes tyrannical, and tyranny, Paul, is the death of freedom. It may cherish its own – but others it destroys; to its own, humane, but to others no better than a savage. To its children, a father, but to others less than a beast. Such men I have met, Paul, and so have you. But when we see a whole people thus afflicted, then we must know that it will perish. And the day is not far off. For it is morally sick. In place of reason and justice there is tyranny – which destroys the destroyer no less than its victims. Robbed of their reason, men lose the power to think, to feel like human beings. Believing themselves to be superior, they sink into physical and moral decay; arrogant and blind in their foolish pride, vicious in their folly, they are sapped of spiritual strength and lose the right to be called men. Then, Paul, you must know that they are fit only for burning.'

Kathie stored in her heart all these things that Paul told her. One thing he had discovered in Farben was a fanatic hatred of women.

'I don't think I like him,' said Kathie when Paul told her this.

'He once asked me about women,' said Paul.

'And what did you say?'

'I laughed at him.'

'Why did he hate women?'

'I think he loved them.'

'But that doesn't make sense.'

'There had been a woman in Europe. I think it was she.'

'Whom he loved?'

'Whom he hated.'

'Where is he now?'

'He went back to Europe. But that was a year or two later. He was my friend until he went away.'

'Did he go back because of the woman?'

'I don't think so. He said he *had* to go back to Europe. He was afraid of this land.'

'A white man, afraid of this land?'

'Yes. That was why. "There is a moral corruption," he said to me. "It seeps into your bones and lulls you to a deadly sleep. I feel it all around me. I breathe it every day. I smell it in my nostrils." '

'What a strange man!'

'No. Not so strange. Only, coming from a place where there are many different peoples – he told me of these things – he saw this land in a clearer light. "There is meaning in this chaos," he said. "It is for you to find it. I leave it to you to think it out for yourself."'

'And have you found it?'

'Not yet. But one day I will. With you to help me, Kathie?'

'Me? But I know so little.'

'You are learning,' he said, and kissed her cheek.

With the easing of his material conditions, at least in one direction, Paul had turned his thoughts seriously to resuming his studies. In this Farben helped him. All his spare time he concentrated on preparing himself for his examinations, which he could take extramurally at the end of the year. He had written meantime to his sister Nonceba, who had recovered her health and returned to her teaching, and had received her forgiveness for his long silence, though not without the accompanying admonitions and scoldings that were an inevitable part of the deep affection she gave him.

'There isn't a woman like her!' said Paul, 'Except you, Kathie,' he added, in time to save himself the little slap he was about to receive for this one-sided appreciation of womankind.

It was Farben who had suggested he should go in for law.

'Paul, you ought to be a lawyer,' he exclaimed one day. 'You have the devil's own cunning when it comes to an argument. What do you say to that?'

'It's a crazy idea,' answered Paul.

'How so?'

'You don't know this country.'

'Who said? You've taught me a lot.'

'You don't know the difficulties for a black man trying to enter the professions. It's as bad as the proverbial camel and the eye of a needle.'

'So you'll sit down and cry till someone invents a needle threader!'

'You can't laugh it off,' said Paul.

'Don't frown at me like that. Is there a law against it?'

'Not exactly.'

'Not exactly! Not exactly! You're weak-kneed, man!'

'You know the force of unwritten law. It can strangle a man to death.'

'Not if he's got moral guts. You must learn to swim against the stream, man. It's the only way to survive.'

'Is that what you do – swim against the stream?' There was a certain degree of challenge in Paul's voice.

'Now and again, though I'm a bit winded.' And Farben laughed a little bitterly. 'But what's that got to do with you?' he added sharply. 'You are you. And on the threshold of life. Get on with it! Why should you stop at this idea of simply becoming a teacher?'

'What's wrong with becoming a teacher?' Paul asked. 'Aren't you a teacher?'

'Me? Good God, man!' And the shoulders heaved even more heavily than usual.

'Aren't we like the Greeks – sitting down to it and hammering out ideas together?' said Paul.

'Socrates to your Plato, eh? We are not idealists, my friend. Our feet are firmly planted in the soil. But there is something in what you say. In fact, you confirm my point about this teaching business. You can't be a teacher in the true sense of the word. You'll have to stuff the heads of the innocents with the kaffir-food you said you refused to eat in the kitchen of the army captain? Remember?'

'I forget none of these things.'

'Well! You see my point?'

'I see your point.'

'Now as to this law business. It'll be a long, uphill fight. I quite realise that. I know the prejudices, the impediments that'll be put in your way, the insults, the silent sabotage – over and above the not un-important fact that meantime you'll have to live. A man has to eat.'

'I'll manage somehow,' said Paul rather quickly. Farben shot him a look.

'Proud as Lucifer, aren't you? Keep it. You'll need it plenty later on,' he replied laconically.

The two men understood each other.

'Of course, don't expect miracles to come out of law either,' admonished the elder man. 'I've noticed you're a bit impatient, you know.'

But Paul was too excited to pay much heed to the warning. From his initial scepticism he had swung to a wholehearted acceptance of the idea and was eager to make a start straight away.

He had to get an ordinary degree first, and without actually attending a university. So he had had to wait three years. Then Farben had used his influence to get him articled to a firm in town. It had been no easy matter, but the head of the firm had agreed to do Paul Mangena a favour and give him a trial in view of the fact that they had a fairly large African clientele. It would help, among other things, with the language difficulty.

This was the last thing Farben had done for Paul before he left for Europe.

'You must miss him,' said Kathie. There was a faraway look in her eye.

'I miss him,' answered Paul. 'He had a mind of rare integrity.'

CHAPTER 13

Paul and Nontando

Paul had become very wary in the city jungle, for he had a strong sense of self-preservation. Yet even here, at great risk, he put out tendrils of feeling. Living in another room in the same house where he first found lodging, was an African woman, Thembisa Sitole, and her son, whom she sent to a coloured school in the district. She was a woman about thirty years of age, thickset, hardened by her life in town. At first sight she was an ugly woman and her voice had a rough quality, as if she had shouted too far over the hillside in her home village to someone who could not hear her.

There was no man in the house; she supported herself and her child by going out charring for the white people and also eked out her living by taking in their washing. It appeared that her husband had killed a coloured man, who had attacked him in a drunken brawl, and he was now serving a term of imprisonment for culpable homicide. Though compelled to live in an overcrowded human den, the woman had not gone under. Towards men she was hard and cynical, but they respected her. She was best pleased when they kept out of her way.

It was between Thembisa Sitole and Paul that a friendship sprang up. Coming home rather late one day, she had found a strange man sitting on the floor playing with her son Keke. Not at all put out by her suspicious glance, Paul (for it was he) had said by way of explanation:

'Your son and I have been having a game together. He seemed a bit lonely, eh? Little boy?'

Whereupon the boy had excitedly told his mother about the new game the nice man had taught him. This obviously softened the mother and she had thanked Paul, making it quite clear, however, that she had no further need of his presence.

After this, it became a habit for Paul to keep an eye on Keke when his mother was out and he happened to be on the spot. Thembisa for her part, while at first on her guard, imperceptibly came to rely on Paul's assistance and now and again found herself scolding him for not looking after himself properly. She expressed scorn for the clumsy way in which he had mended a dilapidated shirt, to which he graciously responded by allowing her to mend it. Perceiving in the garment an old patch, which only loving hands could have sewed for him, she pried out of him the fact that he had a sister, Nonceba – a wonderful woman. This led to her telling him about her husband and how he had come to be in jail.

'He's a good man,' she said. 'Only he's been unlucky. He used to have his rages, but he'd never kill. Never!'

Then she went on to say that her husband didn't even know the drunken coloured man who had burst into their room one night. And she didn't either, though she supposed that he lived in another room in the house. You couldn't know all the people that were always coming and going in such a place. Well, before she knew where she was, the man had whipped out a knife. But her husband was the stronger. He had got the knife into his hand ... And that was how it had happened.

Her husband was a good man, kind to her and the child. She would wait for him, though it was a long time. And she sighed. Her husband had to have a home to come back to, didn't he? And Paul agreed.

As she spoke, Thembisa was standing over a paraffin stove on which she cooked supper for herself and her boy when she came back from her charring in Newlands, one of the affluent suburbs of Cape Town. Watching her, Paul had the impression that her square sturdy legs were a symbol of the simple steadfastness of purpose with which she would keep her home together until her husband came back to it. Herself a townsgirl, she had refused to go to his people in the country or to send her child to them. She had an indomitable will and a fierce sense of pride that scorned to be indebted to any man.

When her neighbour, a vegetable hawker with a wife and two young children, died, his family went to some relatives and the small room they had occupied fell vacant. Thembisa immediately informed Paul and he got the room, much to his satisfaction, for it greatly facilitated his studies to have a room to himself, however small and ill-ventilated. The neighbours were too busy with the stress of living to do more than fling a ribald word or two at this friendship that had sprung up between Thembisa, who was known to have a harsh tongue and a tough hide, and the young greenhorn – as they regarded Paul – with the dew of the country still on his smooth, deep brown skin.

Then one day as Paul was on his way back from Farben's where he had been working late, and had turned into the sandy track leading to his house, he saw a huddle of African children sitting outside the fence of a dilapidated dwelling as if waiting for something. What a disconsolate picture they presented! How forlorn their postures. If men and women were outcast here, on the edge of the town, what of these children? In soul and body denied comfort, bereft of security from the moment of their birth?

He halted opposite the group. Why were they in the street? What were they waiting for? Had they no mother or father?

There was one of them older than the rest, a girl of about sixteen, slight of build, her wisp of a dress accentuating her slimness; her pointed face was of a golden-brown colour, rather lighter than that of most of his people. Her look was sullen, half timid, half defiant, and Paul had the impression that she was poised in flight, yet her feet were chained to the spot. She was standing slightly apart from the others, but obviously with them.

At sight of Paul she turned away, pretending not to notice him. Paul hovered, undecided what to do. Then he spoke.

'Is anything the matter? Can I help you?'

The girl threw him a glance, but did not answer. Then one of the smaller children, a boy of about ten, responded boldly:

'Pa kicked us out. He says he doesn't want any brats around.'

'He's very drunk,' piped up the little girl beside him.

The big girl turned on them in a fury.

'Be quiet!' she said. She looked defiantly at Paul, daring him to mock their shame.

'It's all right,' he reassured her, but her glance did not lose any of its hostility.

Paul thought it wiser to appeal to the boy.

'I live over there,' he said. 'You can come and sit in my room if you like.'

'My mother told us to stay here,' interrupted the girl quickly.

'Where is your mother?' said Paul.

'She's inside. She's making Pa some food,' said the boy.

'Have you had any supper?'

Paul couldn't have asked a question more calculated to win his point, for the boy's eyes gleamed with a look of anticipation and the little girl started to whimper. The eldest of the group, at this sign of weakness, regarded them with angry contempt.

'What about having a bite with me until it's time for you to go inside?' Paul suggested, then without waiting for an answer, he added: 'I'll go in and tell your mother, shall I?'

The girl darted forward. 'No,' she said. Then to her brother: 'We'll go inside.'

The little boy scowled at her. 'Not me!' he said. 'He'll hit me.'

The younger girl whimpered more loudly, while their sister looked from her to Paul with an angry helplessness.

'You go in and tell your mother and I'll take them along,' continued Paul, his tone half peremptory, half persuasive, and, while the girl hesitated, the boy decided the matter by putting his hand into Paul's. Without another word, he took the little girl in his arms, leaving the eldest girl standing.

'My room's right at the end of the passage,' he said to the boy, loud enough for the girl to hear him. If she could get over her hostility he hoped that hunger at least might bring her after her brother and sister.

Paul hadn't stopped to consider what Mrs Sitole would say. Unaware that she had made supper for him and was looking out for him because he was late, he had hoped to slip past her room with his flock, but sure enough she spotted him and regarded the procession with amazement and obvious disapproval.

'What's all this?' she said.

Paul explained what little he knew, and didn't mention the possible addition of a third member to the party, though he found himself wondering if she would turn up.

'I saved some supper for you,' remarked Mrs Sitole.

'Oh, thank you, that'll suit us fine,' replied Paul, thinking of his hungry charges.

'It isn't much,' she added, glancing with scant sympathy at the expectant little faces beside him.

'You'd be surprised what we'll manage to do with it,' he declared and proceeded to light his own little stove where he was accustomed to make himself a meal of sorts when he could no longer stomach the filthy conditions that prevailed in the few eating houses he could afford.

The children didn't need to be told twice to squat on the floor and tuck in. The difficulty was to contrive to save a morsel for the girl whom he hoped would still come.

'What's your name?' Paul asked of the boy.

'Duduudu,' he answered.

'Duduudu!' echoed Paul.

'Duduudu Kubeka,' added the boy.

'And your little sister's name?'

The little one answered for herself.

'Nosisi,' she said proudly, and Paul gave it back to her in the same tone, to her pleasure.

'And your big sister?' asked Paul.

'She's called Nontando,' replied the boy.

'Nontando. That's a pretty name.'

'There's Lolo too,' said Duduudu.

'Oh, is there?'

'That's our baby brother,' explained the little girl.

At this moment, Nontando walked in. Ignoring her reluctant expression, Paul, with an air of careless cajolery, invited her to partake of his hospitality.

'Have some supper with me, Nontando,' he said. 'I waited for you.'

He was rewarded with a gradual relaxation of her tensed-up

manner and had even got her to speak a little, when Mrs Sitole walked in.

She eyed the girl suspiciously, receiving in turn even more than she gave. Neither of them were given to compromise. Paul's innocent air observed nothing and the woman and the young girl perforce sheathed their involuntary, but mutual, enmity. Why should it spring up so spontaneously between them?

Observing the growing interest that Paul manifested in Nontando, the neighbours prophesied that now they'd see what skill Thembisa Sitole had in those sharp-nailed fingers of hers, and waited for the fun to begin. In this they were disappointed. Thembisa's affection for Paul was of a complex nature; she at once admired him, respected him, relied upon him, was puzzled not a little by something in him she could not comprehend, and over and above all felt the fierce protectiveness of a mother for her big son. In so far as there was a deep comfort in having a man 'about the house', he did in a sense replace her husband in her heart; though in this there was no disloyalty to her husband. The fact that her son Keke clung to him, regarding him as the most wonderful of big brothers, strengthened her affection. Yet there is no doubt that it was possessive towards Paul.

While not completely understanding all that prompted Paul to make friends with Nontando, she was perfectly well aware that, whatever she might feel towards the girl, she could do nothing that would offend him. She promised herself to observe and wait. She told herself she knew the type of girl Nontando was; she was very young, but in a district like this there was probably not much she didn't know. Paul might think himself so much older, so much more mature. But he was a fool for all that. Women would always be able to twist him round their little finger.

Besides the challenge which Nontando's hostility had presented to Paul and the consequent pleasure in overcoming it, there was something in her that appealed to the romantic in him – perhaps her smallness, perhaps the blending of timidity and defiance in her manner. Whatever it was, he felt he had to protect her against the perils of the district in which she lived. Having seen so much of the degradation of womankind since he had come to the city – and it had bitten deep into his consciousness – he could not bear to think that this delicate being should be exposed to all the surrounding dangers without some hand to guide her. It was obvious that there was no such hand in her own home; from what he could gather her mother was a harassed, downtrodden woman in whom the impulses of motherhood were necessarily suppressed in the fierce struggle merely to keep alive, while her father was a consumptive who was destroying his already weakened constitution with drink and impotent rage against forces he could not understand. When able to work, he was a labourer at the docks, where he was exposed to every wind that crossed Table Bay. Nontando herself went to work for the white people, but was not in regular employment. Paul mentioned her in his letters to his sister and wished that such a woman as Nonceba was at hand to help the girl.

Thembisa Sitole was right when she surmised that Paul could not know the true nature of Nontando, though she herself was even more deeply ignorant of all that went to make such a child. Both perceived an aspect of Nontando that had a certain amount of truth in it, but neither of them saw the whole nor even the essential part. Paul with his sympathetic understanding came nearer to the truth, yet even he was blind to her essential need. And perhaps, in the nature of things, he could not help himself.

From an attitude of hostility, Nontando quickly came to idolise Paul. She was attracted to him for the very reason that he was completely new to her experience, completely different from the young men around her. Rather soft, maybe – for to her manliness was measurable rather in terms of toughness than in the more subtle sense of strength of character. His very gentleness was a source of wonder to her, so that she ascribed to it – in relation to herself – more than it was wise for her to do. The danger was that she had no key to such a man as Paul was. All she knew was that she was drawn to him by an irresistible attraction and she gave to this new sensation all the force of a passionate nature hitherto frustrated in every natural channel of expression.

In his presence she felt the breath of a new life that she could not well define; she had no language, no thoughts wherewith to clothe it. He appealed to something finer in herself, that which had been smudged over by habitual contacts with what was gross and insensitive. Deprived of any opportunity for intellectual development, she lived very much through her senses; young as she was, she was intensely feminine. Some call it womanly intuition; but there was nothing beneficent in this blind power that was her only guide. It could be as savage as the forces around her, for it was rooted in them and had been nourished by them. In this sense she was the child of her environment.

Nontando had received little more than the rudiments of education, so Paul encouraged her to study, teaching her himself whenever he could spare the time. She was an apt pupil and the thrill of pleasure she felt when he praised her more than rewarded her for the unaccustomed restraints imposed upon her by the effort to make up for the lost years. Through his eyes she began to see a new Nontando growing day by day. If it wasn't the real Nontando, it gave her a sense of pride – mingled with a mischievous feeling of make-believe – to be more and more like the Nontando whom Paul was creating in his mind. He for his part was tender towards this image, allowing himself to be more fond of Nontando than he realised. Without knowing it, she touched the gentlest springs of his nature, that might otherwise have become petrified in the city jungle. Through the thin walls of her room Thembisa Sitole would overhear the young laughter coming from Paul's room where the girl would come to sit of an evening and at the sound a pang of envy twisted her heart. She told herself she didn't trust the girl. Yet now more than at any time Nontando was tasting the innocent joy of her newfound friendship, without alloy, basking in the warmth of a rare trustfulness. Her complete dependence on Paul was something that neither of them realised; the deeper significance of the feeling he had awakened in her did not show itself on the surface nor did it find words, for she had no words to give it.

Paul's life was a full one. Between his work for Farben, his studies and the time spent with Nontando, he had nothing to spare. He had encouraged Nontando to spend her evenings with himself and Thembisa, hoping also that contact with a woman of Thembisa's character would have a steadying influence on the young girl. In this he was thwarted by the tacit but stubborn hostility on Nontando's part towards the older woman, for which he was inclined to blame Nontando, never suspecting the subterranean currents of Thembisa's own hostility.

As the time for the examinations drew near Paul became more and more preoccupied and expected Nontando to occupy herself with her books also – if she didn't feel like joining Thembisa. This piqued the girl, who felt she was being neglected. She became wayward and discontented, telling herself she was tired of him and his seriousness. He was dull; she wanted amusement; she felt a hankering after the company she had been accustomed to before she had ever known him. So she came no more to Paul, hoping he would miss her company, and meantime threw herself with reckless abandonment into her old way of life with the youths of the district who were only too pleased to win her away from this tall intruder with a mighty conceit of himself.

Then the little Spitfire – as they called her – turned on her one-time friends. They made her sick, she said. They no longer satisfied her craving for amusement. She didn't know what she wanted. Bored with them, with Paul, with herself, where could she turn? One evening she strayed into Paul's room, as if something compelled her feet to take that path and no other, though she told herself she didn't particularly want to see him.

As she drew near to his house her heart quickened. How could she have stayed away so long? She was mad! He may have missed her. But then, he hadn't lifted a finger to beckon her back. Oh, how foolish she had been. He was angry with her and wanted to spite her for hurting him. Oh, she would ask his forgiveness. He was not like any other she had ever met.

She quickened her steps. On his breast she would explain everything, safe in his protecting arms ...

At the door she met Thembisa. The woman gave her a silent look, without greeting. She had been hearing stories. With a toss of the head, Nontando passed on and entered the room. Paul was in his usual position at the small table, his head bent over his books. Nontando advanced slowly, the sullenness that the encounter had brought to her eyes yielding to a soft light as they rested on the bowed head.

'Paul,' she said.

'Oh, it's you!'

Immersed as he was in a problem, his tone was still preoccupied, though he was genuinely glad to see her.

'Sit down. I won't be long.'

She did not sit down. Prepared as she had been to fling herself on his breast, she was outraged at this casual treatment. She waited, silent, her fury mounting every moment. Her hands longed to destroy something, anything, to give vent to her angry pride. There she had been, full of contrition, ready to ask his forgiveness, and he calmly ignored her.

'You think you can treat me like a child,' she burst out.

Quite unprepared for the outburst, Paul looked up, surprised. Seeing the angry hurt on the girl's face he went quickly up to her.

'Nontando,' he said. 'I was busy, don't you understand?'

'You treat me like a child,' she repeated.

'Are you such an old woman?' he parried playfully. For in truth he thought of her as a child and it was her childish waywardness that appealed to the gentlest side of his nature.

'Come and sit down.' He took her by the hand and led her to a chair.

'Come and talk to me.'

She allowed herself to be coaxed into the chair.

'Tell me all about it.'

'There is nothing to tell,' she said.

'Why did you not come and see me?'

'You didn't want me.'

'There you are wrong, Nontando.' He spoke gently, yet he was blind to the significance of her words.

She had no weapon against this gentleness, though she was left with a vague sense of dissatisfaction. He was so genuinely happy to see her that gradually he wooed her into a good mood, and recognising that she needed him he relinquished his studies for the evening and devoted himself entirely to her, with the result that he sent her home in a state of renewed adoration, resolving from then on to conquer her wicked moods. For a spell she concentrated on her books with all the fury of her new resolve to please him and prove worthy of his faith in her.

It was at this time that Thembisa, having invited him one evening to partake of her simple meal, took the opportunity to speak to Paul about Nontando.

Closely observing the girl and fearful of her ways and wiles, Thembisa thought it was necessary to warn him. Hitherto, her assumption that Paul's deeper nature was not touched, had lulled her into a grudging tolerance of Nontando's frequent presence. But a man was only human, she told herself. You never knew when the girl, with her artful, feminine tricks, might catch him unawares. Paul had his head in the clouds, poor lamb, so that he was fair game for the likes of her.

Thembisa's own dependence on Paul made her keenly aware of anything that concerned him, without looking beyond that; what this relationship meant for Nontando herself was no concern of hers; she simply wasn't interested. If there was any danger to Paul, she would be the first to attack, fiercely, if need be. That there could be any danger to Nontando in the situation never entered Thembisa's mind. Nor, for all his affection, did it enter the mind of Paul.

It was after supper, then, and Thembisa's little son was fast asleep on his mattress in a corner of the room. Paul looked tired, for he had been pushing himself hard in the matter of late nights. Thembisa, however, had made up her mind to speak.

'Do you think you can trust Nontando?' she asked.

'Trust her? Of course. But what do you mean?'

'Did you ever ask yourself where she was all that time she stopped coming here?'

'I'm not Nontando's keeper. She's free to come and go. It's not for me to force her to come.'

'She's not the innocent you think she is,' said Thembisa.

'Nontando is her own sweet self.'

'Sweet indeed!' she snorted. 'That's what the minx puts on for your benefit.'

'Why have you got your knife into little Nontando?' asked Paul, suddenly seeing Thembisa in a new light. She was stung by his reply.

'You don't see what's in front of your nose,' she said. 'I don't trust the girl.'

'She hasn't done you any harm, so why –' began Paul.

'You'd think butter wouldn't melt in her mouth, so like an angel she is – for the time being. But I tell you she'll never know her own mind. I've seen her with other young men and –'

'Don't you think you might leave me to judge?' Paul said quietly.

Thembisa brought her lips hard together. He had never reproved her in this manner before. And soon after he took his leave.

For a long time she did not again refer to Nontando, though she did not relax her vigilance.

As if to refute Thembisa's arguments, Nontando did indeed

behave like an angel for some time afterwards. There was a charm about her, intensely grave, intensely gay, sullen and a little wild – a vital quality that knocked at Paul's heart even while it did not satisfy the mind that would one day ask so much of the woman of his choice.

The day Paul was accepted as an articled clerk his mind soared into daydreams of what he would do when he was a fully fledged lawyer. He saw himself in court delivering the most eloquent speeches so that friends and even enemies came to congratulate him on his achievement, which he modestly dismissed as all in a day's work. He was sure of his ability to stay the course; nothing would divert him, no impediment shake him from the path of his goal.

His resolution was soon put to the test. It did not take him long to discover that he was completely at the mercy of his employer, the yoke firmly attached to his neck. He was never allowed to forget the enormous favour that he, a black man, had received by being permitted to set foot in such an establishment. Indeed he must be bled dry for the honour. If he was in any danger of having ideas about himself as a white collar worker, the office staff, from the heads of department to the trim little typist just out from school, took care by a thousand humiliating pinpricks to disillusion him.

Paul went doggedly on, unaware of how much he was taxing himself. He missed Farben much more than he would confess to himself. This European had opened up a new world of thought to him; he had stimulated him and sustained him, not only quickening his intellectual being and sharpening his awareness of what went on around him, but helping him to maintain his balance in what he considered to be a mad world. The man's simple humanity spoke to his own, strengthening his fundamental faith in men. There must be other men like Farben, he thought, but where shall I find them? And now Farben had gone; never again would he see the rounded shoulders hunching with his laughter; never again catch a look from the small, quick eye; never again hear the voice taunting him to think it out for himself, warming with pleasure when Paul challenged him over some point, burning with ardour in his dreams of the future when all men – as he expressed it – would live a life worthy of human beings.

A life worthy of human beings! Paul looked around him. Where

162

could he see such men? Among his own people, outcasts from society, outcasts of labour – for they had none of the rights that even a worker has – he saw only the body fettered with poverty, the mind fettered by the sheer stress of existence, capable only of feeling its own pain or a dull, impotent anger … A life worthy of human beings? Was it then the privilege of the white men? The petty official who lorded it over him? The army captain and his wife? The bazaar employee, cackling at his claim to have a name of his own? Or the iron-faced head of the law firm he worked for, hastening from office to court, from court to office in the interests of his clients and his purse? Paul shook his head. These did not live as men should live. Not these either. For they, too, were enslaved.

And still Paul went doggedly on. Thembisa missed his smiling friendliness, since he did not spare her even those pleasant idling moments after supper which do so much to make up for the toil of the day. She tried scolding him for his overwork, even teasing him for taking himself too seriously, only to find her tactics unsuccessful. There was some small comfort in the fact that Nontando, too, was finding the new routine little to her liking.

The girl still came in the evenings, seeking comfort even in his silent company. Striving to live up to his high opinion of her, she would sit beside him very quietly for what seemed to her an extraordinarily long time. She would arrange his books for him, quite unnecessarily, for he would suddenly dive to the bottom of the pile for the book he wanted, leaving all the rest disarranged. With a sigh of conscious virtue she would rearrange them, waiting for the glance of appreciation that would reward her – the sun in which her wayward spirit basked and expanded. But, alas, she waited most often in vain; the beloved face was completely oblivious of her presence, a frown of concentration between its brows. Sometimes she would make tea for him, feeling certain that this would make him stop, toss aside his horrid books, look at her with the warm light of old dancing in his eyes, after which would follow the innocent ritual of drinking out of the same cup with him. That was how it once had been. Now, however, he would let the tea sit until it was quite cold, ignoring the hand that made it. Patiently she would wait, her feelings growing hotter minute by minute as the tea grew colder. At last, unable to bear it any longer, she would spring up, seize her scarf and say she was going home since she wasn't wanted here. Startled out of his concentration and full of contrition, Paul would hurriedly drink his cup of cold tea, not realising that even that gesture failed to placate her. Gone was the happy ritual of sharing the tea out of the same cup, and, without saying a word she would watch him drink his tea alone and then fling herself out of the room before he could make a move to stop her.

But it was not always like this. Occasionally she would pick up one of Paul's books and pretend to pore over it with the same concentrated expression she so often watched on his face. She even reproduced the frown between the eyes, but that was because the words were dancing on the page in front of her – a maddening incommunicable jumble of words that left her out in the cold.

There were yet other times when she was content simply to sit and watch Paul as he worked. Holding herself very still, afraid to break the silence, she fixed her eyes upon him. She noted his small ears, tracing the delicate line from the outer edge to the centre; she noted the high forehead, the tenseness between the brows; she gazed till every line of his body imprinted itself on her memory, stirring within her a strange sensation of mingled pleasure and pain. Holding her breath, she seemed to be playing a magic game, weaving a spell around him and herself so as to shut out the cruel world that might press inward and destroy them. Once Paul looked up and something of the intentness of her gaze caught him unawares. For a second she did not respond to his look, but seemed to be removed from him, her eyes bespeaking an infinite sadness.

'Nontando!' he said.

She started, leapt up and ran to him, clinging to him without speaking.

'Where were your thoughts?' he asked.

'With you,' she answered.

'But you looked so far away.'

'I was with you all the same.'

'You frightened me a little,' he added.

'Did I? I was with you all the time,' she repeated. 'It is you who go away from me.'

'You don't call this going away from you, do you?' he parried, touching his books.

'Yes it is!' she answered. There was a hint of hatred in her voice.

'But you have your books too,' argued Paul.

164

'Oh, I will never learn,' she answered sullenly.

'You know that is not true,' he said. 'You have been learning very fast indeed.'

'What's the use?'

'How can you say: What's the use? I have told you that books open a new world to you. If only you are patient.'

'I don't want to be patient. This new world – it seems so far away.'

'Not so far as you think, Nontando.'

'If you help me, I will try harder to learn,' she said, lifting her face to his.

'I will always help you, Nontando.' His hand rested lightly on her shoulder.

She nestled against him, then with a joyous laugh darted away to put some water on the little stove.

'Let's have some tea, shall we? And while the water's boiling you can talk to me.'

'All right. You always get your own way, don't you?' he teased, falling in with her mood.

'Now put your books away,' she said, pushing them vigorously to the side of the table and perching on the edge of it in front of him. She began chattering gaily, wriggling on her perch, so that Paul could hardly believe that a moment ago he had met her sad, abstracted gaze that had given him a vague sense of fear.

'What a child you are!' he exclaimed.

At his words her gaiety vanished and her whole expression changed.

'I am not a child,' she said.

He smiled. 'You don't need to be so solemn about it.'

'You are smug, aren't you,' she flashed back.

Paul was nonplussed by her mercurial temperament. He did not try to coax her back to her former humour and soon afterwards she left him. The lid of the kettle danced its petulant tune, demanding attention, but Paul meantime had gone back to his books. Eventually he made himself a cup of tea.

Nontando did not come back again for several days.

Was it possible, as Thembisa feared, that Nontando would awaken in Paul the love that a man gives to a woman? She was of his people. She had charm. Indeed it might have been. With his senses outraged by what he had observed between men and women since his coming into town, it is true that he had locked his passions up, but the very fact that she kept alive in him the springs of gentleness opened the door to a warmer feeling towards her. Yet there was an incalculable element in her personality that put him on guard; being so often nonplussed by her mercurial temperament, he felt insecure. It was something alien to him; nurtured as he had been by a sister whose character was rooted in certain human values, it was hard for him to know the wayward being whom the city jungle had moulded, completely uprooted from the moral norms of his people, and with only the shifting sand of a social chaos under her feet. His humanity cherished her, but his heart sought a woman to whom he could give complete trust, who would be his equal in spirit, yet on whose bosom he could lay his head and say: This is my home.

What Paul failed to realise was that in awakening Nontando's aspirations he had awakened also the woman in her.

And then he met Kathie.

It was a meeting fraught with change for several people, but as is often the way with such events, it happened as lightly as a breeze passes over a pool and ripples the reflection of flower and stem that a moment before had been lying steady in the smooth water.

In the first place when he had been invited to the social evening at which he had subsequently met Kathie, he had not particularly wanted to go. He was too busy to have many evenings to spare. A coloured student of his acquaintance had invited him to come along with a partner, and since Nontando, who had naturally sprung to his mind, had a previous date, he had excused himself, whereupon the student had ragged him for being an old stick-in-the-mud and assured him that if he came he would introduce him to some nice coloured girls. Paul didn't like what he felt to be his rather patronising attitude. Ordinarily, it was as unusual for an African to associate with a woman outside his race as it was for a coloured or an Indian girl to associate with an African. The racial barrier – and racial pride – operated on both sides. This the coloured student was hardly aware of, hence his patronising attitude to Paul. However, Paul, on an impulse, had decided to go, without a partner.

And Kathie and he had met and danced and talked together. Their talk had warmed his heart and kindled his imagination. It was a new and wonderful experience.

When he came back after midnight, Thembisa had greeted him as he had passed to his little room beyond hers. But he had not wanted to stand and chat with her, as was his custom. He had wanted to be alone.

CHAPTER 14

Joy and sorrow

The second time they met had been by chance in the Company Gardens at the top of Government Avenue. Tired after a particularly difficult case, Kathie meandered along the paths in the gardens, then lingered beside the fish pond, just off the avenue below the art gallery. It was one of those radiant winter days between the rains when everything gleams with an intensity as if to fill itself with sunlight before the wind and the rain should come again; one of those days when the clarity of the mountain makes you aware that every atom of it is an integral part of the city. Kathie, her mood relaxed, drank of the vital quality of nature around her.

The sun lay couched upon the water lilies, illuminating the reflection of their lilac and blue petals in the pool below. How solid their bed of succulent leaves, floating double, leaf and shadow. Shoals of goldfish drifting head to tail close to the surface wove a pattern of bronze and red and silver-grey, their fan-like tails fluttering like gossamer. The little stone cherub gazing at himself in the pool seemed to catch the dancing motion, for the sunbeams on the water threw back to him the rippling waves so that stone and shadow danced together. Kathie stood fascinated at the sight, unaware that the rippling sunbeams were illuminating her own face.

It was thus that Paul caught sight of her as he approached. His head, if not in the clouds, had been lifted to the towering buttresses of Table Mountain standing in dense blocks of light and shade above the scene. Waiting till he came up close to her he greeted her so quietly that without any movement of surprise she smiled up at him and her first remark directed his glance from her face to the rippling sunbeams on the pool.

'Look at that fat little cherub,' she exclaimed. 'I swear I can see him breathing.'

'Even the stones dance on a day like this,' he answered.

It was as much as to say: 'We have met. Therefore the day is beautiful.'

Sitting on one of the benches overlooking the pool, they spent the next hour together, though neither of them could have said afterwards what it was they talked about.

These two young people had gravitated towards each other with a spontaneity undreamed of in Paul's experience. He had never imagined that a woman like Kathie existed. Ordinarily reserved in his contacts, he had few friends and though young women were attracted to him, they found him aloof. The idealistic streak in his character made him uncommonly fastidious – a factor that the shrewd Thembisa counted on when reckoning the chances of Nontando being able to 'twist him round her little finger'. The woman of Paul's choice would have to satisfy both head and heart. And, lo! the miracle had happened – or so he had told himself.

The bond of sympathy between him and Kathie, the physical attraction enhanced by the rare joy of conversing with a mind that partook of the same eager quality as his own, at one stride leapt over the racial barrier that custom imposed. Not that he deliberately ignored it; it was rather that this alchemy of attraction made any racial barrier meaningless.

When he had discovered Kathie's love (as it then seemed) for Alan Nel, he tasted for the first time the bitterness of disappointed hope, but his devotion burned the more brightly for its secrecy, and the gaiety he infused into their meetings together was the more poignant when he perceived the innocent pleasure that she, too, experienced in his company.

Her love had ultimately found its true home.

It grew into a relationship such as is rarely vouchsafed to any man or woman in any age, in any sphere of life, and was all the more remarkable for the barren conditions of existence in which Paul and Kathie and those around them were compelled to live.

It was a mature womanhood that Kathie brought to this relationship. Until the full tide of it came upon her she herself had never suspected that she could feel as she did. Imagine the sap of life flowing steadily throughout nature, pushing up out of the dark soil in an infinitude of shapes and forms, glowing in the manifold colours of flowers and foliage that give back the light of the sun, drink up the rain of the clouds, deck themselves morning and evening with dew and are visited by the honey-seeking bees and birds. To imagine this sap of life is to know something of what Kathie experienced in her newborn love for Paul. It welled through every thought and mood; it quickened her senses; it gave to the motion of her body and the glance of her eye an indefinable grace.

But this vital quickening of the whole woman, while it made for joy, did not make life any the more simple. Her vision of the world around her took on an intense quality. It was not long before she was to learn that happiness has its price. As her life mounted to its fulfilment, for Nontando it was to bring a drinking of life to the dregs. How soon was this joy to be menaced, not through any fault of its own, but by the sad complexity of human relationship! The fate of these two women, Kathie and Nontando, was inexorably bound together by their relationship to Paul. They stood about him, two embattled forces of joy and sorrow, life and death. There could be no compromise between them.

More than once, when she and Paul were together, Kathie turned the conversation towards Nontando, but found that of late Paul's manner had become constrained. She wondered why. He had become perturbed at what was happening to his young friend and could not bring himself to speak because it seemed to him like betraying a trust to do so.

It is not to be supposed that Nontando's sharp eyes could fail to detect a difference in Paul after Kathie had become part of his life. He told her nothing. How should he? But she had other ways of knowing. She had been increasingly petulant with him lately, and he had set aside his books and hers and was trying to coax her into the Nontando he knew she could be. Poor girl, what a bright flower she was in this smothering atmosphere of turbulent living. How should one know all the wayward thoughts that filled her mind, longing to breathe a little of the free, fresh air? How little he could do to enable her to breathe that freshness, he who was himself struggling for a foothold in the city jungle.

Suddenly one night he became aware that her gaze was fixed on him with more than usual intensity. Was it hostility he read there? But how could it be?

'What is it, Nontando?' he asked.

At first she did not answer.

'You are different,' she said.

'Different?'

'Everything about you is different.' And as she spoke she contemplated him as if she would pierce the inmost secrets of his heart.

He laughed. 'I am the same Paul.'

'I don't think you like me any more,' she said.

'Not like you? Nonsense! That's impossible.'

'You are not the same,' she reiterated stubbornly. 'Sometimes I catch you looking far away. Then you are not thinking of me. You are thinking of somebody else. Are you?' She spoke the question sharply.

'No, Nontando.' Yet even as he answered her, the image of Kathie came to his mind. But he could not speak her name to the girl at this moment.

Nontando stood up, a hard, distrustful expression on her face, her body poised for flight in a characteristic gesture. He remembered it from the first time he had seen her, standing outcast beside her father's door.

'I don't think I can come tomorrow,' she said sullenly.

'That's all right, Nontando.' His quiet reply infuriated her.

'I told you!' she exclaimed. 'You don't like me any more.'

'But, Nontando, you are unreasonable. If you can't come to-morrow I'm not blaming you.'

'Oh! Oh! Oh!' she cried, tears of rage springing to her eyes. 'You make me mad. I don't want to see you any more.'

For answer Paul held out his hand. 'Come,' he said.

With all the strength of her slight body she slapped the outstretched hand.

'Go away! Go away! I hate you!'

Paul's eyes hardened. He immediately desisted in his attempt to placate her. Nontando stood at bay, opening her breast to that cold look as if it had been a naked dagger. With a cry she flung herself on the door, wrenched it open and ran without stopping into the street. Paul followed her down the passage, but realised it was useless to try to call her back.

Making his way slowly to his room, his thoughts on Nontando, he met Thembisa, who had heard the running footsteps past her door.

'The girl is getting wilder and wilder,' she said.

Paul's anxious face half angered her. Why should he waste his time on a worthless young baggage?

'Haven't you ever tried to talk to her yourself, Thembisa? She needs a woman's hand,' said Paul.

'Me? Never! Small thanks I'd get if I so much as opened my mouth.'

'Must you be so hard on her?'

'I may as well tell you,' said Thembisa. 'She hasn't been to work the last few weeks either. I'm sorry for that mother of hers. The girl seems to have got it into her head she's a lady. It's those books you've been giving her to read.'

'Thembisa, there are some things you and I don't agree on; and one of them is the question of Nontando. Let's leave it at that.'

'You know best,' said Thembisa, her tone implying the opposite.

For some time Paul had thought of bringing Kathie and Nontando together. He wanted the two to be friends, for Nontando occupied a special niche in his heart. For him there was room for both; while Kathie called forth the strongest and best he had to give, for that very reason it was not possible for him to be indifferent to the girl who had kept simple human feeling alive in an environment that conspired in every way to destroy it. He was sure, too, that a woman like Kathie would draw the best out of the young girl in a way that even he could not do.

For one reason or another he just hadn't got down to arranging a meeting between them. During Stella's escapade with Alan Nel he had been too preoccupied for Kathie's sake to think of anything else. And now somehow it seemed to be more difficult. He did once tentatively mention Kathie as a young woman he would like Nontando to meet. But the girl had not responded to his suggestion. 'Who is she?' she had asked, at once suspicious, and he had explained, keeping his tone impersonal. Yet he said enough for Nontando to conceive a dull hatred of this Unknown – who was better educated than she was and whom Paul obviously admired. The fact that Kathie was not of his people or hers increased her animosity.

Nontando was labouring under heavy seas. The more she felt herself at odds with Paul, the more she kicked against the preoccupations of the career he had undertaken; and the more she became convinced that this unknown woman, Kathie, had ousted her in Paul's affections, the more insecure she felt. He had beckoned and she had followed into a purer, happier world; she idealised him, revered him, loved him without measure; his gentleness was strange to her, strange and alluring to her senses, yet left her unsatisfied. Urged on by her devotion she had tried to be the Nontando who called forth the tenderness she hungered for, and when with her keen senses she missed this tenderness, then that image which was in her mind – and in his too – was shattered. For all the sympathy that was between them, they did not know each other and had no key to the understanding of the other.

One evening Paul had taken Kathie to see a film. It was a poor show, but at least they had been together. After seeing her home – he did not go in – he crossed the now empty streets of the city and made his way to his own lodging. It was a long journey, but with his senses still warm from the joy of her presence, he forgot the weary trudge of it. On turning a corner not far from his room he observed in an alleyway a man and a woman in each other's arms. There was a giggling and a scuffling and ordinarily he would have passed them by as being no concern of his, but the woman at that moment gave out a shrill laugh that made Paul start and look more narrowly at the pair. The woman was nearest to him and from the light of a distant lamp he dimly made out the figure and the dress she was wearing. The man was in shadow. Could the woman be Nontando?

The memory of Thembisa's warnings, which he had thrust from him at the time, came flooding back into his mind. He recalled

Nontando's strange, petulant moods of late, and the way she had stood in front of him only the other night, her eyes burning, her shrill voice crying: 'I hate you!'

Was this the meaning of it all?

As he drew abreast of the pair he could not help peering into the shadows. The man became aware of him and seemed to recognise him, for the woman suddenly swung round. It was Nontando. As Paul hurried on, the man gave out a guffaw of laughter and the sound rang in his ears even after he had entered his room and shut the door.

How little one may know of others, even when they seem nearest. So thought Paul in the first shock of his discovery, his disillusionment in this girl towards whom he had felt such protectiveness and affection. He had made the error of thinking of her as a child, and but little spoiled by her environment. Now he knew better. The picture he had just seen, the laughter he had just heard mocked him for his folly. But whose was the fault? After the first shock of disillusionment he began to realise that his own mental image of Nontando had lulled him and blinded him to the reality. He who had thought to protect her, how much he had failed! A feeling of remorse assailed him. Yet he was still far from realising the true nature of her need for him.

As he sat pondering, to his amazement there was a quick knock at the door and Nontando walked in. From the defiant look on her face it was clear that she had come, not as the accused or the penitent, but as the accuser, herself opening the attack before the attack she feared should be opened upon her. Before he could speak, she began to speak. It was a Nontando he had never heard before, a spitfire with a tongue that lashed him for his complacency. This was no child speaking, but a woman. If Paul learned anything that night it was that the being who had so often sat by his side, sometimes a charming companion, sometimes wayward, sometimes sullen – was a woman.

The pent-up resentment of months poured itself forth in a flood of words, for love did not know itself from hate. She had a desperate need to protect herself against his accusations, her defiance born of the fear that he would despise her. What if he did find her with Petu? She wasn't doing any harm. And besides, Paul didn't care.

At last Paul took his chance to speak: 'But I do care, Nontando!'

She paused and looked at him. How much did he mean by that?

How did he care? Was it possible that he was jealous of Petu? Ah, that she could understand and forgive.

'Nontando, I have known you a long time. Do you think I like to see you with a fellow like this Petu?' Now that she had spoken the name, he recognised him as a young African of the district with the reputation of a local Don Juan.

'You say that, just because he's a little wild,' she retorted.

'I know the type,' answered Paul. 'They take all from a woman – I'm afraid for you, Nontando. You don't know –'

'You!' burst in Nontando. 'What do you know of Petu? It's you who don't know! What business is it of yours anyway?'

'What happens to you concerns me very much, Nontando. Why are you fighting with me? Don't you trust me?'

As Paul spoke he drew her gently to him. She was silent and trembling. 'Have I done anything to hurt you?' he persisted.

Though her heart was bursting she could not speak. What could she say? If only she could bring the name of this unknown woman to her lips. But she dare not. He would only laugh at her and not tell her the truth.

'Tell me, Nontando. You used to tell me everything. What is troubling you?'

The words trembled on her lips. He waited. There was silence in the little room.

Her eyes looked large at him, her lips pressed together.

'Yes, Nontando?'

She opened her lips, but no words came. She could not bring herself to confide in him her fears, her torment, her love. She was too ashamed. Something stubborn in her nature, too, would not let her speak. To speak was to give herself away, at the very moment when he was already despising her. No, she would not speak. She would keep her secret.

Her passion of defiance was over. She no longer wanted to defend herself. She didn't mean the accusing things she had said to him, but she wasn't going to take them back. He could think what he liked of her ... She felt very tired.

'I'm going home now,' she said, her voice almost inaudible.

'Dear Nontando,' he said.

She almost broke down and confessed all, but already he had accepted her silence, respecting her right to keep her own counsel.

He would not probe further if she did not want to tell him.

Thus it might be said that if Paul had been of less sensitive fibre it might have been possible for Nontando at that moment to unburden herself of all that troubled and bewildered her, easing her pent-up emotion, providing a channel for her pain to resolve itself instead of filling the vessel to bursting point till it could hold no more and action when it came could only be of an ungovernable, uncontrollable nature.

His restraint was least calculated to give her relief, for it made her attack on him look foolish, depriving it of justification, so that she felt guilty in double measure. It deprived her of confidence since she could not read what lay behind it and feared his condemnation. She would even have welcomed an outburst of anger on his part; that was something she could understand. But he did not give her this comfort. The effect of this incident was to leave her more lost than she had ever been.

Without anything more being said Paul accompanied Nontando the short distance to her home. It was very late and the houses were in darkness. From time to time he glanced at her face, so near to him and so dim. It was resolutely turned away from him. At the door of her house he took her unresponsive hand in his.

'Will you be all right, Nontando?'

She nodded without answering.

'Good night,' he said.

'Good night.' In the darkness he barely caught the sound.

As she disappeared inside and the door closed upon her, Paul felt a sharp pang as if he had lost her.

Back in his room, he was unable to sleep for thinking of her. He knew this young Petu she had been with, a tough, handsome young African, town-bred like herself, who contrived – nobody knew how – to dress well and swagger as only a townsman can. Paul recognised in him the wildness of frustrated youth who sought by living dangerously to compensate for the mean pettiness of his existence. All the more reason why he was a dangerous associate for Nontando. His very recklessness must appeal to her, who was given to such wild moods of rebellion. But it was each for himself in this jungle. Petu would take this sweetness and when he had done with it cast it aside as savagely as life had dealt with himself.

If only Paul, knowing so much, had consciously envisaged that it was a battle between himself and Petu for the spirit of Nontando. But under the enchantment of his love for Kathie he had not been sufficiently aware of the turmoil in the wild young spirit beside him, yet so far from him. For some time before Paul's discovery she had been meeting Petu. In her very evasiveness – for her heart sought another home – she excited Petu's lust for mastery. She loved pretty things and with a mere touch of bold colour or the careless fold of a scarf could enhance the golden sheen of her skin. So, with an indifferent air, yet also with the flourish of the lover bestowing largesse on the lady of his choice, he would present her with gifts most alluring to her vanity. The age-old battle of pursuit went on and as long as Nontando felt assured of her place in Paul's affections, she resisted him. But the trend of events was all in Petu's favour. It was not on moral grounds that Paul would ever wean her from the other. The love of a man for a woman would alone do that, and this he could not give her.

How much at cross purposes they were. Deeply perturbed by what he had discovered, Paul came back to the thought of what a good thing it would be if Kathie and Nontando could be friends. A great deal of the girl's trouble had been that there was no woman to whom she could turn. And who could be better for her than Kathie? he reflected. Only, if he did speak to Kathie, he decided not to endanger their relationship by revealing what he had just seen; he would not for the world belittle Nontando in her eyes.

So one day, without any explanatory remarks, he said to Kathie:

'I'd like you to meet Nontando.'

'Of course, Paul,' she readily answered. 'You promised me that some time ago.'

'I can't think why I've put it off so long.'

'I wondered,' she said.

'I'd like you to be friends,' he continued.

'I'd like it, too.'

'You may not find it easy,' he warned her. 'She's a girl of strange moods.'

'Perhaps I'd understand them better than you, Paul.'

'That's just it,' he agreed eagerly. 'I did hope that Mrs Sitole and Nontando would hit it off, but for some reason or other they don't like each other.'

'Is it so surprising?' asked Kathie, who felt she knew the forthright person Mrs Sitole was.

'No, I suppose not,' he answered doubtfully.

'Dear Paul.' Kathie smiled and Paul wondered why she wore such a wise look on her face. 'Have you spoken to Nontando about me?' she continued.

'I have mentioned you as someone she would like to meet.'

'And what did she say?'

'I don't remember.'

'You mean, she didn't really want to?'

'Possibly. But she's not very friendly towards people. She's always on the defensive.'

'Rather like Stella?' Kathie suggested.

'You said that once before.'

'Somehow I think of them together,' said Kathie thoughtfully. 'They are both very young and, I think, unhappy.'

'I wish Nontando would confide in you,' said Paul, concentrating on the problem that was uppermost in his mind.

'If she likes me, she will,' replied Kathie.

Paul slowly shook his head. 'How could she not like you?'

The little barque of Nontando's life was indeed tossing, rudderless, on a full sea when another wave came and well-nigh foundered it.

She had recently been employed as an assistant at a nearby store in the district – a dirty, congested iron-roofed shack where her slight figure flitted to and fro, for she was an efficient little saleswoman. The owner of the store was an African who had promised himself a satisfactory income by trading with his impoverished people. The turnover was almost up to his expectations, but unfortunately an initial burden of debt to a white man who demanded immediate payment, swamped him completely before he could get on his feet. The result was that the white man took over the business, lock, stock and barrel. He decided also to keep on Nontando as a good asset at a very cheap rate. His clients – as he remarked to a friend – might be a lot of dirty, drunken scum of the earth, but with his organisation, a system of no credit and a girl like Nontando – even though she was black – he'd soon turn it into a paying concern. He had also kept on a middle-aged African who was as docile as his master desired.

Nontando had preferred working in the store to going out as nursemaid to the children of Europeans, but with the advent of the new storekeeper, Vadaris, her whole world darkened with something she had never thought possible – even she who in her almost seventeen years had learned to fear much.

Vadaris had a large, pale, thin-lipped countenance, a small body and a paunch too heavy for the rest of him.

Under the pretext of seeing that she did her job properly he would hover over her in a way that filled her with a sickening disgust mingled with fear. Her first impulse was to throw up her job. The dirty, filthy beast, she thought, and mentally spat on his pale, heavy face.

But it was the best means she had so far found of earning a livelihood, always a precarious matter, and doubly so for her, who could never assume the proper docile manner expected by the master and the mistress. She had tried one job after another; she had spells of idleness at home, which – in spite of Mrs Sitole's assumption that she liked to play the lady – she hated even more. For the crowded room where her consumptive father now lay filled her with one desire – to escape, anyhow, anywhere. It had therefore been a relief to herself and a source of great satisfaction to her mother, who all the time fought a losing battle against poverty, when she had been taken on at the store.

But the new boss filled her with such fear and loathing that she was ready to sacrifice her hard won benefits. Everything strengthened her against any temptation she might have experienced in such a situation: her natural loathing and contempt for the man, who could only regard a black woman as a chattel; her attachment to the wild young Petu; above all, her respect and adoration of Paul and her spiritual dependence upon him.

She was thwarted, however, in her attempt to seek safety by removing herself from the man's vicinity. Without stating any reason – she could not bring herself to do so – she announced to her mother that she was quitting the store, whereupon a storm burst over her head. The woman poured forth a flood of reproaches on this ungovernable daughter of hers. She was a selfish girl, she was bad, she was mad to think of such a thing as throwing up her job. Many other girls would be glad to have it; they'd snatch it out of her grasp if they could. Jobs were hard to get these days. Had she thought of what would happen to them all now that her father couldn't lift one foot past another?

Had she a thought for her mother who went out working every day to keep a roof over their heads? Who was going to clothe and feed the children if she, the eldest, could throw away good money just when she felt like it? She ought to keep in with the new boss and he might raise her wages if he wasn't too mean.

Nontando glared at her mother, unbowed by the shrill tirade while the man in the bed turned his face to the wall.

But when her mother began to cry, she looked away. Their father was a sick man, and there was no sick benefit coming in. They might dole out something to a coloured man, but not to the likes of them. He was a sick, helpless man and she was a sick woman, too, and her daughter had no heart. She couldn't stand it any more. She couldn't stand it.

At this, the man lying in the bed broke into a feeble protest. They must settle their quarrelling elsewhere and give him some peace. But it was true, he added, Nontando was a mad, selfish girl. Couldn't she see her mother was all upset?

Nontando looked from her father's gaunt face, petulant with its helplessness, to her mother's contorted features. She shuddered. She wanted to shout wildly that they didn't know anything, that she wasn't a bad girl, a mad girl. What was the use? She held her tongue. She went back to the store. And that same week the boss raised her wages.

Nontando's manner towards the storekeeper became more pert. She told herself there was nothing to be afraid of; she could hold her own against anybody, whether it was her mother or Petu, or Paul himself. But as time went on she felt a desperate need to confide in somebody. The daily contact with the storekeeper, with his half insolently friendly, half threatening manner towards her gave her the sensation of something closing in upon her. Whom could she turn to? Not her mother. Then Mrs Sitole, whom Paul admired? No, the woman always looked as if she had something against her, always watchful, always reserved ... and she had known about Petu for a long time. Never, never could she confide in her. Who, then? Petu? Even as the thought of him came to her mind, she laughed.

No, you didn't tell your feelings to Petu. He was wild and light-hearted and that was the part she had to play with him. Then a mad thought struck her. Petu was quick with the knife. Petu was a man! She saw his fists flaying that large, pale face, she saw the flash of the blade puncturing that flabby paunch ... But he was white. And for Petu that would mean jail ... death. Reluctantly she relinquished this mad hope of a way out for her.

Paul. He was really the only one in all the world to whom she could bring her troubles. Paul? She recalled her last encounter with him, her defiance, his puzzling reserve and her inability to tell him what was in her heart. Then how could she go to him now? What could she tell him? She shrank at the very thought. He did not know about such things, she told herself. That was the part of her life he did not know and had never known. Such things did not belong to his life. If he knew he would despise her still more; he would not believe in her any more. No! No! No! She could not confide in Paul. She dared not. She must lock this new distress in her breast. Which way could she turn? Involuntarily she put up her hand to wipe the slow tears slipping down her cheeks. Shame, too, added to her distress. How different she was from what Paul imagined her to be. He would shrink away from her if he knew. For the first time a kind of fear of him overcame her. He was so far above her and the gulf between them seemed to grow wider and wider as she contemplated it.

Suddenly her mind leapt to the thought of Kathie, going back to the first time Paul had mentioned her and what he had said then. What was her name, Nontando had asked and he had told her. So she wasn't an African? She was coloured. Coloured? Nontando hadn't liked that. She was a very fine nurse at one of the hospitals, Paul had said. Then he had used a funny phrase about her that Nontando tried to recall: 'She's a woman you can talk to. She has a way about her of listening to you, man!' And he had laughed as he said it, like a man remembering something very pleasant.

She's a woman you can talk to. Thus Nontando's thoughts, roving desperately to and fro, brought her back to Kathie – Kathie whom she had never seen. From that day to this Paul had never brought her to see Nontando and for this she was half glad, half angry and suspicious. She was a coloured woman and a trained nurse, he had said. She must be well educated. That would mean a lot to Paul. This coloured woman would probably look down on her if they met. Of course, Paul must be too ashamed to bring her. Sullenly her thoughts settled to the memory of the growing reserve between herself and Paul. How often he seemed far away in his thoughts, forgetting her who was beside him. Thus with the stealthy cunning of jealousy she came always to this unknown figure, this Kathie, whose very vagueness made her loom monstrously in Nontando's imagination ... *She's a woman you can talk to.* A woman you could go to in time of trouble and unburden your heart of all that oppressed it? No! A thousand times, no! Kathie was the last person in all the world to whom she would turn. She would rather die.

Kathie and Paul had decided it would be a good thing if she had an outing with Nontando alone one weekend when she was free. Her mother's house was not suitable and Paul had never invited Kathie to his room, which in any case was the least desirable setting for a meeting between them.

Then one day, before any arrangement had been made, Kathie did come unexpectedly to Paul's house, or rather she came to the street looking for him since she wanted his help in contacting the parents of one of her patients, who was an African.

Having some difficulty in finding the place Kathie went into Vadaris' store and enquired of the storekeeper as the most likely person to direct her. Vadaris had looked this coloured woman up and down with an appraising eye and answered half insolently, half with a grudging politeness, that he did not know.

'Mr Mangena?' he said, echoing Kathie but putting a sneering emphasis on the 'Mister' when he recognised the name as that of an African.

'Yes. Mr Paul Mangena,' Kathie replied coldly.

'Don't know him,' was the abrupt answer.

Nontando from her place behind the counter instantly noted Kathie.

A coloured woman, dressed in the crisp uniform of a sister, and looking for Paul? It must be – her. She quickly stepped forward.

'Mr Mangena. I know where he stays,' she said.

Kathie smiled gratefully.

'Oh, thank you. Is it far from here?'

Nontando explained that it was only a few streets away. Perhaps it would be simplest if she took her there. With this, the girl looked enquiringly at her boss, who had stood listening to their conversation. Ignoring Nontando and addressing Kathie he said: 'Oh, you mean you're looking for the kaffir that lives next door to Mrs Sitole? I see him passing, always with books in his hand.'

The idea seemed to give him amusement, for the protruding paunch shook a little.

The two women were silent.

Then turning abruptly to Nontando, 'You are not leaving the shop,' he said, and walked away.

Nontando flashed a rebellious look at him and returned to the back of the counter.

'Thank you very much,' Kathie said to her. 'I'm sure I'll find my way.'

Nontando did not return her smile.

Watching the graceful figure of the woman as she went up the street, the girl resolved that nothing would stop her from going to Paul's house after her. Conscious that the storekeeper was still keeping an eye on her, she continued serving with great rapidity and efficiency. She bided her time until she saw him going out and across to his house next to the store, then she indicated to the other assistant that she had to go home but would be back directly and if the boss should ask where she was, he must say she was feeling sick. Without waiting to hear the remonstrances of her shop companion, she discarded her apron, fetched her bag and hurried out.

The woman – she judged – wouldn't be gone from Paul's yet. He would probably want to keep her there. She would still be in time and then she would see. What would she see? This she did not define to herself; she only knew that she must see Paul and this woman together.

As she drew near the house she slackened her pace, for she must not let it appear that she had been hurrying, especially in front of Thembisa, who she found sitting on the doorstep of the house in the afternoon sun, with her son beside her.

'Paul has a visitor,' announced Thembisa.

'I know.' Nontando spoke almost triumphantly. 'I have met her,' she added and passed on into the passage leading to Paul's room.

Paul rose as she entered.

'Come in, Nontando!' He greeted her warmly, as if it made no difference to him that she had been avoiding him.

'I want you to meet Miss Liedeman.'

So it is her, thought Nontando to herself.

'We have met already,' exclaimed Kathie and told Paul what had happened at the store.

'Did you come all this way to see if I had found the place'? she asked.

'It's nothing,' murmured Nontando.

'I'm very glad, anyway,' said Paul. 'Do sit down, Nontando. I want you and Miss Liedeman to be friends.'

Nontando sat down stiffly on the edge of a chair and after a few unsuccessful attempts on the part of Kathie to draw her into the conversation, she and Paul carried it on between themselves.

Nontando watched them with a tense, still expression. Not a movement, not a glance escaped her. Fixing her eyes on Kathie she noted every feature and every line of her dress. It was as if she would imprint the woman on her memory, never to forget her.

Kathie was not beautiful, she decided, but she had a warm, friendly smile. What Paul said of her was true.

But especially did Nontando note that when Kathie looked at Paul there was – what was it? A soft, almost shy expression in her glance. Turning her attention to Paul, she watched the movement of his lips and his expressive hands; she listened to the tones of his voice – all of them familiar to her as the beating of her own heart. Familiar, yes, but there was something else, something that she, Nontando, had never seen when he was in her presence. She concentrated her whole being into that listening and watching. Now she knew. He did not need to tell her. He could say what he liked, he could pretend what he liked, he could seem as indifferent as he liked. But she was not to be deceived. She knew. It was his eyes as they rested on Kathie that gave him away most of all.

It was not Nontando that he loved.

After a few moments Kathie became aware of Nontando's intent gaze. She felt drawn to the girl. For some reason she had always associated her in her mind with Stella, a child at odds with those around her. But now she saw that Nontando had a more vital, more untamed quality about her. What was the girl thinking as she sat there so quietly? She must be very fond of Paul. It was a pity she couldn't get her to speak. Next time perhaps, when there wasn't this urgent matter to attend to.

'Come on, Nontando! Where's your tongue?' exclaimed Paul.

The girl smiled to herself. They didn't know her secret. They didn't know she knew. They thought she was only a child.

'I was just listening,' she said.

'I'm afraid I can't stay a minute longer,' said Kathie, rising. 'You'll let me know as soon as you get in touch with these people,' she continued, referring to the matter that had sent her looking for Paul.

'I'll go straight away,' he said.

'I'll be glad. Goodbye, Nontando. I hope I shall soon see you again.'

'Goodbye.' Nontando spoke in a hard, bright voice that gave no clue to her feelings.

Paul escorted Kathie outside, exchanging a word with Mrs Sitole who was still sitting on the doorstep. Nontando followed them slowly. Coming abreast of the older woman, she stood still and they stared at each other. What did Nontando see in the woman's face? Did she also know? But why did she look at Nontando like that? She seemed to be mocking her. Ah how she hated them! She hated them all – even Paul.

Paul had offered to accompany Kathie part of the way. They had already set off down the road when suddenly a figure flashed past them.

'Look, it's Nontando,' said Kathie.

'Nontando! Come back!' Paul called. But the slight figure did not slacken its pace, nor look back.

What had loomed uncertain in Nontando's imagination was now confirmed. There was no more need for hope. She told herself that she had been deceived. Paul did not care what happened to her.

What a fool she had been! She had tormented herself all for nothing when she had feared what he would think of her association with Petu. It was nothing to him what she did.

In the turmoil of her emotions love and hate and fear were intermingled. By day, in the store and at home she assumed a hard, indifferent air, while to the storekeeper she was as rude as she dared. But at night she had bad dreams.

Tossing about in her bed one night, feeling stifled in the close air, the bodies of the younger children pressing against hers, and burning her where they touched her, she suddenly flung herself out and stood barefooted in the middle of the floor. She looked round her, her breast heaving. Dimly she could make out at the other side of the room the huddled bodies of her father and mother. Her father breathed noisily in his throat. She had the impulse to shout at these somehow un-human figures, dead to the world, that she had had enough, she was going! But she suppressed it. Then she lay down in a corner of the room as far away from the others as the confined space would allow and pulled a coverlet over her. The hard floor nagged at her bones, but at last sleep came to her. It was a troubled sleep and in this sleep she had a dream.

She dreamed that as she passed along a road, a thorn bush – not like any thorn bush that grows on earthy soil – stretched out its pronged branches, clawing at her body. Madly she tried to pull herself free, but the thorns drew her nearer, tearing her flesh. Then she cried aloud to a tall figure standing by: 'Paul! Paul!' And the figure only laughed and did not move. She cried out again, waking herself with the cry, and her body trembled, though she knew it was only a dream. She listened, lest anyone had been awakened by her cry, but no one stirred. Despair settled on her spirit.

From now on she closed the door against Paul. It was as if she had been led forward by him to a point of vantage from where she could survey a beautiful land that would one day be hers too. She had lifted up her eyes and had yearned to be there; she had pressed forward thinking she would soon arrive at the longed for haven, when suddenly the hand that held and guided her was cold, like the hand of death; the voice that had filled her spirit with joy, was silent, and then he was gone. She was left standing alone in the gathering darkness, the beautiful land fading in a mist before her eyes, and when she tried to make her way forward her bare feet stumbled on the jagged ground. Bewildered and stricken with anguish, she started to run – she did not know where, it did not matter where, be it stone or sucking bog under her feet. If the stones lacerated them, if the mud defiled them, so much the better. For the pain of the body was not so great as the despoiling of the spirit.

Thinking over Nontando's behaviour on that day she had met her in Paul's room, Kathie had more than an inkling of the girl's feeling towards him, though she was far from guessing Nontando's hatred of herself. Her knowledge of Paul's nature gave her a key to what must have inspired his affection in the first place and she very much feared that he would not realise just how much he meant to the young girl. So clear-sighted in some ways, so blind in others, searching always for the reason of things, and probing into the ills of society, he might easily fail to see that which was obvious to others.

Because Kathie had penetrated at least in part the secret that Nontando guarded so jealously, she hesitated to push her way into the girl's presence. She respected her reserve and thus any hope of breaking down her animosity towards Kathie was almost lost. Kathie did try on more than one occasion to show her friendliness, but could make no headway against Nontando's stubborn aloofness. To Paul she expressed her regret at this failure, without divulging her suspicion of the true reason. She pitied the girl, and knew that pity was useless. Paul for his part was unwilling to speak of Nontando, feeling it was disloyal to reveal to Kathie all that he knew – or thought he knew. That he had failed to bring the two women together caused him more disappointment than he cared to admit. It seemed so reasonable to expect that they should have been friends. And so desirable. How happy he would have been to see them together. But Nontando was not to be led or cajoled. If she came to Kathie it would be in her own good time and in her own way.

CHAPTER 15

Stella meets her cousin

One day Mrs Liedeman was all excitement at an item of news in the evening paper, to the effect that a certain Mr LP Baaskemp from Springfontein in the Orange Free State and a candidate for a seat in the government, was spending a month in the Cape.

'Listen to this,' she exclaimed, rustling the paper and arresting Stella on her way out.

'I'm in a hurry,' said Stella.

'Wait till you hear it –'

'What is it, then?'

And Irene Liedeman triumphantly read out the bit of news.

'It's your cousin Japie!' she declared.

'My cousin Japie?'

Stella came over to the table where her mother was reading the *Cape Argus*. The news made her willing to delay her appointment.

Now the cousinship, though remote, was true enough. When Stella was younger her mother had often spoken to her about a farmer in the Free State who was a relation of her father's (though Johannes

Liedeman himself would never allow him to be mentioned) and now this was the farmer's son, Japie. Hendrik Baaskemp, the father, had been even more determined to repudiate the connection with the Liedeman family than Johannes, for obvious reasons, but to Mrs Fraser and her daughter Irene he had become a legendary figure, symbolising 'how it could be done' – how to scale the invisible wall between European and non-European. It was not known exactly how the old man had managed to purchase a farm in the Free State, though legend had it that there had been some shady deals in the illicit diamond business – and fortune, that fickle jade, had dealt very kindly with Hendrik Baaskemp. He had married a farmer's daughter, who was herself considerably well-left by her father. It is a common thing for money to marry money, on the principle of mutual self-preservation in the important matter of property. He had died in the ripeness of age and left his cattle, sheep and a fine old Dutch farmhouse to his son, Japie.

Many a time Mrs Liedeman had poured into her daughter's ears her daydreams of Stella one day visiting the farm and being accepted as one of the family. For wasn't blood thicker than water – especially when you had the same complexion? It was even within the bounds of possibility that he might marry her. He couldn't be more than thirty-five, which was quite an attractive age. By that time a man knew pretty well what he wanted, much better than those giddy young fellows who only wanted a good time and never thought of settling down. Cousin Japie had been married before, but his wife had died, poor thing, and left him with one child, a little boy. Of course that didn't need to make any difficulty for the new wife, because he could always send the little boy to a good boarding school, if he hadn't already done so. It was rather surprising that an eligible young man in his position hadn't remarried. The farmers' daughters in the vicinity must all be setting their caps at him. But it showed that Cousin Japie was a clever fellow who was in no hurry till he'd found the right wife. And now he was actually standing as a member for parliament. Ambitious he must be and no mistake. But he'd need a wife once he was returned to parliament; he wouldn't be able to put it off any longer. Why, a handsome, managing wife was absolutely essential to a man in his position. Think of all the entertaining she'd have to do – the best in the land, cabinet ministers and maybe even the prime minister himself. Yes, Japie Baaskemp would have to find a wife. And here he was, actually in Cape Town. The papers said he'd taken rooms at the St James Hotel. It was fashionable for people from up country to come to the coast at this time of year. There was no doubt about it, Stella must go and see him.

Carried away by this new flood of hope Mrs Liedeman surveyed her daughter. The child grew more strikingly attractive even as she looked at her; she had a good manner and she dressed beautifully. What more could a man want?

'Just you go and present yourself to him,' she said. 'Catch him after he's had a good dinner. That's the time when a man's in a good humour, if he's a man at all.'

Stella stood listening, but affecting indifference. 'I'm not going to beg any favours from my cousin just because he's well off.'

'Beg favours indeed!' exclaimed her mother. 'You'd be doing him a favour if I know anything about farmers from the Free State.'

Stella allowed her mother to continue for some minutes longer, expatiating on her rosy prospects. She wore a slightly sneering smile. Her mother was so naïve.

'I'll think about it, Ma,' she said, still feigning disinterest.

'Don't think. Just go. You'll never get a chance like it again. I'm warning you.'

'All right! All right!'

'I'll see about making you a new dress. You go and buy the material and I'll start it straight away. There'll be a prayer in every one of those stitches, my girl. And don't you forget it.'

Next day Stella bought the material.

She was ashamed of the way her mother spoke. Why should she go and beg from this Japie Baaskemp? For that was what it amounted to. She was just as good as he was – except that she hadn't any money. He might be a big, beefy-faced *outjie* with dirty fingernails. She hated dirty fingernails. This talk of her marrying her cousin was ridiculous of course. But there were other ways of making use of Cousin Japie. Through him she could open the door into the world she wanted. That was all the help she needed. With that, she could do the rest herself. It wasn't much to ask.

But first of all she must meet him. How should she set about it? She couldn't write to him. He would recognise the name and conclude – heavens! – he would assume the worst and ignore her letter. In any case, what could she possibly say in a letter? Then

190

supposing she went to the hotel as her mother suggested. It would take some courage getting past the management unaccompanied. But if she gave her name her cousin would recognise it and refuse to see her. Would he recognise it? Perhaps his father had hidden the skeleton in the Baaskemp cupboard so that her cousin knew nothing about the coloured branch of the family. It wasn't likely, though. So she couldn't afford to run the risk of going straight to the hotel first. It was unthinkable that the door would be slammed in her face before ever she got started. Everything depended on her meeting her cousin face to face and winning him over with her charm and beauty. But how? That was the problem.

Stella was still wrestling with this difficulty when the newspaper again came to her assistance by advertising a meeting at which Japie Baaskemp, among others, was to be on the platform. She was tickled to death that she would ever set foot in a political meeting, but as she had often heard Hakim say, 'needs must where the devil drove'. So on the appointed evening, dressing with extreme care and telling no one of her intention, off she went to the meeting. If she expected to be bored her expectations were completely fulfilled; she concluded that she had never listened to so much hot air in her life. In fact she closed her ears to most of it – till it came to Cousin Japie.

The hall was almost full when she arrived, but she found a single seat at the end of a row near the back. With a quick glance first at the people round her, she concentrated all her attention on the platform, eagerly scanning the assembled speakers for her special target, Cousin Japie. There was a fair bearded man, massively built, sitting up against a table in the centre. He must be the chairman and she knew that wasn't her cousin. Could it be that reddish-brown man next to him with the bulging shirt front that made him look like a pouter pigeon? Or the one on the other side, a mousey looking guy with a meagre countenance, who had a habit of stroking his chin as if to encourage the as yet invisible growth of stubble on it? No. She decided that her cousin wasn't mousy looking. Somehow it was a reflection on her family if he looked like that. Stella scanned back and forth the row of European male physiognomies that were as varied in shade and shape as any other group in the animal kingdom. But neither by the call of the blood nor by womanly intuition could she smell out her Cousin Japie. She would have to console herself in patience until he was announced to speak. Meantime she could stop her pretty ears as best she may while the windy speeches eddied over the heads of the audience and gusts and guffaws of laughter or groans and execrations eddied back to the row of faces and shirt fronts on the platform.

While she waited for the sign that would reveal her blood relative, Stella did begin to recognise a repetition of certain phrases in all the speeches. She didn't follow any of the arguments, but these repetitions had an effect on her like fireflies dancing over a *vlei* on a dark night; she was at once confused and dazzled by these endlessly repeated shibboleths about the colour problem, the native problem, the menace to white civilisation, the duties of the white man, the doom of the white race, the threat of communism, the misdeeds of liberalism, Apartheid, *Baaskap,* inferiority of the child races, race harmony, race hatred, race ... race ... race ...

Each time they occurred they produced a remarkable reaction in the audience, which did not at such times seem to be made up of ordinary human beings but became a many-throated monster emitting a single sound, a primitive sound, of anger, laughter, fear, according to the stimulus.

At last Stella's patience was rewarded. The chairman announced that Mr LP Baaskemp of Springfontein in the Free State would now address them. Mr Baaskemp, he said, might not be well known to them all. He was a very young man still. But he bid them keep an eye on him, for he might very well be the man of the future.

Stella felt her heart going pit-a-pat. The chairman was speaking about her cousin! And soon she would meet him face to face.

The man of the future, who had been sitting second last in the row to the right, at these words of introduction stood up and took his place at the microphone. So that was her Cousin Japie. Strange that her glance had passed him by. He was a man of medium height, lean, dark-complexioned and rather hollow in the cheeks, making him look older than he was. His hair was dark and well-brushed from his forehead. His shaven face had the perpetual shadow of a growth that defied the application of the razor. His fingernails were probably clean. When he first stood up he had an ingratiating manner, but as he warmed to his speech his voice took on a rasping quality indicating strong emotion. And there was no doubt that, though he was far from being a polished speaker – lacking experience no doubt – his Afrikaans had a crude eloquence that carried his audience with him. Stella strained her ears to listen to the words that fell from his thin lips. She recognised again the phrases she had been hearing throughout the evening, only this time she was able to string them together into something of a coherent whole.

The conclusion of his speech, with the mounting enthusiasm of the audience, was particularly vivid in her ears:

' ... We do not speak in any spirit of enmity towards the coloured people. But one principle must be made paramount in all our dealings with them: the white man is master. (Thunderous applause.) We are determined to preserve the European structure of society and whatever we do, we shall do nothing to undermine the position of the white man as master. (More thunderous applause.) When assistance is given to coloured persons that assistance should be given on the basis of Apartheid between European and non-European. I stand four-square for Apartheid between black and white. (Applause) Anything else spells the doom of white civilisation in this our beloved country. Now I have heard it said, ladies and gentlemen, that this doctrine of Apartheid is unchristian, that it is in conflict with Christian principles. But to those people who speak thus, I say: Oh, no! Now I do not understand at all what you mean by Christian principles. Christian principles, I say, count for very much. But there is another principle, the principle of self-preservation for a nation. It is a sacred principle. I place that principle still higher. (Applause.)

'It is high time, ladies and gentlemen, that we had put our house in order, and decided once and for all that our complex society will be dealt with on separate lines. Without colour bars, our country cannot have that condition of peace and that feeling of security that will enable us to sleep in our beds at night.

'Now I must tell you, ladies and gentlemen, that there are in our midst a certain breed of men who call themselves liberals. They preach the most pernicious doctrines. They preach ideas of equality that make us shudder.' (The speaker's supporters hiss agreement with these sentiments and shout: 'Shame!' while the liberals present protest vehemently: 'No! No!') He continued: 'I go so far as to say, ladies and gentlemen, that it is these people who are sowing dissension between black and white in our country today! ('Shame!')

'We have to ask ourselves: Does the non-European want this equality which their liberal friends would thrust upon them with a wanton disregard of all that has been sacred to our people for generations? I say they do not. We must not forget that we Europeans have reached a higher stage of civilisation than that of our darker brothers. The non-European's mental make-up is different from the European's. He does not think along the same lines as we do. He has not the same sense of responsibility and we must not place unnecessary burdens on his back before he is ready to bear them. I may say I have excellent coloured labourers on my farm. They are the type of person with whom we can leave the keys of our house when we go away on a holiday. But put these people to farm on their own and what would happen to them? I do not think it is necessary for me, ladies and gentlemen, to paint in detail the results of such an action. It would be too harrowing. I am happy to say that none of my coloured labourers at least will ever be put into such a position. I care too much for their welfare for that. (Applause.)

'Let us be honest, ladies and gentlemen, the whole colour problem of this country, I repeat, must be placed on the basis of *Apartheid*. Of course at the same time we must deal with the problem of the non-Europeans in our midst in a spirit of justice and fair play all round. But never losing sight of the fundamental principle: *There shall be no equality between black and white in this land, either in church or state*. It was the faith of my fathers and I am proud to say it is my faith.'

Cousin Japie sat down amid the reverberating plaudits of the crowd. Hands clapped, feet thrummed, voices shrilled approval. The many-throated monster enveloped the platform in a wave of enthusiasm. The chairman broadened in his seat; shirt fronts creaked along the row and Japie's dark face flushed with triumph. Stella felt herself being carried along on this monstrous wave of enthusiasm and clapped her little gloved hands as she had never clapped before. Wasn't he her own Cousin Japie? Suppose she were to shout out there and then: 'Bravo! Cousin Japie! Yes, I'm your Cousin Stella!' But of course not. She was a decorous young lady and would bide her time.

She paid no further attention to the speakers who followed. They seemed flat after her Cousin Japie. Instead she kept her eyes fixed on him until he became invisible from her concentrated efforts to focus his face and she had to blink her eyes in order to bring him back again.

Her thoughts were in a whirl and a confusion. She had been carried along by the crowd's enthusiasm, but all the same she was bewildered when she tried to remember some of the things that Japie had said. After all, she knew – if no one else did – that he was a coloured man. Well, if he wasn't, at least he had the same blood in his veins as she had, and Andrew and Kathie and her father and – there was no need to go further back. It was a delicate matter and Stella did not see her way very clearly.

Stella had always been told to keep away from politics because politics were dirty and in any case she had no temptation to be interested – until now. She had had more important things to think about. Of course it was well known that politicians were adept at speechifying with their tongues in their cheeks without meaning half of what they said. But Cousin Japie had sounded so convincing. She was sure he had meant every word he said. He spoke as if he really was afraid of the threat to white civilisation and was determined to keep the non-European people in their place. He had said that they had a different mentality from the Europeans. She had seen the knotted vein at the side of his head when he was speaking and he had pounded his fist into the palm of his hand. Would a man do that if he didn't mean it? But she couldn't get away from the fact that he was coloured. What would the people in the hall say if they knew? Would they throw him out?

Meantime he was her cousin and she had business with him. She must hold on to that. What was her next step? Was it going to be easy? Somehow she wasn't so sure now that the excitement from her cousin's success had died down and the nature of the speech was beginning to penetrate. There was nothing formidable about him to look at, with his thin cheeks and his complexion every bit as dark as her brother Andrew's, and certainly darker than her own. It was his way of speaking that gave you the impression he could be pretty fanatical about things and that wasn't an easy kind of person to deal with. She knew from Kathie. Ah, well, there was no point in losing heart over imaginary difficulties. She must see him, make friends with him and get him to take her up and introduce her to his friends. Ralph Leighton had let her down, but now she'd have a chance of meeting people who would make him look positively small. Pity he'd gone to England. She'd have shown him just what she thought of him ... Perhaps Cousin Japie would introduce her to a young farmer.

She'd never thought of herself as a farmer's wife before. She was a townsgirl who would pine away if she couldn't taste the pleasures of the town. But of course her husband would have plenty of money. They'd have a car – two cars – one of them for her own use so that she could run up to Springfontein whenever she felt like it.

Having travelled thus far on the wings of fantasy she suddenly became aware that the meeting was at an end and the chairman was pronouncing the benediction. Anxiously she watched the dispersal of the speakers from the platform. There was her cousin moving off, already talking to the chairman and probably receiving his private congratulations, judging from the look of satisfaction on his face. Should she waylay him now while he was flush with victory? No, perhaps not. A political meeting in defence of white civilisation was possibly not the most propitious moment for her particular project. It was rather like storming the citadel when the flag had just been run up and the gun practice was in full swing. On second thoughts she decided to put off the crucial moment. No point in losing all in one rash move.

Being now in a position to recognise her cousin immediately, she came to the conclusion that she could visit him at his hotel in St James. It was not easy for a young woman like herself to enter a hotel lounge and sit unaccompanied for any length of time without exciting comment. Except under favourable circumstances, she had no desire to draw undue attention to herself. So she decided to choose the hour when the hotel lounge was most crowded with people chattering and sipping their cocktails between sundown and dinner time. There would be a great deal of coming and going; hotel visitors would be waiting for their guests and guests waiting for their friends to come downstairs. The actual details of her strategy she would leave to the inspiration of the moment.

A few days later, dressed in the new black and white outfit designed for her by her mother, she sallied forth to meet her fate. For it was thus that it presented itself to her; it was to be the turning point in her life. After a period of frustration, disappointment and unhappiness she saw herself at last getting a break. The long-awaited opportunity had come and she would seize it with both hands. All her mother's dreams and ambitions and her own, all the scheming and planning were about to bear fruit and Stella was not the girl to be unequal to the occasion.

With a sense of elation mingled with a tremor of excitement, she got off the train at St James Station, crossed Main Road and began mounting the steps of the hotel that was set at the foot of the steeply rising mountain. Hesitating, she stopped and looked back over the spectacular sweep of False Bay. She breathed in the salt sea air and smiled.

He was not in the lounge. Nonchalantly she approached the well-groomed woman at the desk and asked for Mr Baaskemp. It turned out that there were two of them. Which one did she want to see?

'Mr Japie Baaskemp from Springfontein in the Free State,' she said, whereupon the European receptionist called an Indian waiter and told him to see if Mr Baaskemp, number 39, was in. There was a young lady to see him.

Stella sat waiting in one of the crimson upholstered chairs at the entrance, conscious of several pairs of eyes being turned in her direction. The waiter reappeared.

'What name please? Mr Baaskemp says he was expecting a gentleman, but no lady, Miss,' he said.

This was bad luck. Should she make an excuse and choose some other time? She was conscious of the waiter giving her a rather bold stare.

'Say Miss Lehnman wants to see him and I won't keep him long,' she murmured quickly.

'Very good, Miss.'

As she waited Stella no longer felt so confident as she had been before. She had already thought of giving the false name. If the necessity arose she could easily explain the mistake by putting the blame on the waiter who had taken the message. But that wasn't what bothered her; it was the remark she had made about not keeping him long.

Now why did I say that? she reproached herself angrily. At once it suggested that she didn't know him very well and was begging a favour. That Indian looked an impudent fellow, too. He seemed to smile secretly to himself as he retreated.

She was turning over in her mind what she would say, when her cousin appeared. She rose, gave him her most charming smile and held out her hand, which he shook limply with his thin fingers. There was a broad question mark on his face, though it struggled with curiosity and an involuntary admiration that her well-groomed appearance usually provoked in the male sex.

'Oh, Mr Baaskemp,' she gushed. 'I listened to your speech at the meeting the other night. It was simply wonderful.'

Cousin Japie was not impervious to flattery. His dark face creased into a grin.

'I'm glad you liked it, Miss – er – Lehnman,' he said.

He supposed she was some young follower of his party who fancied she knew something about politics. These modern young women were up to all sorts of nonsense, which of course was all right when they could carry it off with good looks. A man in his position, he said to himself, couldn't afford to throw away any opportunity of increasing his popularity, though judging from the impression his speech had made he had every chance of being the successful candidate. Baaskemp decided that there would be nothing lost in being nice to his young admirer. His friend would be arriving shortly and meantime he was not above indulging in a little tête-à-tête with an attractive young lady. If a strenuous political campaign brought him these little perquisites, he wasn't the man to refuse them.

'Won't you have something to drink?' he asked.

She smiled. 'With pleasure.'

So far so good. Stella felt an inward flutter of triumph.

Cousin Japie piloted Stella to a table for two and ordered the drinks. Leaning back in his chair, he felt himself a bit of a ladykiller entertaining a strange young *meisie* in this fashion. He'd been in danger of getting into a rut, he reflected, always being tied to the farm and keeping an eagle eye on things himself. To be sure it had paid him handsomely. That was why he'd been able to spread his wings and go in for politics in a big way. But he'd been in danger of forgetting how pleasant it was to relax and have a little fling, provided it didn't endanger his career. What was the good of being a widower if you didn't make the most of it?

With the arrival of the drinks, Stella and Cousin Japie gave each other the flirtatious glance and clinked their glasses together before taking the first ceremonial sip. As luck would have it, the expected visitor was late and Japie was soon ordering another drink, same as before. Stella excelled herself while Cousin Japie got so far as to relate one of his jokes in his good, earthy dialect. Stella was most appreciative and Japie remembered a few more jokes. His dark brow was moist with the mingled pleasure of the brandy, hearing his own voice and entertaining a pretty woman. He sucked in his leathern cheeks as he had a habit of doing when he was excited and passed his hand over his smoothly brushed dark hair.

Stella decided he was a likeable enough man in his uncouth way. She had done nothing about telling him who she was, nor corrected the error as to her name. Things were going well as they were and she was feeling so light-headed and happy that there was no point in introducing anything that might spoil the picture.

Cousin Japie was just warming up to telling one of his more intimate stories when he was interrupted by the arrival of his friend, who gave him a hearty slap on the back. He was a ruddy, square-faced man rather older than her cousin and obviously on familiar terms with him.

'Ah, I see you're busy,' he remarked.

Baaskemp got to his feet and made the introductions.

'Sit down, man. Have a drink,' he said. 'What about you, Miss Lehnman?'

'No, thank you,' answered Stella. 'I really must be going.'

'There's no hurry as far as I'm concerned,' replied her cousin, with a glance towards his friend.

'I'm sorry, but I really must go.'

Stella decided it was best to take her departure while he was still in a state of pleasant curiosity about her. She would almost certainly meet him again – if she knew anything about men.

'Perhaps –' she added and stopped.

'Excuse me.' Japie addressed his friend as he rose to escort Stella to the door. 'Can I take you anywhere? I have my car here?' he asked her as they stood at the top of the steps overlooking a well-laid garden with palms and protea bushes flanking the drive, and the distant twinkling lights of the coast reflected in the indigo of the sea.

'Oh, thank you very much. But please don't trouble!'

'No trouble at all. My friend will wait for me. Have you far to go?'

'No. Not far. I'm really all right,' she answered hurriedly.

'I hope I shall have the pleasure of seeing you again, Miss Lehnman. Could I ring you perhaps?'

Stella promptly gave him the number of the dress shop where she worked. And thus they parted amicably. She thought that he held her hand a fraction too long.

Travelling back in the train she sat in a pleasant afterglow induced by the consciousness that she had been completely successful in the first stage of her plan.

She had trusted her own skill to meet the situation as it came and she had been more than justified in her expectations. Cousin Japie might be said to have fallen for her. What if she should marry him after all? Meantime she'd keep her success to herself and not give her mother the satisfaction of saying: 'What did I tell you!' After all it wasn't her mother's doing. She had managed it all herself. She wondered how soon he would ring her up.

Sure enough, Cousin Japie did ring the next day and arranged to take her for a drive over the weekend. This was good going indeed. Like a fairy tale come true.

Several times they met in this way, skilfully skimming the surface of acquaintanceship, where each side (unknown to the other) looked to make something out of it and enjoyed the immediate pleasures of good company. Japie Baaskemp, farmer, prospective member of parliament and withal a fairly faithful attendant of the Dutch Reformed Church, had the titillating sense of playing with fire. The fact that they knew practically nothing about each other added zest to their acquaintanceship. He had assumed that she had connections with people who were staunch followers of the party, otherwise it was unlikely that an attractive girl like her would show such an interest in politics, and he once asked her what had brought her to that first meeting.

'I wanted to hear you speak,' she answered.

He laughed. 'Only me?'

'Only you,' she answered, quite truthfully.

'Oh, come now, you don't mean to say you came to the meeting just to hear me.'

'As true as God!'

'How did you know? Had anyone spoken to you about me?'

'Yes, that's right.'

'You're being very mysterious, aren't you?'

'You'd like to know,' she teased, taking advantage of his curiosity to keep him on, but deciding that the time wasn't yet ripe for her momentous disclosure.

She hadn't meant at first to delay so long in revealing their blood relationship, her idea being boldly to make use of the cousinship to gain entrance to the world she was determined to conquer. But now his amorousness excited the hope of landing her quarry and marrying him. Yet to reveal who she really was became more and more difficult. She was aware of the secretiveness with which he maintained their relationship – he did not again introduce her to any of his friends – and it gave her no little sense of disquiet.

Then one evening something happened that affected her very strongly. They were about to enter a bioscope (he had booked the seats beforehand) when their attention was arrested by the noise of an altercation going on at the box office. Two well dressed young men were being refused admission to the bioscope, which was reserved for Europeans Only, and they were protesting vehemently that they had every right to enter. One of them expressed his contempt for the gross barbarity of the customs of this foreign country. They were citizens of the Argentine and no man had the right to refuse them entrance to any public place. But all their claims were of no avail; in the eyes of the box office Miss, who first refused them, they bore the stigma of colour stamped on their swarthy countenances. Barricaded by the box office grille and reinforced by the full support of the management, she stood in aloof indifference waiting for events to take their natural course. It was a matter of seconds. Signalling a nearby policeman the manager summarily evacuated them from the steps of his handsome building so that they landed with some precipitation in the arms of the protector of the public who escorted them from the scene with obvious enjoyment in the discharge of his duties. The crowd had hardly been aware of what had happened and the few who had witnessed the scene with amusement or apathy forgot it before they had reached their seats.

As he turned to go inside with Stella, Japie remarked:

'Dirty dogs! Damned cheek of them trying to push their way into a European bioscope. The manager sent them sprawling all right.'

Laughing, he took Stella by the elbow and piloted her through the crowd.

'Perhaps they don't know the custom here.' Stella's voice was harsh and constrained. She withdrew from his touch.

'Oh, they thought they could get away with it just because they're foreigners.'

Suddenly Stella hated the man at her side. She wanted to shout at him before all these people: You fool! You hypocrite! You imposter!

You think you are better than they are, you dull, conceited country bumpkin. You, a representative of the people! You, a defender of white civilisation!

'What's the matter?' he asked, vaguely aware of her unresponsiveness.

'Nothing.'

His discomfited tone made her pull herself together. What on earth was the matter with her? She had got things all mixed up. She wished that these foreigners had stayed in their own damned country instead of coming here to upset any of her plans. Why on earth should she get all het up about them? If she wasn't careful Cousin Japie would be slipping through her fingers.

So she exerted herself to be a more charming companion than ever with the result that at the end of the evening Japie Baaskemp went back to his hotel in a pleasantly excited condition wondering how far he could go. She'd probably be game, he reflected.

But Stella, with the bitter memory of Ralph Leighton still sharp enough to bring the stinging tears to her cheeks when she lay awake in her bed in the cold hours of the morning, proved much more 'difficult' than Japie Baaskemp had anticipated. She had resolved never to give anything without full payment in return, and, if possible, to receive everything without payment at all. In this instance the stakes were high. Everything must be respectable, honest and above board. No miserable, clandestine affair, only to be dropped like an empty dish after serving the desired purpose.

She realised that the time had come to resolve the situation one way or another. She didn't want it to burst like a boil that had come to a head. So one warm evening, sitting on the stoep of an out-of-town roadhouse to which he had taken her, she decided to speak.

'Japie, have you ever asked yourself who I am?'

'Actually I did, at the beginning. But you seemed so set on making a mystery of it, I thought you liked it that way.' He spoke with his usual complaisance, thinking to humour her.

'You remember,' she continued, 'you wondered why I had come to the political meeting.'

He laughed. 'It did seem a queer thing for a sophisticated young lady to do. But,' he added, 'you did say you came to hear me.'

'And so I did, Japie.' She spoke earnestly. 'I came to see what my Cousin Japie was like.'

202

He gaped at her.

'Your cousin –! Well, I'm damned! But who?'

There was no Lehnman as far as he knew in the family tree.

'Actually I'm your second cousin, Japie.'

'My second cousin! Are you pulling my leg? Come on, out with it. I've had enough of all this mystery.' He wasn't smiling any more.

She proceeded to explain, including the mistake over her name. When she had finished he could not at first find speech.

'Then you are – Johannes Liedeman's daughter?' he said.

Stella nodded.

She watched his thin cheeks being sucked in to the gums and his dark face grow darker with anger.

'I see it all now. So that's why you came to the meeting. I might have guessed that the likes of you wouldn't know the first thing about politics. And you walked brazenly into that hotel meaning to impose yourself on me, giving a false name.'

'I didn't.'

'Of course you'd lie about it and not turn a hair. From the word go you meant to impose on me.'

'You're wrong, Japie. You're wrong. I only wanted you to help me.'

'Help you?'

'You're accepted as European, so why shouldn't I?'

For a second she thought he would strike her.

'I see your game. A little bit of blackmail, eh?' A sneer contorted his face. 'Who'd believe you?' he said.

'We'll see!' she shrilled, stung by the insult. 'I'll tell the world what you are. I'll tell them –'

Suddenly sobered by the fear that they would be overheard, Baaskemp looked anxiously round. The woman was becoming obstreperous. He'd better get her out of here as quickly as possible. He'd have to take her into town at least.

'I'm going,' he said.

She did not move.

'We can't stay here all night.'

'Nobody's asking you,' she answered.

'I must get back to town.'

'I'm not stopping you.'

'Don't be a fool. I'll give you a lift.'

'I'll find my own way home,' she retorted.

He shrugged. 'If you will play the martyr, don't blame me.'

She was silent and he moved off. Reluctantly he stopped and looked back before getting into the car.

'Coming?'

She did not even turn to look in his direction.

He started up the car and without another sign moved off.

Stella did not know how she would get back to town, which was some eighteen miles away, and at the moment she did not care. A wild pain, shame, fury, hatred almost a madness – possessed her. A desperate thought entered her mind – to make an end of it all. With a mingling of self-pity, spite and anger she pictured what it would mean to her mother and Andrew and Kathie when they knew what she had done. There was a fiendish need to hurt them even more than the need to get her own back on the clod of a farmer, this Japie Baaskemp. She told herself that everything she suffered was their fault. It was they who dragged her down, they who prevented her from escaping into the world where she belonged.

As she sat, a heavy, middle-aged woman emerged from the back of the premises and eyed her suspiciously.

'We're shutting up now,' she said. 'I thought you were with that gentleman.'

Stella ignored her remark.

'Can you tell me if I can hire a taxi to take me back to town?'

'A taxi? At this time of night? Not up here, Miss.'

At the same moment Stella realised she hadn't enough money to hire a taxi.

'Never mind,' she said.

The woman bustled towards the door as much as to say: I'd be pleased to see you take yourself off.

With a glance of scorn Stella walked slowly away, her head high. She heard the doors being bolted after her.

The night was pitch dark, yet for the first few yards she continued to walk stiffly as if she was conscious of people staring after her. Then she stood stock-still. She glanced up and saw the Southern Cross, low in the sky, the two pointers hanging just above the road she was following. She was alone, alone on the dark highway miles away from Cape Town; there was not a soul to see her, not a soul to care what happened to her; she could walk till her feet were bleeding and nobody would know her desperate plight; and nobody would care; she was utterly alone. Her body sagged.

With every step self-pity grew stronger. Sobs caught her breath, though her eyes were dry. She hastened her steps, stumbling and sobbing as she went. She stood still. An impenetrable darkness pressed up against her body. She was afraid. The only sound she heard was the screeching of crickets, piercing her ears with a hot needle of sound.

The lights of an oncoming car shed a blinding glare into her face. Frantically she waved her arms, but the car ignored her summons and sped on its way. Her arms sank to her sides as the black night enveloped her again. She dragged herself on a few steps further. Indifferent now, her sobs ceased; her face stiffened, though not with the consciousness that many eyes were watching her. She sat down by the roadside.

Another glare of headlights fanned out over the empty road. She made no effort to move. The car stopped. A moment passed before a young man got out. As he opened the door his companion leaned out towards him.

'Do be careful,' she said. 'It might be a trap.'

As the young man approached, Stella looked up, shielding her eyes with her arm.

'Can I help you?' he said.

'I've lost my way,' she answered in a small voice.

'Where are you going?'

'I live in town.'

'Good. Then we'll give you a lift.'

Without any further words Stella got up and went with him to the car. He opened the door and she settled into the back seat.

The next thing she was aware of was the man asking her where she wanted to be dropped. They were approaching the lights of the city. She gave him directions to a spot on Main Road, from where she could walk to her house.

'Can't we take you any further?' he asked, as they drew up.

But she hurriedly refused and thus they parted. The woman had not addressed her.

Quietly she let herself into the house. Mercifully her mother was in bed and merely called out: 'Is that you, Stella?'

'Yes, Ma.'

Kathie must be out on duty, for which she was thankful. Without a glance at her mirror, without performing a single part of her usual beauty ritual she undressed and got into bed. Never before had it seemed such a haven of refuge.

The next morning her mother, who of late had acquired an expression of relaxed good humour, asked her how she was getting on with Cousin Japie. Stella turned on her fiercely:

'You and your Cousin Japie,' she cried.

'What has happened now?'

'I knew from the beginning you were crazy. The world is crazy. I'm laughing because I'm alive.'

'Oh, Stella, you frighten me.'

'Shut up and leave me alone.'

Mrs Liedeman began to cry. The harshness of her child, the sudden disappointment of her hopes on which she had been building so much, the fear of what the man had done to make Stella speak in a manner so unlike herself – all this proved too much for her.

Stella looked pitilessly at her mother. Her own eyes were dry and burning. 'Oh, for God's sake!' she said and went out of the room.

CHAPTER 16

Wedding bells

Andrew was getting married. He was nearly twenty-six and making good money. Having gone into partnership with an older man, who said there was a gold mine in the garage business, he had from small beginnings begun to taste the pleasures of independence and very sweet they were. While he was popular with the girls, he had so far evaded matrimony, but a profitable business suggests getting a wife and settling down; a well-dressed wife and a well-furnished home are the tangible and visible symbols of one's success. As to whom he would marry, perhaps it might be said it was more the bride's decision than the bridegroom's. Andrew was blessed with a shallow good nature that did not think too much, so he was most likely to take the line of least resistance. Of all Mrs Liedeman's children her son had caused her the least worry; his easy-going nature seemed to invite good fortune or at least protect him from the problems likely to beset an uncompromising nature like Kathie's or Stella with her intense ambition. So while he had never shown much sympathy for the social pretensions of his mother and his younger sister, when it came to his choice of a wife he did not disappoint them. Indeed it was a source of great satisfaction to Mrs Liedeman that Annette Gregory, the daughter of a teacher, was as light of complexion as himself. The two young people, by good fortune if not intent, had conformed to the unwritten law of the group. Annette for her part considered herself as having made an uncommonly good match, with the prospect of setting up a home that would stand up to the scrutiny and stir the envy of all her girlfriends, who would flock to congratulate her on her married state.

So the day of the wedding was fixed and preparations for the great event were set afoot. Tradition demanded that it be the business of the bride's parents to launch her into her new status with a wedding celebration as splendiferous as their purse would allow – or rather more.

In this instance the main burden of management fell to Miss Gregory, Annette's aunt, who had kept house for the girl and her father since Mrs Gregory's death some ten years previously. But as luck would have it, Miss Gregory fell ill and the suggestion was to postpone the wedding. Annette was petulantly aggrieved at the mishap since her heart was set on as big a show as possible and she could not possibly contemplate postponing the ceremony. That would mean bad luck. So after a general consultation between the two families Mrs Liedeman agreed to undertake the management of the affair, it being understood that Miss Gregory would at least have recovered sufficiently to help where she could.

Carried out of herself by the happy prospect of one of her children marrying according to her ambition, Irene, who had had so little pleasure in life, accepted her responsibilities in the matter of the wedding preparations with such an unusual wholeheartedness that Andrew was delighted and Kathie was pleased at the rare sight of her mother bustling around and bossing everyone.

So the preparations went on apace. What a coming and a going was there! What a hustle and a bustle! The too long silent house was humming like a beehive with the chatter and laughter of helpers. What a crackling and a sizzling in the busy oven, what a bubbling in the steaming pot, what odours and exhalations to tickle the nostrils and whet the tongue! What pleasing cacophony invades the kitchen as cakes and cookies are miraculously transformed by quick hands out of the soft, shapeless dough; golden egg yolks slide and plop into bowls; forks beat a tattoo bidding the snowy cream froth up to the brim; the red wine gurgles and fruits and jellies shiver against the transparent sides of the fruit dishes. And all the while the young girls giggle and the matrons – those queens of the hive – heave their full bosoms, cackling, scolding, commanding and countermanding. They are in their element; it is their day and everything must be done as it has been done, time out of memory. Heaven knows what would happen if it wasn't done.

The young woman round whom all this activity revolves flits in and out with conscious self-importance, her smiles ever ready to acknowledge the felicitations of friends and acquaintances, while her mother-in-law-to-be, secretly elated, but outwardly decorous, distributes hospitality. Andrew, the mere male, stands at the threshold, but beats a hasty retreat at the sight of this regiment of women. He is not wanted here. Annette follows him out and takes his arm with a smirk of proprietorship sitting high on her cheekbones. She is a very ordinary young woman invested with a brief glow of brightness as the chosen bride of Andrew Liedeman. Once safely married and mistress of her little world, she will lose that glow; it will fade, leaving her with a quality all too common among womankind – a sharp tongue whose edge will become sharper with the years.

Now amidst all the hilarious preparations there was one who turned a cold eye on the proceedings and that was Stella. She could not help but have a pang of envy that it was Annette's wedding and not hers that her mother was busy preparing. It was for her that the house should be filled with good things, for her that all the gifts should be flowing in, not this common faced, conceited Annette, who thought she was somebody because her father was a teacher, and now queened it as a bride-to-be. Andrew had already rented a small house in the district, not far from Annette's people, and the girl was continually holding forth about what they had bought or were going to buy in the way of the latest fashions in furnishings. Stella conceived a dislike for her future sister-in-law out of all proportion to her knowledge of the young woman. Why should she have all these things that Stella wanted, and without any effort, too? It wasn't fair. Whenever the two young women met there was a frigidity in the air. Perhaps it wasn't surprising that the antipathy was mutual, precisely because their battle was the same. Annette for her part regarded Stella as too fast for the norm of gentility to which the majority of her circle conformed. She had heard about the affair with Ralph Leighton and knew more about Stella's association with the wealthy Indian than Stella did herself. Gossip has a marvellous capacity for embellishing the truth. As one social climber to another there was no love lost between the sister and the sister-in-law-to-be.

And what of Kathie in the midst of all these festive preparations? When she was present she did her best to take part in the general gaiety, but for some reason there was a slight constraint in her presence; while the helpers and friends of her family and Annette's were polite, they were not quite at ease with her, as if she didn't quite belong.

The truth is, it is a very particular stratum of the coloured community that has been gathered together for this important event. The members regard themselves as the elite of their society, the guardians of coloured respectability, the wardens of its good name (especially in the eyes of the whites) and therefore the champions of its claim to be worthy of special rights and privileges that approximate to, but are not identical with, those of the whites. Occupying a position between two worlds, neither white, nor willing to be identified with their darker brothers, their lives might be summed up as the pursuit of an alluring but ever unattainable goal. As a group they are distinguished by a common tendency to lightness of colour – while in feature they are as varied as that of human kind. Their offspring, if they are fortunate, are eventually due for promotion to that anonymous band who will successfully cross the line into the camp of the privileged, but they themselves haven't quite made the grade. It is this failure and this common ambition that creates the bond between them even while at the same time there are intense rivalries, jealousies and spites amongst them.

They gravitate together, they know one another's business, they vie with each other for social position in the various clubs where they meet in the pursuit of sport, art and the like. But they know when to rally together, when it is a question of fundamentals, of marriage, of birth and death and family honour.

Pretension is the essence of their existence. For them education is a means more often than an end, a veneer rather than an inward possession; art is not a passion but a fashionable pursuit, and a picture is purchased to adorn a wall rather than to delight the soul. They fear vulgarity more than a sickness, yet are prone to bad taste;

for them religion is a thing of good repute and reputation more than simple kindness. In short, nothing *is,* but seems. Their assumption of careful gentility is all the more precarious, placed as it is between the grinding poverty of the mass of their non-European brothers, black as well as coloured, and the arrogant security of the privileged whites. For while they on the one hand repudiate their brothers, they themselves are open to insult from any member of the master race who should take it into his head to tar them all, light and dark, with the same brush. Thus culture is something that they seek as an avid necessity, something with which to justify themselves, rather than something that springs up and blooms out of the rich soil of society, the flower of a civilisation that embraces all. And all this is forced upon them by the very barrenness of their material and spiritual environment, a blight which affects not only their own people, but the very master race that claims superiority over them. In this little group of respectable coloured people a terrible isolation is the undertone of tragedy to the comedy of pretension and snobbery.

At last the great day arrived when the goodly company made their way to church to see Andrew and Annette united in the bonds of holy matrimony. Then for the wedding reception. Relatives and friends from both sides clustered round the proud couple; speeches were made and the many dainties consumed at a much faster rate than it had taken to make them. The bride's dress was admired and the cost of the bridal veil secretly computed. Outside, a crowd had gathered to gaze at the fashionably dressed company, but when a bunch of vulgar coloured youths pressed in through the doorway, it had to be shut in their faces. These obnoxious *skollies* were known to have spoiled many a genteel party by their unwanted presence. After the dancing had started up the bridal pair stayed the customary length of time and then took their departure, smothered in good wishes and more confetti. The bride looked charming in a sky-blue costume with white accessories.

After a short honeymoon the young pair settled in their new home. The Liedeman house returned to its habitual quietness, the family smaller by one and the three women left without a man in the house. But Mrs Liedeman was satisfied as far as her son Andrew was concerned; he now belonged to another woman but he was not lost to her; in fact with such a wife he was more closely bound to her circle and strengthened her position within it.

If only she could be as happy about her other two children, Kathie and Stella. Uppermost in her mind was the ever pressing problem of Stella, who had become so difficult since that disappointment over Cousin Japie. Tired now after all the excitement of the wedding, Irene regretted that she had been so generous in her offer to help Annette's family out of their difficulty. Suddenly she, too, longed that it had all been for her own daughter instead of this girl, Annette. She sighed. It wasn't her fault if Stella didn't get the man she wanted. She had done all she could.

She sighed again, thinking of Kathie. Her thoughts dwelled on her eldest child with a mixture of pride and uneasiness. Most girls had found their man by the time they were her age. The silly girl had had her chances, but she was too hard to please; and now she must go and become friendly with a native when she ought to know she shouldn't even allow herself to be seen with one. Of course there couldn't be anything in it, but Kathie was so thoughtless in her own interests. She really must speak to her about it.

The very next evening an opportunity presented itself when Kathie was helping her mother to collect some of the dishes that still had to be returned to their owners now that the festivities were over. Stella was out and they were alone together. Mrs Liedeman first of all talked about Andrew and Annette and how nice it was to think that Andrew was settling down. She asked Kathie what she thought of Annette, but Kathie was reserved in her answers. She had a shrewd idea of the type of young woman Annette was and how narrow the goal of her ambitions. She and her mother laughed together in a friendly way at the idea of Andrew being kept in order by that sharp little tongue of hers.

'What about you, Kathie?' her mother asked. 'When am I going to have to prepare for your wedding?'

Kathie looked at her, startled, but said nothing.

'You know that nothing would make me happier,' continued Mrs Liedeman. 'Every mother wants to see her daughter getting married, much more than her son.'

'I know,' murmured Kathie.

'And if I saw you getting a good man – a good, steady husband like Annette has in your brother – then even if it meant losing you –'

'Oh, Ma!'

'You're not so young, eh?' her mother half teased her.

'I know.'

Then Mrs Liedeman assumed a more serious tone. 'There's one thing I'd like to say, Kathie. It's about Paul Mangena.'

'Paul?'

Kathie had never spoken to any member of her family about Paul. She had been too sensitive of their treatment of him, secretly angry at her mother's coldness on the rare occasions when she had brought him to the house. And now with the love between herself and Paul at last fully confessed, she had felt the widening of the gulf separating her from her family. She had not formulated it even to herself, but Paul's coming had brought it clearly into the open. The very fact that they had no home where they could meet as young lovers do gave them a peculiar feeling of isolation which at the same time bound them more closely together. Paul had not spoken of marriage – and Kathie knew he would not while he was still struggling to get his law degree – but he was her man. No words were needed for that . . .

But how could she tell her mother all this? She could not plead on his behalf. If they accepted her they must accept him. That was all.

Her mother was speaking. 'I don't like you to be seen around with this Paul Mangena. Have you thought what it means?'

Kathie was silent, the truth trembling on her lips.

'I know you don't mean any harm by it,' resumed her mother complacently. 'You have a way of making friends with all sorts of people. But take a mother's advice, Kathie. It's spoiling your chances to be seen with a man like him.'

'A man like Paul! Ma, you don't know what you're saying!'

'Oh, don't get it into your head I've anything against him. I'm only speaking for your own good.'

'*I* am the judge of that, Ma.'

'You may think you know better than me, but if you have any sense of what is right and proper – '

'Ma, I can't listen to you. Paul and I intend to get married.'

Kathie had never meant to blurt out the truth in this way and the expression on her mother's face made her regret her words as soon as they were spoken. This was not the time to have done it.

'Is that what he has persuaded you to do?' exclaimed her mother with a trace of fear in her voice. 'You can't have been in your right senses when you agreed to that.'

'I have never done anything I am so proud of,' Kathie replied.

'Oh, you are mad!' cried her mother. 'I forbid you, do you hear?'

Half pityingly, Kathie shook her head.

'What will Andrew say? And Annette and her people?'

'I have my own life to live.'

'And Stella? What will you say to her?'

'Stella will go her way and I will go mine. It is a long time since anything I did mattered to Stella.'

'But she will feel this.'

'Ma, you think only of Stella.'

Her daughter's composure maddened Irene.

'He'll never enter my door again, do you hear!' she cried. 'He has taken advantage of you. That's what he has done.'

'You have a very strange idea of Paul. I wish I could tell you what he is really like.'

'I don't want to hear it.'

'So, there's no more to be said.'

With that, Kathie left her mother and went to her room.

'What it is to have children!' said Mrs Liedeman aloud to an empty kitchen.

She sat and gazed at the unpacked dishes around her, forlorn and full of self-pity.

'After such a nice wedding she has to go and do this!'

When next he met Kathie, Paul could see at a glance that something had happened to upset her, but to his enquiries she was extremely reticent.

What she did say was that she was seriously considering leaving home and finding a room for herself.

This was enough to indicate to Paul that she had had words with her mother. Was it about Stella? he asked. No. Was it about himself?

Kathie nodded, not trusting herself to speak and he did not press for an answer. As to her leaving home, he was not sure what to advise. With Kathie's strong sense of responsibility he knew it would not be an easy step for her to take; no matter the quarrels and the tensions, there were ties binding her to her mother and to Stella, which would be hard for her to break. He wondered what her mother could have said to make her look so stern, as if ready to do battle. It was a look he had seen on her face before and he loved her for it. Yet he hated to think he had been the cause of hurting her. How he wished more than ever that he could take her and give her a home, secure in their love, secure in the approbation of the world.

But it could not be ...

Why must they always have to fight for what they had? How they were hedged in, frustrated, confined!

As to going to live by herself, there was the simple difficulty of finding a room, with thousands looking for accommodation. He would help her look round.

Weddings, they say, are infectious.

This thought put the problem of Kathie out of Mrs Liedeman's mind for the time being. Stella had met a young man not long arrived from upcountry and was having a whirlwind affair with him. If she played her cards well there was every prospect of the amorous gale blowing her little barque straight into the desired haven of wedlock.

Stella, after all she had been through, was under no illusion as to what she could get in the way of a husband. Her ambitious little wings had been singed, with the result that she had acquired a wariness and a hardness that signified, not a relinquishing of her aims, but a recognition of the need to limit them – like a general who orders his forces to retreat and concentrate on a constricted but more advantageous front, thereby winning his main objective.

Stella met Carl Meyers at a church bazaar held in aid of charity, where she consented to assist at a lingerie stall. Her mother's expert hands had made some of the exquisite needlework behind which Stella stood, herself looking the most attractive thing the stall had to offer. At least this is what Carl Meyers thought as he strolled past the various wares put up for sale at the exorbitant prices which anything in aid of charity is privileged to demand. He ogled the dainty young woman, walked on, turned and repeated the process, this time pausing boldly to handle the artificial silk garments lying on the stall.

Stella eyed him at first coldly, with some amusement at his slightly embarrassed temerity in handling the goods. His physical appearance was unattractive to her, even distasteful. He was a big man, heavily built, already too heavy and loose-limbed, considering his youth. She noted his ruddy complexion, obviously very much exposed to the sun; his hair, his eyebrows and his thin lashes were a uniform sandy colour that suggested to her mind an ill-thatched roof. The colour was particularly offensive. She had time to note these things as he bent over the garments in front of her, fingering them with hands that were thick and freckled. He had on a new suit and, in spite of his assumption of the townsman, she guessed him to be a raw countryman.

Looking up to find her gaze fixed on him, he dangled a garment in front of her and asked the price. She put on the smile of the saleswoman for charity and named a stiff sum. He jibbed a bit, but decided to be reckless. She was a damned good-looking girl. After some parleying and the exchange of heavy jocularity, the upshot of the transaction was the offer of a date for the evening – neither accepted nor refused. So during the next few hours the young man could be seen hovering within the radius of the lingerie stall, held by an invisible thread leading to its centre. When the waitresses appeared with tea the bemused young man invited Stella to one of the many tables scattered through the hall and managed to clinch his date over the teapot. During the next few weeks followed a game of hook and line familiar throughout the ages between the lover and the pursued object of his infatuation. Before he knew where he was the fish was landed, gasping but happy.

Stella had sized up her man correctly in that first lookover at the bazaar stall. He had come to town some few months previously from a small upcountry *dorp* in the Western Cape. He was the second son of a large family, he said, but was vague about their circumstances; through the influence of a friend of the family he had walked into a job as shop foreman in one of the Main Road bazaars. It was an easy job, not too well paid, but he hoped to pick up something better soon. He hadn't any friends except this man who had got him the job. He was still a bit bewildered by the city, never having been further than the local small town some fifty miles from his *dorp*, and he was emphatically lonely.

Stella undertook to solve both his problems. Carl had never met such a charming, sophisticated young woman; she made him feel that he was really beginning to live. How he wished that the *kêrels* he had left behind could see what a lad he was. How they would envy him!

Their rendezvous was usually near the dress shop where Stella worked and when he asked where she stayed she put him off with the difficulty of getting there, first by bus and then by train, especially seeing he didn't know his way about yet. When he showed a natural curiosity about her family she was as vague as he had been about his connections: 'Most of my people are upcountry too.' It was nice to think they shared a common loneliness in the big city. She explained that she lived with some pleasant people, but the house was very crowded and it wasn't easy to bring friends along. Of course they were quite nice about it though you were afraid they were just being polite. She preferred to be independent; didn't he? – to which sentiments he heartily agreed. He had come up to town on his own because there was nothing doing in the *dorp*, while here there were plenty of jobs to be had almost for the asking. It was only the stick-in-the-muds who stayed back in the *platteland*. And Carl was no stick-in-the-mud. Not him!

So the affair moved on with lightning speed. The infatuated young man, marvelling at his good fortune, was importunate in his desire to be master of this adorable girl, which of course could only be in one way. He didn't know what his people at home would say to him getting married so soon and in his present state of mind he didn't much care. He had promised to send them a regular sum to help them out, for on the small bit of land his father owned, with its output dwindling every year and the drought to contend with and a young family growing up, they were hard put to it to make ends meet. But Carl had himself to think of. And once he had a better job he'd be able to send his family something every month too.

One night Stella told her mother she was going to marry Carl Meyers. She said it quietly. The two women looked at each other, a world of meaning in their glances, a thousand thoughts unspoken.

'Oh, Stella!' Her mother could not help wiping away a tear.

Irene Liedeman was dying to meet her future-son-in-law. Couldn't it be arranged? She would like to see what he was like. She would like to see him sitting in her parlour and give him a cup of tea at least.

'If he comes,' said Stella, 'it'll have to be when Kathie's not here.'

And so it was arranged. The terrace they lived in was genteel enough and the situation was simplified by the fact that he didn't know the suburbs of Cape Town, with its mixed areas. Where he came from in the country there were no such grey areas; the residential line of demarcation between black and white was clear.

So Carl came to fetch Stella one Saturday afternoon. All unsuspecting, he sat in the little parlour where Stella's father had challenged her grandmother, denouncing what she and his wife were planning for his child. All unsuspecting he sat and drank tea, which Mrs Liedeman brought to him and her daughter. She was not introduced to him and he did not notice the coloured woman bringing in the tray. Stella, on tenterhooks lest some unwelcome visitor should drop in, cut the visit short and the two young people hurried off to the seaside. Carl didn't have a car and they would have to catch the train. They would go to St James, Stella thought exultantly, one of the beaches reserved for Europeans Only, instead of to Kalk Bay, the only beach along the line of rail that non-Europeans were permitted to use. Standing at the level crossing waiting for the booms to lift and let them through, Carl remarked:

'Nice little house you stay in. Sorry I didn't meet any of your friends.'

'I'm sorry, too. But it's Saturday afternoon when everybody wants to be out.'

'You've said it. Let's hurry.'

Left alone, Irene Liedeman didn't wash up the tea dishes. She didn't feel like it. She just wanted to sit.

She had seen the man. And Stella was going to marry him. Was this the fulfilment of her dream at last? Was this the hour for which she had lived and toiled, pinched and scraped, plotted and schemed? After the lean, mean years, the reward, the consummation? True, the man wasn't all that she and Stella had dreamed of. She ought to have done better than marry a shop foreman. He didn't seem to have had much education either – not like Stella – and he was rather coarse in his manners. But he had the main thing ... You must take what you can get in this life and be thankful for the mercies that God in his goodness grants to his toiling children.

So let the preparations for the day of days go forward. It cannot come too quickly. Let the wedding garments be bought. Let the sewing machine, that has taken such toll of the mother's health, now hum and thrum and whirr as it has never done before. Let the needle trill a song of triumph as it runs up and down the artificial silks and satins for the bride.

Or is there a sadder theme that weaves in and out as the needle flies? The song of a mother who in victory suffers defeat; who in gaining the coveted security for her daughter loses filial affection; who in the pride of ambition fulfilled, suffers shame. Who shall sing the song of the violation of filial bonds?

Stella was going to be married quietly in a registry office. Not for her the grand show that Annette could boast of; for Stella only the few intimates of the family would rally, they who knew what was involved.

Andrew, as might be expected, took the news calmly. 'What does this man do?' he asked. And when he was told, he shrugged his shoulders. He was probably making more money a week than Carl Meyers, even though he was white. As for Annette, she was thrilled. Dear Stella, it was too, too, wonderful! To herself she said: He must be a bit of a fool. Supposing he found out about that stuck-up sister, Kathie, the nurse, who goes about with a native. She foresaw plenty of trouble for Stella, though meantime she'd be turning up her nose at Andrew and her and probably cut them dead if she met them in the street with her husband.

Kathie was the last one to be told the news. She too, on the surface, took it calmly. 'What kind of man is he?' she asked and received only a vague answer from her mother. Had her mother seen him? Yes. Then why all this secrecy? Why hadn't she been told sooner? Kathie couldn't bring herself to congratulate her sister; the words stuck in her throat, for there was too much that she didn't know.

The two sisters were unexpectedly left together early one evening, their mother having gone to see a friend for a short time after supper and before it should get too dark, for she never liked to be out late. Stella was sitting in her mother's chair, finishing off by hand a dainty nightdress her mother had made that afternoon. It was a pretty scene; the young bride-to-be plying the busy needle, her face, calm and preoccupied, bent over this pleasant task. How many girls had sat thus in the last hours of their girlhood, diligently stitching their wedding garments and dreaming of the life that lay before them? What were Stella's dreams and hopes? thought Kathie.

'I haven't had a chance to talk to you,' she said aloud.

'No, we're all so busy,' Stella replied without looking up.

'Is everything nearly ready?'

'Very nearly. I have some odds and ends to still buy.'

'Has Ma made everything herself?'

'Yes.'

'Stella, I haven't met the man you are to marry –'

Stella's needle stopped.

'So I don't know what he's like. Is he a good man?'

'What a funny question. Of course he is.'

'I'm glad. And I suppose he's very much in love?'

'He's mad about me.'

'Then it will be all right? Have you told him?'

Stella put down her sewing. 'How do you mean?'

'You know very well what I mean. Does he know what you are?'

'What's all this for?' demanded Stella.

'Does he know?' Kathie persisted quietly.

'You have no right to ask me.'

'But I have, because I want you to be happy. I don't think you understand me, Stella. I'm not against your man because he is white. If he is a good man you can still be happy, and you will make him a good wife. But if a secret lies between you – the secret of what you are – then your marriage will be built on quicksand. Don't you see, Stella?'

'If I told him, it would be the end of everything.'

'Are you sure?'

'It would be crazy to tell him.'

'But you say he loves you.'

'Loves me? Yes!' Stella gave a bitter laugh.

How indeed should love prevail against the fear of colour when a man breathes the poisoned air of it from the days of his childhood? At that moment there flashed into Kathie's mind the memory of her mother's attitude to Paul and the terrible finality of her answer: *I don't want to hear it!* It was natural to her to close her mind against Paul. Why? Why must it always be so?

Stella was speaking again: 'I'm not expecting a bed of roses,' she said. 'But I'm marrying the way I want to and nobody can stop me.'

Once again Kathie had to acknowledge that she had failed. All the suppressed conflict of the years since the death of their father, Johannes Liedeman, culminated in this marriage, with the truth unspoken. It marked Kathie's defeat, which was her father's defeat.

Carl Meyers and Stella Liedeman were married in the registry office. It was a pity that both the bride's people and those of the bridegroom couldn't be present, but it couldn't be helped, since they were two young people living alone in town. The only others present were the two witnesses: the one was Carl's friend, who was a middle-aged man with a preoccupied air that seemed to say: Why must these foolish young things marry, without a thought of what's in store for them? The other witness was a discreet friend of the Liedeman family, Mrs Boyd, a very good-looking woman of about forty, light of complexion, well-dressed and most correct in her manners. She had been very helpful to Irene Liedeman and her daughter during the last hurried weeks and thoroughly approved of the match.

As they parted after the brief ceremony, Stella clung to her. The older woman patted her hand reassuringly and kissed her carefully on the cheek. Then the honeymoon couple went off for a short holiday – all that Carl could get since he hadn't been long in his job – and the witnesses went their several ways.

Mrs Boyd went straight to Mrs Liedeman's house. She found her sitting in the kitchen beside her sewing machine, now empty and idle – just waiting. As she opened the door she had a glimpse of the mother's face caught unawares, and her heart broke at what she saw there. What had her thoughts been as she sat alone, not daring to show herself at her daughter's wedding – she who had set her daughter on the road to this marriage?

The mother looked up eagerly as Mrs Boyd entered.

'Well?'

'Stella looked lovely!'

The mother smiled.

'Everything went off smoothly,' said Mrs Boyd. 'The bridegroom looked a bit awkward, but Stella looked cool and lovely. She was ravishing in the two-piece you made.'

'Oh I'm glad everything went off well,' breathed the mother. 'And did Stella ... ' She was unable to finish.

'The last thing Stella did – she sent her love.'

In this Mrs Boyd lied, but well she knew how desperately Irene needed to hear these words. She was rewarded with another smile that lighted the anxious face.

'Now don't you worry,' she went on. 'Everything will go all right. You'll see. He seems a decent chap. Stella will manage him all right. She's a fine girl. Now what about that cup of tea?'

After first removing some of her wedding finery, Mrs Boyd bustled about and behaved generally as if she was quite unaware that Mrs Liedeman had any reason to be in low spirits. The mother was grateful for it, doing her best to keep up the pretence. It is at such moments that sorrow is cheated out of its worst pangs.

Mrs Liedeman was to be still further bereft in her hour of victory.

Kathie had at last come to a decision. Her mother's ultimatum against Paul: *He'll never enter my door!* removed the last shred of hope that she would ever accept the fact of her marrying him. It seemed to her that she had been living in this house with them under false pretences, and the sheer inertia of habit had prevented her from breaking away – a step she should have long since taken. Now, however, there was no possibility of further pretence. In taking Paul, she had made her choice; to stay where she was meant to be disloyal to him, for if her people accepted her they must also accept him; they could not accept her and turn their back on him.

But that was not all; she might still have hesitated if Stella's marriage had not come hot on the heels of this crisis with her mother over Paul. There was no doubt that the complete cleavage brought about by the marriage marked the end of a period for Kathie. For as long as she had lived under the same roof as her sister, there was still, in spite of the estrangement, the hope of an understanding, at least on Kathie's part. Now she realised that she had been deceiving herself. And if it was her too strong sense of responsibility that had been holding her back, wasn't that responsibility now completely at an end? With Stella's departure, weren't the threads of a lifetime wrenched once and for all? This marriage marked the triumph of her mother's ambition and therefore the final step in the betrayal of her father's last wishes. It was a thought that caused Kathie to harden her heart against her mother at a time when she was already feeling acutely her rejection of Paul.

Kathie redoubled her efforts to find separate accommodation for herself. Nearly every weekend, when she was off duty, she and Paul exhausted themselves in this soul-wearying search, till at last they were successful, and she found a room with a respectable Malay family at the other end of the town up against the mountain and overlooking the sea. She would have a door to herself and thus could come and go – for her hours were sometimes late – without disturbing the family.

One morning before setting off to go on duty at St Mary's hospital, Kathie briefly informed her mother that she had found a room where she could stay by herself. Steadying her voice, though she was trembling inwardly, she tried to speak as casually as she could.

Her mother looked up, startled.

'You are not going, Kathie!' she exclaimed.

'I think it's best, Ma. It's time I was on my own.'

'Why didn't you tell me you were looking for a room?' asked her mother, finding refuge in the smaller grievance.

'I didn't want to bother you.'

'I suppose you never asked yourself if I wanted you to leave?'

'I had to make my own decision.'

'And you don't want to live with your mother any more?'

'Don't put it that way. For a long time I've felt that you and Stella didn't want me here.'

'You know that's nonsense. Besides, Stella's gone now.'

There was a tremor in her mother's voice.

'We don't see things in the same way, Ma. Our ideas are different –'

'But that's no reason why you should leave me,' interrupted Mrs Liedeman.

'I haven't time to argue about that, Ma.'

'Is it this Paul Mangena you're hinting at? Is that it?'

'I am not going to speak about Paul now. It seems to me that there is no need for me to stay here any longer. You have your friends, and there's Andrew and Annette.'

'Annette! My son's wife! What is she to a mother compared with her own daughter?'

Kathie ignored the angry reproach in her mother's voice.

'But I must go away, Ma. I want to be on my own and think things out.'

'You are selfish. Only thinking of yourself. That's what you are.'

Kathie realised that she would get nowhere by arguing with her mother.

'I must live my life,' she answered. 'But it's not as if I'm going away for good. I'll see you often … And now I'm making myself late.'

With this, Kathie tore herself away. And within the week she had left home.

Only the mother lived on in this house, the house by the railway crossing with its flashing red lights, the house where her own mother, the Englishman's daughter, had so long nursed her fanatical dreams, that had now borne their fruit.

And more bitter still the harvest to come!

The mother sat alone, not so busy as she had been. There was no more need. She felt a great weariness and she kept herself to herself, even more than ever, neither visiting nor being visited by more than one or two friends. She saw Andrew and Annette occasionally; Annette was usually sulky when she had to visit her mother-in-law and for the sake of peace Andrew came more and more seldom. As for Kathie, her mother was determined not to go and see her in her new abode, though Kathie made a point of visiting her whenever she could.

Stella the mother never visits; she lives now in a distant suburb of the city, where the only thing in common with her old home is the mountain, which, though from a different angle, still keeps its constant vigil.

But in her thoughts her youngest child's presence continually hovers.

CHAPTER 17

The wheel of life

Paul had finished his two years as an articled clerk and was now a fully fledged lawyer. He hadn't an office, he hadn't a practice, but he had at last achieved the title. It was the fulfilment of a long-awaited ambition, long and patiently striven for under great privation, and like many such achievements, the scaling of one peak found him standing with yet another peak and another before him calling for the same strenuous effort, the same pitting of one's strength against impediment. He had wanted to set up on his own, but this was a step which for an African bristled with difficulties; besides this, being destitute of capital and determined not to make still further calls on the generosity of his sister Nonceba, he was compelled to continue in the employ of the European firm of lawyers with whom he had been articled. He chafed at the way they continued to exploit him – and recognised that as a black man they had the whip hand of him. When would he ever be able to achieve the independence that was the goal and aim of his ambition?

Then a few months after Nontando had come face to face with

Kathie in Paul's room and there discovered that it was she to whom his love was given, an unexpected turn of events took Paul away from the city. The firm for whom he worked decided it would be a profitable move to send him to a recently formed branch of theirs at Lukaleni in the Ciskei in the Eastern Cape, where he could handle cases for the Africans who formed a large proportion of the population. Poor as they were, the non-Europeans were always becoming involved in court cases and would more readily employ one of their own people – by which means the firm would oust any rival in the district, or at least reduce him to a negligible position.

It was a foregone conclusion that Paul would accept the offer. As the firm saw it, no native in his senses could possibly turn down such a chance but count himself extraordinarily fortunate to get it. For Paul and Kathie, however, the issue was not so simple. Their love was young; they were still tasting the wonder of it, conscious of its precious quality, wrested as it was out of the jungle, and they felt deeply the need of being together. Of course Paul recognised the advantages of such an offer. While the money was still inadequate in view of his qualifications, he would gain much in experience and would have more scope, more freedom in the practice of his calling. Added to this was the fact that he would be near his home and none would be more overjoyed than his sister Nonceba to have her Sipo with her again.

Paul and Kathie discussed the proposition earnestly together, and, as might have been expected, she urged him to go. She argued that nothing should be allowed to stand in the way of his advancement; the experience he would gain and the increase in salary would both bring nearer the goal he aimed at – of setting up on his own. So by parting they were actually hastening the time when they would be together. How foolish, then, to be afraid of facing a little bit of loneliness. He could try the job for six months and if he didn't like it he could always come back. Six months wasn't a very long time. Why, they'd both be so busy it would fly past before they knew where they were. Kathie might even contrive to get a holiday and come up and see him and Nonceba. She wanted very much to meet his sister, who had been so good to him. They had faced other difficulties and they could face this one. Nothing in the world could harm them because they were sure of themselves and of each other.

So at last they agreed that Paul should go to the Ciskei and he made his preparations accordingly. It was not without some feelings of regret that he bade goodbye to Thembisa Sitole. She had been a good friend to him at the time when the pressure of the new world of the city had almost overwhelmed him, and he was not the one to forget it. She, for her part, felt his going much more than she admitted, even to herself. He had been almost as a father to her son Keke, who worshipped him, and she knew all too well that a growing boy, especially in such an environment, needs the presence of a man he can look up to and be fond of at the same time. The ties of affection provided the fatherless boy with a sorely needed anchor. She herself had come to rely on Paul as more than a big son to her. The vacant place in her heart waiting for her man to return had been filled by the earnest young student. It was with a sad heart that she helped him to prepare the few things he had – washing, ironing and mending them for the journey.

There was one person whom Paul left behind with a pang of anxiety and that was Nontando. He was aware that she went out of her way to avoid him in these last few months, and when he sought her out he found her changed. He feared that the youth Petu was having a bad influence on her, but when he tried to talk to her she would laugh and put him off. He didn't know this new Nontando, older, harder, more crude and unmistakably hostile to him. While remembering that Mrs Sitole had been strangely unlike herself in her intolerant attitude towards the girl, he thought he would make one more appeal to her to be friendly while he was away.

'You've always had a wrong idea about that girl,' Thembisa exclaimed as soon as he opened his mouth. 'From the very beginning you've favoured and spoilt her and she isn't a child any more. She knows how to keep that Petu dancing attendance on her and I don't need to tell you what sort *he* is.'

'It's because of him that I'm worried about her,' he answered. 'She is too young to know just how much suffering a man can bring her to.'

'As for that, there's not much she doesn't know,' Mrs Sitole retorted.

'There's some goings-on at the store too, if I'm not mistaken,' she added.

'What do you mean?'

Paul spoke sharply and Thembisa realised she had gone too far.

She shrugged. 'Perhaps I'm wrong. I'm a busy woman and I haven't time to go prying into other folk's affairs.'

'But what are you hinting at?' he persisted.

'Oh, it's nothing. Probably some idle talk. Now don't you go worrying your head about the girl. You've enough on your mind as it is.' Thus with an affectation of indifference she put him off.

She had not banished his uneasiness, however, and he made up his mind to ask Kathie to keep in touch with Nontando. His hopes of a friendship developing between the two women had been sadly disappointed. The barriers between them were too great, though he was unaware of the greatest of them – Nontando's jealousy of Kathie. But during his absence, he thought, the two might have a better opportunity of coming together. When he put the suggestion to Kathie she expressed her willingness to try yet again to break down the girl's reserve. She, too, thought it might be easier when Paul was away.

And what did the parting mean for Nontando?

The last meeting between her and Paul has the quality of those mute tragedies that do not lend themselves to words. There is so much in them of frustration and helplessness, of feeling too deep for anything but silence, so violent in its suppression that the sense is numb and assumes the outward mask of calm and even indifference. It longs to sob with uncontrollable sorrow – and is dumb. It longs to plead that this parting is the end of life, but it is silent and only smiles a brave farewell. Life that once flowed in a joyous tide through the veins, ebbs and sinks into a deadly stillness. Only in the tearless eyes such a world of unutterable despair looks out, that the beholder shrinks from what he sees there, and he too is silent.

There was a moment when she seemed about to speak, to confess some burden of the spirit weighing too heavily upon her. But it passed and the words were left unspoken. (Stay, Paul, and listen! It is a silence that will always reproach you.) They parted, with Paul expressing the hope that Nontando and Kathie would learn to be friends before he should return. Then saying a last goodbye, he hurried away to see to the details of his departure.

Paul was gone. Kathie found herself thrown on her own resources and had never felt so lonely in her life. Always keen at her work, she now flung herself into her duties at the hospital with such avidity that one of the sisters asked her what devil was driving her. If she went on at this rate she would have a breakdown and then where would they be, understaffed as they were? Kathie laughed at the very idea since she was one of those who boasted that she had never known a day's sickness in her life. She would drive herself to the point of physical exhaustion so that at the end of the day's work she fell into the oblivion of sleep she longed for. But its balm lasted for all too short a spell. She would awaken in the early hours, take up a book and read, put it down again and try in vain to sleep, while her restless thoughts travelled hither and thither. Paul's letters gave her some cause for anxiety; though guarded in their expression they said enough to show that he was far from happy in his work; he was obviously working under an inner tension as well as against outward difficulties.

It was not simply that Kathie missed Paul's presence and the stimulation of his ever searching mind. It was the potent influence of that contact that directed her own thoughts along channels they had never clearly followed before. She was thrown doubly on her own resources because of her complete break with her home, for this meant breaking with old habits and contacts accepted willy-nilly in that circle, in spite of the fact that she never wholly belonged there. In choosing a black man she had violated the social code of the group (though it was not written in any statute book) and to break with this little world with all its prejudices – which reflected the racial pattern of the larger system of society – was but a logical conclusion of that choice. Henceforward she must forge a path for herself. And it was no easy step for her to take. The new road is uncharted and, brave as the spirit may be, it must shrink from the loneliness this involves. To turn one's back on the old, however frail its props, takes some courage. Every human being needs the comfort of *belonging* somewhere; social approval, social contacts are the bedrock of moral and spiritual security; remove them and it is very likely that the individual may founder. The herd instinctively hates that member who breaks away from it. Together, Kathie and Paul found much that atoned for the privations of their position, separated as they were both from their equals in the white community and from their own people, but now, forced to part, Kathie more than Paul felt the full force of her isolation.

There was the simple problem of filling the gap in her life that his absence entailed, for they had been very much together during the months before his departure. In an attempt to fill those few evenings when she had time to kill, she went to meetings of this and that club she had heard vaguely about. Stimulated by her reading (Paul and she owed much to the bookseller, Farben, in this respect), she was no longer satisfied with what she was able to achieve as a nurse. Too often all her efforts seemed utterly futile in face of the ceaseless suffering she encountered in the lives of those people whom she tended. So she sought something more, though what it was she did not know. She could only grope this way and that in the hope of finding something that would answer to her need. There were dramatic clubs, social clubs, political clubs; she tried this one and that one, but in a rather sceptical frame of mind. It did not take her long to smell out the social or intellectual snob who hobnobbed with art and politics chiefly with a view to social advancement. She had too much common sense to be taken in by the pretentious in any form and found their antics boring.

Then about four months after Paul's departure something happened that put everything else out of her mind.

Kathie was busy at the hospital one afternoon when a message was brought to her that an African woman wanted to see her and was very insistent. Telling the nurse to show her in she was almost immediately confronted by a middle-aged woman she had never seen before, untidy, distraught, her dark face ashen through the brown.

Without any preliminaries she burst out: 'It's Nontando. I'm her mother, Mrs Kubeka. Please, please can you come quickly –'

'What is it?' Kathie asked, rising from her chair.

'Nontando is sick. She's in terrible pain. I don't know what to do.'

'Where is she?'

'I found her on the floor when I got home. She's crying out something terrible.'

'Wasn't there anybody to help her?'

'Nobody. My husband died last month. Oh nurse, please can't you do something to help her? I think her baby is coming, but it's too soon.'

'I'll come at once,' said Kathie. She masked her surprise in the calmness of her voice.

Calling a nurse to fetch one of the other sisters, she asked her to take over her duties. She was acting against regulations, but she would have to risk it. Gathering such things together as she thought she would require, she set off with Mrs Kubeka.

On the way the two women exchanged only a few words. Kathie learned that Nontando's child wasn't due for another two months. She had been ailing of late, but had been at work the previous day, and she had been sleeping when Mrs Kubeka had gone out in the early morning. Nothing was said as to who was the father of the child. On asking the mother how she had known where to find her, Kathie was told that it was not Nontando who had sent her. (No, thought Kathie, she would never send for me.) Mrs Kubeka had done it on her own. First she had run to Mrs Sitole where Mr Mangena used to stay. ('Yes, I know her,' said Kathie.) But Mrs Sitole was not yet home. Then she had thought of the young lady who had once come to see Nontando when her husband was still alive. He'd said she was a nurse and spoke kindly. ('Yes, I remember the day I met him,' murmured Kathie.) 'I couldn't think of no one else to help me in my trouble,' said the mother. 'You being a nurse, I thought –'

'I'm very glad you came for me,' said Kathie.

Hurrying on their way in silence, they at last reached Mrs Kubeka's house. Kathie promptly took charge. Finding the younger children in the room, hovering scared and helpless about the writhing girl, she beckoned to a neighbour who meantime had done all she could, and asked her to look after them.

Nontando had not opened her eyes, but lay across the bed moaning in a way that almost unnerved Kathie, accustomed as she was to tending those in pain. Suppressing her emotion, she examined the girl with cool, efficient fingers. At her touch, Nontando opened her eyes, shrank away and cried:

'No! No! Not you!'

Kathie exchanged a quick glance with the mother, who stood with strained attention at the other side of the bed, then firmly resisted the thrusting hands and proceeded with her task.

'Nontando must be taken to hospital at once,' she said.

'Oh, Sister, is there any danger?' asked the distracted mother.

Kathie reassured her. 'I don't think so. But we must act at once. I must ring up the hospital. Where's the nearest phone?'

'There's one at Vadaris' store – that's where Nontando works.'

'I know where it is,' replied Kathie. 'I'll be back as quick as I can.'

And giving Mrs Kubeka instructions as to what to do during her absence, she hastened to the store.

Realising the gravity of Nontando's condition, which she had not admitted to the mother, Kathie did not let her mind dwell on all that lay behind it nor on the girl's strange attitude towards herself. Instead she concentrated all her energy on the immediate task of saving Nontando and, if possible, the child. First she must get her removed to hospital where at least there were the facilities and the cleanliness essential for the job.

On entering the shop and looking round for the proprietor, she was more peremptory in her manner than she realised and it was only when she caught the look the man gave her that she reminded herself that this was a white man and he saw her as a coloured woman. She did not alter her tone, but all at once she remembered that this was where Nontando was employed. Of course, they must know that she was ill. Or did they?

'Did Miss Kubeka come to work this morning?' she asked.

'Who?' The face twisted rudely on the word.

'That's Nontando,' said the African assistant, who was within earshot.

'Oh, her,' said the storekeeper. 'What about her? Yes, she stayed away this morning.' His tone implied that she had no business to do so.

'She is very ill,' Kathie continued, and was struck by the sudden narrowing of the man's eyes. His expression was not that of sympathetic concern, but on the contrary of indifference – with something else she could not fathom. At the same time she noticed that the assistant, an obsequious individual with the spirit of independence long since crushed in him, had edged nearer and was looking at his master.

Then turning to her: 'I'm sorry to hear that, Sister,' he ventured.

'Get on with your work,' snapped the storekeeper. Then to Kathie: 'I don't like people using my phone. But you can do it this once. And not again.'

'Thank you,' said Kathie.

As she turned away she said to herself: There's something here I don't understand. I don't like it either. But she dismissed the thought for the serious task in hand.

It was even more serious than she had anticipated. After she had given a few brief particulars about Nontando, the voice over the phone declared that the hospital couldn't take her in.

'But you must! It's extremely urgent!' she exclaimed and demanded to speak to a higher authority, only to receive the same refusal. They were sorry, they were full up, couldn't take a single patient more – out of the question – impossible. And then as Kathie reiterated her plea as to the urgency of the case, the sharp click of the phone being hung up at the other end, terminated the dispute.

For a few seconds she held the dead instrument in her hand, her anger mounting, yet she knew how futile it was to beat her head against the stone wall of officialdom. And it was quite true – as she well knew – there were no beds to spare. She hung up. She was considering what to do next when she looked up to find the storekeeper standing quite near her, watching. Why was he staring at her like that? Again she had the sensation that here was something sinister. Or was she just being fanciful? The man with his unhealthy large face and the protruding paunch in the small body, produced a kind of nausea when one looked at him.

She had forgotten him the next moment in considering what was best to do for Nontando. Ordinarily she was competent to take over any such case. Among her people the women did not have a doctor for this most common and universal event; most of them couldn't afford it. If they could not go to hospital their doctor was the midwife, who amid all the crude conditions of their homes brought the puling infant into the world as part of the day's work. In this instance, however, Kathie feared the complications of a premature birth, added to the nature of the conditions under which she had to work. And then of course, it was Nontando. Had not Paul bid her have a special care for her welfare? The responsibility weighed heavily on Kathie. These considerations took but a second to flash through her mind. Then she made a second call, this time to a non-European doctor in whose ability she had great confidence. She would engage him herself for Nontando. Unfortunately the doctor wasn't in so she left a message, giving instructions where to come; the case was most urgent. There was no more to be done for the time being. As she turned away from the phone she again became aware of the storekeeper's watchful gaze. Handing the assistant the money for the calls, she hurried out.

As she entered the room where Nontando lay, one swift glance told her that the doctor would be too late. The girl's life was in her hands. With machine-like efficiency she ordered the mother to help her and the woman quickly and dumbly obeyed. Nontando was not unconscious; but the agony of her travail reduced the whole being to that one centre of burning consciousness as if all her senses were rushing into this abyss of pain, dehumanising, wiping out all memory of love or hate. And in this only was it merciful – she did not know who it was that was with her. The wracked body knew only to cling to those strong hands fighting together with her to bring forth the living child.

At last it was over. A baby boy had been born. He was a puny little thing, prematurely delivered; his life beat feebly in his breast; he did not greet the world with the lusty cry of the newborn infant filling his lungs with this new element – the air. Having left the warm, dark nest of the womb he sent forth a thin wailing cry as if he would willingly return to the dark again.

Nontando lay pallid with exhaustion, her eyes closed, her brow clammy and cold. Kathie's task was not done. With the help of Mrs Kubeka she saw to the child and made the new mother as comfortable as she could think how to do in this room so destitute of the comforts of life. She was in the midst of this when the doctor arrived. Briefly Kathie gave him the necessary explanations and it did not take him long to discover that Kathie had done a very good job of work; in fact there was not much for him to do except to say that the young mother would probably be all right, if she received great care, for she was in a very weak state. As to the child, however, he shook his head. These premature babies needed a lot of looking after and he hoped there was somebody who could do it.

Mrs Kubeka and Kathie looked at each other. He hurried on to say that he himself would try to persuade St Mary's hospital to find a place for the girl and her baby, though he didn't hold out much hope.

'Meantime your daughter couldn't be in better hands,' he said, addressing Mrs Kubeka, who murmured that she knew how truly the doctor had spoken.

'But, Doctor, I should be here all the time,' interrupted Kathie, 'and I'm on duty at St Mary's. Couldn't you speak to the matron for me and get me off for a day or two?'

The doctor shook his head. 'It won't be easy.'

'I know. But I'm staying here all the same. Do put in a word for me.'

'I'll do my best,' he assured her. Then telling Mrs Kubeka not to worry, he hurried off.

When he had gone the room settled to a rare quietness. It is such a quietness as descends after one has been wrought to a pitch of physical and mental exertion and nature lulls the whole being into a half-consciousness while she fills again this human vessel that has emptied itself out completely. It was not only Nontando who was exhausted. Her mother too, who, in witnessing the birth of her first grandchild had suffered the pangs of her daughter's labour as she had never felt her own, had been moved out of her customary apathy. Struggling under a too harassed existence, the woman in sheer self-defence had atrophied in feeling. But now, as she sat quietly beside Kathie and her eldest child – this wayward daughter who had been a source of so much bitterness – her heart flowed towards her and it came over her with an aching regret how little she had ever given Nontando of motherly care and love. Watching the face of the sleeping girl, long suppressed feeling struggled with weariness and there was an uneasy pleasure in letting it take possession of the relaxed body and mind. Towards Kathie she felt nothing but admiration and gratitude. There was a woman! Strange, that Nontando had never spoken about her.

Kathie decided that she would stay the night. Her calling had taught her to snatch rest and sleep when and where she could find them. It was only when she sat down and tried to relax that she realised she had given her all in the last few hours. Involuntarily her thoughts leapt to the birth of her sister Stella – the other birth that had meant so much to her. Then, too, child as she was, the sight of a woman's painful labour had bitten deep into her consciousness, never to be forgotten. There, she thought, lay the root of the calling she had finally chosen. What joy that birth had brought, and in its aftermath, what sorrow! Her mind slipped away from that memory.

Stretching her tired limbs she took a reckoning of the day's work and felt that it was good. She pictured herself writing to Paul and telling him what had happened, and though he would be distressed at the circumstances that had led to Nontando's ordeal, he could not but be glad that it was Kathie who had been with her and seen her through. Glancing over at the baby, lying so still in his improvised little bed, she resolved to do everything to save him. Yes, he had been conceived perhaps in recklessness and foolishness, but he was Nontando's child. Nothing could alter that.

What would the young mother's reaction be towards her baby? If she loved him, all would be well. This thought led to another in Kathie's mind. Who was the child's father? Would Nontando ever tell her? Suddenly for no apparent reason, she recalled that incident at the store when she had gone to phone the hospital. The expression on the storekeeper's face when she had told him Nontando was ill – it had been hostile and watchful. Could this white man be the father? She saw again the figure that had stood near her when she had looked up from the phone. He was a repulsive creature.

A woman could feel nothing but contempt for such a man … No, it could not be!

Kathie bent over the baby and examined his dark, diminutive little features most earnestly. No, his father was an African, whoever he was. Of that there could be no doubt. Having satisfied herself on this point, Kathie felt her eyelids drooping and, after looking to see that all her little company was settled, she too snatched a few moments' sleep. It was a sight that would have brought a great joy to Paul's heart if he could have seen it – the woman he loved and Nontando, bound together by the newborn life lying asleep between them.

On his second visit the doctor expressed himself dissatisfied with Nontando's condition. She was a healthy enough girl, and though the birth had been hard, she had been in good hands, so there was nothing to prevent her from going straight ahead and getting well. But she didn't. Why? She had been a foolish girl, no doubt, but it was nothing to mope about. Let her get up and look after her baby and then she'd forget about herself. The little fellow needed looking after. He'd slip through her fingers if she didn't wake up. There was no likelihood of getting into St Mary's, so she'd better pull herself together and do her best for the baby. Thus with rough and ready cheerfulness the doctor tried to shake Nontando out of her apathy, without success. He was a busy man and couldn't spare any further time, so he addressed a few words of advice to Mrs Kubeka and took his departure, promising himself to have a word with Kathie when he met her. Unfortunately she had had to go back to St Mary's.

Mrs Kubeka looked at her daughter anxiously. Nontando would lie for hours without moving. Her eyes were unnaturally large (for all the world like her father's before he died, thought her mother with a pang of fear) and they would either fix themselves intently on you as if probing your inmost thoughts, or they would have that vacant, incommunicable look of those whose thoughts are entirely turned inwards. Towards the child she showed no interest or affection.

As soon as she was able to get off duty Kathie would hurry to the house and always she was startled by the girl's immobility. At sight of her, Nontando's eyes widened, while she held herself almost rigid. Pretending not to notice this, Kathie proceeded cheerfully with the tasks in hand and told Mrs Kubeka to go and rest. She was aware how the girl shrank from her touch, but she did not speak. At last she sat beside the bed and waited, hoping that the very quietness of her presence would have a soothing effect on Nontando. Yet her own thoughts were far from being at peace. What could be behind all this? The experience had been a profound shock to the young body, but could it account for this abnormal, even unhinged, behaviour? There must be something more. If Nontando herself would not speak, she must try to find out from her mother what it might be. She could not be allowed to continue in this deadly state of passivity; apparently she had no will to get well. But she must, for the sake of the baby. If only she would show a flash of that wild Nontando she remembered seeing a few months ago when she fled past her and Paul. A burst of temper would be less disquieting than this impassiveness. Had she been like this before the birth? she asked herself. Had there been signs already that all was not well? With a stab of remorse she had to admit that she herself had not been in a position to know.

With her mind still anxiously exploring what could be the reason for Nontando's condition, she remembered that in the stress of the immediate task not a word had been said about the child's father. Was Nontando perhaps pining for him to be with her? What did she really know of the heart of this girl beside her? And had she any right to try to probe its secrets? Kathie put out her hand to stroke her forehead, but withdrew it even in the act of stretching it out, remembering how Nontando had shrunk away from her touch. If only Paul were here, he would speak soft words to her and break asunder the iron band that was locking up her spirit.

Next day Kathie put a few guarded questions to Mrs Kubeka, who said she was certain the father of the child was Petu, the young devil, though he would never acknowledge it and they could expect nothing from him towards the upkeep of the baby. As to whether Nontando was fond of him, she didn't think her daughter would break her heart if she never saw him again. But, she continued, didn't Kathie know Petu had been in jail these two months and more. The wonder was that he was ever out of it. In answer to Kathie's question as to whether Nontando had been in any way strange in her behaviour before the birth, her mother admitted that, now that she thought of it, Nontando would have fits of brooding like she had never had before, and then suddenly she'd burst out into such a wildness of laughing, her mother would shout at her to stop because it made her so mad. But then, she reminded Kathie, with her husband sick and dying at this time, she had been in no mind to pay much heed to such behaviour. With all this Kathie felt she had not got to the bottom of Nontando's deep disturbance of mind.

Sitting beside Nontando that evening, she said:

'Nontando, what are you going to call your son?'

To this she gave a scarcely perceptible shake of the head.

'What about giving him your father's name? What was it?'

Nontando reluctantly replied: 'Bantwini.'

'I like that name. Shall we call him Bantwini, then? And is there any other name you would like to go along with it?'

Nontando was about to form the name with her lips.

'Yes?' said Kathie.

Nontando slightly shook her head.

'Don't you love your little son, Nontando? He needs your care, you know.'

Kathie paused, waiting between each remark, hoping for some response.

'Don't blame him because he caused you pain. It's what every mother goes through. And how quickly she forgets it in the joy of having her son in her arms.'

'He has no father,' Nontando said dully.

'But, Nontando, nothing can take your motherhood away from you. There's many a woman who longs in vain to have a son. And you *have* a son. No matter what the world says, you are a mother and you are proud of your son. He is yours. Look at his helpless little hand, see how it wants to cling to you. Take him to your breast. Only you can make him strong.'

At Kathie's words, quickly and softly spoken, an answering gleam at last came into Nontando's eyes, and as Kathie put the child into her arms, the young mother's body relaxed; enfolding him, she bent her face to look at him long and tenderly, as if seeing him for the first time. She herself gave the child his next feed and slept that night with the tiny body nestling in the crook of her arm. Kathie had wanted to put him back in his cot, but the mother would not let him go. She had discovered her child and her motherhood, and with it the life began to flow back to her numbed senses.

To Kathie's disappointment, however, her progress towards recovery fluctuated and her mood had violent changes. Her attitude to her baby, too, was so intense, so anxious, so eager to press on to the day when he should be well and strong, in a word, her life hung so much on that of the child, that Kathie trembled at this new turn of events. Her plan had succeeded almost too well.

Kathie was comforting herself with the thought that time would bring Nontando back to normality, when a chance meeting with Thembisa Sitole brought her nearer the truth of what had wounded the girl's spirit. Alas, it made the healing of it more uncertain.

Kathie was hurrying back to Mrs Kubeka's as usual after coming off duty. Her road took her past Mrs Sitole's house, where Paul had once lived. She had been surprised that Mrs Sitole, as an old friend of Paul's – even if she had no time for Mrs Kubeka – had not so far offered to come and help them, so when she saw her standing in her doorway, she greeted her somewhat coldly, meaning to pass on. Mrs Sitole, however, beckoned her in, and, thinking that she might still enlist her help, she agreed to come in for a moment. Brushing aside the woman's friendly enquiries about herself and Paul, she said: 'You know about Nontando?'

'I know.' The manner was abrupt, even for Thembisa.

'You haven't been to see her yet?'

'I'm not wanted around there, Sister Kathie.'

'I don't know what you mean by that, Mrs Sitole. There's been sore trouble in that house. The baby was premature and Nontando is far from well.'

'Now you are talking just like Mr Paul,' exclaimed Thembisa. 'I know you delivered her ill-gotten child, Sister Kathie –'

'You have no right to speak like that,' said Kathie. 'Nontando is ill. She needs help. This is no time to condemn.'

'You'd sing a different tune if you knew what was going on at the store,' said Mrs Sitole harshly. 'I haven't seen the child, but –'

'You are wrong!' cried Kathie.

In a flash of understanding she flung the challenge back at the woman. The scene in the store leapt to her mind; the man's narrow, speculative look, the insinuating sympathy of the shop assistant and the storekeeper's abrupt dismissal of him. Poor girl – she had been at his mercy. But it was not as Thembisa Sitole concluded. Rigid in her outlook, and in that way holding her own in the ruthless battle of life, she would draw her own simple conclusions about the situation. But she was wrong.

Without pausing to exchange another word with the woman Kathie continued her way to Mrs Kubeka's house. She told herself she had discovered the key to Nontando's deep-seated malaise, her lack of the will to get better. She must get her to talk, break down her barriers, banish the bewilderment and the fears that must be obsessing her mind and thus restore in her the will to live. In her present condition her well-being hung too precariously on that of the child.

Kathie had reason to be hopeful of the success of her further plan to restore Nontando to herself, because of the way she had responded to her a few days previously. She no longer showed any antipathy to Kathie. Her absorption in her baby had apparently banished it, Kathie hoped, for good.

Sitting again at Nontando's bedside in the quiet of the evening, Mrs Kubeka having gone to see the neighbour who had befriended her children, she gently led her on to talk about herself. It wasn't easy. Nontando shied like a startled foal and Kathie went warily, talking first about the baby and his father, Petu. She said she was sure he had his pa's features, whereat the young mother smiled, nodding her agreement as she gazed at the sleeping child. She ventured to ask if Petu knew about the child's coming before he had been arrested.

'Yes, he knew,' answered Nontando. And then a shadow crossed her face. 'If only they hadn't taken him away –' she said, and stopped.

Kathie waited.

'Everybody thought he was bad,' continued the girl, 'but he would have taken care of me. I – '

Her lips took on their rebellious expression. 'But why do you ask me all these questions?' she said.

Kathie did not pursue the subject further that day. She could wait.

Another time, after first remarking on the baby's progress, she came to the point of describing the day she had gone to the store to telephone. At the mention of the storekeeper, Nontando gave her a startled glance. But Kathie deliberately kept her description on a jocular plane, exaggerating the way she had ordered him about and his reaction to it, and expressing her amused contempt of the man. Nontando joined hysterically in her laughter at the picture conjured up. Then, when Kathie went on to ask, almost casually, if she intended going back to the store when she felt better – the floodgates of Nontando's pent-up spirit opened.

'No! No! I'll never go back there. Never!' she cried.

Kathie listened patiently while she poured out the fears and the shames that had pursued her during the months before the premature birth of her child. She was quite sure, she told Kathie, that Petu would have killed the man, but the police came and took Petu away ...

From her incoherent words Kathie learned enough to know that her surmise had been correct.

As Nontando unfolded her story, sometimes crudely, groping for her words, going back to the time when she first met Petu, which had been when Paul and herself were coming together, Kathie began to have a picture of what it had meant to the young girl to feel that she was no longer able to turn to Paul with confidence, having lost her trust in him, her trust in herself, fearful of what he would think of her. How blind Kathie had been – and Paul too. Now she understood much.

Moved by an extraordinary impulse, Kathie bent forward and touched the baby's cheek. 'It should have been Paul's child,' she said.

Nontando looked at her, then buried her face against the little bundle of humanity.

When she was alone Kathie dared not analyse her own thoughts too deeply. What mattered now was that she had contrived to make

Nontando unburden herself of the knotted emotions that had blocked the path to her recovery. From this day forward she would certainly be on the mend till she was able to shoulder the full responsibility of her baby son. Yes, her life was now bound up with that of her child. He needed constant care, which both women gave him, clinging to the hope of strengthening this thin thread of life on which so much depended. Kathie chafed at the hospital duties that kept her away from the young mother and her baby, but she had no choice. Not a day passed, however, when she did not visit them at some time or another.

Alas for the change of fortune that the morrow can bring! Even as one sleeps the doom is wrought; joy turns to sorrow and hope to despair.

Nontando's baby died in the night. Her mother, wakened by a terrible cry and still half dazed with sleep, had stumbled to the bed where her daughter was with her child. She found her on her knees on the bed, holding her baby close to her breast, rocking him and hushing him.

'He is cold,' she said, and strained him closer.

Mrs Kubeka then (as she afterwards related it all to Kathie) had put out her hand to feel him, but Nontando had jerked him away. The baby made no sound and still she went on rocking him, her movement becoming more and more violent. The dreadful suspicion entered Mrs Kubeka's mind that the baby was dead. Placing one hand firmly on her daughter's arm she arrested the ceaseless rocking and put out the other hand. The touch sent a shuddering through her body. The little face was dead.

Nontando broke into a low moaning sound, moaning and swaying to and fro, and the sound struck fear into her mother's heart. She wondered what she should do, for it seemed impossible to take the baby out of her daughter's arms. She longed for Kathie to appear. At last she coaxed Nontando to lie down, though she still clung to the child. It was the doctor who had taken it from her when he had arrived some time later, and she had submitted. She did not utter a word, but turned her face to the wall.

That was how Kathie found her. She recognised the same terrible immobility that she thought she had successfully routed. Nontando refused to eat; to all entreaties she was silent; when Kathie gently touched her shoulder, she shrank away. With her patience running out, her mother spoke sharply to her. But it was of no avail ...

Now Kathie bent over her and with her strong hands under her body, tried to raise her, whereupon Nontando flung herself up, her eyes blazing, and struck Kathie full in the face, then springing out of bed she faced the two women at bay. No word had passed her lips. Breathing strongly, she began with frantic speed to look for her clothes.

'Nontando, you cannot go out. You are not strong enough yet,' said Kathie.

Anticipating her movement, Kathie went swiftly to the door and stood barring her way. Thus thwarted of her purpose, Nontando paused, a desperate hatred in her face, but she did not again touch Kathie, who now began speaking with all the power that was in her, quietly, persuasively, firmly.

Suddenly Nontando's resistance crumbled. Her rigid body, still weak from all she had been through, sagged down, and slipping to the floor, she covered her face with her hands. Within a few minutes Kathie, with the help of Mrs Kubeka, had her tucked into bed with a hot water bottle, with which she had armed herself on the first day of the confinement. Nontando no longer made any resistance, though she still refused to eat.

Deeply perturbed at this new turn of events Kathie considered what was best to do. Should she send for Paul as being most likely to be able to influence Nontando? She could not be sure. Undecided, she promised herself to write to him as soon as possible and tell him all that had happened.

It was with a heavy heart that Kathie was compelled to leave Nontando and go back to her work. Lingering a moment at the door, she gave one last glance at the figure lying inert on the bed, with wide-open, unseeing eyes. She would hurry back, she told herself, and not all the matrons in the world would prevent her from getting early off duty.

Along the pale stretch of sand beside the sea the figure of a girl clad in a thin dress moves slowly yet lightly like a shadow. The wind laden with snow from the inland mountains whips the tender, unprotected flesh as the figure walks unheeding, nearer and nearer to the water's edge. She stops and looks round her at the expanse of sea and sky and the massed clouds moving majestically before the wind, and her gaze, uplifted, lingering, seems to reach out to a freedom and a beauty she had never known and never seen before.

So still and so long she stands, she seems already to be a part of insentient nature that knows nothing of the turmoil of the human spirit. But who can tell what thoughts, fed with the warm blood still coursing through her body, burn in that sensitive brain? What voiceless longings and desires are there, what gropings of the spirit, that eager but bewildered spirit? What visions and terrors of the nameless monsters of life lurking to rend her with pitiless tooth and fang? What desperation and despair?

The waves touch her feet.

She sees, yet does not see, that tumult of mounting waters rolling steadily towards her, for the tumult is within. As if with a last defiant gesture of her wilful heart, she moves steadily forward to meet the engulfing waves.

The waters plunge. She is gone. The massed phalanx of the clouds wheels darkly to the grey horizon. And only the low thunder of the sea sounds her parting dirge.

The spirit of Nontando will never more be broken on the wheel of life.

Book 3

HARVEST

CHAPTER 18

The return

Between Paul and the last surviving member of his family, his sister Nonceba, was a bond of affection greater than that between most brothers and sisters. She had been a mother to him and to her he owed all that he was now. She was a strong woman, strong in body and strong in character, and only those who knew her intimately were aware of the well of loving kindness that kept her spirit perpetually alive. She had never married. The children in the little school where she taught fulfilled all her instincts of motherhood – or nearly all.

When brother and sister met after so long an absence – it was seven years since he had boarded the train that carried him from her away to Cape Town – a mutual, but unexpressed, pleasure underlay the light tones of their greeting. Both knew how much this moment meant to the other; all the privation, all the effort, all the loneliness that belonged to the years between, were here transmuted to the joy of reunion.

She scanned his face with keen eyes and saw there a different Sipo from the youth she had sent out into the world seven years ago;

he was a man. And if he had still a long way to go before he reached maturity, yet she saw already the man that was to be – searching always to understand the world in which he found himself, never satisfied, more stern and more hard than the boy she had nurtured, his cheeks lean and rather sharp on the jaw, the forehead expressive of too intense thought. She did not know the town, but she learned something of what it could do to a man by looking into her brother's face. She told herself that he had come back to his people, still young in years, but mature in wisdom. The old men would give him respect and the young would look up to him. The old men, shrewd with the years, would shake him by the hand and say: *You are a man, my son.* Involuntarily she thought of their mother, who had never known her son.

They were standing together at the doorway of the small thatched house where as a child he had so often run in and out and had never paused to reflect that this was his home, this the land that was part of him and these his people who tilled the soil.

Nonceba spoke. 'How proud she would have been this day,' she said.

Paul knew it was their mother she meant. Their eyes met and he looked out over the land again.

It did not escape her attention that he was much moved by the changes he saw around him.

'Yes, things have changed since you went away,' she said.

'Everything looks so withered and bare, so dried up,' he exclaimed.

'The land is hungry,' she replied.

'Where are the cattle?'

'Yes, where are the cattle?' she echoed. 'They have taken away our cattle. The Native Commissioner says the people have too many cattle.'

'But the people look starved.'

'You have answered,' she said.

'And where are the sheep?'

'They have taken away our sheep and our goats. It is the new order of things.'

'I see only old people since I have returned – the old and the very young.'

'That is because the young men and women have gone away to

the city, as you did, Sipo, because they must. There is nothing for them to eat. No land to plough. The very soil is old and tired. For man no food, for the cattle no grass. The land is hungry and the people perish.'

Poverty. Poverty. He had not remembered it like this. All the way from the station to his home, a distance of several miles, he had been appalled by what he saw; the dilapidated condition of the huts, the barren fields, the few hungry cattle. It is true that when he had left home as a youth his people were poor, but it was never as bad as this. As he stood beside Nonceba, memory painted a picture of his boyhood days when he had lived with his family on the land they had inherited from their fathers. That had been before the drought and the depression years had decimated the stock in the district. Through a golden haze of memory he saw again the fields and hills where he used to roam, the tall green grass with the morning dew upon it, wetting his bare knees; the cattle his father owned – which the boy took to pasture with the other herd boys – the cattle with well-fed flanks, chewing the cud and gazing at him with soft, contented eyes; the young horses he used to ride bareback on the slopes of the neighbouring hills, whinnying as he approached them, kicking up their heels in an effort to unseat him, but finally acknowledging him as master. Oh, the days that have passed and gone! Where once waved a sea of grasses in the wind, now only a few meagre blades struggled to survive on the edge of the jagged dongas. And the cattle? These emaciated beasts lying here and there were but shadows of cattle; they were already dead, for they would never bear young. No doubt it was an idealised picture that Paul conjured out of the past, yet the contrast was sufficiently striking to bring home the truth to him who had been away in the city so long and now came back to see the plight of his people, the rapidly advancing destruction of land, cattle and human life.

'The land is hungry,' said his sister.

What was this blight that hung over their land and their people? Paul asked himself. He looked, and felt a deep anger stir within him. What could he do to change the face of poverty and desolation?

It was not only what he saw around him in that first startling picture of the countryside after his return that told the tale of poverty. In his work at the court he came into still closer contact with it, touched it,

251

smelt it, hated it. In the town he had already observed much to turn his thoughts sharply to question the nature of a society that demands such traffic in human misery. Now, in his home district, battling day after day with the petty cases in which the people became involved, he began to see law in terms of human life itself. What he saw at the court was an intensification of a process that was going on outside the courts. It was that section of the people who bore the badge of colour who received the most assiduous attentions of the arm of the law. To have a black skin seemed to be itself a crime to which many crimes were added so that a black man could hardly move or breathe without running the risk of breaking some law or other. Justice, far from being blind, saw through the spectacles of colour and operated on the assumption that poverty had an inexhaustible ability to pay court fines and lawyers' fees. Inside and outside the courts a monstrous juggernaut was passing over his people. Could the human spirit suffer this and survive?

Battling at the court with all the skill, cunning and eloquence at his command Paul was increasingly aware of his own helplessness.

But without realising it, he was growing in mental and moral stature. The shift to his home district, taken so tentatively, had been a step that was to have more far-reaching consequences than either he or Kathie could have foreseen. He had thrown himself into his work with all the vigour and enthusiasm of the eager young crusader determined to right the ills of the world. Here was something practical he could do to help his people. Here was the work for which he had been preparing himself for so many years, laborious years from which now he hoped to pluck the good harvest. He had mastered the intricacies of the law and with this weapon in hand (he had thought) he would gladly spend himself in defending his people. It was not going to be easy, he knew. Of course he would encounter the hostility of the whites, to whom the idea of a black lawyer was anathema – a violation of that which was divinely ordained.

But for this kind of thing Paul was fully prepared. In his contacts with them he could expect, at best, a tacit truce to open war, a grudging acknowledgment that he could take his place in the legal arena on his own merits, without assistance from the white man. If his lance should be shattered and his brave plumes bite the dust, so much the worse for him. It was what everyone would expect. A black man who contrived to enter a profession and also made a success of it, was, to say the least, a disturbing phenomenon. If such a phenomenon should ever show signs of increase and black lawyers began to infest the courts up and down the country, then indeed there would be cause for alarm. However, one black locust did not make a plague. So he could be tolerated, though not encouraged. To contend with such an attitude was all in the day's work for Paul; in fact it added zest to it.

What he had found disturbing was the peculiar sensation at first of being a stranger among his own people. Not that he consciously separated himself from them. Far from it. He had once observed a teacher, newly come from college, dressed in his fine clothes and browbeating the peasants, and the sight had turned his stomach. Yet at first he found it difficult to make contact with the men and women round him; they appeared different from what he remembered; their world was so much more circumscribed, due to the sheer poverty of their existence; their vision was narrowed to the day-to-day problems of merely staying alive. On the other hand, he too, appeared different to them. He was their son, he was one of their own who had made good and they were proud of him, but he had not only gone to the city, he had entered a white man's profession. His very clothes separated him from them: he was a townsman, while they wore the garments of poverty.

Paul had no doubt that time would break down the reserve that existed between them. Let him conduct a few cases successfully; then the word would spread and the tendrils of communication would soon establish themselves. Thus he had every incentive to throw himself into his work. Besides, he meant to prove to Kathie that their separation had not been in vain. He would rise in his profession unless deliberate impediments were put in his way. The first few months passed more quickly than he would have thought possible when he and Kathie had parted.

Handling cases day in and day out, he came face to face with the burning question that concerned his people more than any other – the land question. The desperate need for land. The city, with its own grim problems, had pushed this question of the land to the back of his mind. Here it was inescapable. It pursued him day and night, in the courts and out of them, in his working hours and in the evenings when friends gathered at his house. There was an atmosphere of discontent in the district; the peasants were restive; one peasant would be tried for breaking down the fences that kept him from putting his cattle to graze on the pasture land that had belonged to the people for generations; another would be fined for refusing to cull his cattle or bring them to the official pound to be branded. For one reason or another there was a continual clash between them and the authorities.

It was not always easy for Paul to defend his clients. He was trained in the law and pledged to carry out its tenets; but he was also a black man and a brother of his people. This created an ever increasing conflict in his mind, pushing him towards a criticism of the very laws within the framework of which he had to work. The new regulations under a scheme to rehabilitate the land hit the African peasants hard. On the face of it, it seemed a laudable scheme to prevent the further devastations of soil erosion by limiting and fencing off pasture land and compelling the peasants to cut down the number of their cattle. But they had an answer to this – to them an irrefutable answer: 'Land! Give us land!' Then and then only would they believe that the proposed schemes were for their benefit and not for their further destruction.

Not once, but many times Paul discovered that the old peasant, illiterate, ignorant of facts and figures, yet shrewd, patient and wise, would brush aside the inessentials with his soil-worn hand and get down to fundamentals, drawing his conclusions with inescapable logic.

One day as he was crossing the fields a peasant called to him from far off and Paul drew near to where he was working in his plot of ground. They all knew him by this time, greeting him by name whenever he appeared, speaking out their grievances with a simple forthrightness of speech.

'Yes,' said the old man. 'I had ten cattle and they took away five. They said I had too many cattle. Look at my kraal. It is empty. Look at the ground, dry as a bone. And when the women want to make fire, where shall they find the cow dung?

'Come here, my son. Look at my unploughed fields. They lie fallow for want of oxen to plough. Look there! And there!' and he pointed to his neighbours' fields lying bare like his own.

'Come with me,' he continued, an eager bitterness to demonstrate the truth to Paul quickening his steps. Paul followed him to the door of his hut where he stooped and entered. In the dim interior an elderly woman and a young girl stood up as they entered and gave greeting, which he returned with courtesy.

Without giving Paul an opportunity to converse with his wife, the old peasant went up to the wall where an empty calabash lay on its side, held it upside down and said: 'If we have too many cattle, where is our amasi? The children no longer know what it is to drink amasi.' Then, beating the calabash with the palm of his hand so that it gave a hollow sound, he cried: 'Let no man come to me and say I have too many cattle. I will tell him he lies!'

With that, he flung it to the ground. The girl silently picked it up and held it against her breast, looking shyly at Paul.

'This is my daughter's child,' said the old man. 'Her mother is working in the town. She is a good girl, though she does not know the amasi, eh, my child?'

Blushing at being made the centre of attention the young girl bent down to place the calabash against the wall again as carefully as if it had been filled with the precious liquid.

After exchanging a few friendly words with the woman, who knew his sister very well, Paul took his departure. And as a parting shot the peasant called out to him: 'They have promised us fine grass for our cattle one fine day – and meantime those things that are to eat their fine grass are being killed off. So much for their promises.'

Confronted with these and similar instances of hardship, frequently challenged in his position as defendant of a peasant who had broken one of the many regulations hedging them in as sharply as a barbed wire fence, Paul was compelled to ask himself what he should do. Prove a man innocent who had broken the law? But upon what argument? Or should he prove guilty the peasant who obeyed a law common to all mankind – the preservation of his children? What shifts must he resort to, searching in all the nooks and crannies of the law by which a guilty (or was it innocent?) man might slip through. And what mean, piddling business was this to one who had set out to master a great calling and at the same time serve his people?

As if this state of uneasiness were not enough, there was old Daniso to plague him in the evenings with his never-ending questions. Daniso was an old friend of the family, a man who had revered their mother and was especially devoted to Nonceba, since between them they kept burning brightly the dead woman's memory. He was a lonely old man, his five children having all left him to go to the town. He and his two youngest grandsons, children of a daughter who had died, were looked after by a relative, a middle-aged woman, who bossed him as assuredly as he liked to boss other people. It was natural for him to take an interest in Paul Sipo as if he were his own son and it became his custom to come round in the evenings to sit with the brother and sister.

Towards Paul he adopted a careless, rough-and-ready, half jocular manner which the young man did not always relish, though Nonceba perceived that underneath his truculence he was proud of this 'son' of his and deeply interested in the way he was shaping. It was not the first time that Daniso had seen young men go off to the town and come back with what he considered a completely distorted view of things, including themselves, and he would shake his head in sad amusement at the conceit of these children. So he was all the more eager to test the understanding of a young man like Sipo – to be sure, only a child, but a child who promised to grow a beard sooner than most. Of course it was right and proper that Daniso should appear rough with him; if the boy came anywhere near his expectations of him, the roughness would do him no harm but only serve to show the mettle of his pasture. He would taunt Paul a little, the more to draw him out of his shell. If this boy (as he dreamed) was one day going to be a leader among his people, he would have to throw off the reserve behind which, he was sure, lay a good deal of latent strength. Meantime he must not be allowed to think that he knew everything.

Very often the conversation turned on the cases Paul was handling.

'So you think you're getting somewhere with this law business,' remarked Daniso laconically.

Paul did not answer directly. 'It was time that a black man stood up in court to defend his own people.'

'That is true, that is true, my son. You think that a black man must be more just to his people than a white man?'

'Undoubtedly.'

'Even if he thinks like a townsman?'

'You have a wrong idea of a townsman, father.'

'Maybe. Maybe. But then I've seen some queer specimens coming back from the town. To see them walking through our village, mincing on their toes with their noses turned skyward, you wonder what manner of place it is that turns a man into a fool.'

Daniso took his pipe from his mouth and laughed the slow, wise laugh of the old who have seen many things. Paul joined in the laugh. When it was over, Paul continued: 'I have seen a white man in court, supposed to be the defending counsel and he argued the case against the accused better than the prosecutor himself. That was because he *thinks* white and not black.'

'You always think black of course?'

'I think as a human being.'

'Ah! Good. If only all men thought as men. Now will you tell me why you took up the law, my son?'

'I wanted to study justice and help our people.'

'Ah!' Daniso puffed hard, then deliberately examined the bowl of his pipe, apparently engrossed with the business of smoking. Paul waited.

'You wanted to study justice?' remarked the old man at last. 'Justice. That is a great thing. So you studied the law from top to bottom. And did you find this justice?'

'I have tried to master the law. With what purpose you know.'

Daniso refilled his pipe.

'I have no doubt that you have the law at your fingertips. And you have a nimble tongue when you like, as I heard in the court today.'

'You heard me, Father?' Paul was pleased.

'That I did,' replied Daniso. 'I've heard better in our own councils. But it wasn't bad. It wasn't bad. There's one thing that troubles me, though.'

'What is that?'

'You said you wanted to help our people. But whose law is it?'

'Whose law?'

'Who made the laws?'

'The lawmakers,' answered Paul.

The old man smiled. 'Yes, and who is this lawmaker?'

'The white man makes the laws.'

'Ah, the white man. And that is the instrument you propose to use for helping the black man?'

'I think I see your meaning, Father.' Paul spoke slowly, almost unwillingly.

'Sipo, my son,' continued Daniso. 'When you said you took up law in order to bring justice to our people, I knew from these words how young you were. You speak like a man who never knew what it is to be conquered.'

'But I do know what conquest is. In my flesh and bone I feel it every day, as every black man must feel it.'

'I still say, you do not know conquest, not as we old men know it. For we who are old, we remember what once we were. We know what we have lost. You, who are young, you know what you want to win. That is the difference between us. You seek, but you do not know how to find what you seek.'

'Can *you* tell us?' asked Paul.

'I can tell you one thing, my son. When a conqueror makes the laws for the conquered, it is not out of a love for justice.'

Paul pondered the truth of this statement. 'And it reminds me of what a white man once said to me – though I did not heed him at the time.'

Daniso made a slight grimace expressive of his scepticism.

'A white man?' he said.

'Yes, Father, we must not make the mistake of thinking that all white men are the same.'

'That may be,' replied Daniso in a non-committal tone.

'I may as well confess to you,' continued Paul, 'that I have been troubled about the work I have undertaken. Too often I seem to beat my head against a stone wall.'

'You are not satisfied?' Daniso gave him a shrewd glance from under his brows.

'I am not satisfied.'

'That is good.'

'You are not very comforting, Father.'

'You are on the road to wisdom, my son.'

And with that the old man rose and took his departure, Nonceba having long since retired to her bed.

All these circumstances were adding fuel to Paul's state of doubt as to his ability to help his people within the framework of the law; living and breathing the land question all around him, day in and day out, he was compelled to take stock of his position. While not fully aware of the nature of the conflict in Paul's mind, Nonceba, who observed her brother closely, from time to time made such caustic remarks that affected him more strongly than she knew and contributed in no small measure to these doubts that assailed him. Now to put certain questions to oneself is no easy matter, especially when they concern the fundamental position on which one stands. A man instinctively shrinks from such a step. Yet given a temperament like Paul's, it is inescapable. It might have taken a longer time, however, if Nonceba had not brought to her brother's notice the misfortunes of a friend of hers, Mrs Dhlomo, whose husband had fallen foul of the law. That the events which followed brought a crisis in Paul's affairs is not surprising. The emotional ties binding him to Nonceba since the formative years of childhood made it natural that she should influence him in such a matter. Indeed it might be said that the keen sense of justice and humanity that was the keystone of his character had been implanted by herself.

One day she related to Paul the story of what happened to Dhlomo when he came back from the city. If she was in no hurry to tell him the essential details of it, he knew he would only delay matters still further if he showed any impatience and tried to hurry her. So, being wise from experience, he let her talk, giving form and substance to the thoughts she had been storing up for many years.

In her long life she had seen great changes come over the face of the land and disrupt the lives of the people, and she was one of the few who had survived. (Yes, thought Paul, survived with a stubborn tenacity that is part of her nature.) She had seen the young men, the strong men go off to the towns. She had seen the women struggling to carry on by themselves, at first with hope, comforting themselves with the thought of the day when their men would return to them. But for most of them that day never dawned. The women would struggle on, their faces hardening, their eyes emptying of hope and at last empty even of memory, existing only in the present, grimly, doggedly, meeting the day's needs, silent, or bitter of tongue. The children about them would run wild, for the little school where Nonceba taught held but a handful of those clamouring to get in and she had to turn them away – she who would have taken them all to her bosom if she could. The boys and girls would also grow restless, disrespectful to their elders, discontented with their lot, hemmed in by the barren soil. And the day came when they, too, looked over the horizon whither their fathers and big brothers had gone and felt the need to follow them into the unknown. Their mothers would reproach them and scold them, fearful of what would happen to them, but could not hold them back. For what could they offer their children but the bitter bread of poverty and stagnant days? And there were taxes to be paid, though a man had nothing. Truly, they that did these things to the people were like the baboons who choke their young to get the food out of their mouths. And so the young men would follow their fathers and many of them would vanish into the big city, never to be heard of again.

Sometimes a man would return and great would be the joy of his returning. Such a man was Dhlomo, whose tale Nonceba proceeded to tell. From far off the children of the village caught sight of him trudging across the fields, dressed like a townsman, and carrying a box on his shoulders. As he drew nearer to the huts the elders gave him greeting, which he returned with a hearty shout, but did not pause till he had reached his own hut. It was empty. Dropping his box carefully to the ground and straightening his back, he turned to the children who had followed at his heels like birds behind the plough.

'Where is the mother of Jamani?' he said, asking for his wife.

One boy taller than the rest pointed to a distant part of the fields.

'She is busy over yonder. I will go and fetch her,' and off he ran, the man meanwhile squatting in the shadow of the hut till she should come. The children clustered round, still staring, curious, at his town clothes.

At last the figure of his wife appears. Dhlomo gets to his feet and walks to meet her. She stands still a moment, then gives a little cry and quickens her step. The husband waves the children off, they scamper away; husband and wife are alone. No man may describe the joy of it.

But in the days that followed, when they who had been forced to live without each other tried to bind up the broken threads again, it was not easy, for they had become strangers to each other. He was no longer a peasant, but had brought back with him the habits and speech of the city. He learned that his mother had died during his absence and at the news a shadow came over his face. In the city he had forgotten his mother; he had not written to his people and he did not know how it was with them. His wife, at the memory of it all, broke into reproaches for his silence, for the loneliness, for the burden left for her to bear alone. He bade her be silent. What did *she* know of what a man endures in the city? Then he asked where his eldest son Jamani was, the stripling who had a strong look of his father and promised to grow into a fine youth. The mother hesitated in her answers, hiding the truth about their son. He had gone off to work for a white farmer, but he was very discontented; he was past managing even before he left home.

'It had to be,' she said. 'We had no choice.'

There was a heavy silence between them.

She had been left to manage their small plot of land herself. She told him she could not get enough out of the soil to feed their children. And Dhlomo bent down, letting the grey, dry earth trickle through his fingers, while memory came back to him who had been so long in the city. There was an expression of pain on his face. In his absence something had gone out of the soil and something had gone out of him too. The silence was heavy between them.

Suddenly he spoke. He will buy a few head of cattle, so that they may till the soil. There is money in the wooden box he has brought back with him. It isn't much, but he has managed somehow to save it. Their hearts stir with hope again and next day he sets out on his mission, his wife waving him goodbye, without fear, for does she not know that her man will come back to her, and with cattle that will give her children milk to drink and oxen for the ploughing? Life is good after all!

In three days' time her man returns with the cattle he has bought; they are not what he would have bought in the old days, not by a long way, but what is a man to do? He had no choice but accept what the farmer offered. Let him not think of the price or it would take away all his pleasure. He'd make it up somehow, even if he had to go back to the town for a short spell. His wife needn't be afraid he wouldn't come back soon this time; let her not be so downcast. Did they not have the cattle? With the oxen they'd till the fields twice as fast. Slapping the flanks of the beast nearest him, his hand tingling with the joy of it, he sees already in his mind's eye the dark furrows sprouting with the young green shoots, he sees the ripening ears waving in the wind, ready for the hand of the reaper, the harvest of all his labours.

So husband and wife set to work.

But one day the police come. What could the police want at his place? Could it be his son who had got into trouble?

But no, it was not his son. They had come to take away his cattle.

His cattle! They must be mad. How could they touch his cattle?

Then the police told him that if he didn't come quietly, him and his cattle too, there would only be more trouble for him.

But what had he done? Dhlomo asked. The cattle were his. Let them not doubt his word. Let them come with him to the farmer from whom he had bought them. But his words were of no avail. The police said they were not there to argue with him. He had bought the cattle without permission of the authorities and they must confiscate them. At this his wife gave a shrill cry, letting out a torrent of angry words on the police.

'Hush, woman,' said Dhlomo. 'This is a serious matter and I must understand it properly.'

One of the policemen was a black man like himself so Dhlomo decided to speak to him and ask him to explain to the white policeman that there was some mistake. The black policeman, however, would not listen and struck him, whereupon Dhlomo lost his temper and struck back.

'You'll never get my cattle from me! Never!' he shouted as the two policemen dragged him off in front of his wife's eyes. Mrs Dhlomo was no longer crying, but stood dumb as if a thunderbolt had descended out of heaven and cracked open the roof of her hut, leaving her exposed to the relentless storm. Dhlomo's cattle were impounded and he himself was thrown into jail for resisting arrest as well as being illegally in possession of cattle.

When Nonceba had finished her tale, there was silence in the room. Paul had not spoken, nor did he make any comment. For her it was a foregone conclusion that he would defend Dhlomo in court. He expressed his readiness, explaining that application would first have to be made to his firm. She was equally certain that he would be able to get Dhlomo off, and not willing at this stage to be too sanguine, he assured her that at least there was a reasonable chance that he would succeed.

'Reasonable!' snorted Nonceba. 'The whole thing is unreasonable. I ask you, Sipo, as a man, not as a lawyer, where was the crime? Is it to buy oxen to plough so that he might have food for his family? Or is it to seize a man for so doing, take his cattle from him and then jail him? Tell me. Who commits the crime?'

'It is true the law is hard on the individual,' said Paul.

'What a way is that to speak? If a law destroys men it is not worthy of men. Such a law is against all human law. But I've no doubt you'll tell them so,' she concluded.

At this Paul laughed ruefully. 'The court has its own way of conducting things, and I'm afraid it is not your way.'

'More's the pity,' she retorted.

Paul laughed again. But when he was alone he pondered over her words. Her uncompromising way of looking at things fitted only too well into his growing self-doubt. Dhlomo's experience was by no means exceptional, only it happened to strike the anvil of Paul's mind at a critical moment so that the question of getting him acquitted of the charge assumed an importance not only for its own sake – for Dhlomo's sake and that of his wife – but in relation to Paul himself. His sister's words: *Such a law is against all human law*, seemed to him to contain a challenge, not only of the law as it was at present constituted, but a challenge to himself.

Meantime it had been agreed that Paul's firm of lawyers would handle the case and Paul undertook Dhlomo's defence.

There is no doubt that he took the case very seriously. In so far as it was a test case, whatever decision was taken would affect the other peasants; if Dhlomo should be acquitted they would know better where they stood; if he were found guilty the law would be more stringently applied against them. The trust placed in him by the peasants put a great responsibility on Paul's shoulders. Of course, to lose a case was part of the ordinary hazards of a lawyer's career, nor would Paul lose prestige through it. Yet he did not take comfort from this reflection. For him the issue was a larger one. It seemed to him that he himself was on trial, before the people, before Nonceba. And what of Kathie? Her fate, too, was bound up with this issue.

CHAPTER 19

The trial

Sometimes at the end of the court session Paul would separate himself from everyone, irked by the atmosphere of the courtroom, oppressed by the tales the people gathered round him poured into his ears, disinclined even to face the affectionate solicitations of his sister when he returned home. One day, with a letter from Kathie in his pocket, he set out across the veld towards the setting sun as if he would pursue it across the horizon. Unattended by a single cloud it hung like tarnished bronze in a pale sky that was gradually misting over to a smoky blue, for it had been a hot day with a hot wind blowing so that the dust of a dying soil tainted the atmosphere. Involuntarily he recalled that first day he had met Kathie under the ramparts of Table Mountain; he saw again the water lilies laving their shadows in the pool; he saw the rippling of the reflected waters playing upon Kathie's face, and at the memory his heart contracted with longing. Had it been wise for them to separate after all? Did they not pay too heavily, letting the days and the nights slip past, never to return? Taking her last letter from his pocket he read it again slowly, savouring every word, tasting every nuance of feeling, both what she expressed and – as he told himself – what she tried to hide.

With the letter still in his hand, he looked up in time to see the sun taking its last stride before disappearing into the darkened earth. And the sight sharpened the feeling within him. It was as if something within himself had gone out. If only Kathie were beside him now. The touch of her hand, the warm glance of her eyes, the quiet tones of her voice. To her at this moment he could have unburdened his mind of its doubts; the sights he had witnessed since coming back to his home village, the stark conditions of his people and his own increasing sense of frustration in his work. How well she would understand and sympathise. Didn't she too, in her day's work at the hospital come constantly in contact with suffering? She also knew what it was to feel helpless as if her weak hands could do nothing to staunch this vast social wound.

Arriving home late he was met at the door by Nonceba, who had a reproach ready on her lips, but contented herself only with the question: 'Where did you go, Sipo?'

'Oh, I just went for a breath of fresh air,' he lied. 'But it's so hot.'

'It'll be cooler inside. And come and eat your food. We can't have you wasting away, you know.'

Paul had no stomach for food, but remonstrance was in vain. He might cut a fine figure in court, but to his big sister he was still the little boy she had mothered with more fondness than a mother herself. Nonceba sat and watched every mouthful.

'And now I hope you aren't going to turn the night into the day,' she said. 'Every night this week you've been hard at it.'

'I want to make sure I've got everything on Dhlomo's case.'

'You'll get him off if anybody can.'

'That's just it, Sis N'ceba. There's such a tangle of laws. If they don't catch a man out with one law they'll dig up another.'

'Keep a clear head on you and you'll manage them. I know you. Now go and have a good sleep, my child, and shut the book.'

Paul decided it was good policy to obey his big sister and retired to bed – with his book.

It had taken Paul some time before he could bring himself to speak to Nonceba about Kathie. He knew his sister would accept her simply because she was his choice; she could not believe that he would do other than choose a woman worthy of his family. She had a very strong sense of family pride that had been her bulwark in her life of hardship and she assumed that her young brother in all the vicissitudes of city life would derive strength from the same source. In this she was in a sense correct; though Paul himself would not have called it family pride, he had an integrity that had been nourished at the fountain of family affection since it prompted an unconscious acceptance of his sister's standards of action.

But Paul, in choosing as his future wife a coloured woman, had done something that his sister might not find easy to understand. Within her own sphere Nonceba's knowledge of life and human relationship was both wide and deep; nevertheless she knew nothing of the city in which, as in a vast crucible, people of different races mingled, married and intermarried. Her conception of what coloured people were like was derived from those few whom she came across in her immediate environment – a poor, downtrodden, landless people, despised by all. In these coloured labourers she did not recognise anything in common with herself. It would not be easy for her to visualise Kathie, a townswoman, a cultured woman, a woman whom Paul would be proud to make his wife.

So first of all when they sat together in the evenings he would talk to Nonceba about the city, painting a vivid picture of a seething, jostling humanity, each one struggling to maintain his foothold. He conveyed to her by his very restraint the anguish of a man in his first impact with such a world: the shock and outrage, the mind bracing itself to meet them, the hardening of the senses. More than anything else his imagination had been stirred by the spectacle of the destruction of human feeling brought about by the racial fears and hatreds which permeated this society of white and black and coloured and Indian.

Nonceba listened while Paul tried to convey to her experiences that she recognised to be the same in essence as she, too, had encountered in this far-off rural district. The scene was more complex perhaps, but the conflict was the same.

'In town or country, Sipo, the struggle of life hardens feeling,' she said.

'It is more than that,' exclaimed Paul. 'It is a madness of the mind that neither sees nor hears, nor thinks nor feels with one's fellowmen. It is a madness that infects the very victims of this racial injustice. For in this jungle, Sis N'ceba, our people turn and rend one another.'

'That is their despair,' she answered. 'But I refuse to believe that even with all this madness humanity is dead. That is not my experience. It is rare, but it burns all the more brightly for the surrounding darkness.'

'I have found it, too,' said Paul, and moved out of his usual reserve he proceeded to tell her about his meeting with Kathie, the ripening of their friendship and something also of her difficulties within her family.

Nonceba listened and watched as he spoke. No doubt it was an idealised picture. How like him, she thought, to give all to such a woman. He had never been one for half measures. Now that the barriers were down he went on to tell her how they had decided that he should take up this job in his home district though it meant a separation for a year or more, if he agreed to his firm's proposals. At the moment he wasn't sure.

'Did she try to hold you back?' asked Nonceba.

'No. It was Kathie who urged me to go.'

'That is good,' she said.

She decided that Kathie, whatever else she was, must be a young woman of character. A selfish woman would have clung to him for fear of losing him.

'I wish you could meet her,' exclaimed Paul. 'Then you would see for yourself what she is.'

'Isn't there a chance that I may?' she asked, smiling at his eagerness.

'Yes. Yes, there is. She is due for a holiday in about a month's time. She could come here. Would you mind, Sis N'ceba?'

'Of course not. But what about her?'

'Oh, she! Wait till you see her!'

Though Kathie had once mentioned her coming to see him he had not thought it would be so easy, partly because he knew he would be busy and more because he feared it would be strange for her, accustomed all her life to the town. It meant bringing her into a strange community where life was simple and even crude. People might not be friendly ... But all the difficulties melted away now that he had spoken to his sister.

There and then he sat down to write to Kathie and put the suggestion to her. He had not written such a cheerful letter for a long time, for the effort to hide from her all his doubts and misgivings had resulted in him writing letters that revealed everything to her, while telling her nothing. His omissions had only added to her anxiety and her feeling of being shut out of his confidence. Now the very act of writing to her after his talk with his sister released some of his pent-up emotion. Now his problems no longer seemed so formidable; perhaps he had been making too much of them, shadow-boxing with monsters, exaggerating obstacles that hardly existed. The very thought of her already at his side lifted the weight from his mind. He resolved that he would hide nothing from her. He owed it to her to discuss fully his present position so that together they would find out what was best for him to do.

Kathie's answer to Paul's letter came promptly; she would be very pleased to spend a holiday at Paul's village and she was looking forward to meeting his sister, though she was a little bit afraid of her, from all that he had told her about Nonceba.

'Now what nonsense have you been saying to Kathie?' scolded Nonceba when Paul read out this passage from the letter.

'I made you out to be the most domineering ogre that ever was!' he declared, ducking in time to escape the flat of her hand on his impudent head.

The following days passed quickly. Paul had two things to occupy his thoughts: the impending case of Dhlomo and the coming of Kathie, and they were in a sense bound up together. He set great store on winning this case for his people, knowing also that whatever he achieved concerned his future and Kathie's. While his experience in the country had made him seriously consider the wisdom of the course he had chosen, at the present moment his mind was in a state of excitement and hope rather than depression. In the courts he was at the top of his form; he argued keenly and well and the whites grudgingly admitted that he knew his job. As for his own people, it was evident that every day increased their admiration of him, their faith in him, confirming Daniso's judgement that here was a young man capable of becoming a leader of his people. Paul could not but catch the warmth of affection surrounding him, all the more because it was expressed in the undertones rather than in the obvious and cheap overtones of popularity. There was so much simple faith and generosity in the attitude of the peasants towards him, their eagerness to take him to their hearts so much revealed the spiritual starvation of their everyday existence, which made his advent so precious to them, that he was both gladdened and saddened by the experience. He felt deeply his responsibility.

. Each time he went to the prison to interview Dhlomo he did his best to cheer him as to the outcome of the case. He found the man bewildered and resentful; already embittered by his experiences in the town, he felt that he had come home only to be caught again on the wheel of the law.

'They hounded me when I was working in the town,' he said, 'and now they hound me off my own bit of land and take from me the very cattle I buy. Yes, and it was blood money that bought those beasts. All those years I sweated for it. Where is a man to live without fear? Where can he lay his head in peace?'

Paul assured him once again that he would do everything to get him off, but felt it necessary at the same time not to be too confident of the issue. The police had also charged him with resisting arrest.

'And it was a black man that laid his hand on me,' exclaimed Dhlomo, spitting at the memory of it.

'When a man puts on a uniform it does queer things to him,' said Paul.

Dhlomo spat his contempt again.

From Nonceba, Paul heard how Mrs Dhlomo was living only for the outcome of the trial and her husband's return.

'Do you think they'll be able to pay the fine if the case is lost?' asked Paul.

'No, they will not,' she answered. 'But do you think they will find Dhlomo guilty?'

'It is not a simple case.'

'If they do find him guilty, it will be a complete miscarriage of justice,' declared Nonceba emphatically.

'Is that a challenge to me?'

'I know you'll do your best,' she said.

As for Daniso, as the day drew near all he said was: 'So you think you can beat the law, my son?' and laughed his slow, wise laugh.

Paul's mood, however, was fairly optimistic when on the very morning of the trial he received a letter from Kathie. Recognising the handwriting, he was surprised at the lightness of the envelope because she was in the habit of sending him a fat letter which it was his joy to spill open and devour its contents page by page. She had a vivid pen and gladly gave him all those little details of thought and perception that fill the gap of time and beguile a lover with the sense of nearness. Paul tore open the envelope.

Nontando was dead.

Briefly, Kathie told him of those last tragic days, the premature birth of the child, the struggle to bring the young mother back to an acceptance of life; then the death of the child, Nontando's despair, her disappearance; the finding of her body.

Nontando – that wayward child – dead, and by her own hand. What despair must have driven her to such a deed? Memory laid her warm hand upon him, revealing Nontando as she had sat beside him many nights when he was poring over his books. He saw again her sombre, intent gaze. He shuddered. How had he failed the child? Could he have prevented this? Turning again to Kathie's letter he thought he detected a peculiar restraint about it. Was it from a desire to spare him? He wished at that moment that he could leave everything and take the train to the city. He must learn more from Kathie about what had happened ... Good God, what madness possessed him! Dhlomo's case was due within the next hour. Time to think of Nontando hereafter.

But the stubborn little ghost of her refused to be banished. The chill thought persisted – how had he failed the child? He told himself he must not allow this to come between him and the task in front of him. All the more reason he must win the case.

The small courtroom was packed to overflowing for the trial of Dhlomo. With the first light of dawn on the horizon the peasants had begun to arrive from far and near, some of them on horseback. The case of Dhlomo was the case of all of them and they had come to hear their son, Paul Sipo Mangena, who had come back from the town, back to his own people, speak for them and defend them in the white man's courts. Just outside the village they left their horses to graze then, sticks in hand, and many with their blankets slung across their shoulders, they made their way slowly to the courtroom which was situated at the centre of the village not far from the local prison. Arrived too early, before the opening of the doors, they stood about in groups, smoking and conversing about the things that most nearly concerned them: the fencing off of the pastureland that had been theirs for generations, the culling of their cattle, the price of mealies which they had to buy at the local store and now the present case of the man charged with buying oxen to till his fields without permission of the authorities.

At last the doors opened and the people streamed in while the orderlies herded them into those sections marked for non-Europeans, and separated from those marked 'Europeans only'. Many of them had to stand at the back and still more outside the windows. They were quiet and decorous, waiting and watching. They had a stolid appearance, for men close to the soil learn to wait for the revolution of the seasons which bring planting and harvest in their appointed times. But these peasants knew the bitter waiting that brings no harvest; the seasons that bear neither seed nor fruit.

When Dhlomo was brought in by the police orderly, men spoke in subdued whispers about the changed appearance of the man, for many were seeing him for the first time since his return from the city. From where he stood his glance passed deliberately over the court and the assembled crowd answered their brother with their eyes. Then as Paul entered a murmur went up amongst them.

'Why,' said one old man who had come from far, 'he is a beardless boy! Can such a young head hold all the wisdom that only the years can bring?'

'Wait till you hear him speak,' answered another. 'He has a tongue as cunning as a serpent when he has his opponent in his nets.'

'Silence in the court!' shouted the orderly, at whose signal everybody stood up while the magistrate entered and took his seat.

And so the proceedings began. With intent faces the peasants listened. Where necessary the interpreters translated.

The two policemen, the one European, the other a black man, gave evidence of how Dhlomo had defied them when they came to arrest him and had assaulted the black policeman. Dhlomo looked particularly incensed while the black policeman gave evidence against him.

'The dog, he speaks false!' he shouted.

Murmurs of agreement were heard through the court, whereupon the magistrate, with a sour look, commanded silence, threatening to clear the court.

When the time came for Paul to address the court he expressed himself at first in clear, measured terms, but gradually allowed his emotion to emerge in full force. He spoke in the language of the people, for it was they whom he was addressing as much as the magistrate, and in defending Dhlomo he was in effect defending the African peasants and giving voice to their grievances. In the courts, surrounded by the incomprehensible trappings of legal procedure they stood dumb and patient, but he gave them back their own voice, let them hear their own thoughts, formulated their aspirations. There was not a sound in court while he was speaking. Those beyond the barred windows pressed forward in the hope of catching his words. All eyes were turned to this tall figure that gesticulated sparingly even at the height of his eloquence.

He painted a picture of the African peasant who for generations had known no other means of livelihood besides tilling the land, and though now, like Dhlomo, he had been driven to seek work in the town, he still looked to the soil as his heritage. His cattle were the very backbone of his existence; they were milk and food to him; they were the bread of his children; from sunrise to sunset the activity of the family revolved about the cattle kraal; in birth and death, in marriage, in war, in celebrations of all kinds cattle were part of the life of the community. How should a man live without cattle? To till his soil he must have a span of oxen. If drought should decimate his cattle what should he do but replenish his stock with new beasts? Such things were an act of God which he must endure patiently. But what if men should come to seize his plough oxen? In resisting the action of the police, Dhlomo was simply, as he thought, defending himself and his family from unlawful seizure of his property. When a peasant was told that such things as the taking away of his plough oxen were for his benefit he found it very hard to believe. Paul went on to stress Dhlomo's ignorance of the new regulations since he was only a week home from the city.

Paul's voice had strengthened and deepened with the emotion that carried him forward to a height of eloquence he had never before reached. There was complete silence in the court as he paused a moment to consult his papers. He then proceeded to outline the legal aspect of the case, quoting authorities to emphasise his point. He had returned to the measured but forceful tones with which he had begun his speech. In conclusion he called upon the court to declare Dhlomo not guilty.

As Paul sat down it was evident that he had carried the people with him. Though there were only a few murmured exclamations, men flashed their appreciation and sympathy with the quick glances of their eyes. Nonceba laid her hand over that of Dhlomo's wife and smiled. Only Daniso shook his head, half proud, half sorry at Paul's eloquence, knowing its futility in such a place. Now the orderly shouted: 'Court adjourns!' and with the exit of the magistrate there was a general exodus; while he and a few other privileged people refreshed themselves with tea the crowd drifted outside, glad to stretch its legs and air its opinions on the case.

It was evident that the free tone of Paul's speech had incensed the white community. It was more than mere curiosity that had brought them to court. There was a general feeling among the local farmers, traders and officials that the blacks were getting out of hand and it would be none too healthy if the Dhlomo case was decided in his favour. Thus during the brief recess there were acrimonious comments flying back and forth. It was agreed that Paul's speech had gone very much beyond the bounds of legal propriety.

'Give a native an inch and he'll take a mile,' remarked a white storekeeper to his neighbour, who was a farmer in the district.

'Ja! That's what comes of letting a kaffir meddle with the law. This *klong* here doesn't know nothing. He doesn't know that a law court's a place for dispensing justice and not a soapbox for a *verdomde* troublemaker.'

'I don't know what the world's coming to,' remarked another. 'The sooner we kick this agitator out of the village, the better. Look at the crowd here today, positively hanging on his lips. That's what comes of educating a baboon.'

'I wonder what kind of firm it was that brought him here in the first place?' asked a farmer who was waiting to be called as a witness in a case of stock theft.

'It's them *verdomde* Jews, you may be sure!' chimed in the storekeeper.

As to the outcome of the case, they decided that the magistrate knew his business and the more drastic the penalty he imposed, the better. Here was a new scheme for rehabilitating the natives' land and they sabotaged it at every turn. 'You'd never teach these natives what was good for them,' they said. 'It would take centuries to pull them out of barbarism.' This was the general opinion of the officials, and they ought to know, they said, because they had to handle natives every day.

'Silence in the court!' barked the orderly, and business was resumed.

The prosecutor now put the case for the crown. In the course of his speech he said: 'The defending attorney has built up an emotional atmosphere by painting a harrowing picture of the sufferings of the natives – a picture which, in my opinion, is extremely questionable. But all this is entirely irrelevant to the case. The court is called upon to decide the issue on a point of law. The accused has without doubt violated the regulations under the new scheme and moreover aggravated his offence not only by resisting arrest but by assaulting an officer of the law. These facts have not been denied ... '

He concluded by asking the court to find the accused guilty. He also went on to ask the magistrate in deciding on the sentence to bear in mind the general unsettled state among the natives at present. The sentence, in his opinion, should be of such a nature as to have a salutary effect on others and teach them to respect law and order.

Dhlomo was found guilty and sentenced to three months' hard labour, or a £20 fine. At the verdict a wave of resentment passed through the crowd of Africans who packed the court and those outside seemed to press too closely to the windows.

'Order in the court!' roared the orderly. The magistrate rose and disappeared through the door at the back of the court; officials and lawyers filed out; without a glance at his white colleagues Paul gathered up his papers and stepped quickly outside where he was immediately surrounded by a crowd variously expressing their anger at Dhlomo's conviction, their praise for Paul's defence and their determination not to be cowed by such verdicts. Mrs Dhlomo stepped forward and thanked Paul with tears in her eyes, while Nonceba for once had nothing to say.

Paul's one desire was to get away by himself for a time. Avoiding Daniso he followed the path he had taken once before over the barren veld that stretched to a far distant horizon hidden in the dusty haze. On this occasion neither sky nor earth spoke to him; the embattled forces within him engrossed all his senses. The conflict that had been lulled by the expectation of Kathie's visit and the preparation of Dhlomo's case now burst into the open and clamoured for some kind of solution. Even though he had told himself and others to be

274

prepared for an adverse judgment in the Dhlomo case, the actual event found him unprepared to take it.

In his present mood he was incapable of realising that while he had lost the case he had won a victory as far as the people were concerned. What he regarded as his failure brought him face to face with himself. Daniso was right, he reflected, when he said: *What is this law through which you hope to help our people. Who made it?* Yes, who made it? Paul was filled with disgust at the part he had played, a part imposed on him by his acceptance of the narrow dictates of legal procedure; he was filled with dismay at his helplessness in face of the people's plight; he was shamed by the gratitude of Dhlomo's wife.

The words of the prosecutor came back to him. From the high rostrum of legal impartiality he had dismissed the sufferings of the people as 'completely irrelevant to the case'. Impartiality indeed! What deception! What sophistry! To hound and harry men in the name of regulations. And all he had been able to do was to fight a legal battle with his suave opponent, with the certainty of losing in legal terms.

Pursued by the furies of thought he hastened over the veld, stumbling against a large ant heap and only just prevented himself from falling. What was the goal he had set himself? he asked. Was it not to serve his people? And how had he succeeded? Must he then take some other road? But which road? That was something he could not answer.

The memory of Nontando's tragic death suddenly leapt to his mind. He had failed there, too ...

How would he explain to Kathie, to whose coming he had so looked forward the root of his discontent?

He longed to tell her and yet he feared it too. If he ceased to have faith in what he was doing, what would become of the proud career he had visualised for himself and which would enable him to marry Kathie? Would he be able to carry on? And what would happen to him if he didn't ... ? He could make a compromise with life. How many men and women could ever claim to do otherwise? Men survived because they learned to compromise. Heaven help them if they didn't! A man must be a fool – or possessed of an iron will – if he didn't learn to yield to forces stronger than himself, in order to save his skin.

Yes, he could continue to make a comfortable living for himself.

But from what? The present system of society and the machinery of the law were sucking his people dry. And wasn't he also getting his cut out of it? Profiting from the ills of his people? A fine fellow preening himself because these poor peasants looked up to him! He smiled bitterly as the truth of his position struck home.

'Kathie, I have been deluding myself!' he exclaimed aloud, and stopped short at the sound of his own voice. He became aware of where he was. Far over at the limit of the horizon a dust devil came riding above the bare veld. What a tormented creature it was, at the mercy of the wind. As he watched its rapid course Paul thought of the precious topsoil that had been whipped up and carried into the air in this fantastic formation. The long drought had withered the grasses that bind the soil so that it lay in a fine dust ready to be seized by the wind when it swept by.

There, said Paul to himself, there is man's last hope of harvest dancing a devil's dance before the wind.

And what had he thought to reap? Was it wealth, honour, happiness with the woman he loved, while his fellows struggled in the pit beneath him?

'Oh, Kathie!' he cried. 'What happiness can there be for you and me?'

Paul was called away soon afterwards to a neighbouring village to collect evidence in connection with another case. This left him no opportunity of meeting Daniso – a relief since he did not want to enter into a discussion with the old man.

On his return he went quietly about his work, outwardly calm. He became aware of two things: on the one hand the people were even more friendly towards him than before and his sister remarked that his conduct of the Dhlomo case had been much appreciated, especially the way he had spoken out. To this he made no comment. On the other hand he perceived an increased hostility in the attitude of the Europeans with whom his work brought him into contact. Previously a few of them at the court at least had made some show of courtesy to a black man who had contrived to enter the ranks of the legal profession. As one lawyer put it, there were these cases of exceptional intelligence among the natives, the *rara avis* who only proved the mental inferiority of the general mass, and you could safely treat these as civilised human beings, provided they knew their place. Unfortunately Paul had shown signs that he didn't and it was time therefore to let him know where he really belonged.

Paul gauged the increased chilliness of the atmosphere by the behaviour of the office typist, a young woman who had previously accorded him an uneasy courtesy, but who now registered a cold yet familiar insolence with which an inferior is commonly treated. In this she was taking her cue from her bosses. The head of the local branch of the firm had reprimanded him for his behaviour in court and hoped that he would in future express himself with more propriety and impartiality as became his high calling, otherwise he would find that his services were no longer required by a firm which had already bestowed on him an enormous favour by employing him at all. He had hardly shown due gratitude for the tremendous privilege he had received. Paul had restrained himself from answering on this occasion. The rather menacing attitude of some of the petty court officials towards him he ignored with contempt.

If outwardly composed, he was far from being tranquil within. Attending the court day after day, he no longer saw things in a normal light. They took on a nightmarish aspect even in the brightness of day, and he began to see the machinery of the law as a monstrous octopus devouring his people from whom society had already sucked all it could. It was not the first time that some such image of what was happening had crossed his mind – indeed he realised that he had been aware of the process long before he had left the city – but only now did it grip his imagination. As he sat in the court day after day it seemed to him that the slow wheels of the law turning indifferently, yet deliberately, were dripping with human blood. He shuddered at the thought, trying to shake off the morbid intensity of his feeling. Looking round him he saw the agents of the law moving like robots who counterfeited men with human features, but they did not have the language or the thoughts of men. Day after day the show was enacted with grotesque solemnity; court officials mumbled or barked their commands; men and women, the accused, shuffled to and fro or stood dumb and bewildered and did not know what was happening to them.

This was madness. He must not give way to such morbid thoughts. Kathie would be arriving at the end of the week. Her quick eyes would scan his face and discover there all that he wanted to hide. He must pull himself together.

The day before her train was due Paul came face to face with Daniso. The old man beamed upon him.

'I've been watching you, my child,' he said, 'though you've had no eyes for me for some time past.'

'I've been very busy,' answered Paul.

'I have no doubt,' said Daniso, and Paul had the impression of a slight mockery in his tone.

'I've been wanting to tell you,' he continued, 'that you did not do so badly in the Dhlomo case.'

'I could have done better.'

'No doubt. No doubt. But you will learn with time. You are on the right road, my son. Let me tell you that the people are still speaking about what you said that day in the court.'

'What are they saying, Father?'

'They are not displeased, my child, at what you said. In fact they are proud of their son.'

'I did nothing to be proud of.'

'That's as you may think,' replied Daniso, 'but the people understand what you said. You spoke after their own heart. They will not forget it.'

'But Dhlomo paid the penalty.'

'What a child you are for all your cleverness! Of course he had to pay the penalty. Did I not tell you beforehand whose law it is?'

'I know that. But that is not the point.'

'It is very much the point, my son. If you know that, you know everything.'

'It is not so simple.'

'Ah, for you it is not so simple; that is what you mean. You think you have something to lose. But I tell you, my son, on the contrary, you have everything to gain.'

'Everything?'

'Yes. Everything,' replied the old man, emphasising each word with equal significance.

'Ah, Father, you do not know.'

'There you are wrong. It will not be easy. But I have faith in you, my son. The people have faith.'

'The people?'

'Yes, my child. The people of your great-grandfathers.'

Paul answered in some confusion, recognising the implied

challenge in the phrase.

'I would like to believe it, but –'

'Ah, there you lie! You do not wish to believe it. But you will have to believe it.'

'What do you mean, Father?'

'It is a great responsibility, my son, when the people put their trust in you.'

Paul had feared to hear these words. He had thrust from him the logic of his own conflict. And now the old man did not spare him.

'You would like to shun that responsibility, because the flesh is weak. But a man does not shun it. The plight of our people is desperate. You know that.'

'I know it.'

'And men such as I am – we are too old. The burden is for young shoulders to bear.'

'Why should it … ? Why should I … ?' Paul had difficulty in putting his thought into words.

'I know how gladly you would put the task from you. You dare not.'

'I am not worthy. I am not fit to take it on,' said Paul.

'You cannot find refuge in humility. You speak falsely because you fear the burden.' The old man's voice was stern and his eyes flashed anger.

'Remember this, my son,' he continued, 'whether you shut your eyes to it or not, there is a grim struggle going on every day, every hour. A struggle between life and death. They may take our cattle to the last beast we have. They can squeeze us into a corner of land no bigger than a grave, but they cannot take our manhood from us. No power, I say, can take our manhood from us. We are men. We are men who can still dream of freedom – yes, and fight for it, too. Think over what I have said. I have no doubt that you will choose the right way. Stay well, my son.'

The old man's words echoed in Paul's mind long after he had gone.

There is a grim struggle going on, every day, every hour …

Could he be indifferent to that struggle? Was it not part of him? Had he not battled in the city? For him, too, had it not been a struggle between life and death? And here, in his home village, had he not already become part of that ceaseless struggle? Had he not already spoken for the people?

Yet I say that no power can take our manhood from us ... We are men who can still dream of freedom, yes, and fight for it, too.

Paul had dreamed of freedom. But was it not for himself alone? Himself and Kathie. If he should turn his back on the struggles of the people would he not be relinquishing something of himself?

You think you have something to lose, my son. On the contrary, you have everything to gain.

If only Paul could believe that.

To see all clearly, with a relentless clarity of vision.

To bear all, as if every man's sorrow was his own.

To shrink from nothing, having once chosen the path he would follow.

It is little wonder that as he contemplated these things Paul tried to forget what Daniso had said.

Tomorrow Kathie would come. Let him forget everything else.

How long had he cherished her in the warm hands of memory!

Let him forget everything else but – tomorrow.

CHAPTER 20

Two women

Kathie felt very much in need of a holiday. The accumulation of events over the space of less than a year had subjected her to a nervous strain which had been rather much, even for her tough constitution. The break with her family following Stella's marriage, the wrench from Paul together with her worry over him – all left their mark on her. So it was with a sensation of rare pleasure that she had received Paul's letter proposing that she should spend part of her holiday with him and Nonceba. And then between this promise and its fulfilment had come the battle for Nontando's life ending in tragedy and failure.

This experience, and her knowledge of Nontando's jealously guarded secret, gave a poignancy to her feeling for Paul. It would never again possess the same innocence. She had thought of their relationship as a thing tender in its strength, a shield against the rage of ruthless living that went on around them; she had rejoiced in its very gentleness, yet, however unwittingly, it had struck a deadly blow at a young, bewildered heart. Why did everything in life demand its price?

Pity and fear overcame Kathie as she recalled those last days when she had tried to win Nontando back to a will to live. What loneliness had driven her feet blindly to the cold sea. What compulsion of hatred for Kathie herself. What fear and shame. Kathie could not but ask herself if Paul or she could not have averted all that had happened. What had his attitude to Nontando been before he had met her? She found herself reproaching Paul for his blindness where Nontando was concerned. Was he not guilty of a certain cruelty? Paul, cruel! Then cruelty was part of life itself. How difficult it was to separate the strands of joy and sorrow, happiness and pain.

Such had been the burden of Kathie's thoughts in the first shock of Nontando's death. But with the near approach of her visit to Paul everything else melted away in the joyful anticipation of being together again. With her savings she bought herself some new clothes. She must look her best when she met his sister, Nonceba. From what he said of her she must be a rather formidable person, though devoted to him. She hoped they would like each other ... There was the difference of race between them and she might not like Paul to go outside his people in choosing a wife. But, oh, she thought, once they met, all that would vanish away. Their mutual affection for Paul would be the bond between them.

It was with a light heart that she bade goodbye to her friends at St Mary's before going off to the station. The nurses had been unexpectedly kind to her, giving her little presents for her journey, and some of the patients who had been there a long time showed such regret at losing her that she did not know what to do between her laughter and her tears. Such moments in life were good. 'I should go away more often,' she said laughingly.

Her journey was like any other journey in a crowded train and travelling in a segregated coach. She had long inured herself to such conditions. In two nights and a day she would be with Paul, so let the wheels revolve faster and faster, let the train eat up the miles like the beneficent monster it was, for did it not bring her ever nearer to her man?

As she drew near her destination she scanned the countryside, thinking: 'This is Paul's home. This is where he grew up. This is his country.' But, oh, how barren it was. No wonder his spirits had fallen if this was what he had returned to. He must come back to the town.

He must come back soon. They had been separated too long.

Her heart beat fast as the train slowed and came to a stop at her station. With her things gathered round her ready for her to alight, she stood at the window and eagerly scanned the people waiting on the platform. Ah, at last! There he was. She smiled as she observed in him the selfsame eagerness as he scanned the windows looking for her. She waved. He spotted her and waved back, running alongside the train until it stopped. The next few minutes were filled with her getting herself and her baggage off the train.

The words they exchanged were trivial and only the eyes spoke volumes as they smiled and laughed a little and then were silent. His face told her a good deal of what his letters had tried to hide. All in good time, she thought, he will tell me what has been happening. For the time being their pleasure in each other's company was enough.

They made their way through the village, Paul carrying her suitcase.

'It's rather a long way,' he said.

'That won't worry me,' she replied. 'In fact it's all the better. I need the exercise.'

They met a number of people as they went through the village and Kathie noted how frequently they greeted Paul and how many curious glances were cast on herself. In the town one could come and go and never a soul take heed of you. Feeling rather embarrassed she laughed at her shoes not being suited to the country roads.

'I ought to have known better,' she remarked.

'I oughtn't to have let you walk,' he responded.

'What would you have done? Carry me?'

Strange that emotion so deep could hang on so slight a thread of words. They were finding refuge in the light badinage tossed from one to the other. But all the time her eyes were darting hither and thither, absorbing the landscape that had so moved Paul when he had first arrived. Only as they drew near to his home did she say softly: 'I am with you, Paul. Have you forgotten me?'

'I have missed you, Kathie.'

It was all she wanted to hear.

'Here we are – home,' he said.

'Home,' she echoed.

As they entered, Nonceba emerged from the other room. Paul introduced the two women to each other.

Nonceba, with the wisdom of her years, appraised the young woman whom her brother had chosen to be his wife. She liked what she saw. Kathie for her part was aware of the scrutiny; she perceived a strong-faced, shrewd looking woman in front of her, and felt a little afraid. Paul had told her that a heart of gold lay beneath the stern exterior, but at the moment she realised that it would only reveal itself if she herself proved worthy of it. She had the fleeting impression that she might have to do battle with this woman for the possession of her Paul, though what the forces were that might be against her she did not yet know.

The next moment all was laughter and friendliness between the three of them. Paul seemed to challenge his sister as much as to say: You never imagined she was all that I described, and more. While Nonceba seemed to answer: Steady on, my child, don't rush me. I like what I see. But give me time.

Kathie was keyed up to give of her best as if playing for stakes even higher than she knew. Paul's very presence transformed her, so that she hardly knew herself.

Soon afterwards they had a visitor, an old man who, Kathie gathered, was very close to the family. His name was Daniso. As soon as she was introduced she was aware of his piercing eyes bent on her with a hostile look. Here is an enemy, she thought, though why she should suddenly feel the chill of an alien presence she could not understand. If he was a friend of Paul and of his sister, he should be a friend of hers, too. She glanced swiftly at Paul, but found his face masked in a way that was new to her. Involuntarily her spirits dropped and, while Daniso conversed with Nonceba, she withdrew into herself. She had no further inclination to play the gay part that had seemed to her so exhilarating on her arrival. She had come to a strange country and it was necessary for her to be wary. After all, she was a stranger. Paul had brought her among his people, but they were not her people. Who indeed were her people? Her sister, Stella had turned her back on her. Her mother – Kathie's reverie was broken by a movement from Paul who had come to sit beside her.

'You must be tired,' he said. 'I've been forgetting you had a long journey and then that long walk home.'

Kathie flashed him a grateful glance.

'Yes, I didn't realise I was so tired.'

Daniso had stopped speaking and was observing her and Paul

together.

'Would you like to lie down and have a rest? I have to go back to the court,' continued Paul.

'The court? How silly of me to forget you had your work. I hope I haven't caused you any inconvenience.'

'Inconvenience!' Paul laughed. 'Did you ever hear of such a thing?'

He turned to his sister. No one echoed his laughter.

'Kathie's going to have a rest,' he said.

'By all means,' said Nonceba.

'Oh, it's not so bad as all that,' protested Kathie.

Within a few moments, however, the little group had broken up into its separate parts, all going their different ways. Daniso was the first to depart and Paul did not bid him wait for him. It was decided that Kathie would visit the court another day when she would be able to see Paul in action.

'You had better go, Sipo,' said Nonceba, and Kathie agreed with her, whereupon Paul protested loudly at this petticoat government but finally took his leave, promising to be back as soon as he could.

With Paul gone, Kathie made up her mind to make friends with Nonceba by speaking about her brother. Besides, she wanted to probe the reason for the evidence of strain she had observed in him.

'Paul must have been working very hard,' she said.

'Too hard,' replied Nonceba. 'You have noticed that?'

'I have noticed it.'

This was where the two women could meet.

'Paul wasn't sure about leaving town,' continued Kathie, 'but we both decided that it would be good for his work.'

With this 'we' she seemed to claim her part in Paul.

'You did well,' replied Nonceba.

'He must have come up against a great deal of prejudice,' went on Kathie, feeling her way.

'From the whites, yes. This was to be expected. But with his own people, you'd not believe what he has been able to achieve in so short a space of time.'

'I can imagine it.'

'Yes.' Nonceba looked at her as if caught by the pride in the young woman's tone. 'Sipo will go far yet.'

'I am sure of it,' Kathie agreed.

'But it will not be easy for him,' said the older woman.

'I know that.'

Again Kathie was aware of Nonceba giving her a peculiar glance as if there was more to the words than appeared on the surface.

'But Sipo will scold me if you haven't had a rest before he comes back.'

Kathie laughed at the picture of Paul being so bold where his sister was concerned, and she also recognised that Nonceba was changing the conversation.

'I will obey,' she said. 'Though you forget that a nurse often has to do without a night's sleep. The journey was nothing, really.'

Kathie and Paul were finding fewer opportunities of being alone together than either of them could have foreseen. It was natural enough that it should be so, yet Kathie found herself wondering if there wasn't some element of design in it too. Paul had changed. Not that she doubted his love for her. On the contrary, she sensed that it had a more intense quality than it had ever had before. Whatever had happened (and she was sure that something had happened) it had not lessened but deepened his need of her. At the same time there was an evasion in his manner; he seemed to be afraid of something – no, not afraid – not Paul ... Then what was it? She could only wait until the time was ripe for him to confide in her. He was withholding something from her. But for what reason? Was he afraid she would not understand? Or could he not trust her? But that was absurd. Then was he perhaps afraid to hurt her? Surely he knew that whatever concerned him concerned her deeply also. It was impossible to keep it from her. So with these questions in her mind, Kathie waited.

One evening Paul said quietly: 'Tell me about Nontando.'

And Kathie told him. She had not thought it would be so simple. She had feared to be the first to speak; the experience was too fresh in her mind and it had excited such conflicting feelings where Paul was concerned. Now the quietness of his manner disarmed her and she found herself telling him everything.

'Oh, the pity of it, Paul!' she cried, overcome afresh at the memory of what had happened. 'All that I could do could not restore her confidence in life.'

'I am not guiltless in all that happened,' said Paul.

'Did you know that she loved you?'

'I failed to think of her sufficiently as a woman,' was his answer. 'And then it was too late.'

'Neither you nor I, Paul, would willingly have hurt her. And yet it was so. Life is not a simple thing. Our actions, once taken, have a power to go beyond what we foresee of them'

How true that was. Neither Kathie nor he had foreseen how his coming here was perhaps going to alter their whole future. Surely this was the moment to speak out to her. He knew he ought to have confessed to the conflict that had been going on in his mind – confessed immediately after her arrival. But to speak at all was to give finality to his decision and this he could not bring himself to do. Now what better moment could there be than this?

'Kathie – ' he began.

'Yes, Paul.'

'There is something I have to tell you.'

'I have been waiting, Paul.'

'You guessed?'

'Silly one, there is no miracle about that. Tell me, what have you been hiding from me?'

'Not hiding.'

'No. The word is wrong. Only tell me, Paul.'

'For a long time – '

Just then the door opened and Nonceba entered. Much as he liked his sister, he could not bring himself to continue in her presence.

Kathie realised that she would have to wait a little longer ...

Next day she slipped into the court without having let him know she was coming. In town she had never had occasion to hear him speak in public, partly because he hadn't had the same opportunities and partly because of her own work. Now, hearing him for the first time in a court of law, she was caught by surprise, even though she had always believed he would make an eloquent speaker.

As she listened to the flow of his words, precise yet persuasive and delivered in a deep, resonant tone, she experienced a strange sensation, a blending of pride and apprehension. This was a Paul she did not know. It came to her that during the time they had been separated it was to this that he had been giving all the strength that was in him. Indeed he was not the same Paul. He had grown beyond her. He did not belong to her.

Glancing round the court, she observed on the faces of the white people a mixture of hostility and interest; but especially did she note the rapt faces of his fellow Africans. Paul had found a place among them. Of that there was no doubt. Then she caught sight of Daniso. How keenly he was watching the proceedings, nodding, scowling or shaking his head at certain points. She wondered if he would recognise her. But when she caught his eye she almost started at the glance he gave her. There was no answering smile but an expression of unmistakable enmity. The man could know nothing about her – why, then, this attitude of positive hostility? She must speak to Paul about it and perhaps he would enlighten her. These were his people and she wanted to be on friendly terms with them all; she wanted them to like her. For as his wife she would belong with them also.

As his wife. The word sounded in her ears with a new music. If only that time would come. When Paul returned to the city he would be certain to get a better job as a result of his experience, even if it wasn't what his talents entitled him to. They could get married straight away. She had no family ties now to hold her back; there was nothing to stop her and Paul from getting married. She would still continue her work as a nurse of course. But Paul and she would be together in a home of their own. Oh, let it be soon!

At the end of the session she joined Paul, who had spotted her as he turned to leave the court.

'Why didn't you tell me you were coming?' he asked.

'I didn't want to put you off your stroke. Do you realise I've never heard you speak before? Paul, it was fine –'

'Nonsense. It was all in the day's work,' he retorted, embarrassed.

'I'm not the only one who was rapt with wonder,' she continued, half jocularly. 'We all were. But especially your friend, Mr Daniso.'

'Oh, him.' Kathie noted his reserve as he answered.

'Paul, he doesn't like me,' she said on an impulse.

'Doesn't like you? What makes you think that?'

'Oh, I have ways of knowing.'

'Then I don't like him,' exclaimed Paul with vehemence. 'And it's none of his business.'

'What is none of his business?'

'Oh, never mind,' replied Paul evasively.

'But I want your friends to like me. And Nonceba, too.'

'She does, Kathie. I'm sure she does, though she may not show it very much. That's not her way.'

They were walking along the main street of the village and Kathie again became aware that the appearance of her and Paul together was attracting the attention of the passers-by. Two ragged coloured youths standing at a street corner stared at them offensively and obviously exchanged a jocular remark. The incident was trivial, yet it stuck in her mind.

These are my people, she thought and was ashamed.

'They have no roots. They do not belong anywhere,' said Paul, as if to answer her and explain the youths' behaviour.

What was the matter with her? She had been happy to think that she was coming 'home' to Paul and his people, but now, far from that being true, she felt that she was a stranger here. She was aware of it through Daniso's hostile coldness; she felt it even in Nonceba's reserve. Yes, Paul's sister was kind, but she withheld herself from Kathie. The more she thought of it the more she became convinced that this was true.

Could this, then, be what was behind Paul's own strangely reserved attitude towards her? If only he would be frank with her.

'Need we go straight back, Paul?' she asked as they passed the last houses in the village.

'I'll take you where I sometimes go,' he said, and led her by the path that cut across the veld.

They walked on in silence for a time.

After a while Paul said: 'Let us sit down.'

He took off his coat and spread it on a mound where she could sit, then stretched himself out at her feet. He was in no hurry to break the spell of silence that enveloped them.

'What has been happening, Paul?' said Kathie at last.

'A great deal.'

'Tell me.'

She listened silently as he described some of his experiences. Then he said:

'I have to confess that I'm not satisfied with what I'm doing. I feel that I have failed.'

'Failed? But that's ridiculous. When I listened to you today, when I saw how the people behaved towards you I knew how much they had taken you to themselves.'

'All the more reason why I mustn't let them down.'

'That's something you couldn't do. I just don't understand you, Paul.'

'If you'd been here the last six months you'd realise how little I've been able to do.'

'You're too ambitious. That's your trouble. You can't expect to move mountains straight away. I'm sure the people around here don't see it the way you do. They have faith in you because they see you fighting the laws.'

'That's just it!' exclaimed Paul. 'For me to think I can save our people simply by defending them in the law courts – well, I'm just deceiving myself – and them too.'

'So what do you intend doing about it?' Kathie's tone was not sympathetic.

'Sometimes I feel like giving up the law altogether.'

'Give up your career? After all you've put into it? Paul, you can't mean that.'

'It has to be more than a career. I must believe in what I'm doing. At the moment I do not see my way clearly. But if I think it's necessary I'll make the break.'

'Then there's no more to be said, is there? It's for you to decide.'

She spoke coldly in spite of herself.

'Not I alone, Kathie. But by your tone of voice you don't want to understand what I'm trying to say.'

'Paul, you can't blame me for not being able to see from your point of view. I tell you, I have observed how the people behave towards you – it made me proud, and more than that. I can't describe it to you. Now you're trying to tell me that what you're doing is wrong. It doesn't make sense.'

'I have to satisfy myself that it is *all* I can do. If there is more, I must take steps to carry it out.'

'Very well, you understand this best, Paul.'

It was clear that she was not at all convinced. In fact she did not understand all that was behind his feeling of failure, which on the face of it was contradicted by the faith he obviously inspired in the people. It was this very faith that was pushing him further, forcing him to examine his position, but the trouble was that he himself was not yet able to formulate his goal clearly. To burn his boats without being able to answer the vital question: *What next?* was a very serious matter. Kathie was not making it easy for him.

'One thing is certain,' he said. 'When I finish my contract with the firm I won't renew it. I must be on my own.'

'Will you be coming back to town, then?' Kathie's tone was distant. How different all this was from her expectations.

'Yes.'

The monosyllable revealed nothing. How could he explain? How could he express all he felt? He had left unspoken the greater part of the problem – their future together. How could he say to her that perhaps they could never marry? If he chose a hazardous path, he dare not ask her to share it with him. But would she ever see it from his point of view?

Their manner had become chill towards each other, their eyes averted. They made their way back to the house, walking a little apart, speaking almost like strangers. Was it possible? Kathie wanted to cry out, but the very depth of her feeling made her tongue-tied.

All her surmises as to the reason for his reserve, which she had vaguely felt but could not name, had not brought her near to this that he had just told her. She was unhappy, because she could not understand him. To her he seemed rather unreasonable. Yet it was so typical of him to be uncompromising in his attitudes; this she could appreciate. It was bound to make things hard for him, she thought, so all the more reason why he must feel that in her he had someone to whom he could always turn. They would be together whatever happened. There were no two ways about that. Of course! That was what she wanted to say to him now. Why, then, was she not able to speak? Why must she allow him to think that she was cold?

Kathie had sensed rightly that old Daniso looked on her with disfavour, though she could not possibly guess all the reasons for his antipathy. Where the knowledge of human beings was concerned, Daniso had the wisdom of his years and a shrewd mind to guide him; but in this instance there were two factors obscuring his vision. As he had lived all his life in the country, his only knowledge of the coloured people – as in the case of Nonceba too – was derived from the few who had to eke out a miserable livelihood as labourers working for white farmers in the district. Seeing them as hirelings and outcasts, without roots in the land as he himself had, he could not but regard them with contempt; he did not wish to understand them; he did not even see them.

And now here was Kathie. She was a coloured woman and Paul intended to marry her – as Nonceba had indicated to him. It shocked the old man. She did not fit into the category he knew, but neither did she fit into any other. Where she belonged he could not say. To him she was a 'foreigner'. Such a woman could not be the wife of his 'son', Sipo, the brother of Nonceba, of the house of Mangena. It was unthinkable. This was enough to make him shut the door of his mind against her, whatever her personal qualities. But there was an even stronger reason.

He had visualised a certain destiny for his 'child' as a future leader of his people, as one who must assume the burden that had grown too heavy for the old. The plight of his people, he had said to Sipo, was desperate, therefore the responsibility of leadership must not be shirked. Of Sipo's capabilities for such a part he was absolutely convinced, only there were certain impediments of youth and a too modest temperament which time and wise counsel would, he felt sure, remove. Nothing else must be allowed to stand in the way of this goal. Having talked with Sipo, having fed with cunning words the divine discontent within him, Daniso felt that his purpose was well on the way to achievement. And now, this woman, this 'foreigner', must appear on the scene, a danger to Sipo, a threat to the destiny he had conceived for him.

Daniso asked himself if he should speak to Sipo himself or should he get Nonceba to do it. He thought that she must feel as he, Daniso, did. Sipo's sister, she who had sacrificed so much to bring up the boy, could not but resent a strange woman coming and taking Sipo away from his people. There would be no use in appealing to the woman herself. He knew women. She would ensnare Sipo in the coils of her affections so that he could not escape; she would blur his vision, turn his bones into water and weaken his will. There was no time to lose. So far he had said nothing to Nonceba and decided to have a talk with Sipo himself.

Paul had a great respect for Daniso and in their previous discussions he had been profoundly affected by the old man's judgement. In this instance, however, Daniso started at a disadvantage. Having allowed himself to be prejudiced against Kathie, he had relinquished that calmness and justice that were the attributes of his wisdom, and Paul, moreover, was aware of that prejudice and was quick to resent it. The whole trend of his development, especially since he had met the bookseller, Farben, had been towards a rejection of racialism whenever it raised its obscene head, whether it was in a vain young woman like Stella, or in a petty white official, or in one of his own people. Besides this, he had not reconciled himself to the implied challenge that Daniso had thrown out to him in the course of their last conversation. He had to arm himself against the old man because he had not yet fought out the battle within himself.

It is a great responsibility, my son, when the people put their faith in you, he had said. And Paul still shrank from that responsibility.

To Paul in this frame of mind, Daniso necessarily appeared more of an antagonist than an ally. And the situation was not made any the easier by the fact that he and Kathie had not yet come to an understanding. But any conflict involving the claims of Kathie as against those of his people, must be fought out between Kathie and himself, and never by means of an attack on her by man or woman. If it should happen that Paul did not marry her, it would be for reasons which both of them faced and understood.

Daniso, knowing Paul's habits, waylaid him next day on his way into the village. Paul would have preferred to hurry on, but courtesy forbade it and in any case the old man was remarkably agile on his feet, considering his age, and did his best to keep up with him. He talked of this and that and then he asked, almost with an assumption of innocence:

'Tell me about this young woman who is staying with you.'

Now to answer that question adequately Paul in a certain mood might have taken a volume written in the finest language he knew, or perhaps, if he had been a poet, one golden image would have contained it all. But at the present moment he was in a combative mood so he answered abruptly:

'She is the woman who is going to be my wife.'

It was a thrust that even the shrewd Daniso wasn't prepared for and he took an appreciable minute to recover from it.

'Isn't it rather soon for you to be thinking of marriage?' he said, masking his chagrin. 'The members of your family were never given to hasty unions.'

Paul did not answer. Daniso tried another tack.

'You've an uphill road before you, my son. It behoves you not to do anything to increase the burden.'

'A good wife is a helpmate to her husband,' replied Paul.

'Ah, but this foreign woman –' The word had slipped out.

'This woman,' said Paul deliberately, 'is as worthy to be my helpmate as my mother was to my father.'

'Your mother!' Daniso's voice trembled.

'I know how much you revered my mother,' said Paul quietly.

In this juxtaposition of Kathie with his mother, so dear to memory, he could not have issued a stronger challenge.

The old man's silence acknowledged the young one's victory.

He began again.

'I once said that the faith of a people puts a great responsibility on a man.'

'I have not forgotten your words, Father.'

'If he accepts that responsibility a man must have a single mind, a single aim.'

'I know it.'

'If you marry this woman, will you not destroy this single-mindedness?'

'What makes you think that, Father?'

Paul waited for the answer.

'She is not as our women are.'

'In what way?'

Daniso refused to answer directly.

'She will take you away from your people, my son.'

'My people are her people.'

'You have a great need to believe that, and your need speaks stronger than your reason,' parried the old man.

'My reason tells me that we are one people. And until you and all of us realise that it is so, we are in chains,' answered Paul.

'Indeed we are in chains, my son, but they are not of our making.'

'True. But according as we think, so do we rivet our chains, or burst them asunder.'

'How so, my son?'

'You once asked me who made the laws,' continued Paul.

'I did.'

'And for what purpose.'

'We know the purpose,' said Daniso.

'Then do not these laws make us all brothers? All of us who in the eyes of the white man bear the badge of colour?'

'There is justice in what you say, my son, but at the moment I am concerned with another problem – that of your future.'

'My argument did not stray from that problem, Father. It is you who sought to obscure the issue. I can do nothing for my people until I see clearly what my task is. And the first thing I must do is to break asunder those chains that not only bind our bodies but also enslave our minds. If I, too, despise my brother for the colour of his skin I am no better than those who deny us both justice for that reason. How can we guide our people if at the very outset we suffer from the same affliction as the lawmakers? Can the blind and the sick of mind lead a people?

'Father, when you speak to me of the plight of our people, I listen as a young man must listen, to the wisdom of the old. When you lay before me the duties of a man, I take heed. If you should advise me against marriage with a woman because of some fault of character or disposition, which bids you warn a man of his folly – then would I also hearken to your words. But when you pass judgement on a woman whom you know not of, then I do not understand you. I do not hear you. Whatever road I take in the future, the decision will be mine and that of the woman I love. I have spoken, Father.'

Paul had never spoken at such length to Daniso before, nor had he ever adopted such a firm tone. The old man was silent.

'I am late for the court. I will have to hurry. Stay well, Father.'

'Go well, my son.'

Paul went on ahead, leaving Daniso, who walked very slowly, deep in thought.

In this battle for Paul's future course there was another protagonist who had not yet played her part. Whatever happened to Paul was very much the concern of his sister Nonceba. Her attitude to Kathie was a very different one from that of old Daniso. She did not shut her eyes to her qualities as a woman. In this her very affection for her brother, combined with her respect for his judgement, made it possible for her to overcome the racial barriers. Sipo had done something unusual in going outside his people for a wife, but, being Sipo, he must have good reason for it. And when Kathie came to stay in her house, Nonceba's observation soon convinced her that he had chosen well, and indeed could be considered fortunate. Kathie was a fine woman.

Yet to say this was not to solve his problem.

If he were in an ordinary position Nonceba saw no reason why Sipo and Kathie should not marry and be happy together. But then Sipo was not in an ordinary position. She, too, had dreams of her brother one day becoming a leader of his people, and like Daniso, she had no intention of letting anything jeopardise that position – not if she could prevent it. There was no doubt that the prestige he had gained as a lawyer who undertook to defend his people in the courts, had paved the way for his acceptance in a more important role. She did not see his failure over the Dhlomo case, for instance, as he himself saw it. At the same time she had become aware of his deep dissatisfaction. There were never many words lost between brother and sister, but there was an understanding born of sympathy rather than knowledge. She was aware also of the discussions that went on between Sipo and her old friend and counsellor Daniso, and surmised their nature. Neither did it escape her that all was not well between the two young people. She did not need to think far to know why, and her sympathy went out to them, knowing that at this age the vision does not extend far into the future, but that the heart can live or die in the thought of the immediate event. For all her sympathy, however, she was in grave doubt as to the effect of such a marriage on Sipo's future.

His absence on business in a neighbouring village gave Nonceba the opportunity she had been waiting for. He had sent a message to say he would be detained till next day and the two women found themselves alone for the night. Kathie had not many more days of her holiday left, so Nonceba must speak now or lose her chance, perhaps never to get it again.

The young woman was sitting at the table under a lamp, her unaccustomed fingers busy with some sewing she had taken up during her few weeks of leisure. With her head bowed over the material that fell in blue folds on her lap, with her eyes veiled, her full lips in repose and the light glowing on her golden forehead, Nonceba suddenly saw her as an image of motherhood, full-breasted and warm, so gentle and so still. With the hunger of her own womanhood denied, she had a vision of Sipo's child, his head pillowed on this soft bosom. Could Sipo know greater happiness than this? Nonceba's heart contracted with pity mingled with doubt of her own purpose.

If the world were other than it was, what trinity of happiness would her ageing eyes behold – her boy, this woman and their child. All the suppressed instinct of motherhood rose up in the older woman to envelop the young.

But this was weakness. She must be resolute, for her purpose was to turn this woman, so ripe for motherhood, away from her intention of marrying Sipo. Her task would be a difficult one and she would need all her skill and wisdom for it. Kathie looked up, caught her look and smiled.

'I believe you went to the court the other day and heard Sipo speak,' she began. 'Were you satisfied with what you heard?'

'Satisfied? It was wonderful!' exclaimed Kathie. 'He holds you as he speaks. He held them all.'

'It is a great power he has.'

'It is all the more strange to me,' continued Kathie, 'that he should say that he has been a failure here. I don't believe it.'

'He has confided in you? I'm glad of that, for his mind has been sorely troubled of late. Did he tell you all?'

'All?'

'What did he say, my child?'

'Perhaps you can understand it better than I can. He seemed to think that he cannot serve the law and serve his people too. He even speaks of having to give up the law.'

'Sipo knows best,' said Nonceba. 'If he should give up the law, have you thought what this will mean for you?'

'For me? It will he harder for us. That's all.'

'Do you think Sipo will be willing to cause you such hardship?'

'Oh, I'm ready to share it with him –'

'But what if Sipo is not willing to see you face it?'

'What do you mean? If he has made up his mind I won't keep him back.'

'I believe that. But when a man like Sipo marries a woman, he will not be content unless he can give her a home and all that goes with it. Security, happiness ... '

'If we are together, it is enough. I am not afraid.'

'You are not thinking of it sufficiently from Sipo's point of view. His pride is strong. If he cannot give you these things it will shame him.'

'That's nonsense. He knows me better than that.'

'Kathie, I believe you when you say you would be prepared to face any hardship with Sipo. But life may ask even more of you than that.'

'I do not understand you.' Kathie's tone was wary.

'You have seen with your own eyes how he can move men. What does that suggest to you?'

Kathie was silent.

'Do I need to tell you? The people need Sipo, my child.'

As Kathie listened, she recalled the scene in court, the rapt faces of the African peasants around her, and she remembered her own pride and her own fear, the strange thought that came to her then that Paul no longer belonged to her.

Nonceba was speaking. 'Kathie, I could wish for no better wife for him than you. This you must know. But there is something else, something stronger than what you or I can wish. I see the future beckoning him. Are you not aware of it too?'

'I think I have known it all the time,' murmured Kathie.

'His path is likely to be hazardous and full of danger.'

'I am prepared for that too.'

'My child, when the time comes, he will not belong to any woman then, neither to me nor to you. He will not belong even to himself. He will belong to the people. Their faith will be in him. Their eyes will be upon him. He must do nothing that will obscure his purpose, nothing that would alienate him from them.'

'What are you trying to tell me?' broke in Kathie.

'If he married you – they see you as a stranger – forgive me – would that be wise for him?'

'No! No! I do not believe you. You are wrong. In this dream of leadership you have forgotten Sipo himself!'

'It is not my dream, my child.'

But Kathie went on. 'You are inhuman. Even if I should give up all you ask of me, what of him? What of *his* happiness? Do you think he will give me up so easily?'

'No.' Nonceba spoke dispassionately, almost as if she yielded to the conflict. 'He will resist it with all his might. You have seen it in his face, Kathie. The battle has been on these many weeks.'

'I saw it and I did not know.'

'His own happiness he will relinquish, if I know Sipo,' went on Nonceba, steadily. 'But for you, perhaps he will give in, for your sake.'

She paused. 'It is in your power to refuse to give him up. Maybe I am inhuman. Then claim your happiness, my child. He will grant your claim.'

'My happiness? You have destroyed my happiness,' replied Kathie bitterly.

'Not I, my child. You are unjust. I only speak of what I know.'

Kathie hid her face in her arms. Nonceba rose and stood beside her, her hand on the bowed head.

'Kathie,' she said. 'There was no one else to say what I have said. We two obey a purpose that is greater than ourselves. And in so doing we suffer. It is the way of life.'

Kathie lifted her face and buried it in the breast of the woman who had never borne a child of her own.

Of all that had passed between them neither woman revealed anything to Paul when he returned. This was not from deliberate intent, but was born of the mutual understanding that had sprung up between them. Nonceba had suggested that Kathie should stay on a few more days if it fitted in with her plans and to this she had readily agreed.

Paul was overjoyed. Such an air of gaiety prevailed in the house when they were all together that he wished it could go on for ever like this. If one could only stay the passage of time! He could not but feel the happy relationship between the two women, for it drew him and occasionally even Daniso into its charmed circle. The old man did not unbend towards Kathie but at least there was a kind of armed truce since his discussion with Paul and she frequently found herself, to her embarrassment, the object of his scrutiny. Paul surmised that the evening the women had spent together had been a fruitful one, though he had no inkling of its nature. It gave him a deep satisfaction to see the growing bond between the two who meant so much to him, proud that Kathie had been able to win over so exacting a woman as his sister and grateful to Nonceba for her generous affection towards Kathie. Kathie, indeed, seemed to wish to be more with her than with him and for this he would tease her, whereupon they would exchange a glance of understanding that made him positively feel that he was the mere male left out in the cold.

Kathie could not have said what prompted her behaviour

throughout this period. Perhaps she had suffered a wound so deep that an instinct of self-preservation bid her lie low until a protective skin should grow over it. Her gaiety was not the spontaneous play of a woman secure in her possession; it had the quality of a fire that burns low in the hearth, consuming something of the spirit that nourished it.

When alone with Paul she was gentle, but slightly aloof, as if desire had drawn a hood over its burning face, deliberately shielding itself. If he could have expressed what he felt at this time, he would have said that somehow Kathie had withdrawn herself from him; she was elusive, slipping out of his hands when he touched her. But these sensations were too fugitive for him to define, for no sooner had he become aware of this tantalising elusiveness than he would the next moment be enchanted by her gaiety. He was discovering this Kathie of his in a new light.

Paradoxically, Kathie herself had never felt so near to Paul, never so capable of understanding him. And perhaps it was this very removal of herself that enabled her to see him more clearly; for desire is unconsciously possessive, seeking first its own need. But an unexpected incident revealed to her that this removal of herself was not so genuine as it pretended to be; the protective skin she had been growing was but a shallow covering after all.

According to her custom now, she had been attending the court for a part of every day. Paul had remonstrated with her, but she had insisted and he had yielded. It was not only that she liked to be with him; she had a desire, half proud, half painful, to observe this Paul whom she had not known until she had come here. It was the Paul who was in touch with his people, arguing, persuading, defending with his powerful voice; it was the Paul to whom, as Nonceba had expressed it, the future beckoned and whom the future would take from her.

One day, then, Paul was outside the court consulting the wife of one of his clients, an African who had been seized for stock theft. Kathie had a fleeting glimpse of the woman, who had a child of about three tied with a blanket to her back. She must have come far, thought Kathie, and carrying such a big child, too. Her experienced eye noted that the woman was near her time; her heavy body sagged with the burden of her unborn baby. Then she moved away, her interest taken up with a group of youths who had obviously come in that morning from an outlying district and were being signed up as recruits for the goldmines. She was struck by their extreme youth, their smooth dark-brown skin giving them a peculiar air of innocence, and she became lost in the thought of the city mines that would so soon engulf them. How ignorant they were of what lay before them.

She was startled out of her reverie by Paul, who came up to her breathless and discomposed in manner, which was very unlike him.

'Kathie, come quickly! I need your help.'

Hastening along, his hand at her elbow, he continued: 'There's a woman taken ill. Thank heaven you are here!'

He led her to an outlying shed where a number of people were pressing in at the door and dispersing them he made way for her to enter. Kathie at once recognised the woman she had previously observed talking with Paul. She was lying on the bare floor, moaning, her blanket lying askew over her body. An elderly peasant woman was bending over her, while in the corner sat the three-year-old, contentedly playing with a knotted piece of rag.

The old woman straightened up at their entrance, looking askance at Paul and throwing Kathie a doubtful glance.

'I have brought a trained nurse,' he explained.

There was not a moment to lose; there was no possibility of moving the woman, nor any likelihood of outside help, so Kathie enlisted even Paul to fly hither and thither for at least the bare necessities for her job. This done, she hustled him out, bidding him meantime to try to get transport so that the woman might be taken to her home.

And now the two women were left alone to their task – the peasant woman and Kathie – the one with hands, though weak and old, that had helped to bring many a child into the world; the other, 'the stranger', skilled and quick of hand, a woman of the city.

When it was over, Kathie put the newborn baby girl into the mother's arms. The woman's look of gratitude was her reward. The old peasant woman nodded with satisfaction and went to hush the older child, who was whimpering in the corner.

It was not long before Paul asked leave to enter and as he stood beside Kathie, contemplating the mother and the newborn infant, something in this timeless, universal scene moved him to put his hand on Kathie's shoulder. Trembling at his touch, she lifted her eyes to his, a world of anguish momentarily revealed. What silent revelation did that moment hold between man and woman. Though his reason told him it could not be so, it was as if he had told her everything – and she to him – and there was nothing more to say. For Kathie it was a moment that linked past, present and future together. It was she who had brought Nontando's baby into the world, the child of whom she had said: *He should have been Paul's child.* And now the thought was heavy upon her that she would never hold in her arms the child that was his and hers. She had forfeited motherhood.

This last incident made Paul decide to have it out with Kathie. So far he had not been completely frank with her. Their future was still uncertain.

It was evening, after supper, and observing his sister busy at something – he did not know what – he remarked with ill-disguised impatience: 'Sis N'ceba, you work too hard. Why don't you go to bed and have a rest?'

When both women laughed at this he looked surprised.

'Since when have you been so worried at me working?' asked Nonceba. 'But I'll go to bed when I'm finished, and not before.'

'Oh, I didn't mean –' he began lamely, and was stopped by Kathie, who put her hand playfully over his mouth.

Nonceba soon afterwards retired, leaving them to themselves. Kathie made no attempt to begin speaking. She would leave that to him; for her it was no longer necessary to urge on events; rather she wanted to suspend time forever in the present. Paul on the other hand felt the urgency to act. He had delayed too long. He had boasted to Daniso that whatever decision he took as to the future it would be only with full understanding between himself and Kathie. So he plunged straight into what he wanted to say.

'Kathie, that day I talked about my plans, I'm afraid I didn't explain to you all that I had in mind.'

'There is no need to explain.'

'Oh, but you don't understand –' he began.

'Are you sure?'

'You didn't seem to be convinced that I was right. I am sure you thought I was unreasonable. You may have even blamed me –'

'I don't blame you and I don't think you're unreasonable.'

Paul was surprised at her acquiescence. It was too easy. He had contemplated a battle and here she was laying the victory at his feet. He wasn't sure he liked it that way. Her attitude had been very different the first time he had spoken. What had made her change? As if answering his unspoken doubts, she continued.

'I know that whatever decision you make for the future, it will be a ... a responsible one. And I won't stand in your way.'

'I never thought of you doing that, Kathie.'

'I'm glad you know it, Paul.'

He was still puzzled at her completely acquiescent attitude.

'But Kathie, you and I ... the choice is not an easy one ... '

She came to his assistance. 'I think I know all that you want to tell me, Paul. Put your mind at rest. I understand more than you think. Silly one, you didn't need to worry so much.'

She hurried on, speaking lightly. 'When does your contract finish?'

'I have at least another six months.'

'And you won't renew it?'

'No.'

'And will you be spending the rest of your time here?'

'Part of it. You know that they asked me to stay on a few months longer. Then I'll come back to town.'

'And when you come to town, then we'll have a good old talk about it all. Time enough then, eh?'

'Kathie, I don't know what to say –'

'Don't try. Goodnight, Paul. I'm taking a leaf out of Nonceba's book. She believes in an early beauty sleep. Goodnight.'

Paul held her back.

'Don't leave me,' he said.

'I'll still be here tomorrow,' she teased.

He enfolded her in his arms.

She stayed a moment and there were tears in her eyes, which she hid from him.

'Goodnight, Paul.'

And she was gone.

When Kathie returned to town it was with the knowledge that she had won a place in Nonceba's regard, second only to that of Paul himself. Paul jokingly commented on what he called her conquest and marvelled at the way women understood each other.

'How did you do it, Kathie?' he asked.
But Kathie did not reveal her secret.

CHAPTER 21

Carl and Stella

Carl and Stella Meyers had rented a small house in what can only be described as suburbia. Suburbia suggests respectability in rather crowded quarters; the small, detached or semi-detached house which aims at privacy but cannot help sitting on top of its neighbour. Its stoeps are matchbox size, but they have the pretentious pillars of the mansion-that-might-have-been if the architect had had more elbow room. Its square gardens (so-called) betray the same compromise and look like playpens, in which, however, no children ever play. They show a brave front, and have a mean backyard.

This European suburbia was only a cut above that in which Stella had lived with her mother; it had the same mixture of pretentiousness with parsimony, but it could claim to be on the safe side of the racial line. To Stella it was her castle and fortress, the symbol of her achievement. After a brief honeymoon she had set about prettifying it and carried it out with such good taste that her husband, unaccustomed to these urban graces, was filled with admiration. He basked in the sunshine of his newly married state under conditions that he could not possibly have visualised a year previously. From his point of view he had made a very good bargain.

Carl Meyers had grown up in a village in the Western Cape in poverty and yet in laziness, which is imposed on the white man because, however poor he may be, he is taught to regard manual labour as the function of the black man and therefore beneath his dignity. He had had little education – much less than Stella – so that his mental horizon was as stunted as the trees on his father's plot of land; he had had no training in any skilled trade, so that the channels of advancement through profitable labour were closed to him. Quite simply he belonged to the ranks of the unskilled and might have found his natural level – and the work for which he was most fitted – if he hadn't been a white man. To be possessed of a white skin meant that a man had to approximate as nearly as possible to the white-collar job or sink into the ranks of the poor-white, a misfortune that placed him beyond the pale, a disgrace to his race. With no capability – or capital – for becoming a farmer, unqualified for any trade, but with enough initiative to get out of the rural rut, Carl had gravitated to the town where he walked into one of those jobs that seemed reserved for his kind. The possibility of advancement was narrow or non-existent, the opportunity for self-development was nil, yet he counted himself lucky in having a fixed job and more money than he'd ever had in his life before. A roving eye and a robust physical instinct had helped him to pick out Stella as an attractive mate – and now suburbia was his home.

Setting up house was a serious responsibility which entailed saddling oneself with debt at the outset, but in Carl's opinion it was worth it. Looking round his small domain with its delightful feminine touches, his ruddy complexion took on a ruddier shade with the satisfaction of the proud proprietor. Carl had a good nature and a capacity for wonder that should have endeared him to any woman.

There was at first a fair prospect of marital happiness for Carl and Stella. Stella was tasting the sweets of her newfound freedom; her position as Carl's wife gave her the right of way into the coveted white world and she enjoyed its material benefits. Carl had struck up a friendship with a young man, Henry Potgieter, who also had a job in the bazaar. His wife Joyce was a fair, talkative young woman and as the two wives were both house-proud, they got on well together in a superficial kind of way. This made it easy to form a foursome in the evening or during the weekends, Stella flirting a little with Potgieter, just to add spice to Carl's sense of possession, while Joyce did her best to lure the rather too infatuated newly-wed, and found it heavy going.

Newly married life indeed had the aspect of a holiday. Stella made it clear to Carl that she didn't want any children. Not for a long time at any rate. Let them have some fun first. This disappointed Carl more than he allowed his wife to see. He loved children and animals and he secretly thought that if he had a son his cup of happiness would be full. Perhaps one day soon he could persuade Stella to change her mind. What wife could be long happy without a child in her arms?

Meantime life put on a very pleasant countenance for Stella and Carl. The satisfaction of her worldly desires made Stella tolerant towards her husband though she had no real affection to give him; the man so obviously worshipped her, needed her, depended upon her, that she could not but reward him with such sweetness as she was capable of. She wove her spell about his heart so strongly that perhaps their relationship might survive all the tensions and tribulations and all the disillusionment of their subsequent life together. Who could say? Unless the social forces about them were too strong they might yet work out their destiny together. Their strongest ally – if Stella had only known it – was a single-minded capacity for affection on the part of Carl himself, call it perhaps a need of his nature, and, once given to her, only her own folly could destroy it. But how hazardous the venture on which they had embarked! How strong the forces ranged against them! For these forces had already moulded them, warped them and become part of themselves as well as operating from without. Stella had apparently achieved her purpose; she had sacrificed filial affection, but she had done what she – and her mother – wanted. She ought to have been a happy woman. Yet she was never completely secure in herself, never completely satisfied. Her restless spirit did not take long to find reasons for discontent.

One day Carl confessed to his friend Potgieter that he had landed himself in a spot of financial trouble. Nothing to speak of. It was just that the instalment on the wireless set Stella had set her heart on was overdue and he didn't see his way to make it that month. Potgieter laughed at his serious face.

'What's Stella saying to it?'

'She doesn't know.'

Potgieter whistled. '*O God man,* that's bad!'

But Carl didn't join in the laugh.

'I'll tell you what,' continued his friend. 'Just go to the races at Kenilworth this Saturday and you'll win enough to pay off the whole damn lot at one go.'

Carl confessed he'd never been to a race and wouldn't know how to back a horse.

This excited Potgieter's amusement more than ever.

'*God man,* don't make me laugh. It's bad for my stitches,' said he holding that portion of his anatomy where until recently had been his appendix.

'I'll come with you,' he offered. 'I haven't had a flutter for donkey's years.'

'But I haven't any money to go to the races,' protested Carl.

'I'll lend you some. And don't worry. You'll have beginner's luck.'

So Carl allowed himself to be persuaded, elated at the thought of giving Stella a surprise, thereby justifying the fact that he was keeping the venture a secret.

Carl and Stella usually went out together in the weekends and if he did go anywhere by himself he usually informed his wife where he was going, assuring her that he would soon return. On the Saturday when he was going to the races, however, he was elaborately off-hand about going out, so much so that her suspicions were aroused. In answer to her questions he said at length:

'It's all right, I'm going with Potgieter.'

'What do you mean, it's all right?'

'Just what I say: it's all right. What's wrong with that?'

'You make me think you're up to some funny business.'

'Nonsense! The two of us can surely go off on our own without you getting all het up about it.'

'I'm not het up. It's you who are acting damn peculiar, if you ask me.'

'Come on, Stella, don't be ratty,' he pleaded. 'I've got a surprise for you, but don't ask me now.'

'Oh, all right. But what's Potgieter up to that you have to be so secretive?'

'Just you wait and see.'

'Well, off you go, then. Only don't you be doing anything foolish.'

'You bet I won't!' And with a peck at her cheek he was gone.

That day the sights at Kenilworth racecourse were better than a bioscope show to Carl, who nudged his companion and laughed at the sheer novelty of it all – the thronging crowds and the shouting; the prancing horses, their sleek polished coats shining in the sun, proudly showing their paces before the race, sometimes shying nervously at shadows as if they had caught the prevailing fever and knew the heavy stakes that were on them; the fashionable dresses of the ladies preening themselves in the members' grandstand, their dapper escorts bending attentively while they discuss the next race. The shout, 'They're off!' The initial hush, the straining necks, the tense faces, the vociferous encouragement of the favourites; the shrieks of joy mingled with the cries of disappointment and then the general exodus as the horses move off the course and the crowd mills round until the next race. Here all sorts rub shoulders, for the gambling spirit is hot enough to melt the colour-bar for the time being. This lively scene under a brilliant March sky with Devil's Peak standing benevolently in the distance gave Carl an extraordinarily strong sense of exhilaration and excitement. He wished he had brought Stella with him after all. This was the life.

But alas! The jade – fortune – cast never a glance at beginners that afternoon. By the end Potgieter was backing recklessly in an attempt to retrieve their earlier losses. Then in one of the minor races Carl spotted a horse called Stella Maris.

'Let's back her. She's sure to win. Stella Maris!' he exclaimed.

'We don't know anything about her,' growled Potgieter, but the superstitious hope won the day. It might just turn out to be the last lucky throw.

Stella Maris came in nowhere.

The glitter and excitement had gone cold; the people had a shoddy air about them; the horses, the race over, were being led away by black and coloured grooms. The crowd was melting away rapidly into Rosmead Avenue.

Without looking at each other the two men left the course.

'Better luck next time,' said Potgieter jauntily as they parted.

Small comfort to Carl, who had the triple weight of his original debt, his new debt to Potgieter and the necessity to keep the truth from Stella. For him the last was probably the heaviest burden of all. Becoming suspicious of his low spirits she probed him until he confessed, but if he expected to find relief in unburdening himself of the shabby little truth, he was rudely disappointed. Stella gave vent to a spiteful rage out of all proportion to his folly and her contempt blazed out in a manner that startled him. It was the beginning of many such incidents between them.

The following Saturday Carl and Potgieter went to the races again.

In the pattern of human relationship change comes slowly, working its way through the soil of daily contact, irritations, insensitivenesses between two people. Sometimes this seems a merciful thing, shielding the nerves that would otherwise snap with a too violent revelation of what time has taken away; but sometimes this very gradualness has a treacherous, relentless aspect, stealthily taking, removing, loosening, till all is lost.

While Stella was determined to succeed in making the most of her new position, her attitude to her husband bid fair to wreck their married life. Carl indeed deserved more of her than he received. For her the man himself was the problem; the nearer she came to knowing what stuff this man of hers was made of, the more discontented she became with her bargain. At the outset she had no real affection for the man who had made her his wife. This might have grown, because he had lovable qualities; but she herself, with her false sense of values, had so little to give.

At first blind to the true state of Stella's feelings towards him, Carl strove to conquer a reserve that both puzzled and attracted him. He had a great admiration for his wife, both for her physical beauty and her intelligence, but gradually he was repelled by the hardness which she took less and less trouble to hide from him.

She had no respect for him; physically he offended her too fastidious senses; she despised his lack of education; her nimble intelligence, nurtured in the city, had no little contempt for his slowness of wit; he didn't earn enough money for her liking nor was he ambitious enough to satisfy her ambition. She even contrived to bear him a grudge for failing to be the man she had once dreamed of marrying.

This secret resentment showed itself indirectly in a thousand petty ways. Carl had an affectionate nature which would naturally cleave to the woman who gave him affection. Such a woman would have brought out the best in him, providing him with the incentive and confidence he needed. But Stella's ambition nagged and criticised this man of hers, becoming impatient at his shortcomings, taunting his stupidities, goading him with complaints. The paradox of the situation was that she was his superior in many ways, though in one fundamental point of character – his sheer goodness of heart – she was his inferior. It was the quality that was of least value to her worldly ambition and rendered him the most vulnerable to her hardness of heart. His good nature was, in her eyes, but another mark of his weakness, another cause for despising him.

His blundering attempts to keep out of debt only plunged him deeper into it. His visits to the races became more frequent and even when common sense told him that though the turn of the wheel might favour him now and again, he must be the loser in the long run, a frenzy of wilful recklessness overtook him as if he were under the influence of a drug. At the same time he told himself that if only he could make more money he and his wife would be happier and she would again become the woman who had enchanted him at the beginning of their married life. Of course his losses laid him open to further recriminations with the result that he experienced a growing resentment which would flare up with the impulse to retaliate in some way, only to subside helplessly in face of the stronger character that knew only too well how to taunt and hurt.

Who shall describe the slow poisoning of such a relationship? The mutual torment that two beings yoked together in marriage can cause each other? At best it is a battle between man and woman, between two natures each striving to maintain some part of itself free and inviolate from the other. Where there is a fundamental affection and mutual respect there is a fair chance of an honourable treaty between them. But let affection die and respect dwindle away, then will the battle between them become naked and unashamed. Mutual need becomes warped with mutual hate, for who can bear the sting of contempt from the being from whom he has sought the joy of loving? It is then that the battle between them becomes pitiless.

Carl, this big, loose-limbed man with an essentially simple nature, found himself up against a character he could not understand. How could he know all the tortuous paths of experience that had moulded

311

the complexities of Stella's temperament, the insatiable desire to excel, to achieve success, which never filled the void of insecurity? Stella herself was unaware of the motivations of her acts; there was compulsion, not freedom in what she did, because she was not free within herself. Thus two human beings, who had it in them to give each other happiness, floundered in mutual misunderstanding.

He had come to the city from the material and spiritual desert of an impoverished rural district; he had found comparative financial security; he had married Stella and life had opened out for him in a way that he had not dreamed to be possible. And then, apparently from nowhere, the bright skies had clouded over, the sun had darkened and the winds of discord chilled his nerves. Left unsatisfied because of the boredom of his daily routine at work, that taxed him neither physically nor mentally, he sought refuge in his home. He was a man who would have been contented with simple pleasures, his wife and children about him, his small garden to potter about in during the weekends. Failing to find the refuge he sought, and bewildered by his wife's incalculable behaviour, he took to drinking. Stella's contempt for him increased; she became frigid towards him. This enraged him as nothing else had done and for the first time Stella realised that she had pushed this good-natured man too far.

And then Stella discovered she was pregnant. At first she could not believe it and then she could not deceive herself any longer. With certainty came a sense of panic. She did not want a child. She dared not. Her husband had wanted one very badly, but she had resisted his importunity with all the cunning at her disposal. And now in spite of her it had happened. Was ever a woman more unfortunate? she asked herself. This unborn, this unknown, had it in its power to shatter her security – the security she had won at such cost.

She must do something. She could not tamely submit to fate in this way. Her thoughts flew to Kathie. Her sister knew all about these things. She could help her. She must! Then Stella's hope sank as quickly as it was born. Kathie would be the last one to help her in such a matter. Kathie could be hard and stern when she took a stand on what she considered was right or wrong ... She could not bring herself to go to Kathie. What about Joyce, Potgieter's wife? Since the affair at the races a coldness had grown up between the two couples, Stella bitterly blaming Potgieter for taking advantage of her husband's weakness. No, she couldn't take Joyce into her confidence. She could never trust her.

There was only her mother. She would go and see her mother.

At sight of her daughter, Mrs Liedeman's face lighted with joy. Stella looked well dressed and handsome.

'Come in! Sit down, Stella!' she said, pulling out a chair and dusting it with her apron, her gestures pathetically eager.

When her daughter did not respond, she looked anxiously at her. There was something wrong. Yes, there was something wrong.

'What is it, Stella?'

Stella told her. The mother was silent. A little grandchild about her knees – it would give her new life and hope. There was Kathie with no sign of her ever getting married, throwing herself away on this Paul. There was Andrew's wife Annette, a selfish young woman who showed no signs of settling down. The young wives these days expected too much coddling. But if Stella had a son, or a daughter – a little daughter ...

'Ma. Why don't you say something?'

Irene Liedeman was left so much on her own that she had got into the habit of talking to herself. Stella was irritated by the absent look on her mother's face. She had expected sympathy. Her mother must realise what this meant to her, more than anybody could.

'I don't want a child,' she said.

'Don't say that, Stella!'

'But it's true. Surely you understand.'

'You should have thought of this before.'

'It was Carl. I'll never forgive him.' She said this with such concentrated venom that her mother was startled.

'Don't talk so wild, Stella. If you live with a man you can't hold that up against him. It isn't natural.'

'I think I hate him.'

'For wanting a child?'

'Ma! What's the matter with you? What am I going to do?' cried Stella, completely nonplussed by her mother's unexpected attitude. Why, wasn't it she who all her life had wanted her to marry white? And now when something threatened Stella's security she must become all sentimental.

'You'll have to go through with it now that it has happened.'

'Isn't there ... some way?'

'Now don't you go and try any tricks,' cried her mother sharply. 'It'll only get you into trouble. I've heard of cases – You're not to do anything to yourself, do you hear? You never know where it will end.'

'But I'm so afraid, Mother. I don't care if it is dangerous.'

'You are mad!'

'Isn't there some doctor?'

'At a price, if your husband had plenty of money.'

'He hasn't.' Stella put a world of contempt in her voice.

'But I won't hear of it, Stella,' said her mother with unusual vehemence. 'It's a wicked thing you'd be doing.'

'Wicked?' Stella mocked her mother for her narrow-minded, religious attitude, but for once Mrs Liedeman stuck to her point and cunningly stressed the danger to Stella of attempting to interfere with nature.

'I'm warning you,' she continued. 'And don't take it to heart so. It may turn out all right. The chances are that it will.'

'If only I knew.'

'Have you told Carl?'

'No.'

'You'll have to tell him. He'll have to accept it, that's all. After all, he married you.'

Realising that she could get nothing out of her mother in this state of mind, which some would call fatalistic – or perhaps it was only matter of fact – Stella went home again to the man whom she now felt she hated more than she had ever hated anyone.

Afraid of the unknown and feeling herself entrapped, Stella was no easy wife for Carl during the ensuing months. She did not tell him she was going to have a child. He drank a little more and wondered how he could bring back those first joyful months of his marriage. He even confided in Potgieter that he was a bit worried as to Stella's state of health. She was so extraordinarily nervy. Whereupon his friend threw back his head to give one of those bellowing laughs that Carl used to join in when they were out on the spree together, but which now struck him as not nearly so funny.

'*God man!* You're the world's biggest fool!'

'Eh?'

'You're blind, man.'

'What you getting at?'

'Ask your wife, man. Do you mean to tell me she hasn't said anything?'

'She says plenty. She has a tongue on her. It's sometimes more than I can stand.'

Potgieter roared again.

'That's why, man.'

Carl stared at him.

'My wife knew weeks ago. And she gave me the hint. You're going to be a bloody father!'

Carl could hardly wait to get home that afternoon. He burst into the house, his big feet thumping along the diminutive passage, his face like an afternoon sun.

'You've been drinking,' Stella said, putting out a hand to ward him off. But Carl was not to be daunted this time. Poor Stella, he thought, he had been misjudging her all this time, while she had been suffering – well, if not in silence, at least she had reason for behaving as she did. And he could forgive her anything.

'Stella, why didn't you tell me?'

She shrank away. But even this he misinterpreted. How could a big, clumsy fellow like himself know how a woman felt at such times? He blamed himself for everything. In his joy at the prospect of a child being born to them, the immediate past with its petty strains, disappointments and follies, fell away. The Stella he had loved – and still loved – was to be the mother of his son. Gratitude, adoration and the thrill of anticipated fatherhood transformed him almost into a sensitive being. He reproached himself for being, as Potgieter so aptly described him, a blind fool. His wife had every reason for being discontented with him. How eagerly he resolved to put an end to his recent recklessness and strain every effort to get out of the rut. He'd look for another job, a job that offered some prospects of advancement, and he'd throw off the incubus of debt that had been weighing on him all these months.

In a state of exhilaration he had already in fancy conquered all his impediments to happiness. Clasping his wife in his arms, he exclaimed: 'If the little one only knew all the preparations that are being made for him. The little rascal!'

When at last the chill of his wife's reserve penetrated his buoyant mood, he didn't allow it to dishearten him, but put it down to the general whimsy of women in this condition. He would do nothing to cross her.

With clumsily gentle hands he wanted to touch this precious body that carried within it the living seed of his loins, and was startled by the violence of her movement away from him. He stood, his hands hanging loosely at his sides, the strong hands grown flabby for lack of the labour for which he was the most suited, labour that would have helped the man to feel he was a man, playing his part in this proud city ...

If his wife had not been so centred in herself and her fears and her resentments, she would have been moved to pity by the hurt look he gave her.

It was the second day of January. New Year's Day for the coloured people. Coon Carnival Day. Through the streets of the city danced the many troupes of capering Coons in their glancing satins of green and gold and black and gold and red and yellow and shimmering blue – a river of wild, singing beauty that spilled over into the night and all night long.

And on that same night a son was born to Carl and Stella. His first lusty cry filled his lungs with a good gulp of the new year air.

He was a big, eight-pound baby, with a tuft of black hair as soft as down. His skin, still creased and damp from the womb, had the same tint that had delighted Paul Mangena when he saw Kathie standing by the pool in the Company Gardens.

This, without any doubt, was Johannes Liedeman's grandson.

Stella lay exhausted, too weary to think or feel, and fell into a deep sleep. In a cot beside her lay the newborn child. Carl stood long looking down at him. This little brown bundle was his. He was a father and this his firstborn. As with all affectionate natures, the instinct to cherish this helpless being moved strongly within him. To hold that which was his against the world.

To hold or cast out?

That night the father and husband fought a battle with all the prejudices he had imbibed through his race.

He moved away from the bed and paced the narrow room that had grown insufferably close, more by reason of the struggle within him than the hotness of the night. The sound of some early morning revellers came through the open window ...

316

To hold or cast her out, together with her child? For she had deceived him. Doubts and hints that had flickered across his mind from time to time, and which he had pushed away from him, were now confirmed as he looked at his child. Men would point the finger of scorn at him, the father. The purity of the white race had been violated. If he were true to the racial creed on which he had been nurtured, he would cast out this woman and her child, back where they belonged. His family would never accept her or the child. Oh, bitter thought! He had dreamed of taking his wife and child proudly to them. And now? His people were poor, but they clung all the more fanatically to their purity of race, because it was all that was left to them in a society that had pushed them to the wall. It was their only badge of superiority.

All his training bid him obey the morals of the herd and cast out this woman. Would he not rather be of the pack than one of those hunted by it?

It might seem strange that this simple-hearted man should have to fight such a battle in the silent watches of the night while his wife and their firstborn lay sleeping. In other times and under other conditions it might be thought a strange and terrible thing for racial myths and fears to warp men's minds. Indeed a kind of madness – to believe that a brown skin houses an inferior soul and a pink skin a superior one. There may come a time when the wind of a great gargantuan laughter will send these little monsters scurrying out of the mind of man. But, strange or terrible, preposterous or absurd, to Carl these racial myths, and the fears and brutalities engendered by them, were real and inescapable. The society to which he belonged had been niggardly in its treatment of him, the son of an impoverished farmer; it had not granted him wealth or education worthy of a man, nor had it given him opportunity for advancement; it had left him intellectually and spiritually stunted. But it had implanted in him certain dogmas, of which the worship of racial purity was the core. The love of man for woman and the instinct to cherish his own – these are powerful human instincts, and Carl had them in strong measure. But who shall measure the blind power of those contrary forces in the society that had nurtured him? For they shun reason as the blood-sucking vampire bat shuns the light of day. In truth they are like the vampire in that they suck reason and human kindness out of men and make sick their moral nature.

Carl was by no means fashioned in a heroic mould. Yet the battle he waged with himself beside his wife and child had something of moral grandeur in it. And the woman who was the cause of it never knew what he suffered in those hours.

How did this fact he had learned alter the woman he had married? He went and stood beside the bed again. How tired, how wan, how weak she looked, lying asleep. In repose the face had none of that harshness with which he had grown familiar; it had a sweetness that took him back to the first days of his happiness when he had met her in the city and life took on a new vigour, a new meaning. He had a tenacious nature where his affections were concerned and this was something he could not forget. The impulse of tenderness that had moved him to cherish the newborn child embraced the sleeping figure of his wife. She was the same woman still, because she had become part of him. He needed her. The very suffering they had caused each other was an inseparable part of that bond. It is not only happiness that unites two people. Perhaps now that there was no secret between them, no deception, they could make something of their life together.

Carl decided to call his son Pieter, which was his father's name.

Carl and Stella remained together as they had been, apparently the same. But they could never be the same. He had once hoped that the coming of the child would end the estrangement between them; he had hoped that a frank acceptance of his position would ease their relationship. He was soon to find that the presence of their son aggravated their tensions and life became even less simple than it had been.

One evening Potgieter came round to see Carl, but he didn't bring his wife. He was all apologies.

'Joyce is awfully sorry she can't come. She has one of her *verdomde* headaches.'

'I'm sorry to hear that,' said Carl, with more sympathy than the occasion warranted. 'I hope she'll soon feel better.'

'So do I. Bloody nuisance, headaches.' Potgieter spoke with rather much gusto.

Stella said nothing. Potgieter then suggested that he and Carl should play billiards at their favourite hotel bar. This was nothing new.

Carl glanced at Stella, who deliberately avoided his look.

'Will you be all right?' he asked her.

'Why shouldn't I?' Her tone was cold.

'Well, so long!' said Potgieter. 'Sorry the wife isn't here to keep you company.'

Stella barely inclined her head as her husband and his friend went out.

When Carl came home she remarked crossly: 'Since when did that woman have headaches? If she's too stuck up to come into my house, you needn't bring her husband here either. I won't be insulted by your friends.'

Carl looked helplessly at his wife. There was much he could have said but he held his tongue.

Potgieter didn't come again. At work he became cool in his manner towards Carl. In fact Carl had a suspicion that his erstwhile friend had said something to the others; he couldn't be sure because it wasn't as if they were actually rude to him, but he didn't feel comfortable. Carl, who had always taken people as they came, now began to withdraw into himself. The Potgieters didn't join up with the Meyers over the weekends any more. Nothing was ever put into words. But Carl and Stella were made to feel that they didn't belong.

It was a situation that strengthened the uneasy bond between husband and wife, yet widened the gulf between them. Possibly Carl adapted himself to it with more equanimity than Stella. He had not clearly formulated why he had acted as he did, but was guided rather by the strong instincts of his nature, and in the same spirit he accepted the consequences of his actions. He did not demand, he did not complain; his needs and his habits were simple, and his weaknesses were such as to exasperate any woman. Stella would almost have welcomed it if he had turned on her with violent recriminations. It would have been something she could fight back. With completely perverted logic she still found it possible to blame him for what had happened. She had never wanted the child.

While she tended the boy with that scrupulous care she had always expended on everything that belonged to her – her house and her person – she withheld from him the tenderness of mother-love. It might have been expected that, since Pieter was so unmistakably of her family, she would take him to his grandmother and let him learn to love her people. But whether from pride or the fear that he would turn to his grandmother more than to herself, she took him to her old home by the level crossing only once or twice when he was small. Her mother obviously doted on Pieter, but she was determined not to encourage the contact.

Carl had insisted on seeing Mrs Liedeman. He wished to know; it was his right to know, he said. And for once Stella respected him. The meeting had been constrained on both sides and neither Carl nor his mother-in-law made any real attempt to break the barriers that separated them. Carl also met his brother-in-law Andrew, together with Annette. The two men measured each other eye to eye. 'Stella didn't get much,' commented Annette when she and her husband were alone. Andrew shrugged his shoulders.

'He might be worse,' he said.

Carl, pursuing his enquiries into Stella's family, learned about Kathie. But Stella never voluntarily spoke about her and never suggested that her husband or her son should meet her sister.

The years were passing. Pieter was growing, and growing out of all his clothes. He had his father's big frame, but in face he became more and more like his Aunt Kathie every day. He was an extremely sensitive boy, perhaps because he missed – without knowing what he missed – the tenderness of a mother's affection, which is so necessary for giving a child a sense of security – that rock on which his unsteady feet must stand if he is to grow into a normal, happy youth.

He learned to read at a very early age and startled his father by the fantastic little stories he invented.

'Where did you hear that one?' Carl would ask.

'In my head, of course,' answered Pieter. 'I can tell you lots more.'

'No, no. Not now. I haven't time to listen,' said his father hastily. 'You go and tell your mother for a change.'

'But she says she's too busy,' said Pieter, pouting.

And thus it often happened that Pieter was left alone with his fancies. He didn't mix easily with other boys. Sometimes he would go up to his father, take the big, coarse hand in his and pull on it with all his might. Awkwardly Carl would take him on his knee and set himself to listen once more.

320

'What a fanciful boy he is,' remarked Carl to his wife afterwards.

'And too lazy to do his lessons.' retorted Stella. 'Don't you go and spoil him.'

Pieter had a little brother, three years younger than himself.

At his birth Carl had said: 'He takes after my mother's family.' And they called him Frikkie.

Pieter adored his baby brother. This might seem at variance with the fact that the sight of Frikkie in his mother's arms excited in the older boy a sensation of being left out in the cold. Yet so it was. Perhaps by the very excess of his affection for the baby, he tried to drive out this feeling which he could not express to anyone, and still less understand. Stella bestowed on her younger son all the affection she had never been able to give to her firstborn. Acting with the blind impulse of her thwarted nature, she did not realise the harm she was doing, not only to the sensitive character of Pieter, but to the younger boy, whom she spoiled. As the boys grew older and could have become companions, it was she who made it impossible for them to get on together. Frikkie, a normal, robust little boy, would tease his brother, who seldom retaliated, except in a rare spurt of rage.

Stella saw to it that her two sons went to different schools, and her husband, while a little bit doubtful that this might hurt Pieter – seeing he was so fond of Frikkie – agreed with his wife that it was probably best that way. It wasn't clear to Pieter why he had been separated from his brother. There were so many things he could not understand, nor could he express them. Sometimes he hated his brother and then he was ashamed. How could he hate his brother? Pieter's inability to adapt himself to others became more marked and he developed solitary habits. Neither his father nor his mother understood the needs of this highly imaginative, intelligent boy, his groping in uncharted ways of thought and above all the deep sense of insecurity that possessed him.

CHAPTER 22

The city speaks

As the train bringing Paul from the Eastern Province to the city wound its way through the Hex River Pass with the naked mountain slopes rising sheer in the morning sun, then made its way down into the wide spreading valley where the laden vines and fruit trees spoke of the Cape's rich husbandry, his nostrils quivered in anticipation of the city so near at hand. The very atmosphere was different; the light was brilliant, but not harsh; instead of a burning aridity, masses of dark and light greens and browns met the eye.

Ah, there at last was the landmark which once seen stamped itself on the mind's eye whithersoever one went: the guardian of the city, Table Mountain. Still far off, the towering ramparts that he knew so well were at first no more than a deepening of the blue distance, but gradually this proud shape assumed solidity and stature. Devil's Peak emerged from its broad bosom and Lion's Head jutted out to look across the sea – the sea that was the pathway to the lands that Paul dreamed of visiting one day, perhaps to meet once more his friend and mentor, Hans Farben.

Clustered at the mountain's wooded base, casting their net ever wider, up the mountain and nearer to the sea, stretched the city's houses and buildings. Seen from the train window, sprawling and untidy, they were no more than the outward form – shadows of the teeming population living and moving perpetually within. His pulse quickened at the thought of becoming again a part of that teeming multitude.

The city! Scene of his first strivings to become a man; where he had suffered in mind and body the shocks of new experiences. The city, where he had trod the hard streets in search of work, shrinking from the still harder hearts of men. The city, which had seen the birth of his ambition and the birth of his love, with all the joy and the conflict that had made it an imperishable part of his being ...

Kathie met him at the station. She greeted him with a quiet but bright-eyed warmth that filled him with a sense of well-being. It was good to be with her again. He gave her greetings from his sister Nonceba.

'When I left home her last words were for you,' he told Kathie.

'What did she say?'

'Tell her there's a place waiting for her whenever she comes back to Lukaleni.'

'Perhaps I shall go back one day,' said Kathie.

Before doing anything else they had to settle first the question of Paul's lodging. Kathie had already been trying to find him a room but so far had been unsuccessful. There was no hotel or boarding house for Africans. There was nothing for it but to see if Mrs Sitole could help him out, though he had no desire to return to District Six. He knew she had taken over his little room and made something out of subletting it. But of course it was most probably occupied.

Thembisa Sitole nearly fell on her neck at the sight of him and led him straight to his old room. She rejoiced at what had seemed her bad luck only a few days previously when a nice young student, whom Paul himself had recommended to her, had had to give up his studies because of family difficulties, and had returned to the Transkei for the time being. Of course she could have got a new lodger the very next day, but she had become very choosy – thanks to Paul. Now it looked as if she had waited on purpose, with him falling into her lap like this. Her ancestors must have been keeping a special watch over her.

Didn't Paul think that her son Keke had shot up remarkably in the year he'd been away? Or was it more than a year? Much more than a year. But Keke had remembered Paul, because he had missed him sorely. So now, with Paul back at last, everything would be pleasant as it had been before. Thus she rambled on while Paul listened with only one ear. The sight of the familiar room with its bare furnishings and the table where he had so often sat poring over his books at the end of a day's work, all brought back the presence of one he would never see again – Nontando.

Paul did not yet feel ready to branch out on his own so he had decided to accept the offer of the firm to continue meantime in their Cape Town office, thus still further widening his experience. It was not that he was satisfied with what he was doing or had changed his mind. In his work, the same sense of futility that he had felt in the country pursued him here in the town and indeed became intensified. It was not only that he was handicapped by being simply an employee of a European firm; however well he did his job it was a case of: thus far and no further. What troubled him most was that he could not effectively assist his people in his present position. He saw himself as a puny puppet in face of the power of the law that sets into motion the dramas and disasters of thousands of lives with their terrors and anxieties.

Yet he was far from being ready to take action as the result of his discontent. It was one thing to know what he did not want. It was much more difficult to answer positively what he did want and to know where he was going. Maturity would not come suddenly; spiritual growth, like that of the seed underground, takes place unseen and unknown; the rain and the sun and the rich, dark soil give it sustenance until one day the stem and the flower appear for all to see.

Paul's sojourn in his home village had begun this process of maturing. It had opened his eyes to many things; he had seen a peasant people being steadily deprived of even the bare elements of their peasanthood; he had seen a drought of the spirit born out of the very drought of circumstance. As old Daniso had said, a grim struggle for survival was being waged every day. For himself, he had grown in self-knowledge, painful as the process had been, but he had also acquired a certain amount of self-confidence; in his discussions with Daniso the two men had frequently crossed swords, while maintaining that courtesy which is proper to two opponents who respect each other. In the courts, too, he had demonstrated his cunning and skill of argument. The people had begun to look to him. Now that he was in the city he was more and more frequently visited by those who had heard tell of him in the country. They came to him as a matter of course. He himself was surprised at the number of times people who had just arrived in town came to him because they had heard about him from some relative in the country. This was perfectly natural. Owing to the system of migrant labour imposed on the Africans, who were excluded from the towns except as a labour force, there was a constant coming and going between town and country; the peasant was willy-nilly the city worker.

Back in the city, Paul looked round him with a keen zest to see, to hear and to make new contacts. He was constantly putting out feelers that enabled him to catch the very pulse of this city life, and he had never been so conscious of all its manifestations. He felt that he was gradually piecing together the apparently unrelated parts of a puzzle, becoming aware of a significant pattern of society. Out of chaos he was beginning to find meaning.

He had an inveterate habit of wandering through the streets during his lunch hour. This he could do with more safety than at night when he was liable to the unwelcome attentions of the police pick-up van on its nightly prowl. The scenes around him intoxicated him with a sense of irrepressible vitality and he never tired of watching the tide of humanity as it eddied round him in an unending stream. What a mingling of peoples was here. Under what a variety of skin colour did the common blood of humanity beat. With what grotesqueness and what grace, what ugliness and beauty did it manifest itself. He felt that here he belonged to an inexhaustible source of life. He was part of it. Yes, he belonged.

To how many of his people, he thought, to how many of his people driven by poverty out of the Ciskei and the so-called native reserves, did the city signify human effort, hope and despair? For fifty years and more they had been coming in a steady stream, in spite of the laws that tried to thrust them back. And for them the city meant new modes of living, new skills of hand and eye, a quickening of coordinated muscles, a faster tempo of living. It meant also a shattering of old relationships that had given the young stability; the confusion and destruction of the moral laws by which men guide their actions. It had meant sickness and madness and death. Yet out of it all, new modes of thought had been born, new strivings, new hopes and dreams of a fuller living.

Vast forces were at work in society, forces which no man-made law could arrest. Let the price be as heavy as it might, a whole people was being precipitated into new ways of living and new ways of thought.

Paul's wanderings took him sometimes to the docks where he was fascinated by the clamour of ships being loaded and unloaded with merchandise. Voices called raucously to one another, cranes overhead creaked and groaned as they swung to and fro over the wharves; men straddled on the ship's deck in the various postures of their labour; shouts from the ship's hold echoed back as case after case disappeared into its gaping maw. Against the gently heaving sides of the vessels in harbour the sea lap-lapped, clucking lazily, while a babel of plaintive bird cries filled the air as the seagulls skimmed, dipped and darted for food and then soared again in an ever-changing pattern of flight. From this busy seaboard, this *Tavern of the Seas* beneath the towering mountain, the mind travelled to all parts of the world. Fruit and grain ripened in the South African sun, planted, tended and gathered by black hands, would find its way across the open sea to other seaboards and then to the shops and homes of Europe. Goods that the rough hands of workers in a thousand harbours of other continents had loaded into ships, were here being unloaded by brown hands and black hands into the trucks that would carry them throughout the Union; the riches of a vast industrial machine, with arteries that linked four continents, passed through these toiling hands.

My people do not reap the fruits of this labour, said Paul to himself, *yet no power on earth can turn our steps backward. We are pledged to the future.*

Such thoughts as these and such sights as these he communicated to Kathie.

'There must be others,' he said to her, 'many others who think and feel as we do, who want to know the why and the wherefore of our present position. We are not alone. We cannot be. We must find them.'

Paul knew that to clarify his own thoughts he must sharpen them

326

against the thoughts of others. Of course one couldn't go out into the highways and byways and expect an answer to what one was looking for, just for the asking. The very fact, however, that Paul was in a questing mood unconsciously drew others to him. He and Kathie together were gradually widening their circle of contacts. She told him – with some humorous details – how she had had a nodding acquaintance with various societies when he had first gone away to the Ciskei and she had tried this one and that one in her search for something to satisfy her. Now literary groups, philosophical groups, political groups – everything was grist to their hungry mill. Paul himself was never entirely satisfied with what he found, but in these groups he had the impression of youth that was insatiable in its need to overcome the frustrations of their present existence. In the nature of things much of this energy, lacking positive direction, consumed itself without achieving anything permanent. There was no doubt, however, that there was a strong intellectual ferment and that this ferment indicated a profound dissatisfaction with things as they were.

The effect of this environment was to make Paul more and more restless. Kathie recognised the signs and realised that sooner or later the day would come when she would have to face that parting which she had already in imagination steeled herself to face, ever since the conversation she had had with Nonceba. Time had been slipping away almost imperceptibly, almost deceptively placid – deceptive because the present seemed to stretch in an endless vista and change hid its face from them. Paul and Kathie were among those rare beings with an infinite capacity for companionship that knows no boredom. Neither of them grasping for possession of the other, their sympathy with each other almost too sensitively attuned, bound together by common interests and a common outlook on life, they were destined – one would have said – to be ideally mated. Kathie told herself it could never be, but of this she said no further word to Paul.

Time slipped past and change hid its face ...

If Paul's brief but potent friendship with the European Hans Farben had quickened in him that process of questioning what most people around him accepted as the natural order of things, then his meeting with the African cobbler James Ndwana, coming when it did, completely confirmed it. And it all happened from the simple requirement of having his shoes mended.

One day he was taking a short cut through a side street leading off Hanover Street, the main thoroughfare of District Six, the home of the coloured people of Cape Town. Hanover Street is a vivacious jade of a street, as raucous as the Cape's famous fish-horn with which coloured fish vendors, perched on top of a perilously swaying cart, split the eardrums of their prospective customers. It was here, within a stone's throw of this strident vitality, that Paul found Ndwana living and working and talking – for before all things he was a great talker. Ndwana was wedded to the District, as he once laughingly said to Paul when they became friends; he had put up with her shrewish tongue for a quarter of a century, and that was how he had learned to be the wise fellow he was.

Hurrying through the little side street Paul caught sight of a tiny window, cluttered like a refuse dump with an array of unmended shoes. This in itself was not enough to remind him that there was only a thin layer of leather between him and the pavement. But at the moment of passing he observed a long, lean hand stretch out from within to take a pair of shoes, and above it, the face of an African that instantly caught his attention. The eyes of the two men met through the window. On an impulse Paul decided to step inside the cobbler's shop, which was flush with the street.

In a space too small to deserve the name of shop, the front consisted of a narrow counter hillocked with shoes at both ends and with a valley between, large enough to allow the passage of yet another pair of shoes to swell the unruly pile. Behind the counter amid a fine confusion of dust and leatherware sat two men. The one Paul recognised as the man – about fifty – whose face had arrested him through the window. He was busy over his last, which had a black and white feminine shoe, fashionably high of heel, perched on it. The other man, rather younger, and shabbily dressed, did not seem to be an assistant, but had the air of a visitor. The two men were conversing, and as neither of them paid any attention to Paul for a moment he was able to observe the cobbler more narrowly.

He was a slightly built man with a high-cheekboned face. The face of a philosopher, thought Paul, rather than that of a mender of shoes. Taking in the lean, sinewy hands, his gaze returned to the face, especially the massive forehead (which was like his own, though Paul did not know it). The cheeks had the hollows of ill health, making the square line of the jaw sharply defined. The mouth was wide, twitching now and again into a smile, but the lips were not very full and the smile spoke more of sadness than of mirth. The eyes must have been large and bright when he was younger, but now the drooping lids veiled them, as if the man found it easier to listen if he drew the lids together.

He was listening now, for the other man had not stopped talking on Paul's entrance. Soon, however, the speaker looked up as much as to say: *What do you mean by interrupting our conversation? We have more important matters to attend to than your shoes.*

The cobbler rose and came towards Paul. Addressing him in Xhosa, he asked him what he wanted. Paul explained, adding that he would have to bring in his shoes the next day, as he couldn't very well walk along the street in his socks.

The cobbler smiled. 'You might find yourself in jail if you did,' he said.

Unwilling to depart immediately, Paul passed some remark and before long the man was asking him the customary questions: 'Where do you come from? ... What is your tribe?'

When Paul answered, the drooping eyes opened in a flash of recognition.

'Ah, you are the lawyer, aren't you?'

'I am a lawyer,' replied Paul.

'And you were working in Lukaleni last year?'

'Yes I was.'

'News travels fast, you see,' said the cobbler, turning to his friend for confirmation.

'Especially when it's bad news,' said the other.

The man laughed. 'And good news, too.'

With the ice thus broken it was not long before the three men were engaged in conversation. The cobbler introduced himself as the son of Ndwana and his friend as the son of Lumko. Both of them, Paul learned, came from the district of Queenstown. They had made their way to the city together in their youth; they had worked in the road gangs, picked up jobs as labourers where they could. Hard as it was to make a livelihood it had not been so hard in those days – they said – to get into the town, not as it was at the present day. Thereupon they launched into the story of how a young African had been arrested because he couldn't produce a permit to show that he was allowed to look for work in the town. The situation was complicated by his having – as the police put it – resisted arrest.

'How familiar I am with that phrase!' said Paul, remembering the peasant Dhlomo, and others.

'We were just discussing the case before you came in,' said Lumko.

'Actually it is the son of my brother who is involved,' explained Ndwana. 'He is very young. He's in jail now, awaiting trial.'

Paul expressed his concern and asked for more details.

'Oh, it was the usual thing,' replied Ndwana. 'It was night-time. He'd just gone to a corner shop to get some cigarettes and was on his way back when he was accosted by two stalwart guardians of law and order, who asked him to show his permit. Of course he had no permit on him, but he assured them he had a job. The irony was that he *had* just got a job and was to have started on the Monday, but he had nothing on him to prove the truth of his words. He repeated that he had a job and produced what papers he had. But the next minute he found himself on the ground, a heel in his stomach and his papers scattered all around. Then a man, hearing the rumpus, ran out of the shop and at the sight of them manhandling the boy –'

'It was a *coloured* man –' interrupted Lumko.

'I'm afraid,' continued Ndwana, 'this coloured man behaved contrary to all rules and regulations. He should have minded his own business, of course, but he didn't –'

'It was only a black man who was being arrested,' chimed in Lumko again, with a sardonic grin. 'The coloured man must have had it drummed into his ears often enough that the black hordes are swarming into the town and eating the bread out of his mouth. But he seemed to have forgotten this. He came up and tried to protect the boy –'

'" ... Arrest him properly!" he shouted to the police,' went on Ndwana, taking up the tale again. '"Arrest him with justice!"'

'With justice!' snorted Lumko. 'Huh!'

'The next thing the police seized him too,' continued Ndwana. 'And my brother's child tried to help him in turn. Then some more people came out of the shop and there was a general to-do. It's difficult to say what happened next. Apparently somebody threw a stone at the police.'

'And then the fat was in the fire,' explained Lumko. 'Whistles were blowing, more police came running up and the batons had a busy time cracking skulls, I can tell you!'

'The upshot of it was that the coloured man and my brother's son were both taken to the charge office.'

'Where is the coloured man now?'

'Both he and the boy are in jail, awaiting trial.'

'You say your brother's son came from the country to look for work.'

'That was his first crime,' answered Ndwana.

'But he had no permit?'

'That was his second crime.'

'It's too bad about that job he had just got.'

'He hadn't a permit. That's all they're interested in.'

'It's crazy,' said Lumko.

'It's the law,' said Ndwana. 'They'll fine the boy and pack him back to the Transkei. It'll break him.'

'When does the case come up?' asked Paul.

'Wednesday next. Will you take it on for us?'

'Haven't you engaged a lawyer already?'

'We only heard yesterday that the boy was in jail.'

'You've come in the nick of time,' said Lumko.

Paul's firm took on the defence of both the African and the coloured man and at least succeeded in reducing the sentence for both of them.

With the bond thus established, the friendship between Paul and Ndwana ripened fast. He got into the habit of dropping into the little shop every other day. Never did he find it empty of someone come to consult the man on some problem or other, and the cobbler was never so busy that he couldn't stop in order to give you all his attention. Often two or three would be gathered there, holding discussions, into which he would now and again throw a pregnant remark or put a provocative question. Sometimes he would work and talk; sometimes the busy hand would be arrested while some particularly knotty point was under consideration. Then of course the work had to be made up some time. Paul wondered when the man slept, for no matter how late he went there he found him either talking or cobbling. He consumed himself all the time, without sparing himself.

Paul's first impression of Ndwana as more philosopher than cobbler (indeed he cobbled vilely) was borne out by all his subsequent experience of him. Here was a man who had never had a chance to be educated beyond the bare rudiments. Leaving school at a very early age he had made his way literally step by step, as farmhand, as labourer on the roads, till he had reached the city, where he had tried his hand at whatever came his way. How he had picked up his present trade Paul had no idea, but the main thing was that it gave him what few Africans possessed – independence. Pearl of great price – independence, freedom, not from toil, but from the bullying breath of the boss standing over you, squeezing the manhood out of you, shrivelling your very brains. It was on this point that he would taunt his listeners, the young men who found their way every evening to his shop. He would survey them with a half mocking, yet bitterly serious severity.

'You have forgotten how to be men,' he would say. 'You have forgotten how to think. Your brains are rotting, like those of your masters. Shall I tell you what sickness you are suffering from? I have a name for it – slave mentality.'

When some of his listeners protested, pointing out that the severity of their conditions made it almost impossible to think and gave them no time to think, he would taunt them again:

'So the slave will wallow in the slough of his slavery for ever?'

Then he would continue more quietly and Paul was startled at the way the man's thoughts coincided with his own; in fact he himself was moved to describe the feeling that this city gave to him of the movement of vast forces bringing change to his people.

Ndwana listened with great interest while Paul was speaking, observing him narrowly through his half-closed lids.

'If only,' continued Paul, 'if only the black worker, too, could share in those riches he helps to produce. But, as I have said, the fruits of his labour are denied to him.'

'That is true,' replied Ndwana, looking round his little gathering of eager ears. 'But it is not the whole truth.'

'How so?'

'I've lived in the town. I've breathed the air of the city for near a quarter of a century. And I'd put it this way – it's not so very different from what you yourself have said. We are toilers. But what the hands touch, what the muscles strain to lift – they are powerful instruments of development in our people. They waken in us new thoughts and new desires.'

'And if we cannot fulfil them?' Paul asked.

'Ah, that very denial quickens our growth. With these hands I have learned it. I know, for I've wielded the pickaxe on the road that was one day to bring me to the city. I've touched the sleek body of a big machine, though I did no more than polish her, and she asleep, not moving at the touch of my hand on the controls, as one day she will. You see that tall building topping the sky, over there, the night lights flashing on her, like a woman in a gaudy dress? I helped to make her, though the drill thrumming under my hand shook the guts out of me as I worked down in the stony rubble. That was years ago, but I do not forget. I know what all these things did to me and thousands like me. As you yourself have said, young man, no power on earth can turn us back – unless it be ourselves.'

'Ourselves?'

'Beware of slave mentality,' said Ndwana. 'It is a cunning sickness. We may have it without knowing we have it.'

'How may we diagnose it?' asked one of the other young men.

'That is a good question,' answered Ndwana. 'He who has the mind of a slave accepts the existing order of things as unchanging and unchangeable, because his master has told him it is so. He does not question it; still less does he try to change it. When he is kicked he cringes; he fawns on the hand that smites him. He begs for crumbs for himself, but not his brother; he slinks into a corner to lick his own wounds, but does not see the wounds of his brother; bullied by his master, he bullies those who are even more unfortunate than himself. Robbed of will and reason, he becomes stupefied and hardened of feeling for others. He loses the very power to think of himself as a man.'

'It is a grim picture,' said the young man.

'Words cannot paint what tyranny has destroyed of our manhood. What do any of you here know of the past of our people? You have not even memories. Our history has been blotted out and stupid lies masquerade as the truth. And you yourselves believe them. You are foolish enough to be ashamed of our past. Ashamed of men who were men, you yourselves are less than men. Go among the old people before it is too late. Go to them and learn from them the truth of how your forefathers lived and fought. But hasten. Time has wings. Our past is dying every day and the dust of oblivion smothers it. Go, study the past so that it may help you to meet the present. But know the present also, for it has much to give you.'

The young man frowned. 'It denies us more than it gives.'

'Only if you are a slave,' said Ndwana. 'You can wrest from it what it has to give, like a miner digging for precious metal in rock and rubble. Arm yourselves with knowledge and understanding. Learn the best that the white man can give you and throw away the dross. I say it must be the best and nothing but the best. You are not children. Then and then only can you begin to build for the future. Remember the future is in *your* hands . . .

'Go home now,' he concluded, his hand across his forehead. 'I have work to do before I sleep. The people must be properly shod in the hard city streets.'

The young men would reluctantly take their leave, some of them looking uneasy under the whip of his tongue; others with their eyes shining at the challenge of his words.

And so the hungry men listened and learned. Paul began to love the little shop, for was it not in a very real sense a workshop of ideas? It drew all kinds of people – all kinds according to the vicissitudes of their daily existence, but one in their common need and in their spiritual hunger. If some came merely out of curiosity they never came again, or they learned to change their ways; for Ndwana had a nose for the charlatan and was merciless to those whom he suspected of seeking first their personal aggrandisement.

'I tell you,' he said once, banging his last in a way that boded no good to the shoe under repair, 'I tell you, there are fools and rogues amongst us, and believe me, the fools do us more harm than the rogues. Give me an honest to goodness rogue and I know how to handle him. I might even have some respect for his roguery – provided I can get the better of it. But beware of a fool. With a fool you never know where you are. A fire-eater one minute, he'll grovel and cringe the next, and then with the following breath he'll stand on his precious dignity. If a rogue zigzags in front of you, you must know that he is doing it to bamboozle you. But if a fool hops now on one foot and now on the other, you may be sure it's because somebody has him by the tail.'

Even as his listeners laughed at the mental picture conjured up by his words, Ndwana waggled his finger vigorously at them:

'I want no fools amongst you,' he cried. 'If we are to emerge as a people we must stand on our own feet. We'll carry out our struggles as *we* think best. Beware of those who call themselves your friends. I don't want to see any of you being held by the tail and dancing to another's tune. And if such a man comes to you, throws up his eyes and swears he is your friend, then double your care of him, for it's then that he's meditating the most mischief, binding you more firmly with the very chains you are trying to break.'

After this discussion Paul went away worried that he had not tackled Ndwana on a certain point that didn't completely satisfy him. Ndwana had said: 'Beware of those who call themselves your friends.' Excellent advice. But it was a point that needed clarifying. So at the very next opportunity Paul put the question to him: 'Don't you believe, then, that it's possible for us to find true friends among the white people?'

'Friends!' Ndwana laughed. 'What is a friend, my friend?' Then, without waiting for an answer: 'You can only have friendship between equals. Now can you tell me a single white man in this country who could ever look upon the black man as his equal? How, then, can he ever be your friend?'

'I think it is possible,' Paul said quietly.

Ndwana shot him a look. 'It has never been my experience in a quarter of a century – yes, and more,' he said. 'I know these so-called friends only too well ... Oh, they may ask you to tea and pat themselves on the back as being very fine fellows for their magnanimity, but, tell me, can you imagine any white man sharing the same blanket with you, my friend, on a cold winter's night? Can you imagine a single one of them coming to you and not seeking to get something out of you? No, my friend. I have never met such a white man.'

But Paul was not satisfied. He proceeded to tell Ndwana about the European bookseller, Farben. He told him how he, too, had asked himself: *What does this white man think he can get out of me?* But he had come to trust this man. The man had loved truth, as Ndwana did. He had wrestled with Paul in argument – as man to man. He had awakened Paul's mind to many things towards which he had been groping. This Farben was a man of integrity ...

Ndwana listened, at first with a sceptical smile on his face, but gradually Paul's earnestness sufficiently convinced him so that he grudgingly admitted: 'Perhaps what you say is true. Only it has never been my experience.'

It was a point on which Ndwana and Paul never quite agreed. Yet in spite of such differences between the two men Paul told himself that if there was one quality which the man possessed in addition to his integrity and his devotion to the cause of his people, it was his capacity to get at fundamentals. He saw with remarkable clarity the true nature of his position and that of his people. While not trained to formulate his thoughts into any clearly defined political system, nevertheless this worker, who derived from the peasantry, had an astuteness of reasoning that cut across all the many forms and manifestations of propaganda from the schoolroom and the pulpit to the hydra-tongued newsprint. He was able to get at the core of things. His reactions to experience were direct and straightforward because throughout a lifetime the truth had been burned into his consciousness by the relentless realities of his daily existence and thence subjected to the scrutiny of an acute intelligence. The result was an absolutely uncompromising attitude of mind; in spite of conditions which of themselves breed feelings of inferiority in those who are subjected to them, the poverty, the shabby coat, the insults of petty officials who at the slightest provocation crack the whip of superiority, in spite of such things Ndwana retained unshaken his sense of manhood. And this he communicated to others.

He is like Daniso, Paul said to himself. *He has the same penetrating judgement of men and things. But something more. He has a wider vision. That is it! A wider vision, sharpened perhaps by the swifter tempo of town life.*

This breadth of vision showed itself not only in Ndwana's formulation of his thoughts but also in his practical activities. Paul marvelled at his ceaseless outpouring of energy, in spite of the obvious weakness of his body that had already been overtaxed by his earlier privations. (Paul feared the inroads of the dread TB germ.) Ndwana had found the time and the energy to found a mutual aid society among a group of Africans. He and his friend Lumko had first organised it for the benefit of those people coming from their own district, in cases of sickness, funeral expenses, arrests by the police and suchlike. It was Ndwana, however, who argued that it should be for the benefit of all Africans, whatever part of the country they came from and whatever tribe they belonged to. Whatever their origins, they all suffered the same disabilities in the city. That was how Ndwana put it. It was a provocative idea to think in terms of one people, more provocative than he himself at first realised, and he encountered some opposition from other members of the society. But he stuck to his point and eventually won the day. So now he had the main responsibility of this flourishing society on his shoulders, an undertaking that called for both skill and integrity. He himself once remarked to Paul: 'My friend, the worst instincts of men reveal themselves in transactions where money is involved. If you ever contemplate being as rash as I have been in undertaking a job of this nature, remember to keep your head and purpose clear above the intrigues that revolve about money.'

What was the dominating idea behind all this outpouring of energy, this tireless assumption of responsibilities, this constant grappling with ideas? Loyal to his friends, he seemed to be inspired by a larger loyalty. Asking himself the answer to this question, Paul found it in a single – and simple – fact. Ndwana had unbounded faith in his people and in the future of his people. This marked the breadth of his vision. Hence his emphasis again and again on the duty of the African to arm himself with knowledge, that knowledge which is the heritage of all mankind and to which every race has contributed throughout the ages.

'We don't want the dregs of civilisation!' he would exclaim, and the veins would stand out on his forehead as he spoke. 'We must acquire the best, the best in every branch of knowledge.'

It gave him great pleasure to see how Paul had wrested his education out of an unwilling system and reached his present position. Only he would shake his head sadly that it should be such a rare, even a startling phenomenon to see a black man reach such eminence.

'Don't let it make you conceited,' he remarked half jocularly to Paul. 'There are many more who should be challenging you in your own field, my boy. Only the odds were too strong against them.'

'I know it,' answered Paul.

Paul had inspired Kathie with an eagerness to meet Ndwana. The result was that they would spend at least one evening every week with him – Paul himself going more frequently. Ndwana had welcomed her with that quiet courtesy he extended to everyone. He never asked them questions about themselves, but when the three of them happened, all too rarely, to be alone, Kathie felt she was in the presence of a man who understood and respected the relationship between Paul and herself. Ndwana's vision saw further than that of Daniso.

Once when Paul, at Ndwana's request, was absent on some business that concerned their society, Ndwana said gently to Kathie: 'When are you and Paul going to get married?'

Kathie was startled and did not know how to answer.

'He is a good man,' he continued, and then, with a smile, 'he needs a wife.'

'I –' began Kathie.

'I know what people say about these matters,' he said. 'There is a great deal of foolish prejudice on both sides. But you and Paul are not children. You know what you do. You need no man's permission as to what you should do. I say it is a good thing that you do.'

Moved to confide in him, Kathie tried to express all that she felt about Paul's future and the need to do nothing that would stand in his way.

'I understand what you mean,' Ndwana said thoughtfully. 'I, too, hope for great things from him in the future. For that very reason I think you should be at his side. If he is worthy of acceptance by the people, they must accept him as a whole. If he chooses you as his wife, they must know that it is a good thing.'

At home Kathie pondered over what Ndwana had said. Was Nonceba, for all her wisdom, perhaps wrong? Paul had a profound respect for Ndwana's opinions, because he trusted his integrity. But in the final analysis he alone would choose what he would do. He had not spoken of his plans for some time.

Kathie was aware that in the period following his return to the city, Paul was approaching step by step to a position of leadership which was the natural fulfilment of his particular qualities and his outlook.

Yet Paul himself was the last to see it in this light. Leadership was something he shunned and even feared. He had seen the people put their trust in men who had proved utterly unworthy of it; they had betrayed that trust because they had forgotten the very people who had raised them to their exalted position.

'The people are too willing to put their trust in these so-called leaders,' he would say to Ndwana, 'and how often have they been betrayed!' The fact that people came to him more and more frequently in the town, while he in turn realised the ineffectualness of his efforts at the courts, goaded him to a self-criticism that was actually in danger of impeding him in assuming those responsibilities which others judged he was ripe for. If Nonceba, Daniso, Kathie and even Ndwana were ready, as it were, to thrust leadership upon him, and regarded it as his goal, it was far from being so for Paul.

The sense of responsibility was stronger in him than that burning ambition which so often drives men on to seek power. For him, leadership was not a goal in itself. It would come inevitably in the course of things if he reached his full development in accordance with the main driving force behind all his actions – namely, a tremendous faith in his people, and provided also there was no counterforce to take him from his purpose. It was the fear of this last danger that had moved Daniso in his enmity against Kathie and that had inspired Nonceba, in spite of all her sympathy, to appeal to Kathie not to marry Paul. The mistake that his old friend and his sister had both made was to think too much in terms of their own ambition for Paul (however disinterested) and too little in terms of his own aims. He would take the road that he felt he had to take, whether or not it led to leadership.

Indeed for him the road was beset with hazard and even danger, once he had pledged himself to the cause of his people. It was this thought, and this thought only, which dictated his unwillingness to ask Kathie to marry him. He knew full well what she was ready to face with him. But was he prepared to ask it of her?

He told himself that he loved her too well for that.

Time slipped by and change hid its face ...

For many years Kathie and Stella never met. For the two sisters time seemed to stand still. Pieter, Stella's elder son, was growing a big boy. So too was Frikkie. Their growth marked the movement of the inexorable dial-hand.

Frikkie was sandy-haired like his father, Carl. But Pieter continued to grow more like his Aunt Kathie.

One afternoon Pieter went along with Frikkie and a group of other boys to see a film show. The ticket clerk let all the boys through, at half price, but Pieter was turned away. And the other boys laughed.

Pieter brooded. There were many things he did not understand.

The day came when Paul fell out with his firm and severed his connection with them for good. He had saved enough to be able to set up on his own and managed to find premises, though extremely cramped, not far from Ndwana's workshop.

'Yes,' he said to Kathie. 'I have decided not to give up the law altogether. I can still give the people the benefit of my legal knowledge. And besides, I must live.'

But law was only to be part of his work. He felt he had something to say to the people, and it must be said. If the people wanted him in the country he would pitch his tent wherever and whenever he felt the need.

The time had come. Paul was ready. And Kathie was ready, too.

'You know what it means, Kathie?' he said.

'I think I do,' she answered quietly.

Then she continued. 'I would gladly come with you, Paul. If you can face the hazards of it, so can I.' As he was about to answer, she silenced him and went on:

'But that is not the only consideration. My presence would make it more difficult for you among your people. I am not one of them.'

'You cannot say such a thing!' cried Paul. 'We are one people, with a common aim!'

'You and I know that, Paul. And Ndwana, too. But the people are not ready to believe it.'

'They are more ready than you think. Do you remember how you and the old peasant woman at Lukaleni helped the mother with her baby? Do you remember how pleased the old woman was?'

'Oh, that –' Kathie shrugged.

'Don't you see? Every day that kind of thing is happening. It's life itself that teaches them to come together.'

Kathie recalled what Ndwana had said. *If Paul chooses you as his wife the people must know that it is a good thing. If they accept him they must accept you.* This was how Paul would see it. Then her promise to Nonceba – didn't it fall away? Perhaps if Kathie had been more possessive she would have decided the matter there and then, sweeping aside Paul's objections to their marriage. It was a weakness of her nature to suspect most what she most desired and give way to the claims of others. It had dictated her relationship with her mother and it explained her long devotion to her sister Stella. Even now she decided it would be better if Paul did go out into the country alone. Let him first establish himself with the people.

And then, later perhaps, they could be together ...

CHAPTER 23

The rising tide

For some time news had been coming in of disturbances among the African peasants in the reserves in the Transkei, the Transvaal, the Free State and in Zululand in Natal. There was clearly a great deal of unrest throughout the country and clashes with the police were becoming more frequent. These incidents were not always reported in the press, but the Africans in town had other means of communication and whenever such news came through, feeling ran high. It was as if two seas were joined by a subterranean channel so that the rising tide of waters from this inland sea surged through it to swell the other. With a group gathered round him studying the report of a clash in a remote district in the Transkei, which had involved the death of several Africans, Ndwana's eyes blazed and the telltale veins stood out on his forehead.

'Out there the peasants are fighting our battle,' he said. 'The battle for all of us. It is a life and death struggle. And what are we doing about it?'

A week later a message was sent to Paul from Eastern Pondoland asking if he would come and defend an African teacher who had been charged with incitement of the people in that district.

Paul handed the letter to Kathie.

'I can go to them at once,' he said. 'I have been waiting for this.'

So once more Kathie faced existence without Paul.

After a time he wrote back to tell her he had won the case, but since he was in that district he had decided to spend some time there investigating what had been happening in the outlying villages where he understood that the people had been up against the authorities. He would pick up a job when the chance – and the need – offered.

Within a few months he was back in town and for a time Kathie was happy in their renewed companionship. It was a happiness made all the more poignant by the knowledge that before long she would have to face life again without him. Thus for the next year or two she steeled herself to endure the winter of her loneliness that followed inevitably on the summer of her joy, half hoping that Paul would one day bid her come to him in spite of his resolve not to ask her to share so insecure an existence. How little he knew of all that was in her heart, she reflected sadly. Yes, even he, with whom she had tasted the joy of a rare companionship. Where in all this, was there security? How many men and women slept on that soft pillow – security? Did Stella, her sister, who had married according to her ambition? No. A thousand times, no! And Paul? He was doing what he wanted to do. He did not ask security.

Throughout this time Kathie found her thoughts turning more and more to Stella. Perhaps it was because she was lonely and not a little tired. Imperceptibly youth had slipped away and she realised that she had always lived at a pace that did not spare herself. Yes, she was a little tired.

One day in February – it was the hottest day of the year – her mother died of heart failure. Up to the last, though she had been ailing, Irene Liedeman had refused to give up working at her machine, declaring that she wanted to be independent and not a burden on anybody who didn't want her. Kathie had visited her regularly, but it was like visiting a shadow. Her feelings had become numb where her mother and Stella were concerned – or else they took refuge in an apparent indifference, like a deep pool covered with ice and a blanket of frost.

On the day her mother had taken ill Kathie had gone out of town to a case, for she was on her own now, having left the hospital some years previously. It was with the greatest difficulty that her brother Andrew had been able to contact her late that afternoon. She had hurried back, but it was too late. Her mother was already dead. Andrew had not yet informed Stella and it fell to Kathie to perform the last services to the dead, a service that had fallen to her hands far too often in the course of her long term at the hospital.

Andrew had suggested bringing help, shamefacedly excusing his Annette, because she was rather highly strung and just couldn't bear the sight of a dead body. But Kathie refused help, saying she preferred doing it alone.

And now it was all over. She had shed no tears. She sat with folded hands in the room of the dead. It was the front room of the house that had belonged to her mother's mother, grandmother Fraser, and which they had always preserved for special occasions.

As Kathie sat in the darkening room she heard the wailing whistle of an approaching train. As it reverberated through her taut senses, almost mechanically she became aware of the reflection of the signal at the rail crossing. In her youth it had become something so familiar that she hardly noticed it. Now she watched the red light flood and fade, flood and fade through the room with hypnotic regularity, and as in a kaleidoscope, came fleeting memories of the past. Poor Ma, she thought. How she had striven and denied herself to keep her head above the city jungle. With what passion of misplaced self-sacrifice had she assisted her younger daughter to her goal, only to be left lonely at the end of it.

Kathie was startled out of her daydream by the sound of the handle of the door being carefully turned.

The door opened and Stella entered. The sisters looked at each other without speaking. Stella's glance went to the body lying on the bed and slowly she went up to it. Kathie did not move, but fixed her eyes on her sister, whom she had not seen for many years. How many? And she forgot their mother as she watched her.

Stella did not look a happy woman. She was neatly dressed – as she always was, thought Kathie, remembering the child who had loved to look tidy and pretty – but her face had a hard, frustrated look, which even this moment of sorrow did not soften. But then Stella had never, except in early childhood, been one to display much emotion. And now affection had been so long petrified that even the death of the mother who had given all she had to this one child, could not move her. Or was she hiding her feelings because of Kathie's presence?

Kathie rose to go out and then she changed her mind. She approached the bed.

'I did not come in time,' she said. 'I was out of town.'

It was as if she wanted to share with Stella the guilt of not being with their mother at the last. Stella gave her a swift glance but did not answer.

'Andrew is seeing to everything,' continued Kathie.

'He told me,' Stella said.

Kathie turned towards the door and, in opening it, nearly stumbled over a figure standing outside in the dark passage. What a forlorn figure it was. And how lost he looked.

She drew in her breath. It must be Stella's son. Her elder son, Pieter. Kathie had not realised that Stella's son could be so big already. How time flew.

'What are you doing all alone in the dark?' she asked him.

The boy did not answer, being more intent on peering into the room, which his mother had forbidden him to enter.

A dreadful curiosity drew him towards the dead body lying on the bed. He must go close up to it and look on this face lying so still and ashen. Before Kathie could prevent him, he went forward quickly, yet stealthily, and stood gazing down at his dead grandmother.

The half fascinated, half frightened look on his face and in his whole posture, startled Kathie. She made a movement towards him, whereupon Stella became aware of his presence. Speaking low, but harshly, his mother said: 'I told you not to come into this room.'

Immediately Kathie took the boy by the hand and led him away. He had an abstracted look on his face, a puzzled look, and her heart went out to him. Shutting the door behind her, where Stella still sat, she lifted her hand to put it on his shoulder, then at the last moment held it back.

'I am your Aunt Kathie,' she explained.

Making her way through the once familiar house, she avoided the kitchen, whence she heard voices talking, and made straight for the little room at the end of the passage that used to be hers and Stella's when they were children. Speaking as cheerfully as she could she tried to make the boy comfortable by putting him in a chair that had been a favourite of her own, though he did not respond to her. He was shy and awkward and at the same time rather sullen, and she told herself that it was probably just his difficult age – about fourteen, if her memory wasn't at fault. Attempting to put him at his ease she began to talk and as he continued to sit with averted eyes, she eagerly took in his every feature. *He is like my father,* she thought, unaware that this was to say: *He is like myself.*

He had the same broad-set eyes, the same forehead, and only the lips were more finely drawn than her own. It was the lips that caught her attention; they were set in a too tense expression like one who was repressed and oversensitive. Of course it might be that he felt the sadness of the present situation, without being able to do anything about it. What should a young boy know of death and sorrow? His mother had spoken harshly to him, but it was natural that she wouldn't have wanted him to come in at that moment. Surely he must understand that. She had done it to spare him and he mustn't be hurt about it.

Kathie found herself wondering why her sister had brought Pieter with her, and not her younger son. What was his name? ... Frikkie. Her mother had once told her he was like his father. Her thoughts concerning Stella and her family were travelling fast, like a frost-bound stream suddenly set free. Her mind leapt to the thought of the two brothers – like Stella and herself. Did they get on together? Was Pieter shut out in the cold, treated as one who didn't belong? Was that the meaning of this closed, intense expression? She must get to know Pieter better. They could become good friends. Kathie stopped short at this thought, realising that her eagerness had run away with her. Stella would make it difficult – if not impossible – for her to make friends with the boy. She wondered if Stella had ever told Pieter about herself. What was he thinking as he sat there so tense and awkward? Did he understand who she was?

Jumping up she went to get food for him. Boys of that age were always hungry, and perhaps his shyness would disappear over a cup of tea and a biscuit. When she came back he was standing over a little bookcase containing some of the books she had had as a girl and which her mother had left in the room undisturbed. Ah, if he was fond of reading, then they had something in common. But at the sound of her footsteps he quickly replaced the book and turned away from the bookcase.

'Don't mind me, Pieter,' she said. 'If there's any book there that suits you, do take it. They used to be mine.'

'No thank you,' he replied.

Pretending not to notice anything amiss in his manner, she proceeded to pour the tea and talk at the same time. He answered mostly in monosyllables, but from time to time he flashed her a look that at last revealed an answering gleam of interest, which made her hopeful that she would make contact with him, if she had the opportunity.

Puzzlement struggled with an involuntary responsiveness to the warmth of her manner.

'You're a big boy for your age. What do you intend to do?' she asked.

'I don't know.'

'What class are you in at school?' It was a simple question, but instantly his face clouded. He answered sullenly: 'I should be in standard nine.'

'And aren't you?'

'No.'

'And why not?'

'The headmaster said there was no room for any more in the secondary school.'

'Oh, Pieter.'

Of course, the two boys would be kept separate; he must be at a different school from his brother. If she knew Stella, Pieter must be a thorn in her flesh. And what of Pieter?

She looked at him, softly, warmly, almost pleadingly. In the long period of estrangement, in the angry pride she had felt against her sister, Kathie had forgotten she had a nephew – a nephew who could turn only to her, if ever he should feel the need. At fourteen he was at the very age when he was at the mercy of emotions he could not understand, feeling the urge of new desires, uncertain and insecure because of them and doubly insecure because of his particular circumstances. Only affection and understanding would help him to come clear of the quicksands. What affection would Stella be capable of giving her son? What was the relationship between Pieter and his father? Kathie asked herself these questions and feared the answers.

The more she observed the boy the more she was convinced that all was not well with him. She felt the anger rising in her. Oh, the blind stupidity of these tormented family relationships. Who should know better than she? She had an impulse to sweep past the boy's sullen reserve and take him in her arms, but for once the full force of the helplessness of simple affection came home to her. He could not yet think of her as his aunt –

Kathie heard Stella's impatient voice from the front of the house. Pieter abruptly stood up. 'My mother is calling me,' he said.

Accompanying him to the door, Kathie said: 'You and I are going to be friends, Pieter. I hope you will come and see me soon. Will you?'

'Yes,' he answered, almost inaudibly.

She smiled. Had she succeeded after all in breaking down the first barrier between them?

'I'll be expecting you, then,' she said.

She stood face to face with Stella as they parted. 'What a fine son you have, Stella. Pieter and I have been making friends, eh, Pieter?'

'Come, Pieter. I must hurry,' said Stella. Then half apologetically to Kathie: 'We have a long way to go and it is very late.'

'Pieter will take care of you,' said Kathie. 'Goodnight, Pieter.'

'Goodnight.' He gave her a shy half smile.

Kathie turned back slowly into her mother's house. What Paul wouldn't do for such a boy? she thought. He would be able to talk to him as she never could. And at such an impressionable age contact with a man like Paul would do him a world of good. Paul would not only direct his studies, but take him out of himself, broaden his mind and clear away those doubts and fears that were written on his face all too clearly.

But Paul was not here. He had gone away to the northern Transkei, to Zaxelwa, where there had been some disturbances recently and a number of Africans were being tried. Paul had undertaken to defend them and he was busy gathering evidence on their behalf. It was no easy matter because the district was still in a state of unrest and the neighbouring European farmers were threatening to take the law into their own hands – an attitude, Paul wrote to her, which made the peasants all the more restive, and suspicious.

Having linked Paul and the boy together in her mind, Kathie yielded momentarily to dreaming of the day when she and Paul would have their own home and Pieter would come often to see them. He might even stay with them ...

With a sigh, she went into the kitchen, where Andrew was waiting, and discussed with him the arrangements for the following day when their mother would be laid to rest beside their grandmother, that domineering woman who had set the pattern of Irene Liedeman's life in thought and outlook.

Kathie had hoped that Pieter of his own accord would come and visit her. She had told him where he could find her and indicated that he could stay with her if he felt inclined. But the weeks passed and there was no sign of her sister's child. Meeting Andrew one day she asked him if he ever saw the boy.

'No,' he answered. 'I shouldn't think his mother would let him. It would make it awkward with his father. If you're thinking of getting at Pieter, you'd better put him out of your mind.'

'I can't get him out of my mind,' said Kathie. 'He's not a happy boy, not by a long way.'

'We can't help that,' retorted Andrew. 'It's none of our business. Let Stella solve her own problems. Why should you worry? She never cared a damn about us.'

'It's Pieter I'm thinking of,' persisted Kathie. 'He's at a difficult age.'

'Oh, he'll get over it like the rest of us. He'll learn sense in time.'

'He looks an extremely sensitive boy to me.'

'So much the worse for him,' responded her brother, with youth safely behind him.

'Oh, Andrew,' said Kathie, 'whatever you have against Stella, don't take it out on the boy.'

'You've got me wrong. I've nothing against anybody. I'm just saying that if the boy's tough, he'll come through. There's no point in mollycoddling him. And we can't do anything about it anyway.'

'I wonder how he gets on with his brother,' said Kathie, stubbornly pursuing her anxious thoughts.

'Need you ask? They probably hate each other's guts. Frikkie'll get all the plums and for Pieter it'll be a kick in the pants every time, wherever he goes. If Pieter has any sense he'll quit as soon as he can and go where he belongs.'

'Where does he belong?' challenged Kathie.

'Oh, I haven't time to argue the rights and the wrongs of it,' said Andrew. 'I'll leave that to you and that Paul of yours. Life's too complicated as it is. Well, I've got to be moving. The wife makes a fuss if I'm late for supper. So long, Kathie. Don't look so down in the mouth.'

And off he went. It was the same old Andrew, reflected Kathie. Henpecked by his pampered Annette, but otherwise taking life as it came.

Soon after Kathie's meeting with her brother, Paul unexpectedly returned. She had never been more glad to see him. Like the slipping off of a heavy cloak, she forgot the sadness into which her mother's death, with all its memories of the past, her meeting with Stella and her anxiety about young Pieter had plunged her. Simply to tell him about her nephew, how excited she had been to meet him, how she had been struck by his abnormal sensitiveness and how disappointed she was that he didn't come to see her – simply to relate all this helped to lighten her sombre thoughts. She concluded that in the mood caused by her mother's sudden death her impressions had probably been exaggerated.

Half playfully, she suggested to Paul that if they had a home of their own, Pieter could come and stay with them. He would be like a son to them. Spoken lightly – for she had long steeled herself to disguise what she most desired – the remark had an effect on Paul for which she had not been prepared.

'Kathie, that word *home*, you don't know how much it means to me!'

He took her in his arms.

'Can you imagine those long, weary journeys on the country roads? Going to a place where no one knows me. Not knowing what awaits me there ... You see, Kathie, we have enemies among our own people – men who do not see the struggle as Ndwana and you and I see it. They forget the people in their enmity towards me ... Strange isn't it? On such journeys my thoughts turn to you in a way you can never imagine. I see you, I touch you, I feel your presence. I talk to you. I see you – how you move, how you smile – oh, you will never know what that means to me! ... You have given up a great deal for me all these years ...'

Kathie shook her head, smiling, not trusting herself to speak.

Paul continued: 'You did so because you thought it was the best for me. Kathie, I want you to change your mind.'

'Change my mind! Oh, Paul!'

'I know you will ask me, have I forgotten all my arguments –'

'Must you explain so much?' she teased him.

Paul had come back only for a flying visit because he had wanted to consult some authorities in connection with his defence of the peasants of Zaxelwa. It was proving a difficult case and local public opinion was violently against them. Paul told Kathie something of what had been happening in the district for some time past. Items of news tucked away in odd corners of the daily press had referred to *Native unrest in a small region of the northern Transkei*, but these gave no idea of what had been actually happening. The Africans had a long list of grievances against regulations affecting the possession of their land and their cattle; they had made dignified appeals to the authorities, which had been ignored. A few individuals had cut fences illegally and they had resisted officials who had come to seize their cattle. They considered that they were merely defending their natural rights as human beings. 'We are men,' they said. 'We have done nothing wrong and we have stolen nothing.' There had been no acts of violence, but, as the press had it, *'The police are standing by'*. What Paul feared was that the local European farmers, anxious for a pretext to use force, would goad the Africans to such an extent that an outbreak would be inevitable. One farmer had been heard to declare: 'Blood will flow here like water!' Altogether it was not the best atmosphere in which to conduct a case, commented Paul with a wry smile. But he would go all out in the defence of the African peasants.

It was against this background that Paul and Kathie snatched a few hours' happiness. They decided that as soon as the case was finished, Paul would return and they would get married. Meantime Kathie would look for a house. Paul was extraordinarily excited on this point: house and home took on an almost violently romantic meaning for him. The wanderer wanted to see in actuality the home he would carry with him in his mind's eye when he went out once more into the country. Kathie and home – symbols of security in a world full of hazard and insecurity.

Paul had contemplated spending yet another day with Kathie before going back, when he received a telegram from Zaxelwa. One look at the hated envelope told Kathie all.

'I must go at once,' he said.

She could not hide her disappointment.

'Who is it from?'

'A friend in Zaxelwa who has been helping me to gather evidence.'

'What has happened?'

'I don't know. He only tells me to come back immediately.'

For a moment she was filled with a fury of passionate revolt.

She wanted to cry out, even in anger. To hurt Paul in some way.

Must she always wait, wait at his bidding? He was relentless, for all his gentleness. It was the eternal conflict between man and woman.

Taking her in his arms, Paul could feel her body reluctant to yield to his caress. She turned her head aside.

'Forgive me, Kathie,' he said.

Instead of her lips, he gently touched her forehead. There was understanding in that gesture – and a great restraint.

With a cry she yielded her trembling lips to his.

The passion of revolt gave way to calm. Was it strength or weakness? Victory or defeat? She did not know. She only knew that he must go.

She would never keep him back.

Kathie found refuge once more in her work. The days slipped past normally. She had a hurried note from Paul to say that he had arrived and was up to the eyes in work. Things were happening – he would tell her all about them when he came back. He ended with the hope – no, the command – that she would have everything shipshape for him when he came – *Home*! Nearly all her spare time was given up to the search for a house and the buying of odds and ends that caught her fancy. Time enough to do the serious shopping when Paul came back and they could do it together.

She had been forgetting Pieter. Now it came to her that she must try to see him, since it didn't look as if he was going to make any effort to come to her. Should she go to her sister's house, after all that had happened in the past? When they had met at the time of their mother's death, there had been no softening in Stella's manner towards her. The very fact that Pieter had not been to see her was probably due to Stella. She recalled how harshly Stella had spoken to him. Poor boy, thought Kathie. It's mothering he needs.

While she was still in an uncertain state of mind as to which course to adopt in order to get in touch with Pieter, events themselves decided the issue.

One evening, having made herself a cup of coffee and some toast, she sat down to read the book she had long promised herself to read – Olive Schreiner's *The Story of an African Farm*. With a positive sense of luxury she snuggled into her chair, nibbled her toast and turned over the pages of the book to get the flavour of it, as it were. She was in no hurry.

A knock at her door followed immediately by the entrance of the intruder, brought her to her feet.

A white man stood on the threshold. He was a tall, loose-limbed fellow and his clothes were creased like those of a man who had bought a ready-made suit a size too big for him. As to his face, it was impossible at this moment to know its habitual expression, because it was the face of a man distraught.

'Are you Kathie Liedeman?' he asked, without any preliminaries.

'What do you want?' returned Kathie.

'It's my son –'

He must be someone who had come for her professional services … though her work was confined mostly to midwifery.

'What has happened?'

'It's my wife,' he began again. 'Stella –'

'Stella!'

'She sent me for you. You must come at once!'

'What has happened to Stella? Please explain.' Her own voice echoed his emotion.

'Not Stella. My son –'

'Pieter?'

He nodded. 'Please. Please come. My wife sent me to fetch you!' he reiterated.

Kathie could get no more out of him, so without another word she threw a few things into a bag and followed him out of the door.

The white man and the coloured woman walked down the street together.

Boarding a bus, the white man hesitated a second and then sat down beside her. The conductor eyed them with cold curiosity. Kathie paid her own fare. Carl did not speak and she did not attempt to do so either. But her thoughts were in turmoil. What could have happened to Pieter? Her sister had sent for her. She had actually sent her husband. Was the boy injured? Or –?

Kathie looked at the man beside her.

'Mr Meyers, you must tell me what has happened.'

Her voice recalled him with a start. He refused to answer her directly.

'We'll soon be there,' he said.

Alighting from the bus, the man and the woman hurried along a typical suburban street, its identical houses packed closely together. The man stopped in front of one of them, opened the gate, went on in front of Kathie and entered without looking behind him.

Making his way to a small back room, from which the light showed from under the door into the passage, he entered.

'I've brought her, Stella.'

Fearing what she was about to see, Kathie went forward into the room. Over by the bed in the corner she recognised her sister. Recognised, though this was not a Stella she had ever seen before. Her eyes travelling swiftly to the bed, Kathie saw a figure almost completely hidden by the blankets. Pieter? But surely – not dead?

Stella was leaning over the bed, her hand lying protectively on the motionless body. She did not get up as Kathie approached, nor did she change her expression.

'Kathie – Pieter – ' The mother covered her face with her hands. There was no sound of tears.

Kathie moved the sheet a little from the half covered face. Thank God, he was alive. She put out her hand and touched the clammy forehead. The face was swollen. With a habitual gesture she made to adjust the sheet, which was still too much over the face.

What she saw there made her start and turn with a question on her lips.

Stella took her hands from her tearless face.

'He tried to hang himself,' she said. 'I found him – '

'*You* found him?'

'I think I found him just in time ... Kathie! He must not die.'

'He will not die,' said Kathie.

'Oh, Kathie, if I hadn't come in time – '

'Poor Stella.' Unconsciously Kathie adopted the tone that brought them back to their childhood days.

All this time Carl had stood looking on, but had not spoken. From the two women his gaze travelled to his son and rested there. He did not seem to have the will to move, but stood there helplessly – a big, forlorn man.

Kathie suddenly became aware of him, taking in the bewildered aspect of the man expressed in every line of his body. Indeed her gaze seemed to embrace all three of them – mother, child and father.

'Stella, you had better go and lie down,' she said.

'I don't want to.'

'But you must.'

'I tell you, I couldn't rest.'

'Then you won't be able to look after Pieter.' Kathie spoke sharply. Stella had no more to say.

Kathie turned to the husband. 'Go and make something for her – and yourself, too,' she said. 'You need to keep up your strength.'

When Kathie later led her sister firmly to bed, Stella fixed her burning eyes on her and said: 'No one must know of this. Tell Carl. No one must know.'

Kathie stayed in her sister's house that night. Stella wanted Carl to make up a bed for her, but Kathie insisted on keeping watch beside Pieter. She would snatch her sleep when she could. She was used to it.

She knew that in time she would learn the story of this terrible act of Pieter's. But between herself and this family there was as yet a world unspoken. A great deal of what lay behind it she could already guess, but now was not the time to explain or think of anything, except bringing Pieter back to health. She dared not yet come to grips with that far more difficult task of healing the mind that had so far lost itself as to seek self-destruction. What despair made such a deed possible? She could not but remember Nontando and shrank from something deeper than her understanding could compass. She could not imagine herself capable of such abandonment of the will to live.

Sitting alone beside the sleeping boy she thought of the violence that such young spirits suffer; the eager spirit flung back on itself, mocked by prejudice, frustrated in its ambition, outraged in its pride, helpless in its anger. And when those nearest to them are themselves floundering in the maze of this social confusion, then are the young lost indeed. To whom can they turn?

What must it be to sink into the icy waters of despair, without hope, with nothing to live for, no one to live for, not even oneself? It was an abyss that Kathie dared not contemplate. It was unknown to her.

Throwing off her morbid thoughts, she made a sudden movement and leaned her head softly against the boy's sleeping body, finding in it warmth and comfort. He stirred slightly, sighed and returned to sleep. He is young, she said to herself, and the young are quick to recover their strength.

She vowed to herself that he would never be lonely again as long as she lived.

The following days, during which Kathie stayed on at her sister's house, were far from being free from awkwardness. In the face of catastrophe, Stella's first impulse to seek her sister had been overwhelming; but those moments when emotion purges everything in its white heat are rare indeed; afterwards one has to pick up again the threads of existence with all their ragged endings, and old habits reassert themselves. It was clear that Stella had been shaken to the roots of her being, yet Kathie could not be sure that her sister did not perhaps regret the impulse that had made her send her husband to fetch her. She was far from admitting to herself, and still less to Kathie, the significance of all that had happened. Neither sister was willing to be the first to speak, if it was necessary to speak. Perhaps everything was spoken in the sharing of the immediate task, the recovery of Pieter. He was the living bond between them.

Each day saw an improvement in his condition and as he grew better he turned more and more to his Aunt Kathie. Towards his mother, though she was more loving to him than she had ever been, his manner was reserved. This was understandable. What he had done, his very failure to carry out his intention, created in him a painful shyness mingled with shame. His act had exposed him to others; it lay like a gulf between him and the rest of the world and it would take him a long time to bridge it. Kathie was determined that his mother, his father and herself, together with Paul when he returned from Zaxelwa, would help Pieter to build that bridge as quickly and soundly as possible.

Kathie had not heard from Paul since that first hurried note sent immediately after his arrival back in Zaxelwa. But his silence did not cause her uneasiness. The faster he worked, the speedier his return, as he had promised. Events had happened so quickly and violently that she had lost the sense of time, yet it was only a week or two since Paul had left. She must not be impatient. She certainly had her hands full now. Once she was sure that Pieter was well on the way to full recovery she would resume her house hunting with redoubled energy, for she had now an added incentive. That dream of hers to give Pieter a second home with Paul and herself was certain to come true. Life did indeed work itself out in strange ways.

Till Paul should return she must proceed with the help of the others to lure the boy back to normality, her best ally being the natural resilience of youth itself. What assistance could she expect from his parents? How much from his father? Kathie had not had much opportunity to observe Carl Meyers. He was away at work all day; in the evening he would hover about his son's room as if he wanted to say something. But what? Then he would bid Pieter goodnight, give Kathie a half grateful, half embarrassed look, and depart, saying that he was going to see his other son, Frikkie, who had gone to stay with a friend while his brother recovered. When Kathie did eventually meet the younger boy she saw that he did not know how to behave towards her and resented his mother's attempt to improve his manners. He was an ordinary insensitive boy merely acting according to the standards of his habitual associates. Kathie reflected sadly on the hopelessly tangled human relationships within this family, to which she herself was bound by ties of affection. She did not need to be told what the relationship between the two brothers must have been like before the catastrophe. Nor would it ever be healed.

How much could Stella help her son? What of her own state of mind? Stella, caught unawares by events, had at first been carried along the stream of an overwhelming instinct to return to the bosom that had sheltered her in childhood. The physical shock alone of finding her son, that day of attempted suicide, had been a severe one. Even now she dared not recall the sight of the apparently dead figure. At one stroke it had shattered the arrogant pretension that she had erected around herself all her life, and had left her exposed and momentarily panic-stricken.

Her lifelong pursuit of self-interest – to come to this? Her insatiable ambition – to end in such defeat?

No one must know of this, she had said to Kathie, and in this revealed the shame that her son's act brought her – and her essential worldliness.

At the same time his act had shamed her in a deeply personal way. If she had not known it before, she knew it now – he was her son. His fateful removal of himself had been the sternest rejection as between parent and child; there had been an uncompromising finality in his action, in thus violently repudiating the ties of the family, which, after all, were Stella's bulwark against a hostile world, in spite of all her discontent and contempt for her husband and her coldness towards her elder son. While the shock had chastened her, making her more gentle towards him, her sense of possession, too, played its part; he belonged to her and she had no intention of losing him again. Coming so near to catastrophe, she was at the mercy of all the conflicting emotions which the contradictions of her position made inevitable.

Time alone would tell if the relationship between Stella and her son would ever become a healthy one. Was she capable of coming face to face with herself after the first shock was over? Her whole life made this unlikely. Even if she faced up to the fact that as a mother she had failed her son, was she capable of realising something even more fundamental – that his attempted suicide contained the fatal logic of all her actions since that first choice to which her grandmother and her mother had guided her? In other words, the racial attitudes motivating her actions had led step by step to the culminating point of this catastrophe. Such self-knowledge would leave her naked.

It was not only the relationship between Stella and her elder son that was affected by what had happened. The family relationship as a whole was rocked by Pieter's fateful deed. The least likely to feel it was his young brother, except in so far as the attitude of his parents towards him would be modified because of a more positive adaptation towards Pieter. Between husband and wife the situation was more serious. As a father Carl had been shaken by the deed no less than Stella; he, too, was conscious of having failed his son and his heart yearned towards him. Yet he felt the barrier of the boy's resentment against him. If Pieter's very existence had wrought havoc in the relationship between his father and his mother, his attempt to remove himself was in no way a resolution of their problems.

Perhaps their common desire to bring their son back to health would bring them more together. There is no doubt that Stella was in a softer mood and this softness embraced even the man who had so often excited her exasperation, her resentment, her hate. Her deeply hidden sense of insecurity, aggravated by the shock, made her turn to her husband, whose attachment to her had never been uprooted in spite of all the storm and stress of their marital conflicts.

These two, who had uttered too many words of the bitterness of their mutual disappointments, and had no more to learn about each other, had, with this experience, touched bedrock. They had touched bedrock, but it had not destroyed them. They needed each other, and now more than ever. In this there was hope for the future. Social forces were at enmity with them and would continue to beat at the foundations of this marriage. But there was that between them, as man and woman, which stood to survive the conflicts. Happiness they could not claim, but they had still something to give each other. Above all there was virtue in the steadfastness of Carl's patient affection.

It was towards Kathie that Stella's feelings fluctuated and wavered like a weathervane. The first impulse, prompted by panic, could not easily survive the day-to-day contact with her sister, with its old associations. Completely to accept Kathie also involved the necessity to be honest with herself over all that had happened to Pieter, and why. And how painful must such a process be!

The two sisters never openly expressed to each other what was in their minds.

Kathie had set aside all her other work to be with Pieter. Before long, however, its demands were too insistent to be ignored. One morning, only she and Pieter being in the house, she broached the subject of her departure. Immediately his face fell.

'Oh, no, Auntie!'

'I'm afraid I must.'

'But you've been here such a short time'

'Not so short! I don't want to leave you either, Pieter, but my patients –'

'Can't these other people wait?'

Kathie laughed. 'Babies don't wait!'

Just then they heard the front door banging and Pieter called out:

'Ma, come here!' And as Stella entered: 'Ma, Auntie Kathie says she's going away. Tell her she can't. We won't let her, will we?'

His mother looked quickly at Kathie.

'I'm afraid we can't make her stay if she doesn't want to,' she said.

'It's not me. It's those babies who won't wait.'

'Ma, tell Auntie Kathie she must come back soon.'

'Of course.'

'Promise me you'll be up and doing your gymnastics by the time I come back,' said Kathie, quickly filling the awkward pause.

'You bet I will!'

'You'll have lunch before you go?' Stella asked.

'Thank you. I'll have a bite here – with Pieter. Anything will do.'

'I like that,' the boy said, so quietly that only Kathie heard him.

Thus amid an atmosphere almost of gaiety, with Kathie reiterating her promise to come back soon, she spent her last morning in her sister's house.

Returning first to her room, Kathie glanced hastily through her mail and found what she was looking for – a letter from Paul. The letter was brief but warm, with a touch of inspiration in the language of his devotion that set her heart singing with the joy of it. He went on to chafe against the delays of the law. The atmosphere in Zaxelwa was tense, he wrote, and this was aggravated by the arrival of reinforcements of armed police – which did anything but inspire the peasants with confidence in the peaceful intentions of the authorities. 'It's hard to convince a shrewd peasant,' he went on, 'that a man who comes up to you with a gun doesn't intend to use it.' He repeated, as in his previous letter, that he had much to tell her, which he would keep till he returned home. And in a postscript he wrote: 'Tell Ndwana to forgive me for not writing. He shall hear all – and how much! – when I return. Tell him: *The future is ours!*

Kathie looked at the date on the letter and found that it had been written four days previously. She sat down and answered immediately, posting the letter on her way out.

With a case on her hands, she had practically no sleep that night and returning next day to her room, she intended to snatch an hour or two to herself before going out again. Pulling the curtains to shut out the sun, she was just preparing to lie down when there was a sharp knock at the front door. She was irritated by the sound. It was probably a fruit vendor and if nobody answered he would go away; she knew there was nobody in the rest of the house at this time of day. Then the knock was repeated, more sharply than before. Putting on a dressing gown, she went to answer it.

A telegram!

'Sister Liedeman?' asked the coloured messenger.

'Yes.'

He bid her sign and she took the brown envelope and hurried to her room.

Her eyes read and did not read the words on the paper in her hand for they struck all her senses simultaneously.

Paul. Was dead.

Shot by the police at Zaxelwa.

She recognised the name of the sender as that of the friend who had sent Paul the telegram asking him to return to Zaxelwa.

Paul was dead.

How she passed the rest of the day she never knew. She was numb.

Paul was dead.

The fountain of life was frozen within her.

Paul was dead.

He had died, and she far away and oblivious of that fatal moment. Not a sign, not a sound, not a quiver of her senses had told her when he had ceased to be.

All the passion of her devotion had not been able to protect him from that violence and the violence of death.

Oh, God, how lonely were the dead! How lonely the living!

Against this rage of death, how helpless and foolish was love. All her hopes and fears, the joys and the adorations, the gentleness and the gaiety of that companionship were gone forever, never to be born again.

Paul.

Was dead.

The fountain of life was frozen within her.

She would never see him again, never touch him again, never see the light of those eyes, glowing as they smiled at her, giving back the light they received from her. All dark and still and cold.

How lonely the dead. How lonely the living!

Nontando had walked by the sea. The waves had engulfed her ...

And Pieter, too, he had touched the chill hand of death.

Now she knew the dread face of despair.

But strangely, it had no fears for her. It was gentle. It beckoned her. It had an all-enveloping cloak. It cast a spell over her quiescent heart, promising oblivion and peace.

Paul was dead.

She passed the night alone.

With the morning she knew that she would pick up the threads of life again. She must go to see Ndwana. She must let Ndwana know. Paul had grown dear to him and this would be a heavy blow ... And what of Paul's sister, Nonceba? Ah, she thought, you who were Mother and Father to him, what meaning will life have for you now? The book of your hopes and dreams is closed. Closed and the tale half told.

Must it always be so?

With the thought of Paul's sister, the spring of sorrow gushed in her heart and with it the pang of a new realisation. Even in death they could keep Paul from her. He was a black man. Life was cheap, and her sorrow was naught. *'Such men become less than human,'* said Paul once. *'Their racial hatreds and fears suck their humanity out of them.'* And it was at the hands of such men that Paul had perished.

A knock at the door recalled her to where she was. How different was this knocking from the careless hand that had summoned her yesterday. Yesterday? The word had no meaning. Sorrow did not know time as man knows it. The knocking came again. It was a timid knock. Who could it be?

Pushing her hair from her eyes, she went to the door and opened it.

There stood Stella. And Pieter.

Kathie drew them in and shut the door.

'Kathie, I brought Pieter with me.'

'You know?'

'Yes.'

'Is that why you brought Pieter?' Kathie said softly.

The boy placed his hand in hers.

It was a moment that redeemed much of all the bitterness of the past.

Stella's glance went to the telegram still lying on the table.

'Who sent this?' she asked.

'A friend.'

'May I read it?'

Kathie nodded. 'How did you come to know?' she said.

Stella took a folded newspaper from her handbag.

'It was Pieter who remembered the place – Zaxelwa. You had told him. And then I saw the name.'

'Let me see,' said Kathie. Her manner was quite controlled.

She read the headlines:

SERIOUS CLASH BETWEEN NATIVES AND POLICE.

ONE EUROPEAN POLICEMAN KILLED. TWENTY INJURED.

REINFORCEMENTS RUSHED TO ZAXELWA.

The report went on: *'This outbreak was the climax to a series of incidents in Zaxelwa in the Northern Transkei, where the natives have persistently refused to cooperate with the authorities. The clash occurred when a body of policemen rode into the Reserve to arrest four natives. They encountered a large meeting of natives (A meeting of more than five is illegal.) The officer in charge ordered them to disperse. They refused and adopted a threatening attitude. Stones were thrown and a policeman was pulled from his horse. The officer then ordered his men to fire.*

'In this desperate clash, one European policeman, Lt van Niekerk, was killed and twenty injured. Reinforcements of police armed with Sten guns and rifles were rushed to the Reserve. The natives fled to the neighbouring hills and all who remained in the valley at dawn were either dead or seriously wounded.

'The exact number of killed and wounded amongst the natives is not known. Three natives died after being taken to the Mission Hospital. One of these was a native lawyer, Paul Sipo Mangena, who had been in the district during the past few weeks ostensibly gathering information for a pending case against the natives, but he was suspected of being an agitator. Order has now been restored in the Reserve.'

Kathie read this report without showing any emotion. She laid the newspaper aside.

'Paul's friend will tell us what really happened,' she said.

CHAPTER 24

The future is ours

In the months that followed, Kathie and Pieter were often to be seen together. The manner of their first meeting, and what had immediately followed, had created a rare understanding between the mature woman and the boy, an understanding born of a mutual knowledge and a mutual need. They had both looked on the face of despair; both knew what a precious thing is life, with all that their natures demanded of it. Their very love of life had made their despair the deeper.

In Kathie's mind Paul and the boy had been linked together throughout those days and nights when she had tended him and dreamed of the home the three of them would set up on Paul's return. Paul more than any man would have taught Pieter *how to live*. How to live as a man. And now? ... Paul was dead.

Now, in the crucible of her thoughts, in the heart of this woman who lived and understood above all things through her heart, the image of the dead man took life from that of the boy who had so nearly perished. And from the dead she took the living spirit, kept burning within her own, and gave it to the boy. Through her, all that Paul had lived for and fought for would be transmuted to new purpose in the will of this young spirit standing on the threshold of life – her sister's son.

Her thoughts stretched to a limitless horizon. Thus would the past be linked with the future and generations yet unborn be kindled by that part of Paul which was imperishable. He who never had a son – this would be his immortality.

Speaking one day to Pieter, she recalled a saying of Paul's which had imprinted itself on her memory, and she recalled the place which had inspired it. On one of those brilliant winter days at the Cape, that come between the rains, she and Paul had followed the path leading along the face of Table Mountain. Its grey ramparts rose sheer above them; before them lay a magnificent panorama of the city, from Lion's Head stretching to the edge of the sea; the harbour full of ships, the gleaming waters of Table Bay beyond, with Robben Island, that stepping stone out to the open sea; then round the sweep of the bay, the teeming overflow of the city reaching out over the plain to the mountainous hinterland, its rugged peaks jutting to the heavens with a pale majesty.

'O lovely city,' said Paul. 'Here I can truly say I have lived, in spite of all.'

He had drunk his fill of the scene and then turning to Kathie he had said:

'The time will come when men will live like human beings. All men, Kathie. That is my faith and I would wish it to be the faith of our son.'

Our son.

Kathie turned to the youth at her side.

'You are our son, Pieter, you and all the youth who stretch out your hands to life, demanding more and still more, till your manhood shall grow to its full height.'

And then she recalled Paul's last message, the last words that his warm hands had penned:

'The future is ours!'

The words had been written, not for her alone, nor for Ndwana, but for all his people.

'The future is ours.'

Dora Taylor
Cape Town, May 10th, 1951

ACKNOWLEDGEMENTS

My thanks go to

My mother, for writing the novel with much passion.

Gwen Wilcox for looking after the precious manuscript.

Alison Lowry of Penguin Books (South Africa), for bringing
to reality Dora Taylor's dream to have her fiction published by
Penguin

Jane Ranger, editor at Penguin, for her enthusiasm and
sympathetic handling of Dora Taylor's work.

Lesley Hart for her continued efforts to promote the work of
Dora Taylor.

Professor Vivian Bickford-Smith for his belief in *Kathie* as a
valuable contribution to South African social history.

And my family for their unfailing help and support.

Dora and Jim, Ivydene Cottage in Rondebosch, 1926

Dora Taylor, overlooking Camps Bay, June 1927
(probably taken by Jim)

Dora Taylor, early 1900s, Aberdeen, Scotland

Dora Taylor

Dora Taylor was born in Scotland in 1899. Orphaned at an early age, she suffered physical abuse and neglect by a succession of indifferent relatives, until eventually she was adopted by the headmistress of the local Aberdeen school. Though this straight-laced Victorian spinster gave her neither love nor affection, she nevertheless gave her the opportunity to develop her intellectual abilities. After graduating with an MA Honours degree in English Literature at Aberdeen University, where she met her future husband, James Garden Taylor, she became a teacher, inspiring new generations with her passionate love of literature. In 1924 Jim, as James Taylor was known to all, accepted a post as lecturer in psychology at the University of Cape Town, where later his pioneering research into perception led to major advances in that science. After their marriage in 1926, Dora joined him in Cape Town, a city that would change her forever and inspire her life's work.

With seeming inevitability Dora was drawn into intellectual discussion in a politically motivated climate where with her pen she was moved to contribute to the struggle for a non-racial democracy in South Africa, collaborating with the African leader, I.B. Tabata. Always careful to keep a low profile, she used a variety of pseudonyms. Her *Role of the Missionaries in Conquest* in particular was greatly valued, a radical history of missionary activity and colonial conquest in South Africa, first published in 1952 under the pseudonym *Nosipho Majeke*. This historical work was reprinted in 1986 and distributed in universities and colleges, devoured by those seeking to unravel the truth, and although now out of print is still sought after.

But ultimately, while in Boston, Massachusetts where Jim had been invited in the early sixties to lecture at Harvard University, Dora was advised against returning home because of a spate of arrests by the S.A. Government. She never recovered from being torn from her beloved South Africa and the friends and colleagues she had left behind, and died in exile in England in 1976.

She was a poet, playwright, short story writer, essayist and novelist; a philosopher, a literary critic, a teacher and a lecturer. As a devotee of all the arts, and hungry for knowledge in every sphere, she was an avid theatre goer, film buff, music and ballet lover, and made frequent trips to museums and art galleries in Europe and

America. She imparted this passion to her three daughters, and to all those friends, young and old, with whom she loved to talk away the night.

She was for many years Literary Adviser to the Junior Literary Society, during which time she was responsible for compiling *The Treasure Casket*, eight volumes of selected literature for children. For this publication she wrote the introductions and chose and edited all the works included in the volumes; she also responded to hundreds of young readers' and their parents' query letters on subjects ranging from birth control to the origin of the universe.

To her sorrow none of her prose fiction was published in her lifetime, though in 1928 four of her early poems were included in *Some Scottish Verse - an Anthology of Contemporary Scottish Poetry,* published in London. Although some of her plays were performed by an amateur group in Cape Town, none was commercially published, and the long, hauntingly beautiful dramatic poem, *Tristan and Iseult*, was never submitted for publication.

However, the bulk of her work was non-fiction, and in the 1940s and 50s more than a hundred literary and political critiques were published in the progressive magazine *Trek*, using several pen names. Among her works of literary criticism is a 148-page piece on Gorky, and an almost complete study of Nadine Gordimer, which she was working on when she died. Other South African writers covered are Pauline Smith, Sarah Gertrude Millin, Olive Schreiner and Alan Paton, to name but a few. In her literary criticisms she always looked at the authors' fundamental beliefs, including their racial attitudes, in the context of the socio-economic backgrounds. This gave her work a wider significance within the political climate of the time, making her a unique figure in the recent history of South Africa.

Dora was a small, graceful woman, nimble in her movements and nimble in thought. A person of intense emotion, exceptionally sensitive to mood and expression in others, she gave the appearance of being shy and reserved, but had great hidden strengths. Her deep concern, her pity and her empathy for all disadvantaged people, no matter who they were or where in the world they lived, or how they came to be in a state of desperation, was the stimulus for all her writing.

Sheila Belshaw, 2007